Sugar *and* Salt

Also by Susan Wiggs

Contemporary Novels

THE LOST AND FOUND BOOKSHOP
THE OYSTERVILLE SEWING CIRCLE
BETWEEN YOU & ME • MAP OF THE HEART
FAMILY TREE • HOME BEFORE DARK
THE OCEAN BETWEEN US • SUMMER BY THE SEA
TABLE FOR FIVE • LAKESIDE COTTAGE
JUST BREATHE • THE GOODBYE QUILT

The Bella Vista Chronicles
THE APPLE ORCHARD • THE BEEKEEPER'S BALL

The Lakeshore Chronicles
SUMMER AT WILLOW LAKE • THE WINTER LODGE
DOCKSIDE • SNOWFALL AT WILLOW LAKE • FIRESIDE
LAKESHORE CHRISTMAS • THE SUMMER HIDEAWAY
MARRYING DAISY BELLAMY • RETURN TO WILLOW LAKE
CANDLELIGHT CHRISTMAS • STARLIGHT ON WILLOW LAKE

Historical Novels

THE LIGHTKEEPER • THE DRIFTER
THE MISTRESS OF NORMANDY
THE MAIDEN OF IRELAND

The Tudor Rose Trilogy
AT THE KING'S COMMAND • THE MAIDEN'S HAND
AT THE QUEEN'S SUMMONS

The Chicago Fire Trilogy
THE HOSTAGE • THE MISTRESS • THE FIREBRAND

The Calhoun Chronicles
THE CHARM SCHOOL • THE HORSEMASTER'S DAUGHTER
HALFWAY TO HEAVEN • ENCHANTED AFTERNOON
A SUMMER AFFAIR

Sugar *and* Salt

A Novel

SUSAN WIGGS

WILLIAM MORROW

An Imprint of HarperCollinsPublishers

SUGAR AND SALT. Copyright © 2022 by Laugh, Cry, Dream, Read, LLC. All rights reserved. Printed in the United States of America. No part of this book may be used or reproduced in any manner whatsoever without written permission except in the case of brief quotations embodied in critical articles and reviews. For information, address HarperCollins Publishers, 195 Broadway, New York, NY 10007.

First William Morrow mass market printing: November 2023
First William Morrow paperback printing: May 2023
First William Morrow hardcover printing: July 2022

Cover design by Alan Dingman
Cover photographs © Shutterstock; © stock.adobe.com
Art by MicroOne / Shutterstock, Inc.

Print Edition ISBN: 978-0-06-291424-8
Digital Edition ISBN: 978-0-06-291425-5

William Morrow and HarperCollins are registered trademarks of HarperCollins Publishers in the United States of America and other countries.

23 24 25 26 27 BVGM 10 9 8 7 6 5 4 3 2 1

For my brother Jon,
the family artist and an inspiration to us all.
I love you so much.

A note to the reader: This book contains scenes depicting sexual harassment and rape. Please be mindful of this content, and, if needed, refer to the resource at the back of the book (page 381) for support and assistance.

Prologue

San Francisco 2019

Margot Salton wondered if there was a way to capture this moment and hold it forever. Could she freeze each detail in amber, encased for eternity like a keepsake to be taken out and held close whenever she needed it? Because this was the kind of rare moment she never wanted to forget.

The man she loved was in the audience along with the family she never thought she would have, and still couldn't quite believe she deserved. Her heart melted at the sight of him—self-assured, beaming with pride. She wasn't sure what she'd done to deserve him. There were friends and well-wishers, colleagues and customers, critics and admirers, all gathered to applaud her achievement.

Maybe it wasn't the biggest moment in her life—that of course stayed buried in the past—but this felt huge, perhaps too big to belong to someone like her, a girl who had come from nothing but secrets and trouble.

After everything that had brought her to this point, she was not a person who scared easily. Yet it was daunting to contemplate the notion that all her dreams—and several things she hadn't even dared to dream about—were finally coming true in the most magical way. But like all magical things, her dreams felt impossibly friable and apt to disappear at the slightest breath of wind.

Until recently, she had not been the sort of person to whom good things tended to happen. She was still getting used to the gentle smile of fortune.

Around her neck she wore a wide, colorful ribbon with a heavy medallion that bumped against her chest when she moved. The medal was almost embarrassingly conspicuous, but she wore it with pride as the newest recipient of the Divina Award, one of the country's highest culinary prizes. It was particularly meaningful to Margot, because it not only recognized a restaurateur's skill and vision; it also acknowledged her contributions to her employees and community.

Still, a medal? Really? A medal was supposed to signify an act of heroism, and she was no hero. Even so, this moment belonged to her. Cooking had saved her. Reading books had saved her. Raw determination had saved her. She'd worked her ass off to get here.

And finally, the right people had noticed. Applause and a few happy shouts crescendoed as she descended from the podium. Camera flashes went off, and people held up phones to capture the moment. Special attention was paid to her signature cowboy boots. Under glittering lights, servers crisscrossed the outdoor banquet area, their trays laden with her finest amuse-bouches and tasty bites, flutes of bubbly and jars of lavender lemonade.

After pictures, she made her way back down to a group of well-wishers who awaited her, along with a bottle of champagne in an ice bucket.

She hugged and high-fived her way through a gauntlet of people—her investors from the Privé Group, who had taken a chance on her. The GM and sous-chefs, line cooks, bartenders, and servers, all of whom had a hand in her success, were there to celebrate her. Food journalists and bloggers, even the skeptics who didn't think she'd make it and who had given her plenty of nervous indigestion, now raised their glasses and beamed with pride.

She paused for another picture with Buckley DeWitt, a senior writer and editor with *Texas Monthly*. He had been the first journalist to notice her back when he was a stringer for the magazine, years before. He wore his considerable girth with good cheer, having built a reputation for finding and extolling the best barbecue in the country. He was the only one present today who knew her from her other life.

He leaned close to Margot and lowered his voice. "We need to talk. It's about Jimmy Hunt."

Just the mention of his name turned her blood to ice. "I already told you everything and you published it," she said. "I've got nothing more to say about the Hunts."

"But—"

"But nothing, Buckley. I'm done with all that." She gathered her composure and turned to greet some of the other guests. In reality, she would never truly be done. But she had moved on, and she intended to keep some distance between past and present.

One woman, a stranger, wove and bobbed through the crowd as if particularly keen to connect with Margot. She waved a commemorative menu in one hand and held a manila envelope and a Sharpie marker in the other. She didn't quite fit in with the earnest civic leaders, tattooed kitchen workers, and fellow Perdita Street merchants. This woman wore battered denim and dirty sneakers. She had long straight hair, streaked with gray. Tobacco stains shaded her fingers and teeth.

With a burst of energy, she darted forward and favored Margot with a giddy smile that didn't quite match the sharp look in her eyes.

"Margie Salinas?" She intoned it as a question.

Margot paused, unused to hearing the name. She frowned, looking from side to side. Her heart skipped a beat. "Sorry, what?"

"Margie Salinas aka Margot Salton," the woman said.

Margot had not heard that name in years. She never thought she would hear it again. She never *wanted* to hear it again.

The world slowed down. The noise of the crowd roared in her ears and then faded to a muffled, undifferentiated babble. She could see a raft of tiny details in sharp relief—the gorgeous setting overlooking the bay, the twinkling lights, the lavish tables, the smiling faces—all the things she wanted to hold forever in her heart. Then, in the blink of an eye, the details resolved into the discomfiting, unfamiliar face before her.

"Who the hell are you?" she asked.

The woman passed her the manila envelope, pressing it firmly into her hand. "You've been served."

Part One

I'm always nattering on about cooking, and about what it brings to your life and your mood, about how it's a force for tranquility in the face of the strange. It's a craft, done with your hands, that forces you to think differently than when you're doing whatever it is you do for work, or to fill your days. Cooking helps turn off your brain for a while. Cooking allows you to heal.

—Sam Sifton

1

The proper balance of sugar and salt was the key to perfect barbecue sauce. Of course, when it came to barbecue sauce, everybody had an opinion about the combination of acid, aromatics, fruit, and flavorings—the ineffable umami—that made each bite so satisfying.

But Margot Salton knew with utter certainty that it all started with sugar and salt. She'd even named her signature product after it: sugar+salt. This sauce was her superpower. Her secret. Her stock-in-trade. When she'd had nothing—no home, no education, no family, no means of support—she had created the powerful alchemy of flavors that made grown men moan with pleasure, cautious women ignore their diets, and skeptical foodies beg for more.

She'd come a long way from the humble home-canned jars she'd started out with back in Texas. These days, a brand expert and designer had created the label and packaging, giving her a high-end, distinctive look. Today she took special care to make sure the gift pack of samples was flawless, because everything was riding on today's meeting. And Margot knew the best calling card in the world was a sample.

Today was the day. Today, her hopes were pinned on the ultimate goal—launching her own restaurant.

The name of the place was Salt, a word that was as clean and simple as the substance itself. Painfully aware of the failure rate of restaurant start-ups, she'd done her due diligence and had tried not to make rookie mistakes. She had sought out gigs and had taken classes at City College. She had interned and externed, and participated in pop-ups and competitive events to showcase her talents. She had learned the business from the back of the kitchen to the front of the house.

It wasn't going to be easy. Nothing worth having was easy, so the saying went. She wondered why it had to be that way. Why couldn't a thing be easy *and* worth having?

She had never worked harder in her life, and she'd never loved it more. The seemingly endless labor didn't daunt her. She'd taken care of herself her whole adult life, pulling herself up by the fingernails sometimes, determined to earn her place through her own actions. Now, after years of planning, conceptualizing, crunching numbers, and vacillating between euphoria and terror, she was ready.

As she donned the recommended business-casual attire—tailored black slacks, white silk blouse, fitted blazer—she was attacked by a hail of faltering nerves. She'd been down this road before, making her pitch to investors.

Several private funding sources had already rejected her idea. *The food is five-star but the concept is weak. The concept is strong but the menu is lacking. The business plan fails to cover all bases. The meat is too salty. Not salty enough. We don't need Texas toast in California.*

Each rejection only hardened her determination.

Maybe that was the hidden benefit of having survived the ordeal in Texas. If she could get through that, she could survive anything.

Today was going to be different. A make-or-break meeting. She had to believe it.

Her couture shoes, an epic thrift store find, were uncomfortable, but she had been advised to present herself as a polished professional to inspire confidence in her investors. No showboating. Business casual. Look the part. Follow the rules.

Margot stepped back and regarded herself in the mirror. Knife-sharp pleats in her slacks, blond hair styled at a salon she could barely afford. "What do you think, Kevin?" she asked.

Her handsome tabby cat yawned and groomed one of his paws.

"I know," she said. "I feel like an imposter. Shitfire. I *am* an imposter." As soon as she'd settled in San Francisco, she had changed her name. The new identity fit her so well that sometimes she managed to forget about Margie Salinas entirely, as if that person were someone from middle school who had moved away between grades.

Other times, when she woke up in a panicked haze, chased by nightmares, the girl she'd once been returned to haunt her. She was back in Margie's skin, feeling bound hand and foot in a cocoon, fighting to find her way out of it. She'd read in a book that the past was never really over. It was never even really past. Even after ten years, she knew this to be true. No matter how much time had passed, grief came and settled into her pores and could never be washed out. She still struggled with the sadness that surrounded those odd moments when she remembered that other life.

Sometimes all she could do was try not to dwell on

what she had left behind—and why. But still she ruminated. Despite her certainty that it was the best decision she could have made under horrific circumstances, she still questioned herself.

Most of the time, Margot powered through those moments and went about her life, showing no one in her new world what lay in the past. In terms of emotional pain, walking away had been as intense as the trauma that had preceded it, though in a different way. There was a part of her that yearned to stay close to the one thing that anchored her to earth. But no. Moving on had been the only viable option, given the circumstances, and given the size and scope of her ambitions.

Her spirit refused to be pinned to the ground. She had picked herself up and changed her name. Her home. Her therapist. Her friends. Everything but her cat. She'd gained elite status in aikido and could fend off any opponent—except the ghosts. Even though the past followed her stealthily and slipped uninvited into her consciousness, she usually managed to focus with laserlike intensity on making a new start.

It seemed forever ago that she'd had the audacity to imagine starting a barbecue joint in the most expensive city in America. This was a leap of faith; she'd found the fire to create the future she wanted.

But still, the sting of failure darted into her. What made her think today's meeting would be any different?

Shitfire. Following the rules had only led to rejection.

On impulse, she kicked off the dress shoes, causing Kevin to skitter away. She shed the slacks and blazer and put on an outfit that made her feel like herself—a short denim skirt with a sugar+salt logo T-shirt, and her favorite cowboy boots. Bare legs to celebrate this sunny summer day that even the fog couldn't conquer.

Then she called Candy—her pitmaster, Candelario Elizondo—and told him there was a change of plans.

"Let's take the truck," she said.

"You gonna take the food truck to the financial district?" he said. "You'll get tagged by the city."

"Not if we don't sell the food. We're going to give it away."

He said something in Spanish that was too rapid for her to follow, then added, "You're crazy."

"I'll meet you there," she said, and gave him the address. She knew he wouldn't let her down. She had met Candy while selling her sauces at the Fort Mason farmers' market. An experienced pitmaster, he was a genial man who had been a successful rancher in Mexico. He'd lost everything in a banking crisis and had come north to start anew. Together, they sourced, smoked, and cooked their meats to perfection, using a whole-log smoker with irresistibly fragrant wood—apple, pecan, mesquite, oak, and cedar. They had launched a catering service and leased a food truck, and their creations quickly won a devoted following. The *Examiner* had even run a feature on them. Margot had participated in pop-ups and competitive events to showcase her talents. The day she sold out of everything and started taking preorders was the day she decided the time had finally come to move ahead with her plans.

She had worked tirelessly on a concept that encompassed location, marketing, service scheme, and concept patterned after the best in the business. She lived and breathed atmosphere, price point, cash flow, press clippings. She was confident. She was ready.

Candy had parked the truck in a one-hour zone in front of the midrise office building. He was dressed for work, with his logo cap and apron that matched hers, his muscular forearms, honed by hours at the pit, flexing as he cranked open the window and awning. "You sure you want to do it like this?" he asked.

She nodded. "Wish me luck."

An understated sign in the building led her to the offices of the Privé Group, an investment firm that specialized in restaurant start-ups. With more than a hundred restaurants under their belt, they had a record of success when it came to launching new ventures. The principals were Marc and Simone Beyle, a French couple who lived in a Sausalito waterfront home. Their reputation was fierce, their taste exacting, but Margot had managed to convince them to hear her pitch.

A receptionist, dressed in the sort of outfit Margot had rejected that morning, led her to a chilly conference room with ergonomic chairs and a glass-topped table.

She felt a half-dozen gazes on her as she entered. The air-conditioning raised goose bumps on her legs. But it was too late to regret her wardrobe choice now.

"I do appreciate you meeting with me," she said, setting out the gift packs of her sauces along with the folders containing her personal story—as much of it as she was willing to tell—along with her mission statement, financials, and proposed plan.

"We're eager to hear from you," Marc said, his French accent subtle and sophisticated. Simone had severe, pointy features, but interest gleamed in her eyes.

"Ask me anything," Margot invited. "I'm an open book. And then I'd like to—"

"Who are your culinary heroes?" Simone asked.

Margot hadn't been prepared for this particular question. Fortunately, the answer was on the tip of her tongue. "That'd be my mama, Darla Sal—Salton." She fudged the name a little. She'd nearly said Salinas. Years after she'd changed it, the name followed her like a stain that wouldn't wash out. It was her mother's name, from an ancient region of Spain where the people looked more Celtic than Spanish. "She worked in a commercial kitchen and did catering down in Texas. Her sandwiches and sauces were famous, and when I was little, I spent hours watching her." She didn't mention the reason was that her mother couldn't afford childcare. "Later I learned barbecue from the best pitmaster in the Hill Country—Mr. Cubby Watson. After my mama passed, he and his wife, Queen, were like parents to me." She paused for breath, then rushed on before they could ask her why she'd left Texas. "Here in San Francisco, my hero is also my partner—Mr. Candelario Elizondo. In fact, he's down—"

They interrupted with more questions—Why San Francisco? Her financials looked questionable. How had she chosen her service scheme? Her marketing plan?

She recognized the look from some of the investors. She saw failure written all over their faces. Shitfire. She felt their skepticism. Her heart sank; this was not working. She figured it was a one-in-a-million chance that a high school dropout from Texas could launch a trendy restaurant in the heart of San Francisco. But oh, she wanted it. She wanted to be trusted, valued, given the responsibilities she knew she could shoulder.

"We usually ask prospective chefs to organize something for us," said one of the board members.

"I realize that," she said. She had tried to barter for an event space but hadn't found anything she could afford. "Y'all, with respect, I know this is unorthodox, but I cook better than I talk. I swear, if you can grow it, I can barbecue it. Would it be all right if you came down to the truck?"

"You brought your food truck?" Simone's well-groomed eyebrows lifted.

"Yes, ma'am."

There was an excruciating pause. The Beyles exchanged a glance. Margot held her breath. Then chairs rolled back and they all headed for the door. The trip down to the parking lot was endless, but the street scene was just as she'd hoped. The truck was swarming with people devouring samples of her barbecue as if they'd been starving on a deserted island. There was even a beat cop who probably could have ticketed the truck, but instead was wolfing down a pulled pork slider dressed with a relish Margot had named Pickle de Gallo.

She locked eyes with Candy and then took her place at the counter, and just like that, she was in her element. This was her zone, creating a delicious experience people wanted again and again. Forget the boardroom and the pretentious tasting dinner. She passed out plates loaded with her signature melt-away brisket crusted with the smoky candy of the fire, links she'd crafted in partnership with a sustainable ranch up near Point Reyes, butter-dipped smoked portobellos, and impossibly tender ribs smothered in her artisanal sauces. Her best sides were on display—cornbread, moist as pudding, from her mother's private recipe collection, beans and greens, peppery jicama slaw, and her signature hummingbird cake for dessert.

The group was quiet as they tasted her food. Margot forgot to breathe as she waited nearby. This was her craft, her life's work, on full display. She'd spent years finding the best locally sourced, seasonal ingredients.

After an agony of minutes had passed, Simone dabbed at her lips. "Well," she said. "You've done something here."

Margot had no idea how to respond, so she waited. Tried not to panic.

"The seasoning on the ribs is unusual."

"Gochujang," Margot said. She'd found the perfect balance of heat with the Korean condiment. It was a risky choice, though. "I can make it with a more traditional seasoning if you like."

Simone pushed away her plate and scanned her colleagues' faces. She and her husband murmured briefly in French. "We don't need to try anything more," she said.

"It's the best I got," Margot said.

There was another pause. Another quick exchange in French.

"So," said Marc, setting aside his napkin and extending his hand to Margot, "where would you like to open your restaurant, Miss Salton?"

"You must be Margot." The real estate agent held out her hand. "Yolanda Silva. It's great to meet you in person at last."

"Likewise," Margot said with a firm handshake. *I'm here*, she thought. *I'm really doing this.*

"Help yourself to something to drink. I need to duck into my office and grab a few things before we start touring the properties." Yolanda looked as polished and organized as her surroundings, with a gleaming manicure and couture glasses.

"Thanks." Margot opened a chilled bottle of Topo Chico from a glass-front fridge and sat in the elegant lobby. She took a nervous sip of the crisp, bubbly water. It was hard to believe, but thanks to the Privé Group, she now had a team. A dream team. The organization had matched her up with a management group to help her through every step of the start-up, from concept to design to grand opening and beyond. After her unorthodox presentation and several more tense, challenging meetings, she had an investor. A goal. A plan. A future.

The contracts had all been signed, the team assembled, the timeline plotted out. The only thing missing from the moment had been someone to celebrate with. When she was a kid, she used to run all the way home from school with an A paper, just to see the expression on her mama's face—that glow of love and pride. As an adult, she had to settle for pouring herself a glass of wine and making a toast to her cat.

It was more than a little depressing that she lacked someone to give her a high five or a hug and say *I'm so proud of you.* She could hear the tone of her mother's voice, exactly, even after all this time. Sometimes those memories seemed to be the only thing keeping her sane—the fact that, at one point in her life, she had mattered greatly to someone. She had been valued. She had been loved.

She was a grown woman now. She would have to do without a cheerleader.

Still, at times like this, it would be nice to have someone.

Lying awake at night, alone with her thoughts, she couldn't believe she had come so far. The road behind her was littered with hardship and tragedy and regrets, and it often seemed impossible to trust that she deserved this new start. She tried to feel her own worth. Sometimes the self-talk and self-care worked. A little bit. Other times, the effort simply drew a wall of loneliness around her. Yes, she had worth. But with no one to share the good and bad times, how could it matter?

Doubts aside, the real work was about to begin. Talent alone was not enough, even though her gift for cooking and sauces was undisputed. Passion wasn't enough, either. She had to be willing to steer the craft, the trade, the business, and the madness, no matter what it took—sleepless nights, endless days, zero downtime, head-splitting, granular study, and the grit to power through failure and setbacks.

"All set?" Yolanda came out of her office, carrying a clipboard and a portfolio. Sharp-eyed and stylish, she worked with clients of the Privé Group, helping find the right venue for a new restaurant. She had promised to find a place that would attract a thriving clientele of both locals and tourists, giving Margot a shot at year-round, long-term success.

Margot's general manager, Anya Pavlova, joined them to tour the properties. Anya had managed some of the best restaurants in the Bay Area. She was a fan of Margot's vision for Salt—a modern, stylish dining room that set it apart from other barbecue joints. They envisioned the kind of place that served mind-blowing food, the kind people were willing to stand in line for hours to sample, the way they had for the truck. Only they wouldn't have to line up at the new place, thanks to an app that would manage the dining room flow with laser precision.

"Based on your parameters, I found these fantastic options." Yolanda handed out sell sheets for each place. Margot and Anya had already studied them online, imagining the restaurant in each location. In her entire life, Margot had never actually toured a property. For her, home was whatever safe place she could find for herself and Kevin. Currently they lived in a rented garage apartment in the marina district.

They narrowed the choices down to three properties. The one near Fisherman's Wharf was close to the Fort

Mason farmers' market. The kitchen had been newly refurbished, and the dining room was surrounded by windows. The expansive view framed an iconic panorama of all the things tourists loved about San Francisco. Its deck jutted out over the water, where umbrella-shaded tables could catch the breeze while diners watched the boat traffic and listened to the sea lions. Margot could picture crowds of happy people gathering here.

"The clientele is heavily weighted toward tourists," Anya said.

"That's not a bad thing," Margot pointed out. "I'd love to see more locals and repeat customers, though."

The next place was nicely situated on Nob Hill in a block that would probably welcome a fantastic barbecue place. There were some inviting retail shops, and the theater district was close by. On the downside, it had a grim, colorless façade and the interior possessed all the charm of the DMV.

"We could make it work," Anya assured her. "I've seen the design team do wonders with the homeliest of spaces."

The kitchen was in good shape, and the service alley roomy enough for deliveries from Candy's pit, which was located in an industrial area.

The third option was a space in a vintage building on a historic block called Perdita Street. In the heart of one of the city's most vibrant neighborhoods, it was an area of worn brick boulevards and tree-shaded sidewalks. Some of the buildings dated back to the early 1900s, and a couple had even survived the earthquake and fire of 1906.

The vibrant, animated neighborhood was popular with tourists and locals and had a Saturday outdoor market. There was a place called the Mehndiva Bar, where you could order a kombucha and sip it while getting a temporary henna tattoo. In the same block were a tasting room featuring Rossi wines from Sonoma, a funky boutique with dog and owner matching outfits in the display window, a memory care center with a shady front garden, and an inviting bookshop in the oldest building in the area.

In a low-rise building across from the bookstore was a gaping vacancy where a popular Mexican restaurant had closed its doors when the owners had retired. The space was dank with neglect, but it had good bones, and Margot could picture the comfortable, friendly atmosphere she had always visualized.

There was only one thing that gave her pause. It had a shared kitchen with the bakery next door.

"It's an unusual setup, but the kitchen is huge, and it was shared for years with a full-service restaurant. The bakery's a local landmark. It started out as a community center in the 1960s," Yolanda said.

The kitchen was dated but sparkling clean, and there was a surprise awaiting them, too. A door marked *Bakery* opened, and in came an older Black woman with thick-rimmed glasses, her hair in a bun and braids. She carried a tray of baked goods and a pitcher of lemonade.

"I'm Ida," she said, setting the tray on a spotless stainless-steel counter.

"You're the bakery owner," Yolanda said. "What a pleasure."

"In name only," the woman said. "I'm retired, now— supposed to be, anyway. My son, Jerome, runs the place, but I still have a stake in the business. I came in today because I like to know who we might be doing business with."

Margot introduced herself, and Ida stepped back to

take her measure. "Look at you," she said. "You're no bigger than a minute. And so young."

"Reckon so," Margot said, "but I've been at it a good while. Started out making sandwiches with my mama for a food truck."

"Is that so? You came up in the business, then."

"Uh-huh. It was just my mama and me, and she was my best friend," Margot said. In fact, her mother had been her whole world. "Her sandwiches were beyond delicious. Pimento cheese, smoked meatloaf, egg salad, roast beef and remoulade, honey butter biscuits and fried chicken . . . Folks lived for her food." Darla Salinas had never made much of a living, not because her food wasn't good—it was—but because she didn't have a head for business.

Ida indicated the tray. "Go on now, help yourself. Have a bite to eat and then in a little bit, I'll show you around the place."

The treats she served were the stuff of dreams—a buttery tart glistening with fresh fruit, a molasses cookie that made Margot almost swoon with pleasure when she sampled it, and tiny, decadent chocolate brownies and lemon bars.

As Anya quizzed Ida about the business, Margot wondered if things would have turned out differently if her mother *had* focused on getting ahead instead of just getting by. One year, Darla's brisket and pepperoncini kaiser—with its not-so-secret ingredient of crushed barbecue potato chips—was named best sandwich in the state by *Texas Monthly* magazine, but she had never capitalized on it.

"I got my own start right here in this kitchen back when it was just a community center." Ida showed them around, opening the door to the abandoned dining room.

It had a dated, neglected air, the walls painted with scenes of old Mexico. The empty restaurant resembled a ghost town abandoned in haste, leaving behind upended tables and chairs, an apron on a hook, a battered soccer poster, tubs of plastic tumblers and flatware, discarded receipts and order slips.

Margot stood still for a few moments, picturing the space transformed into a warm, fresh, welcoming restaurant. In her dreams, driven by a yearning to find a place where she mattered, where she fit in, where she was in control, she had designed every nook and cranny, setting the stage for people to enjoy her food.

Ida finished the tour with a gracious smile. "I hope I see you again soon, Margot," she said.

"Decision time," Anya said when they stepped out into the service alley. The dumpsters were neatly aligned and labeled for trash and recyclables. There was an old basketball hoop above a wall with a fading antiwar mural that appeared to be from the Vietnam era. "We need to go over the pros and cons of each place."

As Margot mulled over her options, she tried to be cold-bloodedly objective about each locale. The buzzy Fisherman's Wharf place, the tony Nob Hill location, or historic Perdita Street.

"What do you think?" she asked Anya.

"Well, it could be challenging to share a kitchen with that bakery. It's clean and roomy, but some of the equipment is dated."

"True," Margot conceded. "But remember, I've been working in a food truck, so I'm good with cramped spaces. This place feels comfortable. Down-to-earth, here in the middle of a city that still intimidates me sometimes. I like Ida. She seems so cool. And what did you say that bakery was called?"

Anya handed her a business card. "Sugar."

Margot felt a smile unfurl. Suddenly she had a sense of clarity, one so powerful that she no longer second-guessed herself. "Perfect."

"Well now, I hope you're happy with the place," Ida said. The lease had been signed, plans approved, licenses granted, and the transformation was nearly done.

"We looked at a lot of properties," Margot said. "Once I found this place, I was done looking. It feels exactly right to me."

"Sometimes it works like that," Ida said. "When you know, you know."

Margot hoped Ida was right. The past five months had been intense, but rewarding. A professional design and development team had turned her vision into a reality. She herself had scouted the vintage Victorian chandeliers, spray-painted them black, and hung them in the all-white dining room. The booths along the inner walls showed a subtle hint of color, accented by a single apple-green napkin tucked into a stemmed glass, glowing against the arctic white. The overall impression was clean but not stark or intimidating. The place still smelled of plaster and paint, but soon it would be filled with the smoky sweet aroma of barbecue.

The kitchen and prep areas had been refurbished and updated. Personnel hired and trained, technology in place, menus agonized over, tested, and curated. The playlist featured old and new music that was audible but unobtrusive. Her freshly trained bar staff would soon be serving craft cocktails like the Baja Oklahoma and the Wild West martini. She had attended to every detail she could imagine, all the while being fully aware that the trouble would come from a source no one had anticipated. This was the nature of the restaurant business. This was the reality she had to accept. And that just might be what made it so exciting to her.

She and Ida sat at the gleaming bar, which had been reclaimed from a 1908 hotel.

"I brought you some samples from the pit and smokehouse." She offered Ida a carryout package with brisket and links and her favorite sides. She also included a few jars of sauce.

"sugar+salt," Ida said, studying the label. "And now we're neighbors. Isn't that something?"

"I took it as a sign," Margot said. "I came up with that name for the sauce when I was a kid."

"Did you now? My, my." Ida leaned in with genuine interest. She listened with a friendly tilt of her head. She always seemed like a person comfortable in her own skin. "Something your mama showed you?"

Margot found Ida easy to talk to—which was something, since Margot rarely felt at ease with people. "She let me experiment in the commercial kitchen. Once I was on my own, I started making sauce in small batches for a barbecue place I worked at years ago. Cubby Watson's Barbecue, it was called, run by him and his wife, Queen. In the Texas Hill Country, barbecue's practically a religion, and the Watsons were always in need of kitchen help. I started on dishwashing detail and prepping ingredients for their classic sides, and when Cubby saw how serious I was, he showed me every aspect of the trade, from tending the firebox to tending the bar—which I was too young to do back then, but he was a fine teacher."

"Sounds like a good place to start," said Ida.

Margot nodded. "I loved it, even the hard parts. Cubby's one of the best pitmasters in the world. His brisket is so falling-apart tender you'd swear it was cooked in butter. Folks would travel miles to sample Queen's house-made sausage, her vegan portobello sandwiches with creamy remoulade, and her Texas sheet cake."

"How wonderful. I can see what inspired your menu," Ida said.

The phone rang and she stepped into the bakery office to take the call. Margot was seldom so chatty, but she felt as if she'd made a friend. In several ways, Ida reminded her of Queen Watson—a woman with a sturdy spirit who seemed like she could withstand any storm. Both were women of color, so Margot was sure they'd encountered their share of storms. Queen's fortitude had inspired Margot to survive when she was at her most vulnerable, and she sensed a kindred soul in Ida.

Margot had been sixteen when she showed up in the Watsons' kitchen in Banner Creek, Texas, looking for work, any kind of work.

Her story was one of uncertainty and desperation, but she'd held her head up and looked them in the eye—first Cubby, mild-faced and quiet-spoken, with busy, talented hands and burly arms that could manage the big cuts of meat in the outside pit—and then Queen, whose impassive regard measured Margie from the top of her blond head to the bottom of her skinny legs.

"You're mighty young to be out on your own," Queen had observed.

Margot—Margie, back then—wasn't quite sure what the rule was for minors. She missed her mother so much in that moment. She missed the way they'd stay up late together on Saturday nights, talking and giggling about everything and nothing. Even when Mama had her sick spells, the two of them were best friends and life was simple, nothing remarkable about it—until Del came along.

Del. Delmar Gantry. At thirteen, Margie had been told that they were a family now. She asked her mother what they were before, and Mama broke out laughing. Margie had never understood the joke. Del talked slick and didn't have a job. He looked like a movie star, and he and her mama together were like a Hollywood golden couple. They reminded her of the couples you saw in *People* magazine, looking glamorous even if they were just getting coffee or watching a Lakers game.

Except unlike the Hollywood couples, Mama and Del were always broke. Then one day, as Mama was teaching her to drive, she pulled off the road and said she had a headache. She passed out and wouldn't wake up, and by the time the police came, she was already gone. An embolism. Mama had always been sickly, but the doctor at the hospital said it was totally random, with no underlying cause and no way to stop it.

Both Margie and Del were so destroyed by shock and grief that they couldn't function. They were like pieces of a boat that had broken apart, drifting aimlessly away from each other, attached to nothing. Mama had been the glue that held the family together. When she was gone, so was the bond.

Then one day Margie noticed Del looking at her in a certain way.

"How old are you now?" he asked.

"Sixteen." How could he not know that?

At night she heard his footsteps in the hallway outside her room. The footsteps paused next to the door. She didn't breathe for a long time. Not one single breath. Not until, thank god, the footsteps shuffled into silence.

The looks Del slid her way didn't go away, and sometimes after he had a few beers, she heard his tread outside again. He'd softly scratch on her door. The feeling in her gut warned her to leave and so she took off in her mother's car. She took along a suitcase with a few changes of clothes, some key kitchen items, and the only thing of value her mother had left behind—a thick, food-spattered binder crammed with her handwritten and annotated recipes.

"My mama died," Margie had explained to Queen, keeping her eyes low. "And her boyfriend, Del, he wasn't a good guy."

After that, Cubby and Queen hadn't asked too many questions, which was a big relief, because she hadn't wanted to talk about Del.

Now she remembered the Watsons with deep gratitude, wondering if she would ever be able to repay their many kindnesses. When they discovered she was living in her car, they'd set her up in a garage apartment near the restaurant's smoke shack at the edge of town.

Within a few years, she'd proven herself in every aspect of the service and was an eager student of the art of barbecue. Cubby jokingly called her the son he never had. In fact, he and Queen were childless, and when they'd started bringing Margie to service on church Sundays, they'd raised eyebrows for sure. A blond-haired white girl, she had never set foot in a Black house of praise. But Queen was a church mother and Cubby a deacon, and the congregation of the Church of Hope made her welcome in a way she'd never been welcomed anywhere else.

Thanks to steady wages and tips, and the proceeds from her small-batch sauces, she managed to pull together enough of a life to rent a little furnished cottage by the creek, with a cat she'd rescued from a box of kittens in the H-E-B parking lot. She had settled into a life of quiet contentment, until the night everything fell apart.

Ida returned from the office and put the carryout box in a thermal carrier. "Smells like pure heaven," she said. "I'll take it home for dinner."

"Let me know what you think," Margot said.

"Right now, what I think is we're going to get along just fine." Ida grinned at Margot's expression. "Don't worry. I really am retired. I won't be sticking my nose in your business. Have you met Jerome?"

"I've been really busy. We haven't crossed paths yet."

"You will, no doubt. Mind if I share this with him and his boys?"

"Not at all. And there's plenty more where that came from."

"Jerome's a single parent," Ida said. "It's a challenge, but he's a fine daddy."

"I hope to meet him soon," Margot said.

"I like having them over," Ida said. "They're good company."

"Is there a Mr. Sugar?"

"There was. We divorced a long time back," Ida said, "after Jerome finished high school. All Douglas left me was his name. He remarried and passed away five years ago."

"You never married again?"

"I never did." She paused, seeming to hover on the edge of a larger explanation. Then she shrugged. "Got to liking my own company. Too much, if you ask my son. Jerome, he worries about me."

"Wait a minute—he's single, and he worries because you're single?"

Ida chuckled. "Projecting, I suppose. He knows I get

lonely sometimes, and I suppose I do, but . . ." She looked off into the distance. "My heart's stuck in the past, I guess." Before Margot could ask her about that, Ida asked, "What about you? Single? Dating?"

"Yes—single. And dating? Not at the moment." *Not in a lot of moments*, she reflected. Guys asked her out and sometimes she said yes. She'd had a couple of first dates that hadn't gone anywhere. She did want to find someone. She wanted that feeling of letting someone in, but opening her heart proved to be more challenging than opening a restaurant. There was always a tiny part of her that stood firm against vulnerability. A part that could never move beyond the past that haunted her every day. Focusing on other things was a form of avoidance, but it was simpler to concentrate on meeting with the investment group and planning strategy, working with her new staff. "Getting this place up and running has been my whole life lately," she told Ida. "Anya, my GM, warned me that the general rule of thumb is that things will take twice as long and double the money." Margot sighed. "My original three-month window stretched out to six."

"One day, it'll seem like the blink of an eye. I was young like you when I started the bakery," Ida said. "It was all I ever wanted to do. The neighborhood was a lot different back in the seventies. This space was a church-run soup kitchen. We bought the building for next to nothing. I set up a playpen for my little boy, Jerome, right over there by my desk." She gestured toward the office. "We like to say we've been partners in crime ever since. His boys are eight and ten now, and they're just about the prettiest things you ever did see."

"Spoken like a proud grandma." Margot had only vague, indistinct memories of her own grandparents. When her mother had died, Margot had contacted them and they sent a sympathy card. But they hadn't shown up for the sad, hasty service to bid their daughter farewell.

When she thought about her mother's parents, she could only come up with a vast nothingness. She pictured them like strangers on a commercial for a reverse mortgage, benign and generic. "I hope I get to meet your grandsons one day," she said to Ida.

"I'm sure you will. Just watch out—they eat like a plague of locusts, those two."

"My favorite kind of folks." Margot had a good feeling about Ida and about this place. Apart from Miles, it was the hardest, best thing she'd ever done.

One week until opening day. The deadline loomed, as keenly anticipated as Christmas morning and as dreaded as judgment day. Late at night, Margot keyed in the door code to the kitchen delivery bay behind the restaurant and let herself in. She was too wound up to sleep, so she decided to take advantage of the nighttime quiet and get some work done.

It was a good thing that she loved the work, because there was no end to it.

Her kitchen was ready, her staff trained, her menu set and ready to go. Finally. Tomorrow night would be the first dinner service, a trial run. It was a complimentary dinner for her executive committee and their guests, so they could sample the food and toast the new enterprise. Just the thought of opening the doors gave Margot wave after wave of nervous chills.

Something about the kitchen workflow had been nagging at her. A long wait for an order could ruin a meal, even if the food was delicious. A smooth flow from station to station was essential.

Over and over, she simulated an imaginary order,

timing each part of the sequence from prep to plating. While working the line, she scarcely noticed the time passing. This happened to her a lot. When she was into something, time seemed to stop and wait for her.

She found a possible bottleneck at the far end of the kitchen. There was a tiny desk area that had become a catchall for unsorted objects—mail, utensils, charging cords, odds and ends. She was still organizing the space, but so far, her only accomplishment had been to install a corkboard above the desk. She'd tacked up a photo of Kevin, looking totally luxe curled up in the window of her apartment, and another picture—one of the few she had of herself with her mother. It was an old photo booth strip they'd made the one time they'd visited the beach at Corpus Christi. She could still remember that day, the two of them riding bikes along the seawall and playing in the waves, then getting cones of soft serve and plugging quarters into an old pachinko machine. They'd crammed into the booth, making faces and giggling together. *We looked so much alike*, she thought. *We looked like sisters.*

On the back, her mother had scrawled a message: *You're my happy place.*

Under the desk was an old wooden cabinet. Margot slid it out, replaced it with some stacking bins, and cleared off the work surface.

The upper drawer of the cabinet was empty except for dust and lint. The bottom drawer was stuck, and she struggled to pull it out, jimmying it back and forth. She gave a final heave and the drawer broke free. She fell backward onto the floor, and the contents scattered every which way—yellowed papers and ancient mail, receipts, half-used order pads, matchbooks, boxes of clips—the flotsam and jetsam of decades. Maybe some of it had belonged to Mr. Garza, the former restaurant owner.

She found a few odd tools, like a pie fluter and a nutmeg mill, some small notebooks with scribbled numbers, and too many pens and pencils.

In the bottom of the drawer, something had broken, unfortunately—a large picture frame. She emptied the shards of glass into the trash. The image in the frame was a faded certificate from the Department of Health in 1975.

The brittle wooden frame came apart, and a folded newspaper section fell out onto the floor. It was a special issue of the *Examiner*'s Sunday magazine.

Preserved in darkness, sandwiched in the frame behind the certificate, the paper was in pristine condition.

She took it over to the recycling bin. She was about to dispose of the old paper when something caught her eye. The headline read, LOCAL CIVIL RIGHTS GROUP PARTNERS WITH ANTIWAR ACTIVISTS. It was dated 1972. The Vietnam War era.

Under the headline was a picture of a crowd of protesters jamming the street. The scene, though decades past, looked weirdly reminiscent of recent times—people holding hand-lettered signs, wearing T-shirts and hats with slogans, fists in the air as they shouted or sang or chanted.

Then Margot noticed the backdrop of the photo. It was Perdita Street, definitely more rough around the edges than it was now, but still recognizable. The body art shop was a hardware store back then. The Lost and Found Bookshop had a sign that said THE APOTHECARY TYPEWRITER COMPANY. This very space, as nearly as she could tell, was the home of the Perdita Street Gospel Mission.

Her curiosity piqued, she laid the paper on a stainless-steel prep counter to take a closer look. There was an in-depth article about a civil rights group combining forces with an antiwar group organized by Berkeley students. On an inside page, another photo jumped out at her. It was a headshot of a young Black woman with thick-rimmed glasses and the caption *Miss Ida Miller, niece of Sgt. Eugene Miller, is a key organizer of the joint action for civil rights and antiwar events.*

On the following page was a color photo of an outdoor concert surrounded by people dancing, eating, or lounging on blankets spread for acres on a hill with the Berkeley campanile in the distance. The band was called Jefferson Airplane and the event was described as a "cook-in."

There was another picture of Ida with a tall white guy with long hair and John Lennon glasses. They were holding each other and seemed oblivious to the crowd around them, so absorbed were they in each other. They looked as though their emotions were propping up the sky.

An unbidden sigh escaped from Margot as she gazed at the old picture. To have someone look at her like that, even for a moment, seemed like an impossible dream. It *was* impossible. That kind of romance never worked out in the long run.

She reminded herself that she had a full, exciting life. Her beloved cat and aikido dojo. There were friends and people she would be working with in this amazing new enterprise that was finally taking shape. *Let that be enough*, she thought. *Quit asking for the moon when you have all the stars in the sky.*

She put the newspaper section aside to show Ida later.

Still wound up with nervous energy, she reorganized a serving rack. There was a box of new glassware that hadn't been unpacked. She took out the glasses, washed and put them away, broke down the packing box, and carried it over to the recycle container. It was full, so she unlocked the exterior door and wheeled the container outside to the large waste management bins in the alleyway. The security light came on, then flickered and went out. It was almost too dark to find her way across the service alley to the bins.

Something about the San Francisco fog added a thick chill to the air, making the dark seem somehow darker. Margot fumbled with the key, opened the bin, and put the cardboard inside. Then she locked the container and turned, nearly slamming into her worst nightmare—a large, menacing male.

Backlit by the faint glow from the kitchen window, his silhouette loomed against a swirl of fog.

Her reaction was instantaneous, honed by her years of training—a four-direction throw. She had practiced the *shihōnage* a hundred times and more. And just like those hundred times, the assailant went down on his back, slamming against the pavement. A pair of heavy-rimmed glasses skittered away. The air rushed out of him like a deflating balloon.

She used the precious seconds to run back to the building, frantically pressing in the door code. Then she plunged inside, slammed the door shut, and locked it. Her pulse had kicked into overdrive, and her breath came in gasps of panic. Oh god oh god oh god. Her phone. Where the hell was her phone?

2

Jerome Sugar saw stars, even though the night was seething with fog. His head had slammed so hard against the pavement that he couldn't focus. For several alarming seconds, he couldn't breathe, either. He dug in his pocket for his Ventolin. No luck; he'd probably left his asthma medicine in the car. Wheezing, he managed to roll to one side. His glasses had flown off when he fell. He was practically blind without his glasses.

Struggling to breathe, he groaned and dragged in a deep breath, then got up on his hands and knees. He patted the gritty pavement with his hands, groping for his glasses until he found them a few feet away. One of the lenses was cracked. Awesome.

He got up, feeling a goose egg starting to form at the back of his head. Damn. Being body-slammed by a nutty girl with a ponytail had not been on his dance card tonight.

Jerome went over to the door leading to the kitchen.

He hadn't planned on coming in tonight, but Verna was out sick. Since the kids were with their mom, Jerome had offered to fill in. He'd never liked working the first shift back when he was a youngster starting out, but Ida B had insisted that the way to learn every part of the business was to work in every part of the business.

He stabbed the lock code numbers into the keypad and let himself in.

The girl stood with her back against the counter, cell phone in hand. Okay, she was a woman, not a girl. A young blond woman in a short denim skirt and cowboy boots and bare legs he might appreciate if he were in a better mood.

"I'm calling 911," she said, holding up the phone. Her thumb hovered over the screen.

He gave a weary sigh, rubbing the back of his head as he shrugged out of his jacket. Then he went to the sink to scrub up. "To tell them what?" he asked. "That I showed up for work?" He glanced at her in the mirror over the sink and tried to see himself through her eyes—tall and broad-shouldered, square-jawed, Black. Wearing heavy-rimmed glasses with one cracked lens. He put on a white chef's coat and turned toward her. "Go on, then," he said. "Call the police. Wouldn't be the first time. I guess it'd be the first time it happened in my own establishment."

She put down the phone and stared at his coat, with *Sugar* embroidered on the upper pocket. "Oh my gosh. *Jerome.*"

"And you must be Margot." He dried his hands, eyeing her up and down.

"I'm really sorry," she said as he took off his glasses and polished them with a cloth. The crack angled straight across one of the lenses. "I'll pay for a replacement," she offered.

He put the glasses back on. "I got a spare pair at home."

"I can't believe I did that. I'm so sorry," she said again. "I was doing some last-minute organizing, and I thought I was all alone here . . . and you startled me."

"I could say the same." He eyed the ponytail, the big blue eyes, the worried pink lips. He tried not to check out the legs again. So this was the new restaurant owner. His mother had spoken well of her—itty-bitty white girl, cute as a puppy and smart as a whip. Ida B had not mentioned a violent streak, though. "Where'd you learn a move like that, anyway?"

"Self-defense class." Her cheeks flushed and she ducked her head, looking sheepish. "I'm sorry I treated you like a threat."

"Most girls who look like you think the worst when they meet a guy who looks like me," he said. The indignities were familiar, but wearying.

"I'm not . . . I didn't think at all. It sucks that I had that reflex. I don't want to be that person. I wasn't expecting someone to sneak up on me at one in the morning."

"I wasn't sneaking."

"It was dark. And again, I'm really, *really* sorry."

"Just a thought," he said. "When you're here by yourself at night, maybe don't go out into the alley."

"You're right," she said. "I didn't think ahead, which means I failed the first rule of self-defense . . . Is your head all right? Do you need some ice, or . . ."

"I need to get to work. I'm covering for somebody tonight."

"Oh! Can I help?"

His face must've shown something, because her cheeks turned an even deeper shade of pink. She said, "I mean, I'd like to be helpful. I feel real bad that we got off on the wrong foot."

"It's one in the morning," he reminded her.

"I'm wide awake. Nervous as hell about my opening day. I swear, I'm good in the kitchen. I'd like to help."

Jerome jerked his head toward the row of clean jackets hanging on a rack by the door.

Margot flashed a smile that seemed to light the room, then quickly swapped the cowboy boots for kitchen clogs. Damn. He could watch her do that all night long.

Then he checked himself. This was work. He was at work.

She scurried over to the sink and scrubbed. "I knew I wouldn't be able to sleep," she said, "so I came in to get some things done. I'm a bundle of nerves these days."

He remembered those nerves. Years ago, when he'd taken over the bakery, his first project had been to shut down for refurbishing. It was risky, making changes to a place that had been a community anchor since the seventies.

"Artisan loaves first," he said, bringing out the bins. "The long loaves are usually the first to go." He felt her tracking his every move. Then she started assisting him and emulating his movements as he filled the spiral mixers to mix and knead. He could tell she had kitchen skills—the assured motions with her hands, the attentive look as she emulated his technique. While the dough hooks rotated, they prepared the proofing racks—cornmeal for the baguettes and sesame seeds for the Italian loaves. They put the dough onto a table for bulk fermentation.

"I imagine you'll do all right," he said. "My mom brought home some samples of your food. It was outstanding."

"Thanks. I'm glad you liked it."

"My boys gobbled it up as if they'd been starving in a prison cell."

"Your mother is a big fan of those boys," she said. "Asher and . . . Sorry, I forgot the other one's name."

"Ernest," he said. "Named after their granddads."

"That's nice," she said, her Texas drawl sliding over the word. He didn't know much about her, but Ida B had mentioned that she came from Texas. He'd read in a local trade magazine that the new start-up had the backing of a prestigious private equity group that specialized in launching restaurants. Maybe Margot Salton was one of those privileged, trust fund princesses who wanted to play restaurant. He'd seen the type before—people who were more in love with the idea of a restaurant than they were with actually doing the work to make it happen. Watching her now, efficiently measuring the dough into loaves, he realized he might have to revise his opinion.

She looked like a fairy princess but she was a hard worker, pitching in as he showed her how to score the different loaves and move them into the proofing area. Maybe she wasn't so bad after all. Working side by side, they relaxed into a conversation.

"What about yourself?" Jerome asked. "You got kids?"

Margot's shoulders stiffened, maybe. There was a beat of hesitation, maybe. Which was strange because it was a yes-or-no question.

"Nope," she said. "It's just me and my cat and the herb garden on my deck."

"Ida B says you moved up from Texas."

"You call your mom Ida B."

He nodded. "I started working here when I was four-teen and didn't want people thinking I was special just because she was my mom."

"I worked with my mom, too. I've been planning my own place for a long time." She gave a shudder of nervousness. "Can't believe it's finally happening."

"Salt," he said. "I like the name you picked."

"Thanks. I guess I picked the name before I picked anything else."

"Well, it sounds like a good one, if you ask me."

"I hope people like it. Actually, when I was scouting venues, I knew this would be the one because of Sugar." She brightened. "Be right back." She scurried to a storeroom and returned with a jar labeled SUGAR+SALT ARTISAN SAUCE. "I've been making this since my first barbecue gig, back when I was a teenager."

"Places have been founded for crazier reasons."

"Oh, so now I'm crazy."

He rubbed the goose egg on his head. "Aren't most of us in this business?"

The kitchen door opened, and Omar showed up. "I heard that," he said. "Who you calling crazy?"

As Jerome made the introductions, he could tell Omar was trying not to gawk at her.

"Want to take a break and have a look at my place?" she asked Jerome.

"Sure thing," he said, his curiosity piqued. He'd spent a good bit of his childhood haunting the kitchen and adjacent restaurant, called La Comida Perdita. He used to hang out with the Garza kids. They ran around the neighborhood and played endless games under the basketball hoop on the back of the building.

These days, Asher and Ernest played there, when they were with him. Jerome wondered what memories they would carry, his boys. They seemed to be taking the divorce in stride, but he knew it was hard on them. He and Florence had started out with the best of intentions and the highest of hopes. Their marriage had ended not with a sudden crash, but a slow erosion of the love that used to feel strong enough to keep the universe intact.

She had already remarried, and the boys maintained

a wall of silence between the two households. Jerome staved off the loneliness by working too much and spending more time at the marina where his mother had taught him to sail.

Margot opened the door to her dining room and turned on some lights. Ida B had said it was mighty nice, which turned out to be an understatement. The place *glowed*. It had a friendly, comfortable vibe and a good layout, nice lighting and acoustics. The focal point was the bar. It came from the old Winslow Hotel in Oakland, Margot told him, a place where recruits had been enlisted to serve in the Spanish-American War in the Philippines.

"I like it," he said. "When I heard 'barbecue place,' I was picturing roadhouse decor and funny tin signs."

"Please. The designer would have quit on me. So you really like it?"

"Uh-huh." He perused a set of lighted shelves stocked with jars bearing her SUGAR+SALT label. There were smaller jars of seasoned rubs and flavored salts as well.

"Looks like you're ready to go," Jerome said.

"I'm not," she said with a weary smile, "but I can't let that stop me. If I waited until I was a hundred percent ready, I'd never open."

They went back to the kitchen together. The air hummed with the whir and clack of the mixers and cutters as the morning shift got underway. "I better get to work for real now," said Jerome. "Thanks for the preview."

"Of course. Oh, hey, I found something earlier tonight." She handed him an old news magazine. "This was pressed behind an old framed certificate. It's from 1972, and your mother's in it. Look how young she was."

Jerome scanned the article, his curiosity piqued. Ida B had come of age in the seventies, the daughter of a preacher and a teacher. The pictures showed her as a teenager at some kind of protest rally, hanging out with a tall white dude. She'd never had much to say about that time of her life, only that she eventually put the foolishness behind her and did what family tradition and the good Lord meant for her to do—marry and settle down. The marriage had ended about five minutes after Jerome had left for college.

"Thanks for this," he said. "I bet she'll be glad you found it."

Margot put her coat in the hamper. "I'd better get going," she said. "It was nice meeting you, Jerome. I mean, it wasn't nice at first . . ."

"I get it. Good to meet you, too," he said.

She bent over to pull on her boots. Those legs. He looked away quickly as she straightened up.

"Sorry again about—" She tilted her head toward the back door.

"I'll survive."

"I owe you a pair of glasses."

"Don't worry about it."

3

Jerome's last task of the morning was to deliver a tray of baked goods to the bookshop across the street. The owner, Natalie, took a few dozen every day to serve at the coffee bar in the bookstore. He tapped at the door and she let him in.

"Hey, Sugar man," she said, standing back to make room for her very prominent pregnant belly. "What do you have for us this morning?"

"Only the best. Morning glories, pull-aparts, butterhorns, croissants, black-and-white cookies."

"Fantastic," she said, helping herself to a still-warm pull-apart. She took a bite and closed her eyes briefly. "I like this eating-for-two business."

"Glad to be of help," he said.

She peered out the display window. "So the new place next door to you is called Salt."

"Yep. Grand opening's coming up soon."

"I know. Peach did the restoration work on the antique bar. Did the installation, too. He thinks it turned out great."

"Do you guys like barbecue?"

"At eight months pregnant, I like everything. And Peach is from the South, so yes, he loves it. Have you made friends with the owner yet?"

"I, uh, met her. A woman named Margot Salton."

"And?"

"And she did this." He pointed out the cracked lens.

"Yikes. I hope it was an accident."

"It . . . Yeah, sort of." Jerome told Natalie about the incident in the service alley. He still couldn't believe the woman had slammed him to the ground.

"Well, just think, you'll have a story to tell about the first time you met."

"It's not a very good story."

"Depends on how it ends." She gestured grandly to a display of new fiction on a table. "So is she . . . young, old, single, married, what?"

"Young. Single." *Hot.*

"Ooh, might be a match."

"Knock it off. You're as bad as my mom." His mother kept wanting him to find someone. So did his friends. So did he, but what people forgot was that finding someone was the easy part. Keeping someone, loving someone, trusting someone—that was the challenge.

"We all just want you to be happy, Sugar."

"I'm working on it." He felt the fatigue of the night stabbing between his shoulder blades. "See you later," he said. "You take care now."

Jerome went home and had a shower and a snooze. Then it was back to the office for a planning meeting, inventory check, payroll, and paperwork. He found himself scanning the premises for a glimpse of Margot Salton, but he didn't see her.

After work, he met his mother at the dock for an evening sail. Sailing was a hobby she had enjoyed ever since her youth. It was an unlikely pursuit for a Black girl back in the day, Ida sometimes said, but it was a passion of hers, and she had a talent for it. He'd inherited that talent and hoped his boys would embrace the sport, too.

There wasn't a wisp of fog except in the usual area known as the Slot. It was just the two of them, the way it had been many times when he was a kid. His parents had been good to him, but in retrospect he realized there had been a quiet, excruciating tension in their marriage. Although they'd rarely fought, their divorce had surprised no one.

"It's nice having you all to myself, baby boy," his mother would say, and the fondness in her smile always struck him like a ray of sunshine. It was no wonder he came to like the things she did—sailing and baking.

Jerome had grown up with a lot of advantages, and he hoped he appreciated that enough. His folks had worked hard and bought a nice house. The local school was a good one—and of course "good" meant mostly white. Sometimes people said he was lucky to go to that school. Did they tell white kids they were lucky, too? Of course they didn't. Jerome understood exactly why they said it.

He also understood exactly why they expected him to be the center on the basketball team and the fastest running back on the football team. And he knew exactly why people were so surprised when he tried out for the interscholastic sailing team, determined to prove himself. By his second season, he was raising eyebrows by winning trophies in the whitest sport in the world.

Tonight there was no hurry. Sailing was a pastime Jerome always enjoyed with his mother. They headed around the back side of Angel Island, and there was enough wind to get up Raccoon Strait. In her windbreaker and purple beanie, Ida B looked as young now as she had when he was a boy, her face lifted to the sky, her sturdy hand assured on the tiller. On the return, they sailed downwind at hull speed, refreshed and hungry for dinner.

They picked up fish and chips to take to Ida's house. Her kitchen was full of memories. This was where she demonstrated the god-given talent and craft that had made Sugar a success when she'd founded it at the age of twenty. This was where she had perfected her techniques and recipes—the dense Detroit pound cake, the light-as-air pastries, her signature champagne torte, and the bestselling kolaches had all been developed here in the homey old-fashioned kitchen. Biscuits, she often said, were the purest test of a baker's skill. The ingredients were simple and technique was everything. Use flour from winter wheat and sift it twice. Keep a cube of butter in the freezer and shred it with the box grater. Wet your fingertips with buttermilk and handle the dough as if it were as fragile as a soap bubble. At his mom's side, Jerome had discovered what he was meant for.

Working at the bakery was like entering a beam reach—the fastest point of sail. He liked everything about bakery work—the urgent pace, the smells, the sounds, the camaraderie with the other helpers and vendors, the customers. He was fascinated not just by the craft of baking, but by the business itself. What did customers want every day? For special occasions? Which items had the best profit margin?

By the end of high school, Jerome knew what he wanted his future to look like. In college, he studied hospitality and entrepreneurship. He took a year off to travel, eating his way across Europe and Africa and Asia. He took classes at Lenôtre in Paris and went to Berlin to learn to make bienenstich. He sampled the rich custard tarts of Macau and savory pastries in Cape Town. He learned to make butter on the isle of Jersey and discovered the wonder of the Nanaimo bar on Vancouver Island.

It was the Nanaimo bar that had led to his marriage. At a crowded Victoria café, he'd been jockeying for a place at the counter when he noticed the woman next to him savoring a cream-filled, chocolate-covered confection, bite by tiny bite. When she learned that he had never tried one, she insisted that he sample hers.

He had fallen in love with the Nanaimo bar that very moment. He took a little longer to fall in love with Florence. They counted that as their first date.

They married a year later, and then a while after that, the boys came along. Jerome's parents had raised him to make something of himself. To build something in his community. To have a family and keep his loved ones safe.

He'd accomplished two out of three, he supposed.

Another few years passed, and Florence wanted out. She wasn't happy and hadn't been for a long time. It was both validating and depressing that, deep down, he'd been feeling the same way. Each of them had been warily circling around the issue, waiting for the other to speak up first. For the sake of the boys, and for the dream they'd once shared, he and Florence had hung on until the happiness turned bitter. So although the bakery was what he was meant for, it hadn't defined *who* he was meant for.

His mother turned out to be his ally in the slow, sad undoing of his marriage. "If you can't find a way to make it right," she said, "maybe it wasn't meant to be." He understood that she spoke with the wisdom of personal experience.

Now they sat at the Formica table in the kitchen nook with its funky seventies wallpaper, savoring the ultrafresh fish and chips.

"So I met our neighbor," Jerome said. "Margot Salton."

Ida B dabbed at her lips with a napkin. "Mm-hmm," she said.

"She is . . . not quite what I expected."

"Mm-hmm," she said again. There was a world of meaning in Ida B's *mm-hmm*s.

"What?" He crunched down on a plank of fried fish.

"She's a pretty little thing, and she's single."

"Oh, no, you don't," he said. "She's way too young for me."

"How old is she?"

He shook his head. "Too damn young, that's how old she is. You want to set somebody up, start with yourself." He'd been trying to get his mother to date for years. He'd even signed them both up for ballroom dancing lessons just to get her out every once in a while.

She wrinkled her nose. "That's different. I'm set in my ways. You're just getting started."

"You're not so set," he said. Lately, he worried about her. Not about her health. She was youthful and vibrant. She wrote a column for *Small Change*, a free community newspaper. She had a circle of friends from church and was active in her sailing club. She kept notes in an old leather-bound volume with *Ship's Log* embossed on the front cover.

She seemed distant sometimes, though. Unmoored. When Jerome asked her about it, she just smiled. "I'm not sad," Ida said. "Woolgathering, I guess."

"What does that even mean, woolgathering?"

"Beats me. Gathering memories, I reckon. We old folks do that."

"Knock it off. You're not old."

"I'm not young."

"Hey, speaking of memories, I have something to show

you." He took out the old newspaper and laid it on the table. "Margot found this when she was organizing the kitchen. It's a magazine from the Sunday paper back in the seventies."

She adjusted her glasses on her nose and leaned forward, studying the article and pictures. "Oh my sweet lord," she said. "Doesn't that take me back? Heavenly days, I was younger than the dawn, wasn't I?"

She slowly turned the page and came to the picture of her with the white guy. In that moment, Jerome saw her whole face and body change. Her posture softened, and her mouth curved into the sweetest, saddest smile he'd ever seen.

"Who's the dude, Mama?" he asked.

She glanced up at him with dreamy, unfocused eyes. "What's that, baby boy?"

"The guy," he repeated. "Who is he?"

Part Two

Having a mind that cannot stay quiet,
I've never been able to meditate without going
stir-crazy. But give me a ball of dough and
the not-so-distant dream of a piping hot cherry
tart with a beautiful lattice-weave top and a
generous sprinkling of confectioners sugar,
and a feeling of serenity washes over me.
My mind instantly hushes.

—Cheryl Lu-Lien Tan

4

"Francis LeBlanc" was printed on the boy's name tag. He had a long swoop of blond hair that made him look like a movie star, maybe like one of those guys in the Butch Cassidy movie. Sundance. The Sundance Kid. Ida had gone to see it at the Palisades at least four times because it had been held over. She'd had to sneak, of course, because her parents were strict about movies with swearing and shooting.

Francis LeBlanc didn't look like he did much swearing or shooting.

As she stepped up to the table, she pronounced the name under her breath. It felt like a sugary marshmallow in her mouth.

Maybe he heard her, because he grinned and said, "That's me, Francis LeBlanc, with a capital B, if you want to get technical." His name tag designated him a volunteer. He handed her a registration form.

As she gazed down at him, she was startled to feel a beat of . . . something. Recognition, maybe, although she was certain she'd never met him before.

"I'm okay with getting technical," she said, carefully writing her name on the form.

"And you're Ida B. Miller," he said, tilting his head to

see her name, then writing it on a tag. "With the Perdita Street Gospel Mission Kitchen."

She set down a cardboard bakery box. "I brought cookies for the volunteer table."

His blue eyes lit up. "Mind if I sneak a sample?"

"Sure." She untied the string and opened the box. "Made 'em myself. You like black-and-whites?"

"Oh, man." He tasted one and offered a blissful smile. "Thank you. This is the best cookie I've ever had. Seriously." He handed her a name tag. "How's your day going, Miss Miller?"

"It's fine," she said, feeling a bit bashful. She had always been shy around boys. Especially white boys. Now that she was done with school, that had not changed. She'd only ever had one serious boyfriend—Douglas Sugar. He was two years older, and when he graduated, he left her behind.

She squared her shoulders and tilted her chin up, determined not to look as bashful as she felt. "I'm here to help with the joint action today."

"Racial equality and antiwar," he said. "You came to the right place."

Ida definitely wanted to find her right place. She had just finished school and kept expecting some kind of magical transformation to take place. So far, this had not occurred. She had a job she liked at a small commercial bakery. On Sundays, she went to church and sang in the choir, serving biscuits and chiffon cake afterward. Three days a week, she volunteered at Perdita Street. But so far, she was the same girl she'd been fresh out of high school. A girl who read too many books and baked the best cookies in town and listened to music that made her parents roll their eyes.

She lived the most ordinary life. She had never been

much of a student, although she was a fine writer as long as she was writing her own opinions for the school newspaper editorial page. Her father was the pastor of the Mission Gospel Church and her mama was in charge of the ladies' forum. The children at the mission said Ida was their favorite. Her boss said she was the best baker he'd ever had on staff. She liked going out with her friends.

Still, she kept waiting for life to surprise her. To become extraordinary.

"So, Ida B. Miller," said Francis, "were you named after Ida B. Wells?"

She was impressed. Not many people would make that connection. But she noticed he was wearing a Berkeley T-shirt. A smarty-pants from Berkeley.

"She was one of my mother's personal heroes," she said.

"What brings you to the march today?" he asked.

"I took the Fulton Street trolley."

He grinned. She could watch that smile all the livelong day. "I mean, which group are you with?"

"Oh!" She felt her cheeks grow warm. "Black Veterans for Peace," she said. "My daddy's brother won combat medals and a Purple Heart. He went to the Cow Palace last night, piled them up, and burned them to protest the war."

Francis LeBlanc glanced down at her name again. "Is your uncle Eugene Miller?"

She straightened up, proud that he knew. "That's right."

Uncle Eugene was a friend of Stokely Carmichael, who protested that a big majority of Black men were drafted compared to whites. It seemed wrong that men who were still struggling for equality at home were being shipped overseas for a cause most people didn't even understand. Uncle Eugene had been at Stokely's side when he'd stood onstage at the Greek Theater and yelled, "To hell with the draft."

Ida knew plenty of boys who had been drafted. Her former boyfriend, Douglas, had qualified for honorable discharge when he lost the hearing in one ear during basic training. People said he was lucky, but was he really, if the cost of his freedom was a permanent disability?

As Ida fell into a conversation with Francis, she forgot to be shy. He said he had a job at a local marina, teaching kids to sail. She told him she'd been to Berkeley, laughing at his astonished expression. Five years before, her daddy had taken the whole family to the campus to hear Dr. King speak on the steps of Sproul Hall. Small and nimble, she'd climbed up into a eucalyptus tree for a better view of the great leader.

"I wish I could have seen that," Francis said. "I was still a schoolboy in Maine, messing around in boats."

To Ida, Maine sounded like the ends of the earth.

They made their way together to the assembly area. Something happened to her that day. She could feel it all the way down to her bones. When Francis LeBlanc looked at her, it was like feeling the warmth of the sun on her bare skin. They walked side by side in the march, and when the crowd pressed them together, they held hands and didn't let go all the way to Golden Gate Park.

They sat on a blanket on the slope facing the stage. There were speeches and music, and people hugging and chanting and smoking marijuana, but Ida scarcely noticed, so absorbed was she in getting to know Francis. They talked endlessly about everything. She told him about baking and her family and how much she loved this city. She talked about the kids at the mission and how she wanted a better world for them. He said he was studying to be a doctor. She thought he was the smartest person she'd ever known, and she told him so.

"You know what you are?" he asked, gazing into her eyes with that goofy sweet smile. "You're the most beautiful person I've ever met, and it's not only about the way you look. It's about the way you look at the world."

"You know what you are? The Sundance Kid."

"From that movie?" He tossed his head back and roared with laughter. "I hope I don't end up like him."

"Don't even think it."

Even though they'd only known each other a few hours, she felt as though she'd known him forever. No one had ever seen her the way he saw her. He understood what she dreamed about, and her eagerness for her life to unfold. He looked into her eyes and he listened as if she were the most important person in the world.

At the end of the day, while Sly and the Family Stone played their brassy, bluesy hits, Francis turned to Ida and cupped her cheek in his hand and kissed her. It was a long kiss, soft and searching, and every little thing inside her awakened to a new level of consciousness.

They stayed out past dark, and he insisted on escorting her home, even though it was miles out of his way. He drove a tangerine-colored Karmann Ghia with the top down, and he took her right to the front door. She clung to him, not wanting to say goodbye.

They traded phone numbers and he kissed her good night and she never wanted it to end.

The light over the front door switched on and startled them apart like a pair of foraging raccoons. There stood her father in his robe and slippers, reading glasses slipped down his nose.

"Daddy, this is Francis. From the march today."

"Mr. Miller." Francis held out his hand, and they shook.

Daddy's cheeks went hard, like blocks of carved wood. Never a good sign. "I appreciate you seeing her home."

"Yes, sir. And with your permission, I'd like—"

"Good night," her father said. "Ida, it's late. You'd best come inside."

Ida's father's chilly exchange with Francis set the tone for the next few months. Yet she didn't let it steal the magic of her unexpected romance with the intriguing stranger. When she woke up in the morning, she thought of him. When she went to sleep at night, she thought of him. They went all over together, attending rallies and concerts and sit-ins. Francis confessed that he knew little about the city and they went exploring. She cringed at the storefront theaters and peep show booths around the Presidio and the Centre and Regal on Market Street, where the shop windows displayed things that made her wonder about people. She showed him some of the places where *Dirty Harry* had been filmed.

Francis wanted to show Ida around his world, too. He took her to hear music in Union Square—the Steve Miller Band and Santana and the Doobie Brothers, all so different from the jazz her parents and their friends listened to in the Fillmore area.

He took her to Cal, the most famous place in the country for protests and riots. There were teach-ins nearly every day. She had not set foot on a college campus since the time she'd seen Dr. King years before. To her, it was like going to a foreign land where everyone looked like Francis, wearing colorful clothes with beads and fringe, long straight hair and bell-bottoms, arms loaded with serious books. Every conversation was deeply earnest, as if each person had something of utmost importance to say. They talked about the war and social justice as if they were running for office.

When she confessed to Francis that she felt out of place and awkward among the students, he regarded her with astonishment. "You seem like a woman who could run the world, Ida. You can take your place with anybody."

"Sure," she said, "just as soon as I enroll as a student."

"You could, you know."

She chortled and shook her head. The very idea of college seemed as far away as the moon.

Francis conceded that it was expensive. He himself had to take a semester off so he could work more hours and save up for his final year. After that, he would go on to medical school.

They had endless conversations about everything. Life and death. War and peace. And yes, Black and white. This was something they couldn't deny or avoid, not in the world they lived in. Some part of her understood that the world was not ready for a love like theirs, but the larger part nurtured that love with fierce, unwavering defiance.

She went with him when he did volunteer work at the VA hospital on the west side of town. His deep caring was evident when he sat with patients and invited them to talk. Most of them, Francis told Ida, simply wanted to be listened to. And all of them had something of value to say.

There was a tense moment when one Vietnam vet, a red-haired guy with big fists and a tattoo on his neck, reached out and grabbed the front of Francis's shirt. "I got a warning for you," the guy said.

Ida glanced out into the hallway, looking for help, but Francis shook his head and addressed the patient. "How's that?" he asked. "What's on your mind?"

The guy kept hold of his shirt. "Listen, if your number comes up, you resist, do you hear me?"

"You mean the draft."

"I sure as hell do. You resist. Promise. Don't go to 'Nam. Those folks never did a damn thing to you. We got no business there, and if you go you'll only add to the problem and the suffering."

"I hear you, brother," Francis said.

The guy shoved a card into Francis's hand. "Hang on to this. If you get drafted, it'll hook you up with a group of folks who can help you." The card said something about the peace train to Canada.

"You won't be drafted because of your student status," Ida pointed out later.

"Nixon is planning to mine the main ports of Vietnam, and that means a surge. Sometimes students have to go."

"You're not going," she said, feeling a chill of apprehension. "You need to stay right here with me."

"I'd like nothing better."

She took him to the mission on Perdita Street, and he threw himself into the volunteer work, lending a hand in the soup kitchen and helping with the kids. It didn't seem to matter what Ida and Francis did, so long as they did it together.

On a breezy, sunny afternoon, Francis introduced her to sailing in a boat he had borrowed from a friend. He'd grown up sailing back home in a Maine seacoast town. He was on the sailing team at Cal, and he wanted to share his love for the sport.

She'd grown up on the bay but had never been in a sailboat. He buckled her into a bulky life vest that smelled of mildew and told her she looked like a natural. Maybe he was right, because she loved every moment of it, even the scary parts when the boat heeled over and skimmed along close to the surface. After a few lessons, he said, she'd be handling the sloop like a pro.

There was a true art to sailing. Once Ida was able to navigate the bay by herself, Francis handed her a flat box. "I got you a present. To commemorate your first solo sail."

The box was marked WEEMS & PLATH. Inside was a pen and a blank book bound in leather. Embossed on the front cover were the words *Ship's Log*.

"You need a logbook of your own," he said.

"A logbook."

"To keep track of where you've been."

She had not been anywhere until she met Francis. "On the water, you mean."

"That's right. You keep track of the hours you spend on the water. That way, when you want to charter a boat, it's a record of your experience. Once you get certified, it's a fine chronicle of your accomplishments."

"Charter a boat," Ida muttered, gesturing at the colorful fleet moored at the docks. "Who's going to charter me a boat?" She didn't want to seem ungrateful, so she hugged the book to her chest. "When the time comes, I'll be ready."

One day, the two of them took a group of school-age children from the mission day-care center to the marina. The kids, from the underserved neighborhoods of the city, were rowdy and ready for adventure. When they arrived at the dock, they let out a cheer.

"Finally," one boy said, "a break from the same old parks and museums."

They tumbled out of the van, eager to explore the docks. There were brown pelicans and sea lions, anemones and barnacles clinging to the planks and pilings, and silver flashes of schooling minnows in the shallows.

"You're going to love being on the water," Francis declared, leading the group to the boat shed. He and Ida helped them strap on life vests, and he gave them a basic safety talk. He showed them how to rig and launch the two-man laser. The plan was to take them out one at a time while Ida supervised the others on the dock. They scampered around, lying on their bellies to dip a net into the water, hollering with excitement when they found a crab or small fish.

At first, Ida paid no attention to the other people around the marina. They were the usual crowd in Dockers and Weejuns and polo shirts. Then she realized they were watching her kids, shading their eyes and squinting, then leaning into a huddle. She felt a warning prickle at the back of her neck, which she tried to ignore. Francis set sail with his first student, a boy named Leon who shrieked with joy when the wind filled the canvas. The others watched from the dock, a couple of them wide-eyed with apprehension.

A short time later, the harbormaster came striding toward her, along with a cop of some sort. His shirt was embroidered with a badge that said *Marine Officer.*

Here we go, thought Ida, waving to bring Francis back to the dock. They quickly came about and tied up. Leon wobbled a bit as he clambered out of the boat while the laughing, excited kids surrounded him. "That was so cool," he said.

"Can I go next?" someone asked.

· "No, me," said another boy, and the squabbling started.

"Do you have authorization to use this park equipment?" the harbormaster asked Francis.

Ida perfectly understood the meaning underneath the question.

"I signed out the boats, same as anyone else," said Francis. "Is there a problem?"

"The boats are the property of the parks department."

"And I signed them out, the way I do every time I come here. So now you're saying I can't use these boats?" Francis didn't raise his voice, but she could hear a sharp edge forming.

"I'm saying you can't conduct sailing lessons without a permit."

"How about that group out there?" Francis gestured at a crew of white folks out on the water, messing around in the park-owned boats. "Do they have a permit?"

The harbormaster pursed his lips. "The point is, you can't bring just anyone here to use our boats. You need to apply for permission."

"I've been coming here for the past three years," Francis said. "I've brought guests with me—kids, students, adults. I work here as a sailing coach. No one ever said I needed to apply for permission."

The guy's neck and ears flushed red. Ida recognized the sign.

She stepped forward. "Sir, if you would give us that permission form, we'll get it filled out for you right away."

The harbormaster glanced over at the marine officer. Then he eyed the clump of observers in their sherbet-colored polo shirts and looked back at Ida. "I'll have to check with central administration on that."

"All right, then," Francis said. "We'll just be out here with the boats while you go check."

"Sir, you're going to need to leave the premises with your guests while we straighten this out," the marine officer informed him.

She saw Francis's fists tighten. It was an anger she had experienced on occasion all her life. For him, this was probably the first time.

"Let's go," Ida said, placing her hand on his arm. "We can come back once we sort out the rules for this *public* park." She held the two men in her glare, then turned to stare pointedly at the white observers.

She and Francis quietly helped the kids return their life vests to the shed. There was a chorus of complaints about not getting a turn. "We're going to come back, I promise," Francis said. "I'll make sure everybody gets a turn. Come on, let's go find an ice cream truck."

"Ice cream!" The children, at least, were easily diverted.

"I can't believe we're going to let them treat us like that," said Francis as they drove away.

She realized then that there was no "us" in this situation. A white man using the boats would not attract a moment of attention. A group of Black children was regarded as an infestation.

"You learn to pick your battles," Ida said. "You learn what hill you're willing to die on. When I was the age of these kids, my friends and I went swimming at Roosevelt Pool. The white folks there had a fit. They didn't want to swim in the same water or even use the same towels as us. Starting a fight over that did nothing. Eventually, the rules were changed, but not by fighting. We did it through the system they created." She let out a sigh.

"It must get exhausting," he said quietly. "I'm sorry. Tell you what. Let me make this not exhausting for you."

She didn't know what he meant until a week later, when they went again to the rec center and he had all the kids pile into the van.

"You're not taking them sailing again," she objected

when he turned toward the bridge that led across to the marina.

A cheer went up from the kids in the van.

"It'll be fine," Francis said. "You'll see." He kept checking his watch. They pulled up at the marina, and then Ida understood. They were greeted by a reporter and photographer from the *Examiner*. A week after that they were featured in the Sunday magazine.

Her father was not pleased. "We don't need some white boy interfering on our behalf."

"Maybe we all need each other."

"You'd best stay away from boating. Only reason to go in a boat is to get somewhere."

She folded her arms and jutted out her chin. "I like sailing. I'm good at it. And that's got nothing to do with race."

He slapped his hand down on the magazine, which was spread out on the table. "It's got everything to do with it. The only reason you were allowed to go there is that a white man let you."

She flinched. "That's not true. I—" She cut herself off, knowing her voice would break with hurt. Knowing that her father was right. Knowing she would never be able to persuade him to support her love for Francis.

Her mother put it in gentler terms. "Baby girl, it's just the way things are. I'm sorry they're not changing fast enough to suit you."

She heard their skepticism like the lyrics on a broken record—*Ain't nothing there for you but heartache.*

"You don't understand," she told them tearfully. "This is something special, like nothing I ever felt before. We're meant to be together. I just know it."

"Do you think his family will accept you?" her mother asked.

"I fell in love with Francis, not his family."

"You can't separate the two. When you love someone, you become part of his world."

"And he becomes part of mine," Ida said, prickling with resentment. "I don't know if his family will accept me, but it seems like *my* family already made its mind up about him."

Francis invited Ida to go sailing without the kids, and she felt defiant as she helped him rig the boat. He was so self-assured, and she reveled in the heady pleasure of being on the water. A breeze puffed through the balmy day, and the sun struck glints of light off the water like shimmering golden coins, and nothing in the world seemed impossible.

Sailing helped her forget her troubles, because it placed her in the moment and nowhere else, and she thought only as far ahead as the next gust of wind. She had come to love sailing the way she loved him—with unfettered joy and abandon.

Windblown and salty, they finished their sail. Francis took Ida to an area of private boathouses, where his friend's dad kept a boat called the *Andante*. Not a sunfish or laser, but a true cabin cruiser—a Catalina. It was a perfect capsule of luxury that felt completely insulated from the rest of the world. And it was all theirs.

He held out his hand, palm up, and brought her aboard. She looked around a dim, cozy room—the saloon, in nautical terms—and then they went to the stateroom in the bow of the boat. He laid her back on the angular bed, and she welcomed his embrace. He promised to treat her like the most precious thing in the world because that was what she was. It wasn't her first time with a boy; there had been a few bumbling encounters with her high school boyfriend. She knew just enough to know that making love didn't really work without the love part. This was the first time Ida understood what it was meant to feel like. Francis made her feel cherished and special, and she dared to think they were meant to be together forever.

Afterward, there was a long silence. Then she turned to him and pressed her cheek into the palm of his hand and smiled at him.

"I saw stars," he whispered. "I swear I did."

"Francis. The things you say." She paused, nestling against him. "Do you go to church?" she asked.

"Not really. I mean, when I was a kid, most people went to the First Congregational Church in our town. It was deadly boring. A bunch of prayers that made no sense and a couple of joyless hymns. They wanted us to be good Christians but there was nothing good about a forty-five-minute sermon telling us we would burn in hell if we didn't obey every blasted rule. Which is my long-winded way of saying no, I don't go to church. Why do you ask? Do you go?"

"Joyless?" she asked with a smile. "Boring? Honey, you've been going to the wrong church."

"You mean there's a right one?"

As she waited outside the church for Francis, Ida's stomach felt like the sail of the sloop, curved outward with a puff of wind and fluttering with nerves. He had shown her his world, and she wanted him to experience hers, too. Bringing him to Sunday services was a bold move, but she didn't want their love to be a secret or a cause for concern, which was what her parents kept telling her.

Church was for everybody, she reminded herself.

Even for white boys who went to Berkeley and talked fancy and said they didn't like going to church?

Everybody.

Still, she was filled with trepidation when he parked his Karmann Ghia across the road from the church and got out, unfolding his long lanky frame from the low-slung car. There was no denying how different Francis was from the rest of the congregation. He wore beige slacks and a shirt with a wide tie and penny loafers. But he also wore his big friendly smile and twinkly blue eyes, and he introduced himself to folks with an enthusiastic handshake.

Even though her daddy's church was small, a mighty sound rang from it during worship. She loved seeing the surprise and delight that lit Francis's face. He swayed and clapped his hands, awkward as a pendulum on a tall clock, but that didn't seem to bother him or anyone else.

When he saw the spread of food in the reception area after the service, he said, "This is heaven, right? I've died and I'm in heaven."

He didn't appear to notice the inquisitive looks he was getting. The ladies were downright thrilled to see how much he enjoyed the homemade food.

"Ida, your flaky biscuits are going to haunt my dreams. I swear," he said.

"When I open a place of my own, they'll be on the menu all the time."

"I like hearing your plans," he said. "I like the way you're laying out a path for yourself."

It was gratifying to hear him say that. Most people she'd gone to school with were already married, and a good many of them had babies. It seemed as if every time she turned around, some busybody was asking when she would settle down and get married. She'd been a bridesmaid so many times, she was running out of room in her closet for all those terrible dresses she'd probably never wear again.

It was just the way of things. Ida wanted something different, though, and a lot of people didn't understand that.

During his semester off, Francis stayed in touch with his friends on campus. He invited Ida to a rally at the People's Park, a place where the university administration had once planned to build dormitories. Student protests made them turn it into a playing field and public gathering spot.

By now, Ida realized that Cal was a hotbed of protest, and most of the activists weren't even students there. The rally got out of hand and the police showed up with their dogs and their teargas canisters, and they were backed up by the National Guard. Alarmed, Ida clung to Francis.

"This happens a lot," he said. "Governor Reagan sics the guard on us all the damn time."

"How do we get out of here?"

"This way," said Francis. "I see an opening." He towed her toward a parking lot. Several others surged into the opening, too, and she lost her hold on his hand.

Something heavy hit her shoulder and she cried out. A canister rolled underfoot, spewing a cloud of gas. Instinctively she picked it up and lobbed it with all her might.

"Good work," someone yelled. "You threw it right back at those pigs."

She coughed and covered her stinging eyes with her forearm. Francis found his way to her, and they broke free of the crowd and burst out onto the barricaded street.

"That's her," yelled a cop. He and another cop flanked her, shoving her and Francis apart.

"You're under arrest, young lady," growled the cop.

"What? No," she blurted out. "Get away from me."

They didn't get away from her. They didn't let Francis

anywhere near her, even though he tried. They arrested her and took her away to the substation jail. She was terrified the whole time, freezing and trying to hide her tears of terror. The women around her sang and yelled and stomped their feet while Ida wanted to curl herself into a ball. The minutes seemed to drag until at last she was allowed to call her father.

His expression was thunderous when he came for her. He managed to get her freed without being charged, because the arresting officer had not filled out an arrest report.

On the way home, she told him what had happened. "We weren't doing anything," she insisted. "They just started throwing these canisters. One of them hit me so I lobbed it back."

"Nothing at all would have hit you if you'd been minding your business."

"And nothing will change if nobody takes action against injustice. Remember when you and Mama took me to hear Dr. King speak? Remember what he said? 'We die when we refuse to stand up for justice.'"

"Then you stand up for justice," he said. "You don't go following a bunch of dope-smoking white folks around, pretending you're one of them."

"That's not what I did, Daddy." Ida stared out the window of her uncle's car. Shame crept from deep inside her, because maybe, just maybe, he was right.

"I'm not supposed to see you anymore," Ida whispered into the phone. She had pulled the cord of the hall telephone as far as it would reach and was crouched on the front stoop, hugging herself tightly against the cold.

"Aw, baby," Francis said. "I don't blame him for being protective. I never meant for you to get in trouble."

"It's not fair," she said, feeling a yearning so intense that it made her chest hurt. "I need you, Francis. I'm drowning without you. Can't we run away together, just the two of us?"

"Away." His voice was rough with an emotion she hadn't heard before. "Ida, there's something—"

"Ida B. Miller," called her mother. "Where you at?" The phone cord tightened like the tug on a fishing line.

"Listen," he said. "Meet me at the *Andante*. There's something I need to tell you."

The intensity in his voice worried her. "Three thirty, when I finish at the bakery."

"*Ida*." Her mother gave the cord another yank.

Ida slammed the phone into the cradle and went inside, shivering with cold and ducking her head to hide her tears.

The hours at the bakery crawled past, even though she was making her favorite sourdough kolaches. The manager let her spend time developing recipes, and this one had turned into a customer favorite. Later there was a big delivery of sweetie pie baking pumpkins at the back door. The deliveryman was none other than Douglas Sugar. He had been making eyes at her, reminding her of their high school days. He was superstrong and had a smile like a lit-up billboard. At any other time, she might be tempted to return those doe-eyed looks, but her heart would forever be with Francis. She just knew it.

When her shift was over, Ida took two buses to the marina and waited outside the gate, because a code was needed to get to the docks. *Please be here, Francis. I need you.*

He wasn't there. She paced up and down the water-front, her hood lifted against a damp, darkening fog. Maybe Francis wouldn't come. Maybe he would agree with her parents that they were not meant to be together.

But how could something that felt like this be wrong? This was the purest, truest thing she had ever experienced and she literally could not live without it.

Endless minutes dragged by. Weepy and defeated, with the evening closing in early, she started to trudge back to the bus stop. The vaporous orb over the kiosk painted the scene in depressing tones. More interminable minutes passed as she waited for the bus. When it lumbered out of the twilight, she dug in her pocket for a token. She had one foot on the first step when she heard her name and turned to see Francis running toward her.

They came together like a pair of powerful magnets, slamming into each other and holding fast. Then he took her by the hand and they raced back to the marina, relieved laughter unfurling behind them like a long invisible banner. They went to the *Andante* and tumbled aboard. Since the first time they'd made love they'd returned to the boat every chance they got, their private, romantic refuge. He turned on the heat, and they dove onto the bed in the stateroom.

The intensity took her breath away, and at the very edge of pleasure, she sensed something else. Fear? Desperation?

He held her extra tight in the aftermath as she drifted to earth.

"There's something I need to tell you."

Those words, spoken in any tone, never boded well. She lifted her head from his chest and looked up at his face, studying its angles and shadows.

To her shock, she saw that he was crying. She'd never seen him cry before.

"Francis?"

"Something happened."

"My lord, what? Tell me."

"Ida. My number came up."

She stopped breathing. Her mind absorbed his words like a blow, and a numbness spread through her whole body like a fast-acting poison.

My number came up.

Everyone knew what that meant. Everyone. The number on his draft card. It meant that in the lottery draft, a man's date of birth was drawn, and he would be forced to submit himself to the Selective Service System. Just because he had ceremonially burned his card didn't mean he'd escaped the system.

"No," she whispered. "You can't—it's not possible. What about your student status?"

"I took a semester off," he reminded her.

"It's not fair," she said, her mind flooded with memories of the returning soldiers at the VA hospital where Francis volunteered. Thinking of the men there, the physically wounded and emotionally broken, she felt terrified by the idea that he would be forced to go. "You're going to be a doctor. They can't send you to Vietnam."

"Oh, baby. I wish you were right."

The US was now mining the main ports of North Vietnam. It was like throwing kerosene on an already burning fire. The flames of war were sure to shoot higher. More men would suffer and die in a war that would never end.

And now Francis was going to be flung into the fray. The very idea filled her with dread.

"Don't go," Ida said. "Francis, I'm begging you."

"I tried for an exemption based on conscientious objector status and was denied."

"I'll ask my father to write a letter. He's done it lots of times. He—" She stopped, seeing a flicker in his face. "Oh, lord. You asked him, didn't you?"

"He tried, sweetheart. It wasn't persuasive."

Her temper flared. "You can't go. You can't. Please, Francis. I'm begging you."

He sat up and held her by the shoulders. "I have to leave, baby."

Leave. She heard something in his tone. Was he going into hiding? To Mexico or Canada? "Yes," she said. "Yes, you have to go away. Do whatever you have to do to stay out of this war." Then she clung to him. "Take me with you," she said. "We'll go away together."

"Honey, no. I'm not going to take you from your family. Your friends. Your church. I can't promise you a future. I can't promise you anything."

"Then I'll wait for you. When the war ends we can be together again."

He pressed his lips to her forehead. "I love you with every piece of my heart, and I always will. I'll never forget you, Ida B. Miller. But we're done. It's the way things have to be. There's no coming back from where I'm going."

For days afterward, Ida walked around like a wounded victim, with no appetite for eating or for work, for her friends or even for prayer. Her mama told her it was all for the best, and that would be clear to her one day. She and Francis were too different. Their lives and their families were too different and if they had stayed together, there would have been nothing but trouble for them.

Grief and loss were exhausting. She went about her routine like an automaton. The kids at the rec center would swarm around her and she tried to put on a cheerful face. When a freakish spate of springlike weather blew through the Bay Area, the children begged her to take them sailing. She couldn't, though. She wasn't certified.

She was too new to the sport. She was too Black. Her ship's log was unwritten.

A glimmer of hope came from an unlikely source. Douglas Sugar joined the volunteer team at the mission as a van driver. He was good with the kids, and he had a creative flair they found mesmerizing—music and magic tricks and made-up games. He and Ida took the group on a field trip to Chinatown to get some kites. Her mood was lifted by the kids' wide-eyed expressions as they took in the exotic wares of the unusual shops. They went to the beach when the tide was out, leaving a long, flat, windswept expanse of wave-hardened sand. Eventually all the kites floated cheerfully overhead, colorful banners against the deep blue sky.

Afterward they let the children run through the shallows, shrieking as the foamy cold water swirled around them. Then they went back to the mission kitchen for the community dinner service. Douglas offered her a ride home in the van. Twilight had fallen hard and fast and she readily accepted.

With Douglas, she finally felt more like herself again, bruised by heartache but determined to go on. He stopped at the crest of Kite Hill overlooking the Golden Gate Bridge, and they got out and sat on a bench to watch the sun go down. He slipped his arm around her, and she turned to look at him, and the loneliness inside her reached out, and it went away a little bit when he kissed her.

5

"Are you sure this outfit is okay?" Margot asked Anya. It was opening night, and they were in the dining room, where the staff had gathered for her final pep talk.

Anya, in her understated black-on-black, gave her a once-over, then a nod. Margot had opted for a black denim skirt, black cowboy boots, and a white silk blouse. "It's your signature look—boots and a short skirt. You're the only one who can pull it off, though."

"Thanks." She smoothed her hands down the skirt. Her stomach churned. *This is it.*

"Good job on the hair and makeup, too," Anya added.

"I went to a salon. It's not too much?"

"For tonight? No way. This is a special day for you. Do you have plans for after?"

"Besides emotional meltdown? Not really."

"Make sure you do something special for yourself."

"I'll try." Margot paused. "Thanks for looking out for me." She and her GM weren't close friends, but they'd been working hand in glove for the past few months, and they knew each other well. Anya had served in the navy as a logistics specialist. She was a single mom with three kids and had launched several restaurants. Nothing fazed her.

Everyone was assembled for final instructions—the people from the front and back of the house, handpicked and trained by her and Anya. There was no room in the budget to hire seasoned professionals, so instead, they had sought people of good character to invest in. The employees were mostly young, some as young as Margot had been when she'd started at Cubby Watson's. They came in different sizes, shapes, and colors, and she had pinned all her hopes on them.

"Here we go—finally," she said, standing with her back to the bar and surveying the room. "Y'all have been terrific through the training and practice service. Last night's dry run was great. I hope your friends and families enjoyed it."

As a final practice run, she'd invited everyone to bring a guest. The service had turned out fine, considering all the moving parts involved. She loved seeing people savor the dishes she had worked so hard to create—the gorgeously cured meats from Candy's pit, the handcrafted sauces, the variety of sides, the tempting desserts.

She believed they'd found the perfect bartender. Casho, a Somali American woman, had a photographic memory for hundreds of cocktails and managed inventory like a logistics expert.

They toasted with her nonalcoholic shrub—a bubbly concoction of fruit and herbal infusions. "I'm good at cooking, not at speeches, so I'll be quick," Margot said. "I've dreamed of tonight since I was a teenager, and it's finally happening, and I can't thank y'all enough. I'm beyond grateful that you're here. And if I talk anymore I'll hyperventilate and maybe cry, and that wouldn't be good for any of us, so let's get the room ready and open the doors."

Glasses clinked, and people burst into action.

Outside, there was a hand-lettered tent board announcing the grand opening. A handful of people mingled on the sidewalk, curiosity seekers from the neighborhood who had been watching the preparations for weeks, people who had a coupon from the website, and passersby who had probably noticed the bouquet of black and white balloons attached to the sign.

Margot felt as if she was on the verge of either tears or hysterical laughter. Everything she'd hoped for was about to begin. But she needed a moment.

During the bustle as everyone put away their glasses and straightened the tables and chairs, she stepped out back into the alley, the one place that didn't seem to be overrun by rushing people. Leaning against the wall of the building, she closed her eyes and tried to catch her breath. Her stomach churned and her chest ached. *Breathe* . . .

"Hey." Jerome's voice startled her, and her eyes flew open.

He stepped back, holding up a hand. "You're not going to clock me again, are you?"

She studied the ground. "Maybe. I might."

He tapped his glasses. "Thanks for this, by the way."

"I owed you." She'd given him a gift card to cover the cost of new lenses for his glasses.

"You didn't have to. But thanks. And by the way, you forgot what I said about coming out into the alley by yourself."

She nodded, folding her arms protectively around her waist. "Yeah, I just needed a minute."

"Opening-night nerves?"

"Full-blown panic attack."

"Damn, girl. How can I help?"

The kindness in his question nearly broke Margot.

She looked up at Jerome's face—soft eyes, soft expression, soft lips.

"I'll get through this," she said. "I've dealt with anxiety before. I'll get through it."

"I have a confession to make. First time I saw you, I didn't give you a snowball's chance in hell. I figured you had sweet-talked your way into playing restaurant. I fully expected you to realize you're in too deep, and then bail."

"Yeah, thanks for that."

"Just saying. You changed my mind. I mean, not that it should be your job to change it, but I've watched you put this place together and you're the real deal. A force of nature."

She offered a tremulous smile. "Right."

"I'm six feet tall. I weigh two hundred pounds. You threw me on the ground like I was a pocketful of loose change."

"I didn't mean—"

"I know. I wanted to remind you of your own power. It's your night. Own it, Chef."

She pushed away from the wall. "Thanks, Coach."

"Hold on a second." He took her arm.

She almost—*almost*—reacted. Even after so much time had passed, a sudden touch made her jump. She hoped he didn't notice. "What?"

"Your skirt got dusty." He lightly brushed her backside with his hand. "I'm not getting fresh on you."

"Closest thing I've had to a date in a long time."

"I'll keep that in mind."

His tone made her feel a ripple of . . . something. A kind of interest she wished she had time to explore. "Now you'll have to excuse me, I've got a restaurant to open." Margot lifted her chin, squared her shoulders, and went back inside, passing through the kitchen, where ev-

eryone was ready at their stations, and into the pristine
dining room that suddenly looked too vast and empty to
ever fill to capacity.

Cubby used to say a restaurant was only one service
away from its best or its worst night. And if it happened
to be the worst, you had to fix what needed fixing and
try again the next time.

She caught Anya's eye at the host station, and they
shared a flutter of nerves. Then she went to the entryway,
turned the sign to Open, and flung the door wide.

"Welcome to Salt," she said, stepping aside as a handful of people trickled in, scanning the place with uncertainty. No one wanted to be the only party present, the
awkward target of a too-attentive staff. Margot wasn't
concerned, though, since it was early yet. She perked up
when a few more couples arrived.

The hostess seated folks according to the plan they'd
made with the latest software. The subtle sounds of a
mellow playlist drifted from hidden speakers. Casho
busied herself pouring the night's complimentary cock-
tail, a jalapeño and smoked-salt margarita in a standard
and nonalcoholic version.

The trickle of people slowly increased to a stream
steady enough to be encouraging. Some were friends
and neighbors and associates. Margot's therapist came
in with her partner, probably eager to see what Margot
had been wringing her hands over in their weekly sessions. Natalie, the bookseller from across the street, arrived with her husband, Peach, the contractor who had
installed the restaurant's iconic bar.

"This might be our last night out before the baby
comes," Natalie said. "With our other little one, we'll
be plenty busy soon, so we've been looking forward to
a night out alone. I brought you an opening-night gift,

for luck." She handed Margot a book. "By one of my favorite authors."

"*Acts of Light*," Margot said. "I'll be diving into this soon." She tucked it away under the hostess lectern. Reading had been her refuge ever since she'd discovered the public library when she was a kid. She felt lucky to have a bustling bookshop in the neighborhood.

A few other guests arrived who'd had a hand in bringing Salt to life—her wood supplier for the pit, the graphic designer of the menus. She was thrilled to welcome them all. She just wished there were more of them. When there was a painfully prolonged lull, the panic started up again. Margot beat it back by staying busy, checking each dish before it left the kitchen, and circulating through the dining room. Taking care not to annoy the diners, she tried to discreetly see that their needs were being met—and tried not to be too obvious about hearing their comments.

There were compliments on the food, the drinks, the decor. People appreciated the serving sizes and the ultrafresh bread, rolls, and thick slabs of buttered Texas toast, all supplied by Sugar. A few patrons noticed the emphasis on local supplies. Several mentioned the unconventional decor for a barbecue joint.

There was a moment—a long, leisurely moment when she stood near the switchback hallway that led to the kitchen and looked out over the dining room—that Margot wanted to capture forever. In that moment, everything was perfect. Her place was exactly as she'd imagined it would be, only this was better. This was real.

She saw people digging into their meals and raising glasses to toast. Guests were laughing and chatting, relaxing, and clearly enjoying themselves, some even rolling their eyes in delight when they sampled the food.

And she thought, *I made this happen, Mama. I did it. Finally.*

A wave of pride swept through her, and even brought an unexpected lump to her throat. But there was no time to feel sorry for herself, because in the blink of an eye, the perfect moment passed. Soon after it was gone, the disasters began.

A guest sent back her dish because the duchess potatoes were mushy. A busboy collided with a server in the kitchen alley, and the noise it made sounded like the start of World War III.

And during that crescendo of sound, Gloria Calaveras arrived with a group of friends. No one was supposed to recognize the renowned food critic whose reviews had the power to make or break an establishment. Her identity was an open secret. It used to be that critics arrived and dined anonymously, but staying anonymous was impossible these days. Glamorous in a dark silk tunic and designer shades, with coiffed hair and sharp, shiny nails, she wielded words like a chef with his favorite knife, slicing into the essence of a restaurant and expertly carving an assured pronouncement into the digital world.

The Privé Group's publicist had advised Margot that Gloria had one of the most refined palates and largest followings in food journalism. But no one had warned her that Gloria might show up on opening night.

"What the hell?" Margot whispered under her breath to Anya. "She couldn't have given me a shakedown period?"

"Relax. She probably will. Critics like to give places a few weeks. But they always worry about getting scooped, so they come early in order to put out the first word on a place. And look at it this way—maybe tonight she'll be blown away and the review will be a love letter."

They smoothed things out in the kitchen alley and moved on. Not long afterward, there was a loud shriek from the restroom. Necks craned and heads swiveled toward the sound. The door lock had failed, and some guy had walked in on a woman. Two women, actually, and beyond that, Margot hoped never to know the details.

"What's that I hear?" she asked Anya, trying not to hyperventilate. "Is that . . . the sound of my love letter?"

Fortunately, her contractor was still in the house—Peach Gallagher to the rescue. He did a quick fix on the lock. Margot barely had time to thank him when they ran out of sourdough for the Texas toast. Her signature thick slabs, slathered with gourmet herb butter from Point Reyes, were an essential accompaniment to most of the menu items.

The beer keg jammed. A large group of diners argued loudly over their check. A server pissed off one of the line cooks, not realizing what a bad idea it was to piss off the line cooks. The cook's salty response made the server burst into tears.

The rest of the evening was a wild ride that mostly felt like a train wreck in slow motion. By the end of service, the place looked like a war zone. One of the dishwashers had already quit. Eventually, Margot found herself alone, finishing up the last rack of glassware. She set it in the rolling cart and let herself out the back. The cold orbs of light created a bleak scene, making it resemble an Edward Hopper painting without the humanity.

Lifting her collar against the chilly mist, she made her way to her car.

A citation for a parking violation had been slapped on the windshield. She snatched it off with a furious, white-hot expletive and stuffed it into her pocket.

"Talk like that'll get you banned from church."

She whirled around. "Jerome."

The bar was called Pulp, and it stayed open until two A.M. According to Jerome, it was divey enough to be called cool, but not so sketchy as to cause worry. It was in an old building near the Lyon Street stairs, and the hostess greeted Jerome by name.

"You're a regular?"

He gave a slight shrug, then said, "We'll sit there."

There was a curved booth, the plush bench covered in gold fringe and velvet upholstery. As he placed his hand at the small of her back and guided her, the light touch didn't startle Margot. The startling thing was that she *wasn't* startled.

She slid into the booth and studied the menu.

"The place specializes in craft gin," he said. "All their drinks are good."

She fixated on the Last Word—gin, chartreuse, lime, and kirsch. "Three shots of alcohol," she said. "I can definitely use that."

He ordered something called a Hanky Panky made with gin and Fernet-Branca. The server left a bowl of snacks, and Jerome folded his arms on the table. "So. You want to talk about it? Or do you prefer to avoid the subject?"

"Nice of you to ask."

"I'm nice."

"So your mother told me."

"She did?"

The drinks came promptly and Margot took a sip, letting the tart, herbal flavors slip over her tongue. "I wish I was the kind of person who can shrug off a bad day and move on."

"But you're not."

"Nope."

"Welcome to the human race."

Maybe it was exhaustion. Frustration. Maybe it was that first sip of gin. But whatever it was, she felt drawn to him like a magnet. Yes, he was good-looking, but it was more than that. The timbre of his voice. The shape of his lips. His hand on the stem of the martini glass. It occurred to her that here in the middle of her biggest, busiest career moment, she had developed a crush on this man.

Which was idiotic under the circumstances. She needed total focus now, as she was trying to launch a restaurant. She needed a friend, not a boyfriend. "Everything looked so good when we opened. The dry runs went really well. I had a happy dining room. Everything was flowing. It was so great. Until it wasn't."

She told him about the chain of disasters that had unfolded, one after another, some concurrently. When she got to the bit about the shrieking women, she could see him struggling not to laugh.

"Hey."

"Sorry. Beginnings are hard."

"Did I screw up, hiring mostly newbies?"

"Adds an extra layer of challenge," he said.

"Start-up wages are all I could afford."

"Then make sure you find good people and invest in their development," he advised. "Or do what Ida did and hire family."

"I don't have a family. I have a cat." She stared glumly into her drink.

"Look, I'm sorry things didn't go so well this evening. It's one night out of the gate. Stuff is bound to happen. You know that. How long have you been in the business?"

"Since I was old enough to hold a butter knife."

"In that case, you know bad days happen. So do good ones."

"True. I really, *really* wanted tonight to be perfect."

"'Course you did. Who wouldn't? First week I started at the bakery, I climbed up on a ladder to get a fifty-pound bag of flour and dropped the damn thing twelve feet to the floor. It exploded on a cutting cart. It was like a mushroom cloud after a nuclear blast. All the alarms went off, and we had to evacuate the building. I looked like the abominable snowman."

"Oh my gosh, Jerome." Margot nearly choked on her Last Word.

"You laugh."

"That's an amazing story."

"There were write-ups by the Health Department *and* Labor and Industry. But the point is, I survived. So will you." He finished his martini.

"That's the plan. That's always been the plan." She sipped her drink. "I can't stop thinking about the plate of brisket that got sent back to the kitchen. That's probably the one that bugs me the most."

"I have an idea. Tell me something good that happened tonight."

"You sound like my therapist."

"I'll take that as a compliment."

"It's not. She annoys me, mostly. Asks hard questions. Not tonight, though. She and her partner came to dinner and they loved their meal."

"See, there's something good. Tell me more."

Margot went back over the day. Yes, there were moments. Plenty of them, now that she thought about it. "Why do we remember the bad stuff and not the good?"

"Human nature. I try to focus on the positive whenever

I can. So your mom's back in Texas? I bet she'd be proud of you."

Margot looked off into the distance. "She passed away when I was sixteen. I miss her every day."

"I'm real sorry. Must be hard."

"It's . . . Yeah. I mean, the doors opened tonight and it was this huge moment in my life, and I didn't really have anybody, you know?"

"That's too bad, Margot. Not close to your dad? Siblings?"

She shook her head. "It was just my mom and me. When I moved to San Francisco, I didn't know a soul. The work consumed me and I forgot to have a life."

"How about I remind you?"

"I have an app on my phone for that."

"All this loveliness and you want an app?" Jerome gestured at himself dramatically.

"I mean, I don't want to be a bother."

"Then how about you be a friend?"

She studied him across the table. Muted jazz music floated through the room. Glassware clinked as the bartender mixed drinks for last call. "Yeah," she said. "Okay."

"Okay."

"I wanted it to go well," she confessed. "I wanted everything to be perfect. And I knew better than to have such high expectations, but I couldn't help myself."

"Nothing wrong with high expectations. Ida B says that's what keeps both her and me single."

"Your expectations are impossibly high?" she asked, intrigued that the topic had shifted. "So high they'll never be reached?"

"So high I'll never have to put myself out there, you know?"

She grinned. "You're pretty self-aware. For a guy."

"I got a therapist, too. Had one. Haven't had a session in a while."

"Why don't you want to be out there?" she asked.

"The divorce did a number on me. I don't like to fail. And I don't like to hurt."

"So if you stay single there's no chance of getting hurt."

He stared at her, and then his gaze skated away. "What about you? Ever been married? Single by choice?"

"Never married," she said. "Not even close." She hoped he didn't dig deeper. Experience had taught her to be cautious about what she shared.

Her phone vibrated, indicating a notification. Margot glanced at the screen. "Oh boy."

"Let me guess. You have your phone set to ping you every time someone mentions Salt."

"I'm not going to hide my head in the sand." She opened the app. Several dozen mentions floated into view.

Jerome covered her hand with his, hiding the screen. "Promise me something."

His hand was warm. Gentle. "What's that?"

"If there's a crappy review, you won't fixate on it."

"Deal. I'm a grown-up. I can handle it."

"I'm here for emotional support. Just in case."

She couldn't help smiling. "Don't you have to go to work in the morning?"

"I got time for a friend."

She pulled her phone away from him. "Thirteen reviews," she said. "Not sure I like that number. Gloria Calaveras showed up tonight—you know, that food blogger with a massive following?" Margot cringed, remembering every last dinner service mistake. Then she took a deep breath. "So. The first one is four out of five. 'Beautiful space, delicious food, slow service.'" She ran through a few others. He shifted closer to her on the bench to read over her shoulder. He smelled nice—martini and shaving soap.

Her gaze fell on a single star on the screen, like a zit in the middle of a face. "Damn," she said, reading from the screen. "'Waffles have no place in a BBQ restaurant.' Oh, and this one. 'The hot sauce was too hot.'" Her heart sank as she found a few more choice comments. "'Based on the decor, I expected fine dining. But it was just barbecue like you get from the food truck.' 'Server mumbled when she spoke.'" Margot gulped down her drink and glared at the empty glass.

"Honey, you can't live or die by every gripe," said Jerome. "That's a quick trip to crazy town. If you see a pattern, maybe pay attention."

"You called me honey."

"Is that bad?"

Margot shrugged.

"Is it sexualized conversation? I try to be careful about that shit."

She wasn't honey. She wasn't sweet. He might not know that yet but she wasn't.

She reminded herself to focus on the reviews. *Real Texas barbecue, at last. As good as the food truck but more expensive. The barbecue of your dreams has arrived.* There were a couple more thorns among roses— *Overpriced, watered-down drinks. Too salty. Not salty enough. Got my order wrong. Too noisy. Too quiet.*

Her favorite was a five-star rave. *The Next Go-To Spot. The tender brisket, with a crust as perfect as praline candy, will make you want to brave rush-hour traffic to just to sample it. The sauces are smooth as silk and layered with infusions of spice. Rather than being an afterthought, the sides deserve a life of their own. Margot*

Salton is a sorceress, wielding her unique mastery over wood and smoke and fire.

"Wow," Margot said. "That's a damn love letter. Thanks, sugarman74." Then she focused on the name. "Sugarman. That's you, isn't it?"

Jerome didn't say anything, but a light danced in his eyes.

"Well, thank you," she said. "It's really nice of you."

"Like I said, I'm nice. But I don't lie. Your food is incredible and I hope this goes well for you."

She could look at his eyes all night long. But she gave herself a shake. "I hope so, too. And now, I need to let you get home. Really."

He signaled for the tab and took out his wallet and phone. Both were pink, with sparkles.

"You like the color pink?" she asked.

"No preference," he said. "In certain situations, it's just better to have a nonthreatening color."

She wasn't sure what to say to that. He was one of the nicest people she'd ever met, but that would not necessarily be someone's first impression of him. It certainly hadn't been hers, she thought. All the little things a Black guy had to consider, things white people never thought about. "People who don't know you might think you're a threat."

"Sometimes," he said.

"Snap judgments suck. Shitfire, when folks hear my accent, they shave twenty points off my IQ."

He paid the tab and they walked outside together. The city at two in the morning was like a different planet, preternaturally quiet, lit by the fuzzy orbs of fogged streetlamps, the cars few and far between.

Margot unlocked her car and Jerome held open the door for her.

"You can apply for a parking permit on the city website," he said. "They grant extended hours to merchants."

"Good to know."

"Be careful going home."

"Always."

There was a moment. If she was reading it correctly, it was a moment of hesitation, in which they were both thinking the same thing. *Should we touch? Oh, shit, kiss?* She tried not to fixate on his lips. But ah, they looked so soft.

He stepped back then, and she took it as her cue to slip down into the seat.

"See you later, Margot," he said. "Get some rest."

She was too keyed up to rest. In her mind, there were a hundred things she wanted to improve about the restaurant. But more than that, she wanted to think about Jerome.

6

Salt was not an instant sensation. But neither was it an abject failure. According to the management team, the restaurant was hitting all the marks in terms of bookings and covers, website clicks, media hits, digital ad tracking, engagement on social media, and customer satisfaction. And most important of all, in its first year of operation, Salt was meeting revenue goals. She was able to pledge support to the Amiga Foundation and Planned Parenthood. There was even some talk of a Divina Award, one of the most important in the industry.

Margot left such matters up to the PR firm. She kept her head down and focused on the quality of her food and service. It was amazing how much of her identity was bound up in the restaurant, though. Sometimes she couldn't separate the two. Her sense of self rose and fell with the restaurant's fortunes, which was not great for her mental health, but hard to avoid.

There were nights when she went home in a stupor of exhaustion, collapsing on the bed next to her cat for a few hours of blackout-quality sleep. Other nights, nerves kept her awake as she worried about staff problems, supply problems, bookkeeping problems, regulatory problems. Lately, though, as Salt trended upward, she was starting to relax a little, and sometimes she was able to sleep like a normal person.

Remembering Anya's advice, she made time to do things that weren't restaurant related. She went on drives to the beach at Point Reyes and meandered through wine country. She joined a book group and actually read each selection, remembering that at several places in her life, books had been a refuge. She volunteered at the Perdita Street Memory Center, reading aloud to the residents. The bookshop across the street hosted a bird-watching fundraiser for the Audubon Society, and she hiked around Tomales Bay to observe nesting shorebirds.

She made it through the winter and felt the hopeful embrace of springtime. Over the months, Jerome Sugar became a friend. A good friend, although their work schedules didn't sync up at all. He started early and spent weekends with his boys. Margot's workday began in the late afternoon and usually didn't end until after midnight. Yet something seemed to draw them together now and then. She thought of him, more than she should. His kindness and humor, and the way he listened to her. When he invited her to go sailing with him on the bay, she felt such a rush of eagerness that she realized she'd been waiting for something like this for a long time.

"I don't know the first thing about sailing," she confessed.

"I do," he said. "I think you're going to like it."

It seemed incautious to take up with a guy whose kitchen she shared. Then Margot thought about how kind he was, how funny, and how undeniably good-looking, and she couldn't help herself.

"Yes. Yes, please. I'd like that." She pictured the boats on the bay, with sails like graceful wings as they plied back and forth on the jade-green water. She met him at a small community marina where he and Ida kept a sailboat. He said they'd owned it for years.

"You're wearing that?" He eyed her scoop-neck T-shirt, snug shorts, and flip-flops.

She'd agonized over what to wear, wanting to look athletic, but also sexy. "Something wrong?"

"You need layers. Sorry, I should have told you." He grabbed a sailcloth bag from the boat and took out a shapeless windbreaker and pants. "You'll want to put these on. Even on a hot day, it gets brisk out on the water." He also handed her a life vest.

So much for looking sexy. Then when they launched the boat, she forgot about looks entirely. As they got underway, Margot was grateful for the extra layers. The wind rippling off the water cut like a knife. Jerome introduced her to the basics, and it wasn't like anything she'd ever done before—awkward and challenging, slightly dangerous.

With endearing enthusiasm, he showed her how the wind moved the boat. He taught her the way to trim the sails so that they formed an airfoil to lift the hull in the direction she wanted it to go. She learned to use the tiller to keep the sloop perpendicular to the wind and the mainsail filled. While he demonstrated, he sat close to her and covered her hand with his to help her work the tiller, and she forgot to tense up when he touched her. There was a moment of triumph when she got the shape of the sail just right. The wind moved fast over the curved cheek of the canvas and lifted the boat along in a way that was utterly exhilarating.

The first time Margot sailed upwind was even more thrilling. There was a shushing sound as the sail filled with a fresh blast of wind. Jerome pointed out a big boat going past, creating a wake. "Don't be intimidated," he advised her. "This is the fun part." The closeness of his mouth at her ear was a different kind of thrilling. A welcome kind of thrilling. She'd always assumed that physical closeness was not her thing. But maybe it was.

They cut across the wake of the big boat. Her breath caught as they heeled to one side. He assured her that the boat wouldn't capsize if she kept her wits about her and simply used the tiller to turn into the wind. Still, the heady motion took her breath away.

"Yikes," she said.

"The keel will keep us from going over," he said. Another gust hit, and Margot shrieked and clung to a cleat.

"You feel like puking, go to the leeward side," Jerome said with a wicked grin.

"What if I fall overboard?"

"If you go in, don't panic. The vest will inflate when it gets wet. Just stay put. It might look as though I'm sailing away from you. I have to sail away to come about and bring the boat around. You have to trust that I'll always come back for you."

She looked over at him. That jawline was her new favorite daydream. "I trust."

She learned to take her cues from the wind and water and from the boat itself. Before long, she was able to handle a gust of wind and a big wake on her own. When she heard the sail luffing, she trimmed it. She watched the movement of the water, knowing its muscular shape would foretell an imminent shift of the wind.

There was a moment when she got everything exactly right on her own, without any help from Jerome. The canvas went quiet and all she heard was the sound of the hull rushing through the water and the breeze pushing past. She felt an almost primal connection with the waves. A sea lion popped out of the water like a punctuation mark of delight, and Margot laughed aloud.

"I like hearing you laugh," Jerome said.

"Keep bringing me out here, and you'll hear that a lot," she told him. The spray had probably ruined her hair and makeup, but she couldn't stop smiling.

When they finished their sail, Jerome helped her up onto the dock. She felt unsteady, and he caught her against him, lifted her up in his arms, then set her down.

She looked at him in a daze. He took an inhaler from his pocket, inhaled two puffs, and put it away with a shrug. "You take my breath away."

Her cheeks and ears heated with a blush. "That's corny."

"That's your fault," he said. "Let's go get something to eat."

Margot went sailing with Jerome every time their schedules and the weather permitted. She learned to work the sails and sheets and rudder, to read the wind and waves. Every day was different. Every day was new.

She learned that Ida had been passionate about the sport ever since she was a young woman. She'd taught Jerome to love it, too, and when he was a boy, it became their thing. He told Margot he'd been on the sailing team in high school and college, and now he was teaching his boys the sport.

"Did you play sports in school?" he asked her.

She snorted. "Only if you count running from bullies," she said. "I didn't go to fancy schools like you did."

"Oh, so now I'm fancy."

Though he didn't know it, the advantages he'd had would have blown her mind. Sometimes she was tempted to tell him more. She resisted, though. She was enjoying this too much to put it at risk.

After Margot made her first solo run, they sat on the aft deck and Jerome opened a bottle of prosecco for a toast. "To getting out of the kitchen," she said.

"This is the best feeling," he said. "Doing the one thing I love while falling in love."

She nearly coughed up her prosecco. "Hey."

"What, you don't like hearing that?"

The fact was, she did like it, even though it was impossibly romantic, startling. He wasn't like anyone she'd ever known. The way she felt about him was like sailing—filled to brimming, buoyant, sleek and swift. It was magical.

He must have felt her staring at him, because he smiled and frowned simultaneously, kind of a grimace. "I'm trying to figure out what you're thinking."

"I didn't know how lonely I was until you came along and showed me what loneliness *wasn't*." The admission just came out. She kept a lot of things hidden but she wasn't a liar.

He set down his champagne flute, turned to her on the bench, and cupped her cheek in his hand. "I'm not sure if that makes me happy or sad."

"Choose happy. I'd never want to make you sad."

"The way I feel right now, you never will."

"Never is a long time."

He chuckled. "You sound like my mama."

"I'll take that as a compliment."

They were quiet together for a few moments. Then he asked, "What would you think about me finding the guy—Francis LeBlanc—from that old article that was hidden in the kitchen?"

"I'd think it was a long shot. And even if you were to find him, what would it serve?"

"My mom's been alone for a long time. Maybe she's hanging on to whatever it was she had with him."

"Sounds crazy to me. They're not the same people they were when they fell madly in love. He probably has a family, a life. Or he might be dead. Could be he was killed in Vietnam or came back hopelessly damaged by trauma."

"Love your optimism," said Jerome.

"I just think she's bound to be disappointed. Or even heartbroken. I bet he broke her heart when they were young."

"In that case, maybe she'll find closure."

"After all this time? You want her to go on a quest for her old love?"

"Maybe she should."

"Maybe it would open an old wound, ever think of that?"

Jerome stretched out his long legs and draped his arm along the gunwale behind her. "That's why I haven't told her yet that I found the guy," he said.

She nearly choked again. "You're kidding."

"Hand to god. It wasn't that hard, actually. He changed his name to Frank White, and he's a doctor at the VA hospital."

"Here in the city?"

"Yep."

"And you haven't told her."

"Not yet. I don't even know if she'd welcome the information."

"You won't know until you ask." She hesitated. "Did you talk to the guy?"

"No."

"Could be he's happily married. Or married and miserable. Could be he's actually a jerk. Do you really want to mess with her head, dredge up old memories, if he's somebody best left in the past?"

"Well, I can think of a way to find out," he said. "Let's pay him a visit."

"Seriously?"

"Sure. If he sucks, I won't have to bother Ida about him. On the other hand, if he seems like somebody she might want to see again, then I'll let her decide."

"Paging Dr. White. Please report to checkpoint four east."

Frank White didn't react to the page as he palpated his patient's belly and then listened through his stethoscope. He was relieved to hear normal bowel sounds and to feel nothing amiss in the abdomen.

"Isn't that you?" asked Mr. Johnson. "Dr. Frank White?"

"It is. We're nearly finished here. Keep improving, and we'll talk about discharging you."

"Sounds good," said Mr. Johnson, a former staff sergeant in the army. "I'd like that."

"Bet your grandkids would, too." Frank had noticed a snapshot of the man posing with three grinning children and a sandcastle. He always tried to connect with his patients on a personal level. Most physicians no longer did inpatient rounds, leaving the chore to hospitalists, but Frank still followed his primary care patients like a hen over a clutch of eggs. He'd been eligible to retire for several years, but preferred to stay on the job. It was a way to fill his day.

As he headed to the meeting point, he squared his shoulders and tried his age-old method of letting go. Breathe in. Breathe out. Look up.

It had been a tough morning. He had to pronounce the death of a patient—a second lieutenant who had served in the first Gulf War and had come home with wounds that plagued him for decades. He had finally surrendered to the pain and exhaustion of the fight. The family had been called in. The mournful tradition of draping the body with the flag ensued, and the gurney made its slow exit, accompanied by taps as the health-care workers gathered in the hallway. A few of the ambulatory patients joined the salute from their doorways. The civilians laid their hands on their hearts. The veterans on staff offered a military salute.

Though he'd been through the cycle many times, Frank never got used to it. He was probably better at handling it, though. His life's work had been to care for the men and women who had taken care of the nation, and after all this time, he hoped he'd done some good.

He found two people waiting at the east lobby checkpoint. There was a blond woman who was all legs and cowboy boots, and a tall Black guy in Dockers and deck shoes. Family members, maybe? They didn't seem to match any of his patients.

"I'm Dr. White," he said. "Can I help you?"

"Dr. Frank White?" The guy stuck out his hand, and they shook. "I'm Jerome Sugar and this is Margot Salton. We just need a few minutes of your time."

Frank flicked a glance at the lobby clock. "Sure," he said. He motioned them over to a seating area littered with brochures and magazines.

"We don't want to waste your time, so I'll get right to the point. My mother's name is Ida B. Miller. I think you knew her a long time ago."

7

Frank knew draft dodgers were seen as selfish. Cowardly. Unpatriotic. Maybe he was all those things. But maybe he resisted because of the pointless and cruel deaths—hundreds of thousands of Vietnamese, Cambodians, Laotians. Tens of thousands of Americans. And there was no end in sight for a war the US had entered based on a huge lie—the Gulf of Tonkin incident.

The draft notice instructed Francis LeBlanc to go to the induction center. Back then, no one knew that particular lottery would be the final draft before the war ground to its messy halt. The underground newspaper published by the SDS (Students for a Democratic Society) spelled out ways to evade the draft. A patient at the VA hospital had given him a card with a phone number on it—the Peace Train.

He questioned himself constantly. Was he a coward? Had he failed his country? Should he have submitted to the draft like so many others? He didn't fear a fight. He didn't fear military service. No. What he feared was being part of a war machine that had no call to be there, raining destruction down like napalm on innocent civilians, for a cause that had long since been lost. His application for CO status had been rejected. His claim of asthma was deemed unsubstantiated. He wanted to kick himself around the block for withdrawing from school because his funds had run out. He'd set himself up for this disaster.

On that last day with Ida, he knew he was saying goodbye to her for good. He could tell she knew it, too. For right or wrong, he had to make a choice. Either option meant the end of them. And he had to find a way to retool his life with the choice he made.

Living in Canada was a strange sort of exile. It was the start of a new journey, for sure. He changed his name to Frank White and sent a note to his mother through an underground mail system devised by a draft resister organization made up of ex-pats. His mom might be under surveillance, so it was best to be careful. He settled in Vancouver and found a job in a hospital, humbling work that sustained his passion for healing people. He attended medical school, eventually graduated with top honors, and bought a beat-up old orange-and-white VW microbus. Though he was tempted to contact Ida, as his heart ached for her, he forced himself to resist. She deserved to be free to build a life without him, never looking back at the time they had shared, never having regrets.

The only choice was to move on emotionally, and he hoped she had done the same. As time went on, he dated women who worked with him at the hospital, and others who attended medical school with him. A couple of them said they were falling in love. One of them, a soft-eyed pediatrics resident, wanted him to settle with her up in Nelson, where land was cheap and an enclave of ex-pats had gathered, forming loose communes and working on farms. The rural area needed doctors. They could make a life together there. She was a lovely woman and he was tempted. But he realized his heart wasn't with her. Maybe it was his fate to spend the rest of his life searching for the kind of love he'd shared with Ida.

His specialty as a doctor seemed preordained. He wanted to believe in some kind of grace. His career would be a lifelong penance to atone for the decision he had made. He pledged himself to serve veterans, those who had been broken by the war he had refused to take part in. Canada had its share of wounded men and women. They taught him much, these people who had been mangled by physical and psychic pain. None, he believed, were beyond help. But none would ever fully recover and resume the life they had led before the war.

He was with one such patient when the news of President Carter's amnesty broke. His patient, Albert Baynes, was a serviceman whose unit had provided peacekeeping and support in Vietnam. In a town called Hue, he had been caught in the cross fire of a battle fought during the Lunar New Year. The experience had left him with long-term effects from shrapnel wounds.

"So that means guys can go back to the States if they want," said Mr. Baynes, staring at the grainy TV screen in the ward.

As Frank listened to the announcement, every cell in his body seemed to spring to new life. "Never thought this day would come," he murmured. *Amnesty.*

At first, he wasn't sure what he should do about it. He'd made a life for himself here, had a busy, fulfilling career. Yet deep down, he wanted to go back to the States. Not to Maine, but to the Bay Area, where life had begun for him.

He packed his Volkswagen microbus and headed to San Francisco. The first day he arrived, he drove past the places he remembered—the marina where he and Ida had gone sailing and made love in the cabin of a boat, the campus where they'd marched, the concert venues, the street where they'd volunteered at the mission.

The world had changed almost beyond recognition. The Perdita Street Gospel Mission had closed. Now the building housed a bakery called Sugar, and there was a Mexican restaurant next door. The typewriter shop across the street had hung out a sign advertising rare books. None of the passersby looked familiar to him.

As soon as he met all the licensing requirements, Frank signed on with the VA medical center on Clement Street. He knew what he was doing was risky, but it was nothing compared to the guys who had served.

As he started this new chapter, he yearned to know what had become of Ida. Years had passed and their lives had diverged, but he thought of her every day, and a small, undisciplined part of his heart still held out hope.

He struggled with whether or not to intrude on the world she had created for herself. What did that world look like? Maybe, just maybe, she wouldn't regard it as an intrusion. Maybe she would flash that light-filled smile and welcome him home.

One Sunday morning, he drove to her church. He still remembered the stern looks from her father and the uncomfortable feeling of being an outsider. He parked the van across the road and rolled down the window to wait for midmorning service to break. As strains of music escaped the building, he remembered the rollicking congregation there, and those moments when his sense of otherness was drowned out by the joyful noise and praise.

He often wondered what would have happened if his number had not come up. Maybe her family would have softened toward him. Maybe they would have seen him as a man who loved their daughter and wanted only to make her happy.

Maybe that was still a possibility.

He switched on the radio and listened to David Bowie singing "Golden Years." After a while, the church doors opened and worshippers flowed out like leaves in a stream, the men in their crisp shirts and the women in candy-colored dresses and beribboned hats, little kids running everywhere.

Then Frank spotted Ida, recognizing the lively flip in her step and the proud angle of her chin. She wore a crisp white-and-navy-blue dress and a hat with matching ribbons, and even from a distance he could tell she was smiling.

His heart tipped over in his chest. The palms of his hands started to sweat. Should he approach her? What should he say?

She came down the church steps and turned slightly, holding out a gloved hand.

A small boy in a navy-and-white sailor suit skipped down the steps and took her hand. A moment later, a man joined them and held the child's other hand.

The little family made a sweet picture as they walked together, the little boy swinging between them. Frank's chest ached as if someone had struck him there. It took him a moment to catch his breath.

Of course, he thought. Of course she was married, with a child. There was no reason she would have put her life on hold for him, for a future that might never come. He had urged her to move on, believing he would never return home to her. No one knew if the war would finally end or if the men who had fled would be welcomed home.

Ida had done exactly what he told her to do in that last painful conversation. She'd moved ahead with her life. Maybe she'd forgotten about him or tucked him away like a keepsake.

They were different people now. She was a wife and mother. He was a physician, still constantly questioning himself. *Did I do the right thing? Am I a coward? Is this an atonement?*

Now, as a sad Elton John song came on the radio, he knew he had to find another path.

He pulled away from the curb. In his haste to escape the haunting past—or maybe it was deliberate—he punched the accelerator and peeled out, his tires screeching on the pavement in front of the church. In the rearview mirror, he saw her stop walking and tuck the child against her, glaring at his speeding van.

Each day, Frank tended to the men and women who had served their country. When he helped them, sometimes even healing them, there were moments of grace. He bought a run-down marina-style house in a section called the Richmond and fixed it up. Though he tried not to, he couldn't escape reminders of Ida. When he went out sailing on a bright spring afternoon, he thought about the life they might have shared, and he was hit with nostalgia. He set the sails and relaxed, drowsy from the gentle waves and the mild weather, and took himself through the key exercises he advised his troubled patients to practice.

He visualized letting go. He untethered himself from the past like a cloud moved by a puff of wind. Let go and breathe. It wasn't a magic formula but after many repetitions, it eased his heart.

He met Donna in a class on transcendental meditation.

As it turned out, they both struggled with concentration. They soon found other things in common—a love for reading historical fiction and the music of Led Zeppelin. Riding bicycles and doing volunteer work. She was beautiful and kind, and she said *I love you* before the notion crossed his mind.

Yet when he said it back, he knew it was real and true and it felt powerful enough to last. The emotion was different from the hectic, insatiable love he'd experienced with Ida—a tumult of intensity that consumed him like wildfire. What Frank found with Donna was a quiet, steady emotion, one he trusted to endure.

She helped him renovate the house and took a job teaching English at a nearby high school. Theirs was a quiet contentment founded on stability. Predictability. Two kids—a boy and a girl. A succession of pets loved and laughed at and lost and mourned. They spent three weeks every summer in Maine, visiting his mom and sister. His son, Grady, became a teacher and his daughter, Jenna, worked for a nonprofit.

As a family, they went through all the moments that went into a life well lived.

There were holidays and celebrations, losses and joys, triumphs and frustrations. The heady blessing of grandchildren reminded him what true joy felt like.

Frank kept the tiniest of secrets in his back pocket. He never missed the Sunday issue of *Small Change*, a longstanding community newsletter. Each week there was an essay by Ida B. Sugar. He wasn't sure if that was a pen name or her married name. She wrote clever, insightful commentary and observations about the world near and far. There was always a delicious-sounding recipe at the end, with insightful tips and stories. Each time he read something she'd written, he would imagine hearing her voice, her laughter, her irrepressible spirit. But only for a moment. His own family and work kept him happily occupied and fulfilled.

Donna left him too soon, snatched away by one of the enemies a doctor could not vanquish—cancer. Frank grieved deeply, but his son and daughter propped him up. The three of them comforted one another through the dark, gnawing sadness of loss. He rediscovered joy and delight with his grandchildren, teaching them to sail the way he'd taught the mission kids so long ago.

He could not regret the life he had found. Not for a single moment.

His friends regarded him as a young, vigorous widower who should meet someone. As if the elusive *someone* would fill his life once again. What his well-meaning friends and his busybody daughter didn't know was that he had long since dismissed the possibility. Maybe it had never existed in the first place. Maybe the still-remembered feelings that had engulfed him when he was a young man, crazy in love with Ida, had been an illusion, like the watery visions he'd had when he tried LSD that one time.

But the moment Frank realized he might see Ida again, the moment he thought about taking her hands in his, the whole world lit up.

8

"You go on now," Ida said to Jerome, sending a scowl his way. She was already nervous, and he was making the tension worse. "I don't need a chaperone, for heaven's sake."

"I'll wait right here for you," he said.

Ida looked away. She resisted the urge to check herself one more time in the visor mirror. Then she got out of the car. "You'll do nothing of the sort," she told Jerome. "We agreed you'd pick me up at five. And I'll see you at Friday dinner and we can have a nice chat. It's First Friday. Maybe we'll go to music in the park."

"You call me, you hear? For any reason at all. Any time. I mean it, Mama."

"Stop your fussing," she said. "I'll be absolutely fine. Run along, now." She shouldered her backpack and walked down past the harbormaster's office, following the dock with its rows and rows of berths. She'd agonized over what to wear, though she realized it was silly. She'd been sailing for decades and knew exactly what to wear—crop pants and nonskid Ilse Jacobsens, a light shirt and windbreaker, hat and sunglasses. It was probably the same outfit she'd worn the last time she'd gone sailing with Francis, decades ago.

Still, she had taken an hour to get ready, and a good part of that hour had been spent staring at herself in the mirror, trying to get in touch with the girl she used to be. She was eighteen. A baby. And the love she'd felt for him burned all the way to her soul. When he'd left, she had put away the feeling like a flower pressed between the pages of an old book, out of sight, deeply hidden, but never quite forgotten.

Jerome had brought this meeting about, a kindness from the most loyal son the lord had ever made. But he had done so without knowing that he had reopened a hidden door to the past, one that concealed her deepest secrets. She knew there would be difficult conversations to come; she had never mentioned Francis to her son. There had been nothing to say. The man had disappeared. Soon after that, Douglas Sugar returned to her life, and he wanted to marry her. They'd both been too young to know their own hearts, but Ida felt so alone, and Douglas filled up the empty space inside her, and she was eager for her life to begin.

Not one person, not one single soul, not even Douglas, had said a word when Jerome came along after they'd been married for seven months. Only Ida's doctor had privately noted that the baby was a full-term, healthy infant. He was light-skinned, but so were Ida and Douglas, their heritage every bit as troubled as any Black person's in America. There was only one man who could be called Jerome's daddy, and that was Douglas Sugar. This was the only truth her son had ever known.

Ida wasn't familiar with the marina south of the city in Oyster Cove. Francis—Frank—kept a boat here. She scanned the dock letters and slip numbers, her steps slowing down as her heart sped up. When Jerome had told her that he'd made contact with the man in the photographs in that old newspaper article, she had been thrilled. Mortified. Elated. Terrified.

Francis LeBlanc had been her first true love, and she remembered that feeling as if she'd tucked it into her backpack and carried it around with her everywhere she went. This was both a blessing and a burden. A blessing, because this love had shown her, ever so briefly, that heaven could be touched. A burden, because it was a reminder of something she had lost.

He called himself Frank White now. He was a doctor, a father, a grandfather. A widower. He'd told Jerome that he would welcome a call from Ida.

She'd stared at his phone number like a teenager needing a date for Sadie Hawkins night. Then she'd poured herself a shot of Fernet-Branca and called him up.

"I want to hear everything," he'd said.

"It's been forever. It'll take us forever to say everything."

A whole lifetime had passed since the day they'd told each other goodbye, resigning themselves to the inevitable. Marriage, work, children, grandchildren. After all the twists and turns along the way, were they different people entirely, or was there some essence of who they were that had never changed?

He had a boat, he said. Let's go for a sail, he said.

Frank was standing at C-dock, slip eleven, next to a beautiful, sleek sailboat that was far nicer than the park district ones they'd used. Ida sensed a certain tension in his stance when he saw her coming toward him. She felt herself tense up as well. This man had once been her whole world, the missing puzzle piece of her young heart, the Sundance Kid. Now he was a stranger.

He looked much the same, but older, of course. Settled comfortably into that lanky frame.

What did he see when he looked at her? She was

softer, her hair relaxed instead of twisted into neat, shiny braids, and her face was lined with a road map of the life she'd lived. Her heart was pounding even though she approached him slowly.

"Well," she said. "Well, now. Isn't this something?"

His eyes smiled before his mouth formed into a curve. It was an old man's face of crags and shadows, yet the young man she'd known shone like the sun breaking through the clouds.

"I never thought I'd see this day. You look so wonderful to me, Ida."

"Francis. Does anyone call you Francis anymore?"

"Only you." With a slight, almost chivalrous bow, he held out his hand, palm up—a posture she remembered from the past. As he helped her aboard, she remembered the touch of his hand. She remembered everything.

When he opened the box of cookies she'd brought, his face lit with a smile. "Black-and-whites," he said. "Still my favorite."

"I thought they might be."

His boat was lovely, reminiscent of the Catalina where they'd hidden away together all those years ago, making love in secret. They worked in tandem now as they set sail, following the counterclockwise flow of the popular cruising route. As the city fell behind and water hissed past the hull, their nerves and hesitation ebbed. Ida felt something inside her unfurl and sensed it in Frank as well. They began to talk, and she was amazed at how effortless it was.

The words and stories tumbled from them without ceasing, one thought leading to the next in a strangely familiar rhythm. The rhythm of the cruise was familiar, too. They headed north to cross the bay on a port-tack reach. Away to leeward, she shaded her eyes to gaze at the campanile at Cal, majestic and unchanged from the days of their youth. Then they turned to look at each other, and he took her hand.

"This is nice. Even nicer than I ever imagined it would be," he said.

"You imagined this?" she asked.

"Many times." He hesitated, then said, "I did see you again, but you never saw me."

She frowned. "I don't understand. You saw me?"

"Right after the amnesty. Prior to that, I thought I'd spend my whole life in exile, but when President Carter announced the amnesty, I came back here to the Bay Area. I went to all our old places, and I wondered if I should try to find you. I should have known better, but I wanted to learn what had become of you. So I went to your church one Sunday just as services were ending. I stayed in my car, listening to the radio, sweating bullets, trying to work up the nerve to approach you. And then . . . I saw you. Coming out after the service. You looked so pretty, Ida, in a navy-blue-and-white dress and a hat with ribbons."

She remembered that dress, the way women usually remembered their favorites. She'd bought it from I. Magnin, crisp and new, to match the little sailor suit she'd bought for Jerome.

A gentle sadness softened Frank's smile. "You walked out of the church with a little boy and your husband, the three of you holding hands. Right then and there, I knew I had to leave you be with your family. I had to let you live your life."

"Oh, Francis. I never knew . . ."

"If you had, would anything have changed?"

She was quiet for an agony of moments. He'd seen her. He'd seen Jerome.

Then he asked, "What about you? Did you ever think about looking me up?"

"Oh, Francis. I don't know. I thought of you. Remembered you. But finding you again . . . it never occurred to me."

"I understand."

He didn't. There were things he didn't know. Things that could cause everything to change. They had talked about their lives—his happy marriage that had ended too soon. Her marriage that had ended at the right time. He was seeing possibilities. She was seeing difficulties.

"Ida, I'd like to see you again," he told her.

Her heart spoke before her mind had a chance to catch up. "I'd like that, too." *Heavenly days*, she thought, *what in the world is starting up here?*

She smiled all the way back to the marina, and they talked some more while she waited for Jerome to pick her up.

"I was so happy when you called me," he said. "I thought I was hearing things that day your son and his girlfriend came to see me at the hospital."

She sent him a sideways glance. "Girlfriend?"

"Oh, then Margot's his wife?"

Ida had not been aware that Margot was Jerome's anything. "Girlfriend," she said, making a mental note to look into the situation. A girlfriend for Jerome. Fancy that.

"Well, anyway, I'm grateful that he made the effort to track me down."

"Me, too, Francis. Frank," she said, trying out the name. It would take some getting used to.

When she saw Jerome's car pull up in front of the harbormaster's office, she turned to say goodbye to Frank, and it felt like the most natural thing in the world to lift up on tiptoe and give him a hug.

Maybe this was going to happen, she thought, reveling in the unfamiliar feel of a man's arms around her. If so, there were some things she was going to have to settle—and not just with him.

"I like this, Mama." Jerome handed her a jar of sweet tea and crushed ice from the cooler they'd brought to the park. "Glad you thought of it."

Ida wrapped her hands around the cold jar and regarded her son in the evening light. They'd attended summertime First Friday concerts for as long as she could remember. When he was a boy, Douglas had traveled a lot for work, so it was often just the two of them.

"It is nice, isn't it?" she agreed. "We should do it more often." She relaxed on the old plaid mackinaw blanket they used for picnics and gazed out over the East Bay. It was a lovely evening, and despite the milling crowd and the strains of music coming from the amphitheater, it felt private and safe here. Through the years, she and her son had spent many happy hours here, talking about his studies, his future, her divorce, his marriage, his kids, his divorce. The circle of life.

They'd never discussed tonight's topic, though.

She couldn't imagine how to broach the most difficult conversation of her life, so she plunged right in. "It was awfully nice of you to find Francis," she said. "Frank. Frank White. It was so unexpected. I thought he'd be forever lost in the past."

He chuckled. "Nothing's lost, now that we have the internet."

"When I was eighteen, fresh out of high school, I fell madly in love with him."

Jerome nodded. "Didn't we all fall in love at that age? I'll never forget Linda Lubchik—remember her?"

No, she didn't. Ida took a deep breath and forged ahead. "Well, I just plainly thought Francis was as romantic as a storybook hero. We had a love affair, as I'm sure you guessed. More than a love affair. It changed my life. My parents didn't approve of him, though. He was a college boy from Maine. A white boy. They thought he was nothing but trouble."

"Yeah, I guess Pappy Miller would have had something to say about that."

Ida nodded. "It was a different time back then. I was so young, and full of dreams. He was a premed student at Cal, and he looked like Robert Redford in his prime. I thought we'd go on forever, the two of us. But he was called up for the draft. It was a horrible time. He went to Canada."

"He was a draft dodger, then."

"I encouraged him to go. The war ruined people and I knew it meant I'd lose him, because there was no coming back from that. But I didn't want him to go to war."

"What about his student exemption? Wasn't that a thing? Especially for rich white boys."

"He wasn't rich. He took a semester off because of money."

Jerome sat back, arms folded. "Daddy got drafted, and he answered the call."

"He did, and I'm proud of him for it. What happened to him in basic training was terrible, but the hearing loss saved him from having to serve. But I would have told him the same thing I told Francis. Same thing my uncle Eugene, who was a decorated veteran, told boys—don't go. It's not right."

She watched a pair of brown pelicans soaring over the bay. "Douglas and I got together after Francis left for good. I was working at a bakery, and Douglas drove a delivery truck. He courted me properly, and I did love the man. When he said he wanted to marry me, it felt . . . right. The right thing to do. He was a good man, and my parents thought the world of him. I was young enough to feel the same way. When you came along, everything seemed just perfect. I believed the three of us were a fine, happy family, and I pray you felt that every day."

"Sure I did, Mama. I'm not going to lie—I was disappointed when you split up, but I've had a long time to get over it."

She took a deep breath for courage. "I was pregnant with you when your daddy and I got married. Times were different then. It was a terrible shame on the family when a baby was born out of wedlock."

"I know that, Mama. I've known ever since I was old enough to read a calendar."

"All I'm saying is, your daddy is your daddy—Douglas Sugar, the man who raised you. The man who celebrated every milestone, brushed you off when you fell down, and loved you with his whole heart."

"I know that, too." He frowned a little, clearly wondering what was on her mind.

Final breath for courage. "Son, what I need to tell you is that he was not your *biological* father."

"My— Okay, what?" He held himself completely still.

"Your biological father is Francis. That's what I'm saying."

"Whoa." Jerome stared down at his hands, turning them over. His dark-honey eyes narrowed. "The hell you say."

"Baby—"

"Do you hear yourself right now? What the hell are you telling me? My daddy is *Daddy*."

"Absolutely," Ida said, forcing herself to look her son in the eye. "One hundred percent. He was exactly that, every day of your life, right up until he passed. That will never change for you."

"Now you're saying you were pregnant by some other guy. A draft dodger."

"Yes."

"Did Daddy know? Is that why you split up?"

"I . . ." Ida hesitated. She and Douglas had been so thrilled with Jerome. They had tried for more children—repeatedly, with no results. Douglas and his second wife had never had children together, either. "We did not discuss it. Honey, he was my husband, and you were my baby, and we were a family."

"Oh, Mama. A white guy? Seriously? You're blowing my mind." He looked down at himself, at the backs of his hands.

She hadn't realized she was pregnant when she first took up with Douglas. Then she'd put it out of her mind as if it might magically resolve itself, and when he said he wanted to marry her, she convinced herself it was meant to be.

"Who else knows?"

"The doctor who delivered you and your pediatrician both told me you were a healthy, full-term baby. No one else ever questioned anything. No one asked or let on. Back then, it wasn't considered proper for folks to count the months. Lots of girls got in trouble—that's what they called it, *trouble*. I was young and scared, and I did the best I could, and I'll always be grateful to Douglas for being such a good father to you."

"He never knew? Ever?"

"He never said. He loved you with all his heart, Jerome. His feelings for you were obvious to everyone, and that never changed. He was always a fine father."

Jerome drew his knees up to his chest and turned his face away. He was so handsome and strong, and he held himself with unstudied pride. Sometimes, folks said he looked just like his daddy. That was probably because the two of them had been such a pair, close through thick and thin.

"Did you tell Frank?"

"No. And I won't, unless you say it's all right. I never thought we'd be having this conversation," she said, trying to figure out what was going through his head. "I imagine now you're sorry you found him for me."

He blew out a long, audible breath. "Just . . . give me a minute."

Ida studied him, looking for Francis in the handsome, square-jawed face. She kept thinking about what Francis had told her at their reunion—he'd seen her coming out of church, holding Jerome's little hand. Father and son had unknowingly crossed paths. She didn't tell Jerome, though. That was for another time, perhaps.

"So," Jerome said now, "he's . . . You were happy to meet him again."

It was hard to describe the overwhelming sensation of seeing him. All the feelings of her youth had rushed back as though she were still that starry-eyed teenager. "I think we might start seeing each other," she told him.

"You think."

"It's very new. Maybe it will amount to nothing. Maybe it will be . . . something."

"Something." He shook his head and looked away.

"Yes." Ida felt so torn. She hated the idea that finding happiness with Francis could drive a wedge between her and her son. "I didn't know if the feelings would still be there. I still don't know for sure. I've been alone for so long. But I think . . . I hope I've found what I've been missing all these years."

"Well," Jerome said, and when he turned back to face her, his eyes shone on the verge of tears. "Well, now. It's about damn time, Mama."

On the night Ida had chosen to tell Frank about Jerome, she fixed dinner for him. Chicken and biscuits, creamed greens, thick tomato slices that didn't need anything but a pinch of salt, and a pitcher of iced tea. It was gratifying to feed a hungry man and to see the appreciation written on his face. After he ate, he leaned back and said, "Thank you. If nothing else happens to me for the rest of my life, I will die a happy man."

"Stop." She poured them each a Fernet with a ginger ale chaser. A digestif to settle the stomach. Then she showed him a framed triptych of photos of Jerome—his college graduation, a picture of him with his sons, and a shot of him holding a regatta trophy. "He's my proudest achievement."

"I'm so grateful he came looking for me. He's a fine-looking man. Looks so much like you, Ida."

"Seems like he wanted to check you out before telling me."

"He's protective of you."

"Yes. But there's something he didn't realize," she said, shifting in her chair. "If he had . . ." She squared her shoulders. Cleared her throat. "He was born nine months after you left."

His white skin turned paler and grayer, the blood perceptibly dropping from his face.

"I told him yesterday," Ida went on.

"Before that, he never knew?" Frank's voice shook.

"It was one of those things that was easy not to mention. Maybe I should have said something sooner, but honestly, we were living our lives as a family. My husband was the only daddy he ever knew. Anything else would have been confusing. I just never focused on it. I focused on my boy. But . . . well, now that you're here, I had to tell him. And I'm telling you."

Frank stared at the photographs, seeming to drink them in with his eyes. She showed him a few more in an album, fading images of happy moments.

"My god," he said. "If I'd known . . ."

"If you'd known. Then what?" She brushed off the what-ifs. "We did what we did. We lived our lives, and so did our families. But this"—she gestured around the kitchen—"changes things. He—and you—deserve to know the truth."

He nodded as if the slight movement gave him pain. "That day I told you about, when I came back to the States and waited outside your church . . ."

"Francis . . . Frank—"

"Now I look back and I'm seeing that day through a different lens." He rubbed his eyes. "That was my first glimpse of my son. My flesh and blood. It breaks my heart to realize how close I was to him that day. That little boy—that man—is a stranger because I kept my distance. Never saw him grow up. Never had a hand in raising him."

"I was married. We can't change the way things happened."

"I know." He covered her hands with his. "I do realize that. Tell me about him, Ida. Tell me about my son."

"The man you met, the man who came to find you at the hospital, is exactly who you think he is. Best thing about my son is his big, soft heart. When I told him you're almost certainly his biological father, he was shocked. And also happy for me. I've been alone for a long time. He's always wanted me to meet someone, to find love again. He knows this might be my chance."

"Ida. I believe it is. For both of us."

9

"What are you doing, Daddy?" Ernest sat down on the back stoop next to Jerome. He picked up a flat metal jar. "What's this stuff?"

"Shoeshine," said Jerome. "I'm shining my shoes."

"Those are your church shoes," Ernest pointed out. "I never saw you shine 'em before."

Jerome buffed the leather with firm strokes. "I used to shine shoes for tips when I was your age."

"Huh?"

He chuckled. "I was a go-getter. Used to shine Pappy Miller's shoes for him on church Sunday, and he'd give me a dollar. That was a lot of dough when I was a kid."

"I wouldn't do it for less than five," Ernest said.

"Ha. You're cheeky." Jerome showed him how to apply the paste just so, and how to use the polish and brush to get the sheen exactly right.

"That's cool. But you still haven't said why you're wearing your Sunday shoes on a Monday."

He didn't look up. "I got a thing tonight."

"Is that why we're going to Mom's tonight?"

"You're going to your mom's because that's our usual schedule."

"Lobo said schedules can change."

Jerome felt his teeth clench, a common reflex. Lobo

again. His ex had married the guy a year ago. Lobo was New Daddy.

He forced his jaw to unclench. It was to be expected, even desirable, that he and Florence would move on after the divorce. It was a kind of death, the final blow to a relationship that had been on life support for too long. When they parted ways, he'd known his attractive wife, ten years his junior, would find someone. And she had—a guy who worked in tech and had a taste for fancy cars. Jerome had made his peace with the idea that his kids would spend half their time with someone he didn't know. He and Florence both hoped the divorce wouldn't turn their boys into emotional roadkill. As far as he could tell, the kids seemed to be dealing with the change, navigating between two families with relative smoothness. His household and Florence's were like two disparate islands inhabited by entirely different tribes that never overlapped.

He wondered what his ex would make of Margot. If things kept going in the direction he wanted them to go, he might be introducing her to them.

"It's not changing tonight, buddy," he said to Ernest. "You and Asher need to be ready in half an hour. Don't forget your library books. Your mom said they're overdue."

"I'm still reading *The Crossover*." Ernest dug a stick into the dirt by the steps. "I can't help it if I'm slow."

"Hey. Poems are supposed to be read slowly, right? Nothing wrong with taking your time, bud."

"Yeah. Tell that to Asher."

"He's just doing his job as a brother. Trolling you. Builds character."

"What does that even mean, builds character?"

Jerome held up one shoe, making sure it gleamed.

"Lot of things. Like having confidence. Owning who you are. Just because you take your time reading doesn't mean there's something wrong with you." He knew it was hard, having a brother like Asher. That one was a whiz in school, a straight-A student from the moment he had started kindergarten. Ernest had trouble making sense of letters and words, and no one was surprised by the diagnosis of dyslexia.

Jerome tried to remember himself at that age. He went sailing with his mama. He and his daddy tinkered with cars and sometimes went to Baker Beach to poke around the Battery Chamberlin gun installation. Had Douglas Sugar ever looked at Jerome and wondered? He was a smart man, and he could count. Jerome could only conclude that the absence of blood ties had not mattered to his daddy.

Thank you for that gift.

"You didn't finish telling me about the shoes," Ernest reminded him. The boy struggled with reading a book, but not with reading people. He was always the first to know when Jerome had something on his mind. "What kind of thing you got to go to with shiny shoes?"

Jerome grinned. "You and your questions."

"You and your nonanswers."

"I met a girl," he said. "I got a crush on her."

"What kind of girl?"

"A woman," he corrected. "I invited her to go to the New Century Ballroom with me." He had been mulling over the idea for days, trying to talk himself out of it. She was too young for him. Too white for him. He wasn't good at relationships. But his mind kept circling back to that moment when he walked her to her car after the gin bar, and the even better moments they'd spent sailing on the bay.

So Jerome had asked Margot out and she had said okay. Already, this felt different from the other relationships he'd tried to launch after his divorce. *She* was different. Smart, confident, but shy. She held things back with a kind of caution that made him want to find a way past the wall.

He put away the gear in his shoeshine kit. Ernest stared at him. "You're taking her dancing? At that place you took Granny Ida?"

"Look, I want to impress her. These shiny shoes will show her how pretty I look all dressed up."

"So she'll like you more."

"It's a way to show I care about her opinion."

"Is she pretty?"

That would be a *hell yes*. Big soft eyes, full pink lips. Legs and tight skirts. And those damn cowboy boots. And the yoga pants and bra top she wore sailing. Long blond hair—at least he thought it was long; she always kept it wound up and clipped in a messy bun. He'd dated white girls before, a time or two. But never someone *that* white, from Texas. Or that young. She was what, fifteen years younger, at least. An itty-bitty thing who could throw a grown man to the ground.

"Yeah," he said. "She's real pretty."

They went inside. Asher was standing in the kitchen guzzling OJ straight from the jug.

"What part of *use a glass* do you not understand?" asked Jerome.

"I'm going to drink it all," Asher said with a shrug.

"Dad's getting prettied up for a date," Ernest reported. "It might be serious."

Asher polished off the juice and belched. "Yeah?"

"Let's not get ahead of ourselves." Jerome nudged Asher to put the bottle in the recycle bin. He was relieved to hear the sound of a car horn out front. "That's your ride. Make sure you have everything."

There was a brief scramble for backpacks and books, Ernest's stuffed cheetah that went everywhere with him, Asher's bag of Fritos in case he starved to death on the drive to their mother's.

Jerome kissed them both goodbye at the door, already missing them—their noise and messy energy, the laughter and even the squabbling. When he and Florence had first separated and put their parenting plan in motion, this had been the wrenching moment he dreaded each week—saying goodbye to the boys and then going back inside a house that roared with emptiness. Once Jerome heard the thud of car doors in the driveway, he faced a life he didn't recognize anymore. He would stand in the living room and make a slow turn around a space that used to be where a family lived, vibrant with their collective energy and spirit.

It didn't get easier with the passage of time. But he found ways to deal with it. He went to therapy. He distracted himself by working on the bakery's business and marketing plan. He also spent time getting back into shape the way he'd been in college, as a member of the sailing and rowing teams. It was a relief to find his own shape once again. Because somehow, in the busy whirl of family life, he had begun wearing dad jeans and looking like . . . a dad. With a doughy soft center like Ida B's bestselling kolaches.

Rowing and running had cured that, and he felt a bit like his old self again.

The other distraction was girls. Louise, the general manager of the bakery, had shown him all the dating apps. His nervous fingers had swiped over too many smiling, eager, earnest women, their self-conscious selfies grabbing only a nanosecond of his attention. It was a strange, cold-blooded exercise, knowing that behind each profile was a human story that was as complicated and wrenching and hopeful as the one he himself had posted with such trepidation.

He'd met several nice women. There had been a couple of false starts, and then for some reason, he would realize it wasn't going to fly. Whenever Jerome got discouraged, he reminded himself that in the course of a ten-year marriage, he had learned some things. He knew what it felt like when a relationship wasn't working. He learned to pay attention to the chilling inner voice that admitted it would never work, no matter how hard he tried.

One of his girlfriends, who had said she was genuinely in love with him, also taught him that there was kindness in honesty—and in being prompt. Letting the wrong thing linger wasn't fair to either party.

Jerome shut down the troubled thoughts as he shucked off his clothes and showered. Enough about the past. He might just be onto something new. Something different and unexpected. Something with a Texas twang and big blue eyes. Something that didn't feel wrong yet.

Jerome could tell that Salt was developing a following, not just in the immediate neighborhood, but tourists and casual passersby, and people from other areas of the city who had heard about the place. There were some weeks when Margot seemed overwhelmed, but she always managed to pick herself up. He knew there would always be problems—it was a restaurant, after all—but Margot was gaining confidence. She listened to her customers and staff, and she built relationships with her suppliers—including Sugar, the source of her baked goods. He was gratified to see the orders climbing, week by week.

When she finally announced that she was going to give herself one night a week off, he invited her to the New Century Ballroom. For dancing, he explained to her. Ballroom dancing. At first, she thought he was kidding, but he convinced her to give it a try.

He picked her up at her place, an apartment above the garage of an older home with a security gate and a call box. She'd said to send her a text message when he arrived, which he did.

When she came outside, walking along a flower-lined pathway, he forgot to breathe. Unlike their first unfortunate meeting, he didn't need his Ventolin this time. He had always known—hell, everybody knew—that she was an objectively pretty woman. Tonight, wearing a fitted dress with a flared skirt and sandals with heels, her hair in loose waves and her makeup done, she looked like something out of a dream.

She pushed a button on the gate and stepped outside. "Hi," she said.

"Wow," he said. "You look fantastic."

"Thanks. And what about you? I *mean*."

The down-up-down look she gave him was gratifying. He held the car door for her. A couple passing on the sidewalk glanced at them, and it was one of those glances. Thankfully, it didn't happen so much anymore, but even here in the city there were a few who still gave interracial couples that look.

He shook it off, because that was what he always did. Margot appeared not to notice, because white people rarely did. He held the car door for her. "Ever had a dancing lesson?"

She laughed. "Me? Not unless you count doing the

Cotton-Eye Joe in a line with a bunch of drunk cowboys."

"This is a bit different."

"What got you interested in ballroom dancing?" she asked.

"I guess it must seem like a weird choice, but I have my reasons. A while back, I won a series of lessons in a fundraiser raffle for my kids' school. I talked Ida B into going with me. I thought maybe it would be a way for her to make some new friends. Maybe even a boyfriend, or at least someone to ease the loneliness, you know?"

Her gaze flickered. "I know."

"Yeah, so it didn't work out that way, the lessons. Turned out, she didn't much care for the dancing. But I did, unexpectedly. There's something about getting all duded up and learning the moves that made me feel human again after the divorce."

"So Ida gave up on it and you kept going."

"I did. Got to be honest. I also thought it would be a good way to meet girls."

"Oh. And is it?"

"Turns out it's not the best demographic for dating. I'm usually the youngest one in the group, unless it's one of those nights for couples practicing for their wedding dance. It's cool, though. Something different. Something to get me out of the house when the boys are away."

"Alrighty then. I'm excited."

"How about you?" he asked. "What do you like to do for fun?"

"I read books," she said. "Like, all the time. When I saw that bookshop on Perdita Street, it made me even happier with the location for Salt."

"What kind of books do you like?"

"The kind of books that make me forget my own life for a while."

Jerome glanced over at her. "Why do you need to forget your own life?"

She held her purse in her lap, worrying the strap with nervous fingers. "I have a past."

"Everybody's got a past. Want to tell me?"

Margot hesitated, then said, "Maybe. I might."

"No pressure. I mean, you don't have to. I'm a good listener."

She looked out the window. "You are. It's really cool."

Margot was going to meet Jerome's boys for the first time. She and Jerome were taking it slow, like the delicate dance they'd practiced at the ballroom—pulling together, moving apart, lingering close, turning away, turning back. They would take a few tentative steps toward each other and then feint away, only to be drawn together again. Nothing in her experience had led her to trust a man, and Jerome seemed to sense that. He didn't push. He gave her patience and space. He made her want to get closer. He was gaining her trust, little by little, in a way that almost felt safe.

He'd invited her for an afternoon of sailing with his boys. He'd borrowed his buddy's boat, a sloop with a picnic deck and small galley. This was, she forced herself to acknowledge, a Step. According to Anya, a guy didn't introduce a girl to his kids unless he wanted the relationship to move forward.

The question was, did *she* want that?

The answer was yes. An unequivocal yes.

It wouldn't be simple. She knew this. There was still the nagging issue about her past. She kept that door closed to everyone except her therapist. But if she really wanted to follow her feelings for Jerome, she would need to let him in. The problem was, he came with a past, too. A couple of kids, an ex-wife who might not look kindly on having someone like Margie Salinas in her boys' lives.

Margot faced the day determined to have fun. To avoid overthinking. Ernest and Asher were excruciatingly cute, all big grins and bright eyes and restless energy.

"I don't know many kids," she told them. "Other than their eating preferences at the restaurant, I don't know much about them. But you're people, right? I have good people skills. You can let me know how I'm doing."

"Uh-oh," said Jerome. "These boys have opinions."

"I've been reviewed a thousand times on Yelp. I can handle opinions." Margot had armed herself with a picnic lunch. "I brought food," she said, setting the cooler on the aft deck.

"Barbecue?" Asher asked.

"Oh, I heard you like my barbecue," she said. "But no. We're having Reuben sliders today, warm from the oven. I think you'll like them. And even though your dad is better at dessert, I brought something from my home state of Texas—a chocolate sheet cake."

That was all it took to bring her into the fold. "Can we eat now, Dad?" Ernest asked.

"We're going to moor at Angel Island. We'll have lunch there."

"Can they have some snacks to hold them over?" Margot asked.

"Good idea," said Jerome. "It'll keep them from starving on the way."

"Honey lemonade and chili cheese Fritos," Margot said. "That should hold you over."

As they cruised north to the island state park, Ernest

was full of questions—how old was she, what kind of car did she drive, did she have a dog, did she know how to swim—a barrage that made her feel as if she were on a game show. Asher, a year older, was cheeky and sharp-eyed, noting things like the scar on her arm from a childhood bad decision, and the fact that she was right-handed. At the state park, they hiked up to a meadow covered with soft grass and golden poppies. Jerome spread out a blanket, and they lazed in the sunshine and had their lunch. The sliders and sheet cake were a hit, as she had known they would be. The sandwiches had been a food truck staple—thin slices of house-cured pastrami, garlic dill kraut, Swiss cheese, and Russian dressing, the rolls slathered with herb butter and crunchy seeds and salt.

"Thank you for lunch," Ernest said, unprompted by his dad.

"Too bad you only brought twelve sliders," Asher said. "You're a really good cook."

"She is an amazing cook," Jerome said, "but I bet you don't know she's an expert at self-defense."

Both boys turned toward her.

"You mean like *Cobra Kai*?" asked Ernest.

"No, for real," their dad said.

"Don't oversell me," Margot cautioned.

"You could give them a demo."

"I could. Or I could have another glass of lemonade."

"Show us," Ernest said.

Margot stood up. "All right. The first rule of self-defense is to avoid getting into a fight at all." Their crest-fallen expressions made her smile. "But let's say there's a situation you can't avoid. Then you have to use your opponent's energy against him. Also, one of the first moves to learn is how to fall. Because when you're in a fight, you should be prepared to fall without breaking something. You want to slap the ground with your forearms. Slap, don't crash." She showed them, holding their rapt attention as she fell flat, demonstrating the safe landing. Then she had them practice, starting on their knees, then falling from a standing position. They kept wanting to do more, so she taught them a couple of basic moves. It didn't look as fancy as TV martial arts, but they were into it. When Jerome announced that it was time to head back, there were audible groans.

"Maybe we'll do more another time. The gym where I train has a kids' program."

"We'd rather have you show us," Ernest said.

"Yeah, we're in enough programs," Asher added.

Jerome sent her a what-the-hell look. "Well, excuse me for signing you up for stuff."

"My mom never signed me up for anything," Margot said. *Other than free lunch at school*, she thought. "I didn't even know it was a thing. I learned aikido after I was an adult." She quickly added, "My mom taught me other things, though. I learned my way around a kitchen and a barbecue pit, and I can make any sandwich known to man or beast. Those sliders you had for lunch? My mom's recipe."

They made their way back to the marina and moored the boat, tired and satisfied from their day on the water. "I have something for you," she said to the boys when they got back to the car. "I had these made to sell at the restaurant, and the first run just arrived." She took out three matching folded hoodies embroidered with the Salt name and a stylized logo featuring a salt molecule. She unfolded the smallest one and held it up for Ernest. "What do you think? Want to try it on?"

To her surprise, Ernest exchanged a worried look with his brother.

"I think it's your size," she said. "Do you want a different color, or—"

"We don't wear hoodies," Ernest blurted out.

"Oh!" She hadn't been expecting that. "Um, I didn't realize you don't like them." Confused, she glanced at Jerome.

"A Black man has to think about how he'll be regarded if he puts on a hoodie."

Margot's heart sank. "I'm an idiot," she said. "I didn't think. And that's the problem—*my* problem. Guys, I'm really sorry." A horrible thought hit her. "I gave these out to everyone who works in the back of the house. Damn—er, darn it. I'm going to call every one of them."

Asher held up his sweatshirt. "How about we wear them to bed? And around the house?"

"That'd be okay," Jerome said. He patted Margot's shoulder. "Let's get going."

She felt so bad, and she had no one to blame but herself. Though familiar with the term *white privilege*, she foolishly hadn't believed it applied to her. *Privileged* was the last word she would use to describe herself. She had grown up poor, with a teen mom, and she'd been a school dropout. Jerome had been raised in a loving family that gave him a firm foundation, an education, a solid career.

Yet despite all the advantages, he and his boys struggled with matters she could barely imagine.

"Know what else?" Ernest said. "When we go to the store, we're s'posed to keep our hands out of our pockets."

"And no running when you're outside," Asher added.

"Running where?" she asked.

"Anywhere," the boys said together. They rattled off rules white kids didn't have to think about.

Margot came to understand that this was the world they were growing up in. And the world Jerome had grown up in had been even more extreme. All his life, he'd had to work harder to prove he deserved his success.

When they went to drop the boys off at their mom's house, she watched Jerome as they tumbled out of the car with their stuff and ran up the driveway to the back door. Jerome stared straight ahead, expressionless, jaw visibly tightened.

"Must be hard," she said.

"I'm used to it now. I do wonder what kind of stories they take home to her and Lobo."

"Lobo? Her husband's name is Lobo?"

He pulled out of the driveway. "Can't make this stuff up. He's okay. Afro Latino guy, works in tech. For me, the toughest thing about the divorce was knowing my kids would have another life, separate from the one I'm giving them. So far, the boys seem to get along with him. They told me this morning she's pregnant."

Margot felt a lurch of anxiety. Even now, she had a strange reaction to the idea of pregnancy, wondering what it might be like to plan for a baby, to expect joy. "Oh. Uh, how do you feel about that?"

Jerome shrugged. "I don't get a vote. It could be nice for the boys to have a little brother or sister. Florence should have told me herself, but we're not always the best at communicating. I get most of the news through the boys."

"What stories will they take home about me, I wonder."

"They'll probably say you're Cobra Kai."

Margot chafed at the idea that the boys' mother might have questions about her, and that she might not like the answers. "Well, they seem like great kids, so whatever you're doing is working for them."

"Hope so. That's the plan, anyway. Know what else I can't make up? Ida and Frank, that's what."

"Ida and Frank are happening?" The prospect delighted her. She'd been skeptical at first, refusing to believe that a long-dormant romance could be revived, but Jerome had been hopeful for his mom's sake. And Frank had seemed so nice. A widower. A doctor looking after veterans. It was lovely to imagine that they might end up together after all. Ida had once told her life was full of surprises.

Margot felt a small measure of satisfaction that she'd played her part in the reunion. If she hadn't been working late, if she hadn't dropped that framed certificate and found the old newspaper article, Ida and Frank might never have met again. It was a singular fantasy, a lost love reunited.

"So it appears," he said. "They've been inseparable. He's got a big, fine sailboat. Turns out he's the one who got her hooked on sailing. I never knew that." He paused, looked over at her, then back at the road. "There's a lot I never knew."

"She's happy, then?"

"I've never seen her like this. She's been single since I was in high school, and I never saw her date a guy seriously until now. She's always been a happy person, but this . . . it lights her up. No idea if it'll last, but I like seeing her this way."

"That's really cool. And good for you for making it happen." She saw Jerome's jaw tense again. "What?"

"It's good, yeah. But also complicated."

"Complicated how?"

His grip on the steering wheel tightened. "She had his baby. How's that for complicated?"

"*What?* Holy cow, Jerome, what are you saying? She had a baby with Frank White?"

"Yeah."

"So, the baby . . . the child. Did she place it for adoption?" This was the first place her mind went.

He gave a snort of laughter. "Nah, she decided to keep me."

Margot thought her head might explode. The old white doctor? And Ida? "You? And . . . That guy is your *father*?"

"Biologically speaking, yeah. Neither of them knew she was pregnant when Frank took off for Canada. She was young and scared, and a good man came along—my father, Douglas Sugar. He was my father, and that's the way it's always been, as far as anybody knew or cared. But now that Frank's in the picture, Ida B didn't want any secrets."

"Wow. Are you . . . How are you feeling about this? Are you sorry you looked him up?"

"Like I said, he makes my mother happy. That's what's important. That's why I can't regret tracking him down."

"What about you? Are you upset?"

Jerome's jaw looked rigid. He kept his eyes on the road. "It's weird to think of Frank never knowing me, and me not knowing him. I mean, I had the best dad in the world until the day he died. It takes nothing to father a child. It takes everything to be a dad."

That was painfully true, and no one knew it better than Margot. "Do you feel different, knowing it was Frank and not your dad?"

"Nah. Should I?" He shrugged his shoulders. "I've walked around my whole life with the guy's DNA, and I never knew it until now. Does it matter a little? A lot? I don't know. It explains why I suffer from asthma, maybe. Why I wear glasses."

"Frank has asthma?"

"Yep."

"Holy cow, Jerome. It's a lot to take in."

"I met his kids—Jenna and Grady. He's a teacher, married with a couple of kids. She's a lawyer for a non-profit organization. They say they're happy for their dad. I guess I don't really feel the connection, but they seem fine. And my mother's about as happy as I've ever seen her. He lights her up."

Margot absorbed the information, thinking of the lives that had been affected by that long-ago event. Not just Ida and Frank, but Jerome and Frank's kids, Grady and Jenna, and Ida's and Frank's grandchildren as well. All this drama, just because she had come across that old, preserved Sunday magazine. "So you really think they're in love."

"My mom calls it a September romance. Seeing them together . . . they seem the same as they were in those old pictures." He glanced over at her. "The way he looks at her . . . it could be me, looking at you."

His words were like a song. Even so, it took a mighty effort to give up her customary hyperalertness. She had learned to be overly cautious, sometimes feeling threatened when she got close to him.

"Was it hard, learning about Frank?" she asked.

"Not after I got over the initial surprise. My dad was my dad. Frank is my mom's boyfriend. I have to admit, I was startled when Ida B told me what happened, but no, accepting it wasn't hard. My mom . . . she did what she did. It's not for me to judge what a person did in her past. That belongs to her and her alone."

"You give people a lot of grace, Jerome. It's really nice."

"Everyone has a past. It's who you are right now that matters."

Margot thought about the fact that things unsaid had

kept Ida and Frank apart for decades. Then she turned slightly in her seat and studied Jerome. Did he look like Frank, even a little? He looked like a dream to her. He was like no one she'd ever known, someone she thought could exist only in her imagination.

"Can you find a place to pull over?"

"Sure. Do you need a bathroom, or . . ."

"A place to talk. There's something I need to tell you."

The muscles in his forearms tensed. "That sounds serious."

"I'm serious about you, Jerome, and I want to talk about . . . a few things."

"Look, if it's about the hoodies for the boys—"

"Well, there's that. Shi—shootfire. But . . . Jerome, there's . . . This is something else."

"Okay, now you got me worried."

Margot didn't say anything. Didn't try to mollify him or minimize the impact of the things she had to say. Though it might scare him off, he needed to know the truth. He needed to know exactly who she was, even if it meant losing him, the way she'd lost other people who found her past too troubling. A few years back, there had been a guy with a nice haircut and a big laugh, who loved live music, her cooking, and long hikes. As they grew closer, she'd dared to tell him what had happened. He'd said he understood, he sympathized—but then everything shifted between them and they went their separate ways, like two people on opposite sides of a fault that had cracked open.

Jerome took Sea Cliff Avenue to China Beach, where sea-bitten cliffs towered above the rocky coves and sandy inlets. They took a switchback trail, passing an ominous sign for Deadman's Point with its dire warning—*People have fallen to their deaths from this point.*

They hiked down to a viewpoint overlooking the beach, with the Golden Gate Bridge and the Marin Headlands in the distance.

Jerome sat cross-legged on the dry grass and drew her down next to him. "One of my favorite spots," he said. "My dad used to bring me here. I'd get all sweaty at the playground at Golden Gate Park, and then we'd come here for a swim, and afterward, we'd get burgers and milkshakes at Zim's. Ever been here?"

She shook her head, envying him the fond memories of his dad. "Feels worlds away from the city."

"It's a good place to talk. Now. What's on your mind?"

She hugged her knees up to her chest, but he shook his head and brought her close to him, his long arms encircling her. He was being so tender with her, she wanted to cry. "It's a lot," Margot said.

"I got nothing but time right now."

"There are things about me," she said, feeling impossibly nervous and vulnerable. "Things I don't talk about. But I *am* serious about you and I just met your lovely boys, and this is starting to feel very real to me. Like, it could actually be a thing."

"Then I must be doing something right."

"Aw, Jerome." He always said the sweetest things. "I want you to know who I am."

"I talk a lot," he said. "But I'm also a pretty good listener."

"You are. It's really nice. I think you should know what happened before I moved up here from Texas. Because it . . . You might change your mind about me." If he did, he wouldn't be the first. Margot regarded him steadily as she spoke, aware that it could be their last conversation. The breeze tossed her hair, and he leaned in close and gently smoothed it out of her face.

"Honey, there's nothing in the world that would change my mind about you."

"I . . . If I'm going to be around your kids, you need to know this."

He sent her a sharp look, and she winced. Then she took a breath, inhaling the scent of the ocean and the crooked cypress trees on the bluff. "There's a reason I turned myself into an aikido expert."

"And here I thought it was just general badassery."

She took another breath. Listened to the crash and thud of the waves against the craggy rocks. She had been keeping the beast behind the door for far too long, because she knew that if she ever brought it out, everything would change.

Go there, she urged herself, gazing down at the pristine cove from the dizzying height of the steep cliff. *Just tell him. If he's really who you think he is, it won't scare him off.* Then again, if it did, she could go back to thinking she wasn't the kind of person a good man could love.

Ever.

Part Three

Three things cannot be long hidden:
the sun, the moon, and the truth.

—Buddha

10

The proper balance of sugar and salt was the key to making perfect barbecue sauce. Of course, when it came to barbecue sauce, everybody had an opinion about the combination of acid, aromatics, fruit, and flavorings—the ineffable umami—that made each bite so satisfying.

But Margie Salinas knew with utter certainty that it all started with sugar and salt.

So when Cubby Watson gave her the chance to produce her own special sauce for his restaurant patrons, she named it sugar+salt. She printed off sets of labels at the county library, because she couldn't afford fancy paper. Someday, she thought, she'd have a professionally designed label, one that made her sauce look as special as a bottle of fine wine.

At the end of her waitressing shift in the dining room, she went to the kitchen supply closet, where she stood back and regarded the row of mason jars filled with the deep burgundy sauce, flecked with the spices she toasted and ground in her tiny kitchen.

"That stuff's selling like watermelon on a hot day," said Cubby, coming into the supply room. His shirt and apron were redolent of mesquite smoke from his roaring outdoor pit. "I hope you're up for making plenty more."

She sent him a weary smile and tossed her logo apron into the kitchen hamper. "I'm up for it, don't you worry," she said. "I'll start a batch tonight when I get home. Let it go until morning in the slow cookers."

"Reckon we sold a dozen pints of the stuff today." He handed her a zippered bank bag, thick with cash. "Your cut."

"Thanks, Cubby. You're the best." He really was, and she remembered to be grateful every day for him and his wife, Queen, who had given her a chance just when she thought she'd run out of chances.

In the staff locker room, Margie put on her street clothes—denim skirt and cowboy boots—and greeted Nanda, who had just arrived with the cleaning crew. She loosed her hair from its bun and checked herself in the mirror. Yellow hair in need of a cut she couldn't afford, freckles from too much time in the sun at her farmers' market booth. Next to the mirror was a framed article from *Texas Monthly*, the most admired magazine in the state. There was a review by a writer named Buckley DeWitt, with a special mention of her barbecue sauces. Buckley had discovered her sauces at the farmers' market, and he kept coming back for more. She could tell he was sweet on her, maybe just a little. When he talked to her, his ears turned red and he stammered. He was a real good writer, though, and he was especially good at writing about barbecue. A good review from *Texas Monthly* could cause a stampede.

What Buckley really wanted, he confessed to her, was to write about justice. Crime and punishment. He even ran a blog on the web, separate from the magazine, called *Lone Star Justice*, publishing it under a pseudonym on account of the fact that some of the stuff he said got folks riled up.

Outside the back door, Cubby was enjoying his nightly Black & Mild and a shot of Hennessy while gazing up at the stars. "My place is on a utility easement," he said. "I ever tell you that?"

She scarcely knew what an easement was. "Is that a problem?"

"Means the county could build a skyscraper right on top of me, and I'd have nothing to say about it."

"Cubby. Nobody's gonna put a skyscraper in Banner Creek."

"You say." He tipped back in his chair. "Hope you're right."

"'Course I'm right. See you around," she said.

"Take care, now."

In the front of the restaurant, a couple of the girls were heading out on dates, jumping into pickup trucks with guys who would take them over to Greene's Dance Hall or night swimming at Blue Hole. Sometimes Margie and her work friends would go all the way into the city for a late set by the Austin Lounge Lizards.

"Where's Jimmy?" Ginny Coombs asked, waving at Margie. "Y'all want to go for a dip?"

Margie turned away slightly, ducking her head. "Jimmy and I didn't work out so good," she muttered.

"You're kidding," Ginny said, taking a drag on her Virginia Slim. "Damn, girl. You didn't even give him a chance. I've seen bananas with a longer shelf life than your boyfriends."

Margie grinned, picturing Jimmy Hunt as an overripe banana. "I guess I'm back to playing the field."

"Shit, what happened? Y'all were so perfect together. And . . . c'mon, Jimmy Hunt." She spoke his name with the reverence afforded a conquering hero.

And he was, here in these parts. The Hunt family

was well known for big oil, good looks, and powerful influence, keenly felt in a town like this—a place small enough for everyone to know everyone else. And since Banner Creek lay within shouting distance of the domed capitol in Austin, the influence of the Hunts stretched all the way to the state legislature.

She'd first met Jimmy when she'd gone to a dance hall with some of the girls. He'd caught her eye with his sculpted body, wavy tumble of dark hair, square jaw, and twinkling eyes. He was a star player for the Texas A&M Aggies—one who actually played nearly every game. He was easily the most talented kicker in the league, by all accounts.

She'd been taken in by his easy humor, his smooth presence on the honky-tonk dance floor, and his drown-in-me blue eyes. Afterward, he'd driven her home in his late-model pickup with Waylon on the radio, a long gun on the rack behind the cab, and an open bottle of Shiner beer cradled between his thighs. Enjoying a beverage while driving was never a problem for a Hunt, he'd explained with a baritone laugh. His sister was a sheriff's deputy and his favorite cousin was chief of police. His older brother, Briscoe, was eyeing a run at the DA's office. All one big happy family.

Margie wouldn't know what that felt like. A family. A big, happy family.

After their date, she'd invited him in and they'd talked about football—the coming season would be his last in college but he was being scouted by the NFL—and then they'd made out for a while. He told her she was so damn pretty she was making him forget he was a gentleman.

He was fun and she was lonely so she invited him back on her next night off, promising him a home-cooked dinner. She'd served him chicken and wine with a dollop of fangirl adulation, because she was a Texas girl through and through, and she loved her Aggie football. He was earnest and charming when he talked about himself, his family, how successful they were. She told him her mother had died but he didn't seem much interested in that. People tended to shy away from the grief of others. Maybe that was why she liked church Sundays with Queen and Cubby. Folks there weren't shy about grief.

She let Jimmy make love to her because he had soft lips and he smelled amazing and she was tipsy and so damn lonely. She gave him a condom from the drawer in the bedside table—don't expect a man to remember, her mama always said—and he chuckled agreeably, but in the morning she found the packet on the floor. It was open, and the condom was still inside.

When she challenged him, he gave her that sexy chuckle again—*I don't like taking a bath with my boots on.*

Well, next time—if you want there to be a next time—you're going to have to do that, she'd told him while fixing bacon and eggs for his breakfast.

She opened her birth control pill container, intending to double up on the dose as a precaution against the previous night's carelessness, but the container was empty. Her prescription had expired. She'd spent all her money on rent and sauce ingredients and hadn't yet gone back to the clinic for a renewal. Some months, it happened that way.

He invited her out to the range for shooting practice and she was intrigued since she'd never shot a gun before.

Maybe, she said. *I might.*

As he peeled away from her driveway, his tires spat gravel at the porch, scaring her cat. She scooped Kevin into her arms to soothe him. Through the dust, she could see a Confederate flag bumper sticker and a Kappa Alpha frat symbol on his truck.

Pouring the cat out of her arms, Margie turned away. Then she picked up the towel Jimmy had thrown on the bathroom floor, washed the breakfast dishes, and swept the dirt he'd tracked in the night before.

She thought about the unused condom and the fact that he had not asked her one thing about herself. If he'd asked, he might have learned why she was broke and how she planned to dig out of the hole she was in. What she thought about and dreamed about.

And she thought about the fact that while he held her in his arms and made love to her, she'd felt lonelier than ever.

She called him later that day and begged off the shooting range date. Then she took a deep breath and told him she didn't want to see him again.

"Well now, that's a damn shame, babe," he said. "Also a mistake. It'd be a shame for you to miss out on all the fun. I know how to treat a woman real good."

"I get that," she said, even though she'd seen little evidence of the claim. "You're probably right, but I'm just not in a good headspace right now. I hoped maybe I was but I realized I was wrong." She knew she was trying to soften the blow. Her explanation was meant to spare his feelings, as if it was her job to spare his feelings. *It's not you, it's me.*

What she should have said, if she'd had the spine to say it, was that he'd acted like a jerk about the condom, showing complete disrespect for her. She should have told him that this kind of deception was a fatal flaw in any relationship, even a casual hookup. Maybe if her mother were still around, she would have given Margie more advice about men—how to hold yourself up when your urges were at war with common sense. How to find guys who treated you right. Or maybe Mama wouldn't have been much help. When it came to men, Mama hadn't exactly made the best choices.

"Well now, that's too bad," Jimmy said.

"Thanks for understanding. I'm really sorry, Jimmy."

"Right. See you around, babe."

Now Ginny Coombs gave her a nudge. "Are you double, triple sure you don't want to give Jimmy Hunt another chance? Who knows, it might turn out to be the real thing, and you'd be sitting pretty. The Hunts are made of money. You could kiss waitressing goodbye."

"To be honest, I like waitressing. And Jimmy . . . he and I are just not a match," she said.

"Well now, I guess that's okay. You're young yet." Ginny stubbed out her cigarette in the outdoor ashtray and popped a stick of gum in her mouth.

"Thanks for understanding," Margie said. "Could be I need a break from all guys, at least for a while. Y'all have fun tonight."

Jimmy had been sending her text messages all evening. Another one pinged in her hip pocket as she got into her car to drive home. She took a moment to block his number, then pulled out of the parking lot.

She headed away from town along the narrow, winding farm-to-market road, keeping her eye out for mule deer and armadillos. Banner Creek trickled over the roadway at the ford, spraying the car's undercarriage as she passed between the concrete guard posts.

Her little house by the creek had once been a fishing cottage. It was as plain as Texas toast, a way station for a person who didn't really know her place in life yet. It was her first real home since her mom had passed, just a place to put her things. But it had a good gas stove, and the landlord didn't mind the cat.

The Pratts next door had several noisy teenagers, but they weren't much of a bother. As she unlocked the door, Kevin jumped down from his perch on the railing and swirled around her ankles.

"Come on, buddy," she said. "Let's go make some sauce."

He slipped in ahead of her and she turned on the light. Kevin was a homely little thing and he'd been a skittish kitten, but she'd brought him home and coaxed him, bit by bit, into her life. Now he was her best friend. He watched her every move as she hung up her backpack and put the bag of cash in her junk drawer. Cubby paid her in cash when he could, because she was always hovering just above flat broke, her wages garnished by a medical billing company after her accident the year before. She had been hit by an uninsured driver and suffered a spiral fracture of her leg that required multiple surgeries. Lacking health insurance, she was put on a payment plan that ate up a huge portion of every paycheck.

She cracked open a Shiner stubby and turned on some music. She wasn't old enough to buy beer, but Jimmy had left a six-pack behind in her fridge.

Margie's whole kitchen was organized around sauce production. Four slow cookers lined the counter, and she kept a pressure canner and a water bath canner on the stove. Herbs flourished in pots on the porch, and she roasted and ground her own spices.

She loved to experiment with her sauces. Everything started with sugar and salt. There was often vinegar and onions and tomatoes involved, but then she tried all kinds of ideas. A touch of bourbon, maybe. Stone-ground mustard. Chiles in adobo. Crazy stuff like a vanilla bean from Madagascar, bitter chocolate, Coca-Cola, coffee, star anise, tamarind, or Florida calamondins. She made careful recipe notes and kept track of the most popular flavors, adding her recipes to the most valuable treasure her mother had left behind—a massive file of clipped and handwritten recipes.

Onions used to bring on streams of painful tears, but she'd learned that the trick was to chill the onions and dice them fast with a supersharp knife. Singing along with Brandi Carlile, she took out her ceramic knife with the razor-thin blade and got busy peeling and chopping, taking sips of beer now and then. Tonight's batch would feature fresh Granny Smith apples, the shiny green ones she'd picked up at the farmers' market. She wanted to try caramelizing the apples and onions before adding them to the pot. The big cast-iron griddle spat droplets of grease, so she took off her nice rayon blouse, because one grease spot would ruin it for good. Then she tied her bib apron on over her bra and continued working.

While getting everything ready for the slow cookers, she planned the perfect evening—a soak in the bathtub while reading a book. Next to cooking, Margie loved reading more than anything in the world. She read books that took her to faraway places. Books that let her live a different life. Books that made her see the world with new eyes. If she hadn't had to leave school because of Del, she probably would have read her way right into college, unlikely as that seemed for a girl of her background. Her high school counselor kept telling her she was college material. As if the scratch to pay for college might somehow magically appear.

A gleam of headlights swung briefly across the room, washing past the discount-store furnishings that had come with the place. Probably one of the Pratt kids.

Then, in the pause between Brandi Carlile and Dave Grohl, she heard the thump of a door slamming and saw someone on her porch.

The screen door slapped open and Jimmy Hunt stood in the doorway, his hip cocked to one side, a thumb hooked into his belt loop, and a smile on his face, eyes vaguely blurred, probably from drinking or weed. There was a box of Swisher Sweets stuck in the upper pocket of his denim jacket.

See you around, babe, he'd said when she told him she didn't want to go out with him anymore. She had not taken his words literally, but apparently she should have.

Her heart sank. What part of *We're done* did he not understand? "Hey, Jimmy," she said.

"Hey now, I don't like the way we left things. I think we should talk." In the half-light, he looked a bit mysterious. And menacing. And utterly sure of himself as his gaze moved over her, focusing on her bare legs.

"Aw, Jimmy," Margie said, feeling a wave of goose bumps. "We don't need to talk. It's like I said. You and me, we're . . . It's just not going to work out."

He sauntered over to the fridge and grabbed a beer. "Girl, you hardly gave us a chance. I can be real nice to you. I swear, you are the prettiest thing I ever did see."

He wouldn't be the first to tell her that. She took after her mama, and like her mama, she learned early on that looking pretty wasn't always an advantage. Sometimes it attracted the wrong kind of attention. "I'd appreciate it if you'd leave," she told him. "Now, please."

"I haven't finished my beer." He took a long, thirsty drink.

She faced him now, standing across the room, looking around as if he owned the place. The back of her neck felt prickly with awakening fear. "Let's not do this," she said. "I'm busy here. For the last time, Jimmy, I'm asking you to leave."

He guzzled the beer, set down the stubby brown bottle, and offered her a crooked, slick-lipped smile. Then he focused his gaze on her skimpy bra, which was barely covered by the bib apron. "Girl, your lips say no but your sweet bod says yes."

Margie rolled her eyes. "Oh, please. I don't want to get into it with you." "Hey There Delilah" was now playing on the radio. She flicked a glance at the phone, which she'd plugged in to charge on the kitchen counter. Surely she wouldn't have to call the cops on him.

And if she did? She might get to meet one of his cousins.

"Sure you do," he said easily. "I can be good to you, babe. I can be good *for* you. I bet you don't know what people around these parts say behind your back. They think you're strange. Cooking up your witch's brew, going to the Black church, thinking you belong. You must stick out like a sore thumb there."

Margie didn't reply. It was pointless to engage him in conversation.

The scent of caramelizing onions and apples pervaded the air. Reflexively, she turned off the flame under the cast-iron skillet. More than a little annoyed, she said, "Look, I'm busy. Go find a party somewhere. Some of the girls from work are headed to Blue Hole, or—"

"I got your party right here," Jimmy said, and in a swift surprise move, he pulled her against him, pressing so she could feel his erection. He bent down and kissed her hard.

She shoved herself away from him and backed up against the kitchen counter, shocked and hot with fury now. "Back off, Jimmy. Or I'll—"

He laughed and unbuttoned his jacket. "You'll do what?"

She snatched the knife off the counter. Anger flamed through her, driven by fear. "I mean it," she said. "Go on home."

"That's cute." He reached out to grab the knife.

She flipped the sharp edge toward him. Clearly he had no understanding of the surgical sharpness of a ceramic blade. It sliced his flesh like butter, right in the crook of his thumb.

"Oh my gosh, I'm sorry," she said as blood welled from the wound. "I didn't mean to hurt you."

"Shee-it," he said. "I figured you were dumb, but not that dumb."

She grabbed a roll of paper towels. When she turned back she saw him pull a gun from a side holster under his denim jacket.

"So dumb, you brought a knife to a gunfight," he said.

Margie gasped. The knife dropped to the floor. She could hear it shatter. That was the thing about ceramic knives. They were lethally sharp, but fragile. Her pulse spiked, loud in her ears. She could feel the fear thudding deep in her gut. Maybe the gun wasn't loaded. Maybe it was a toy. It looked like a toy. Maybe the safety was on. She didn't know what a safety looked like. She didn't know the first thing about guns. All she knew was that she'd never liked them. She'd never known anything but grief to come from a gun.

"Come on now, Jimmy," she said, "I'm not looking for a fight with you. Put that thing away." She held out the wadded paper towel. "Here, clean your hand. I'll help you. Really, I didn't mean to hurt you."

"I reckon you didn't," he said. The round black eye of the gun was aimed straight at her chest.

"I'm asking you to please put that away."

"Nah," he said easily. "I don't think so. You're not being very nice to me."

Oh. He wanted her to be nice. "You're right, Jimmy," she conceded, struggling to keep the tremor from her voice. *Yes, go along with him.* Because she sure as hell couldn't overpower him. "I haven't been very kind, and I'm sorry. Tell you what. Let's go out. It's Saturday night. How about we go into Tierney and hear some music?"

He smiled again and slipped the gun back into its holster under his left arm. "Now that's more like it."

Her knees wobbled with relief. "Sure, Jimmy. I-I just need to change real quick." She sidestepped around him and moved toward the bedroom. It was only a few steps to the doorway. It pissed her off that he was making her uncomfortable here, in the one place she was supposed to feel safe.

He followed her. "That's mighty cute," he said, reaching for her. "The way you got that apron on over your bra."

She sidled away. "I need the bathroom. Wait out here. Run some water over that cut. Have another beer." She had no intention of going anywhere with him. But she was stuck in her own house. She had to find a way out.

Jimmy didn't wait. Instead, he followed her. "We had some fun here the other night," he said, herding her toward the bed. "Let's do that some more."

"Maybe later. There's always someone good playing at Tierney."

"There's someone good playing here," he said with a slow smile. He blocked the way to the door.

She tried to duck under his arm. He stopped her with a motion so quick it was like a trap snapping shut. Even drunk, he had a powerful athlete's quick reflexes. His arms went around her, hard-muscled and unyielding.

"Whoa there," she said, trying to keep her head. "Let's go out. Have some fun, okay?"

"Girl, I'm already having fun." He thrust her backward and shoved her onto the bed. Hard. So hard that she bounced back up, almost comically. The breath left her in a rush.

"Damn it, Jimmy, I thought you said you were a gentleman," she snapped.

"Oh, I am," he said, pushing her back down on the bed. He pressed his knee into her groin and pinned both of her wrists above her head. "I am that. Gentleman Jimmy, that's me."

She tried to twist away, but he held her fast, his hand an iron clamp.

With his free hand, he ripped away the apron, yanking it to one side so the strap bit into her neck like a noose.

"Hey," she said, her voice loud and sharp. "That's *enough*."

He broke the front closure of her bra and stared down at her boobs. "Now that," he said, "is nice."

"Seriously, knock it off," she said, pushing the words past the panic crowding her throat. "You don't have to be so damn rough." *Mollify him*, she thought. Her mind raced. "Let's do it the way we did the other night, nice and slow."

"Yeah, that's good." He kissed her hard, tongue pushing in deep.

She held still, held her breath, waiting for the kiss to be over. Then she whispered, "I need the bathroom, okay? And let me get you another beer."

"Beer sounds good." He let go of her wrists.

"I'll just be a minute," she said, pressing her palms to his shoulders. "You wait right here."

He rolled off her, stretched out on the bed, and lounged against the iron frame.

She nearly melted with relief as she stood, clutching the apron against her bare chest. Her boot heels clicked on the floor as she went to the kitchen. Kevin crouched by the door, twitching the tip of his tail, eyes shifting back and forth. He was shy around strangers.

Margie opened the refrigerator and took out the last bottle of Shiner. Her phone was on the counter. She grabbed it, flipped it open, and her thumb flew over the keypad.

911, what's your emergency?

Her hand was on the door handle when she felt Jimmy grab the apron strap behind her neck, yanking so hard she fell backward against him. The phone went spinning away. The bottle of beer hit the floor and rolled, but didn't break.

"Somebody help me," she yelled as loudly as she could, hoping the neighbors would hear. Maybe by some miracle the 911 operator was still on the line.

"Come on, babe," he said. "Quit your hollering." He scooped her against him, lifting her clear off the floor and stalking back to the bedroom. She scratched at his hands, reached back to scratch his face and neck. "Ow," he said. "Don't you fucking do that." He reached the bed in two strides, turned and slammed her onto her back.

She screamed again, an incoherent animal sound. He pulled the neck strap tight, cutting off her air. Cutting off her voice. She couldn't breathe. She couldn't breathe. He yanked up her skirt and pulled the crotch of her panties until they tore.

The strap was strangling her. Her pulse pounded in her ears. She arched her body, twisted from side to side. He smacked her across the face, and she saw stars. The stars turned into butterflies, fluttering away. Maybe she passed out. Because when she blinked, his pants were open, her legs were open, he went in full force.

She bit his shoulder. He roared and hit her again, the same side of her face. She felt something dislodge. Bone. No, a tooth.

She managed to twist her right hand from his grip and went for his eyes, but he shoved his head into the pillow and emitted a muffled groan. His elbow dug into her ribs. No, not his elbow. That was his gun, the gun in its holster under his arm.

Don't bring a knife to a gunfight. Don't bring . . .

She worked her hand around to grasp some part of it—she didn't know which part—but he kept pumping and she couldn't breathe. She didn't know the first thing about guns but she knew what a trigger felt like. She knew what drowning felt like. She knew what choking felt like. She wanted to pass out. She wanted to sleep forever.

Her middle finger slipped through the trigger guide. Maybe the safety was on. Maybe it wasn't loaded. Maybe—

She pulled back with her middle finger. Squeeze. Nothing.

Ahh. He exhaled as he came. She remembered that purring sound he'd made from the other time. *Ahh.*

His lower body relaxed into hers but the stranglehold tightened as he gave the strap another twist. She felt her pulse hard in her eyes as if her heart was trying to beat through her eyes and she saw stars and she squeezed her finger again tighter her middle finger squeezed and then

bang.

11

The paper crinkled on the examination table under Margie, butcher paper like the kind that wrapped the meat deliveries at Cubby's. He took especially good care of the meat because that was his stock-in-trade, the thing that brought throngs of people to his place. He practiced safe food handling like a religion, and he made her and all the staff observe the rules of safety and cleanliness every step of the way.

When Cubby realized Margie was serious about learning the craft of Texas barbecue, he told her the first step was to source the very best ingredients—grass-fed, pasture-raised, hormone-free. He took her to Meister's organic farm where the slaughterhouse practices were certified. She thought she would flinch but she didn't, not even when the carcass was hoisted and drained. That smell was all over her now, sharp and deep like copper or iron.

Now she was a piece of meat. She was a piece of meat on the white butcher paper and she was cold, maybe not as cold as Cubby's meat locker but oh so cold, almost convulsing with shivers. And sticky wet, so sticky, the blood like tar smearing her stomach and bare legs, caked in her hair. She tried to rear up from the table, to run fast and far.

Her hands were tethered to something and she panicked. Restraints? Why was she being restrained?

Her hands. Her wrists. Jimmy Hunt had held her hands pinned above her head.

"Undo me," she said. No sound came out but she kept trying to speak and yank free. "I need my hands."

A woman in scrubs and a lab coat murmured something to the other woman present, who went over by the brown curtain and spoke to someone.

"We can't," said the other woman. Her smock had a badge from the Hayden County Rape Crisis Center. *Brenda Pike.* "I'm really sorry. When we finish here, the police will need to talk to you."

"The police," Margie rasped. Yes. She had tried 911, hadn't she? Then Jimmy's mean streak had leaped out at her like a pouncing wildcat.

She flashed on terror and pain. Screaming. The screaming made him hit her, and then he strangled her until she stopped. When she had tried to scratch and he hit her again. And again. Hands flailing, she bumped up against the holstered gun and then

bang.

"I need you to hold still, please. I promise, you're safe here." The woman's voice was firm but not unkind.

The woman. *Angela Garza, RN,* according to the ID badge clipped to her lab coat. She had a nose ring and a wrist tattoo. Eyes that moved over Margie as though reading some sort of code. "I'm with SANE—Sexual Assault Nurse Examiners—and SAFE—Sexual Assault Forensic Examiners. I specialize in performing this type of exam."

A cloud of unreality fogged Margie's brain. *I'm Angela and I'll be your sexual assault service provider today.*

"Do you know where you are?"

A clinic somewhere. Ceiling tiles. Brown curtain. Beeping noises and the whir of a fan. She shook her head.

"You're at St. Michael's Catholic Hospital. It's in Alameda City."

That was a few towns away from Banner Creek. Margie didn't know how she'd made it here. All that blood, rivers of it. Passed out. Woke up a hundred years later.

Strobe of lights through the window. Police and EMTs in her house. *Get him away from me.* She'd tried to scream but her voice was gone. Someone cut the apron strap, covered her with a space blanket. Placed a mask over her nose and mouth, instructed her to breathe.

Tense voices murmuring back and forth. The crackle of a radio.

On my count, one-two-three, and she was on the transfer board, up and out. Cervical collar around her neck and Velcroed under her chin. It was choking her, inducing more panic. She flailed, tried to breathe, and then there was a flash and then nothing.

"I'm sorry this happened to you," Angela was saying. "I hope you'll give me as much information as possible about the incident. Reporting can help you regain a sense of control."

Words seemed to drift down from the ceiling tiles. More initials: There was a SART. Sexual assault response team. They would organize the investigation. The information gathered speed and flew past like the objects in Dorothy's tornado in *The Wizard of Oz*. Flashes and floaters. Whirlwinds.

Is there someone we can call?

No. No one.

A friend?

Kevin was her best friend. Kevin was a cat.

"I need to feed my cat," Margie said, but no sound came out.

The nurse had a checklist. An assistant came in with

paper sheets and bags. A rolling tray. A fine-tooth comb. Printed forms. A clipboard and camera. Test tubes and clear dishes. A roll of printed labels. Swabs long and short, lined up and ready to probe. Weirdly angled scissors. A hemostat. They swabbed her hands and bagged the swabs.

"I have to pee." Margie's words wafted out on a whisper. He had strangled her. Silenced her voice. Erased it until it was nothing but a wisp of terror.

"Try to hold it," said the nurse. "It's hard, but I need you to hold it just a while longer."

"I need— I have to pee, I—" Too late. She peed herself. She had never done that before, except . . . except for last night. When he was choking her. She had wet herself then.

They cataloged every piece of clothing she had on— apron bra boots panties skirt. The bra and panties had been ripped to shreds. They took pictures, tallied up all the wounds, bite marks, fingerprint bruises on her breasts, a broken nail, evidence of strangulation, wounds indicating she'd been hit multiple times and held down by force.

The blood was a river of sticky tar. So much blood. Had he split her in two, made her bleed like a fire hose?

Angela narrated each step in a flat voice, dictating the injuries. Calipers measured her face lacerations. There was a lamp like the kind used at the dentist. Margie had only been to the dentist one time when she had a tooth that ached so bad it gave her a fever. The school nurse had taken her in because Mama was too sick to do it.

An abscess, they called it. Take it out, pull it out, make it stop. She tried to beg. Anything to stop the pain.

There was some discussion about fees and finally the

school nurse said *Oh holy hell, Earl, I'll take care of it myself then.*

The long, deep needle stick had made her scream. Then the tooth came out on a river of pus that spattered the lamp, and the relief was immediate. They sent her home with pills and said she should visit the dentist regularly. As if her mother could afford it.

Nurse Angela took a picture of her neck. *Evidence noted of asphyxiation.*

Scrapings from under her fingernails went onto a small glass plate and into a container.

Questions. So many personal questions. Her history. She was twenty years old. She had no history. She grew up in a trailer park called the Arroyo in a scruffy brown suburb west of Austin. She had never met her father. He was a kid, like her mom, when Margie was born. Really, her parents were just ordinary folks whose only flaw was that they were too young. "He didn't want anything to do with us," Mama explained when Margie was old enough to ask. When Darla told her parents she was pregnant, they made her leave. They were old-school. Said they couldn't handle the shame.

The nurse and her assistant packaged everything for analysis—hair, clothing, saliva. Noted a chipped tooth and a molar knocked loose.

Swabs everywhere. In places she'd never think of putting a swab. Internal exams of her mouth, vulva, anus.

"Have you ever had a pelvic exam?" asked the nurse.

She had no voice. She shook her head.

Angela explained each step of the pelvic, which didn't make it any less shocking and painful. She noted mucus, which indicated high fertility.

Rushing footsteps came from somewhere outside.

"Where is he?" a banshee scream roared down the hallway. "Where is my son? Where's my Jimmy?"

What? Margie looked around frantically. *Jimmy Hunt was on the loose? Where? Where?*

"Octavia, please," someone else said. "You can't go in there."

Octavia. Where had she heard that name before? Octavia.

"I need to see my son," the woman screamed.

Jimmy was here? Where? Margie panicked again, looking around wildly.

"You're okay," said Angela. "You're okay. You're safe. Nobody's going to hurt you. We're finishing up with the exam."

The voices faded. Finally it was over, the poking and prodding, the swabbing and needle sticks and testing.

"Can I go home and get cleaned up? Please." Her voice was a whisper made of pain.

"They'll let you use the shower here."

She used to love her bath at home. It wasn't much, an old-fashioned clawfoot bathtub with a few rust streaks at the drain. It was plenty deep, though. Queen had given her some nice soaps and towels for her birthday and it was her place to relax and read books. She was in the middle of reading *The Book Thief* about a girl in Nazi Germany surviving something horrific.

"Just a few more things to go over," said the nurse. "You're entitled to treatment for STIs."

Margie nodded. She'd never had an STI. She practiced safe sex.

But Jimmy Hunt did not.

"Can you tell me if you're pregnant?"

"No."

"No, you're not pregnant, or no, you can't tell me?"

"No."

"When was the first day of your last period?"

"I don't remember." Her voice sounded whispery and strange. "Wait, I do. It was a church Sunday." She'd been getting ready to meet up with Cubby and Queen, and she was rushing around when she realized her period had started. That seemed a hundred years ago. "Two Sundays ago," she said.

The assistant went behind the curtain again and came back carrying a pink plastic tub and a tray with packets of pills and some amenities—a comb and a toothbrush. "From the pharmacy," she said.

"Can you swallow a pill?" asked Angela.

Yes.

There was more than one.

"We're giving you treatment to cover any STIs including HIV. We did a pregnancy test that will show if you're pregnant from an act of intercourse two weeks or more before. You're getting emergency contraception— one pill now, another in twelve hours."

"Okay."

"You have to take these pills exactly as directed. Can you do that?"

"Okay."

"It's important."

Brenda Pike produced a pamphlet: *Not Your Fault: What to Do in the Aftermath of Sexual Assault.* What to do? All Margie wanted was to sleep for a thousand years.

". . . to take a statement from you," Angela was saying.

Margie was too tired to ask her to repeat it.

New voices drifted in from the hallway.

"She needs a shower," Angela said to someone outside the curtain area.

A mumbled response.

"Oh, come on," Angela said. "She's covered in . . ." *mumble mumble.*

". . . see if there's a female officer to . . ." *mumble mumble.*

Margie dozed for five seconds or five hours. The curtain swung aside and a woman came in unannounced. She wore a uniform, her hair in a bun. Angela and the rape center woman scowled but stepped aside. An Asian woman in scrubs unlocked the wheels of the gurney. Out of the curtain room and down the hall. Lights overhead, computer stations and whiteboards swooshing by. A giant cargo elevator bore them up one floor, two floors, then out. Turn the corner, through a wide doorway designated *Shower Room.*

There was a changing area adjacent to a tile-lined shower with a clear curtain and pump dispensers marked *Soap* and *Shampoo.* There were towels and some amenities, and a shrink-wrapped pinkish garment to put on after.

The uniformed woman unlocked the handcuff on one side and then the other. What? The restraints were handcuffs? Why was she wearing handcuffs?

She flexed her wrists. Everything hurt as she pushed herself up on her elbows and then sat. The gel and the slick ointment Angela had used were sticky. She touched the sheet and gown covering her, then looked at the cop.

"Excuse me," Margie whispered.

"How's that?"

"Can I have some privacy? For my shower?" She tried to enunciate clearly.

"I'll be staying right here."

She was too tired to argue. She felt sick. She had already been poked and prodded like a prize heifer at the county fair. Everyone in the exam room had observed every crease and crevice, probing her most secret places and capturing her essence in bags and tubes. One more woman observing her was no big deal. Nothing was a big deal anymore.

She felt light-headed as she stepped down from the gurney, dropping the sheet and peeling away the soft, faded hospital gown. Flakes of rust sprinkled the linoleum floor. Her feet were filthy. Rust under her toenails, fingernails, long brownish streaks down her legs.

She stepped into the shower and turned it on. The cool water made her shrink. She stepped back and waited for the hot. The rust reconstituted into blood and flowed in wavy rivulets down the drain, circling slowly like a scene in a scary movie.

So much blood. Was it coming from between her legs? Did her period start? Was it from her insides? Without warning, she puked. Yellowish bile circled the drain.

Margie was plunged into a cloud of steam and she lost herself there, not thinking of anything. She tilted her face up to the spray and let it rain and breathed in so deep she nearly choked. Her knees wobbled and she groped blindly until her hand found the railing attached to the wall. She soaked her hair and shampooed it, scrubbing and scrubbing every inch of her scalp.

Then she methodically scrubbed each part of herself—face, ears, neck, chest, arms, thighs, crotch—everything. She went through the whole ritual twice more. The soap and water stung her wounds and she gloried in the pain. She was cleansed by the pain.

"Best wrap it up now," the officer said, fanning the steamy air with a clipboard. "You've been in there way too long."

I'm staying here forever.

Then Margie thought about home. Could she go home, knowing what had happened to her there?

"My cat," she mumbled. "I need to feed my cat." She shut off the water and wrapped herself in a towel. It was stiff and rough, chafing her skin. She wrung out her hair and tried to finger comb it. The side of her head was tender. He had yanked her hair so hard she thought he'd pulled it out.

There were some weird paper undies. The pink scrubs were marked XS but they still hung on her, impossibly loose. She cinched the waist with the drawstring, put on the yellow socks with the no-slip dots on the bottom, and stuffed her feet into the plastic scuffs.

The tub they'd given her held a toothbrush and a tiny tube of toothpaste, a comb and some lotion. The mirror above the sink was fogged. She used the side of her fist to clear a spot.

Margie gasped at the image looking back at her. The creature in the mirror was a grotesque parody of her former self. One eye was swollen nearly shut. Bruises shaded her cheek and jaw. A bruise-colored handprint marked her throat. She now knew what a *face lac* looked like. There were bite marks on her neck and shoulder. No one had ever bitten her that she knew of. No one human, anyway.

She looked down the V-neck of her top. More bruises and bite marks discolored her breasts. *You're so pretty, you make me forget I'm a gentleman.*

Stop.

She tried to curb the abhorrent thoughts swirling through her mind. "I need to go now," she said. "My cat. And I'm doing a lunch shift at work." Yes, work. Something normal. Then she hesitated, realizing that she had no way to get home. No wallet, credit card, or cash. No phone. "Um, I have to call somebody. To give me a ride." What time was it? Or was it morning? She had no idea. She hadn't seen a clock. Or a window. She didn't know if it was night or day.

The cop hesitated. "We're going to the station. You need to make a statement."

I need to sleep. She swayed on her feet.

"They have to get a statement from you."

"A statement." Her voice squeaked and cracked.

"About the incident."

"Is the rape crisis woman still here? Ms. Pike? She said she would stick with me."

"Let's go," said the cop. "We have to get down to the station."

Margie was too exhausted to keep batting words back and forth. After what had just happened, it was probably better that she stick with the cops.

12

Broad daylight outside. Margie blinked like a prairie dog emerging from its underground bunker.

The police station was in the municipal complex with the town hall and courthouse, the old section of town that hosted the farmers' market each Saturday morning. She counted herself lucky that she had never been inside the station. Going inside meant something was wrong. You'd lost a precious belonging, or somebody broke into your car or messed with your property, or you yourself had done something illegal.

There was a clerk behind glass in the reception area and notices on the walls about safety. A community bulletin board was studded with business cards and announcements. Bail bonds in a hurry. DWI Defense Lawyer. Pamphlets from the Chamber of Commerce, including a menu from Cubby's Barbecue. The cops loved his barbecue more than their own mamas' cooking, and officers and clerks were often found among the lunch crowd.

They took her to a small, bare office and a woman greeted them—Detective Glover. She had what Margie's mama used to call that Austin-hippie look—long gray-streaked hair, no makeup, skin wrinkled by sunshine and cigarettes.

"I'm here to help sort out what happened last night," she said.

Margie didn't say anything. Her head felt heavy. Everything ached. She was so, so tired.

"How are you doing?" Ms. Glover asked. "I know this is a really tough time. You must be exhausted. But it's important to hear from you."

Margie looked back at the door. Glass with miniblinds. There was a mirror on the opposite wall. A two-way mirror, obviously. Cubby's place had one behind the main register.

"You're safe here." The detective gave her a bottle of water. "If you're hungry—"

"No." *I'll never eat again.* "The woman—Brenda. Ms. Pike. From the rape center. She said she'd be here."

"I can have someone give her a call." She got up and cracked open the door and spoke briefly to somebody. Then she sat down at the table and took out a clipboard and some forms, a couple of pens and a pad of yellow paper. One of the manuals on the desk was labeled *Policies and Procedures for Survivors of Sexual Assault.* She set a small object on the table. "I'll record this to make sure we have everything."

Margie eyed the two surveillance cameras mounted in the corners of the room. "Looks like you got everything covered."

"It's for your protection."

And yours, too, probably, Margie thought. She'd seen videos online.

"Let's start with your name and address."

The basics were simple. Marjorie Salinas. Nickname Margie. Address, place of employment, education. Started working at Cubby's four years ago. Moved to a furnished cottage over by Banner Creek last year.

"Now. Can you tell me a bit about yourself? Take your time."

She stared at the surface of the table. Scuffed green, like the top of a teacher's desk. Margie had always liked school. She loved reading books. While her mother was busy making sandwiches, she would curl up in a corner and read to keep herself company. In school, she took accelerated math. She loved studying Spanish and practiced it with the helpers at the commercial kitchen. Several teachers encouraged her to try for college. That seemed as likely as trying out for the Olympics. She was sad to drop out before graduation, but she didn't have a choice.

Mama was sick a lot, and they spent all their money on her meds and care. *Oh, Mama, I need you so bad.* "When I was thirteen years old," Margie said in a rasping voice, "we moved in with Del. Delmar Gantry."

"Del is your stepfather, then."

"Nah, they weren't married. Del and I, we lost touch after Mama died." Margie didn't mention the looks Del gave her. "We . . . we're still not in touch," she repeated.

"Margie?" Detective Glover spoke quietly, showing lots of patience. "Do you have his number still?"

"It's in my phone. Where's . . . I need my phone."

The woman went to the door again, and a few minutes later, the phone arrived in a plastic zipper bag. She took it out and set it in front of Margie. It was filthy, with dark flecks on the case. She flipped it open and the tiny screen showed a picture of Kevin. She arrowed down to Contacts and showed her Del's number. The detective made some notes. "Thank you. Now, let's move on. I need to hear from you about last night."

Margie reined in her wandering mind. She told the detective that it was a typical night at Cubby's. He always closed at ten, even on a Saturday. Nothing good ever happens after ten P.M., he used to say. Banner Creek had once been a sundown town, one of those places where Black folks had to observe a curfew at sunset, or take their chances with the rednecks. Cubby said his daddy remembered those days all too well, and they didn't sound like a party.

She explained about the girls inviting her out for some fun after work.

"Do you usually go out after work? Drinking? Clubbing, dancing, that sort of thing?"

"Sometimes."

"Every night?"

"No. Once or twice a week, maybe."

"And do you meet men on these outings?"

"Sure."

"Do you have sex with these men?"

"How is this about last night?"

"I'm simply trying to get a sense of the background."

"I know what you're asking. I'm twenty years old, and I'm a high school dropout. I work as a waitress and I make barbecue sauce. Sometimes I go out with guys. Every once in a while I hook up with someone. I'm no different from lots of other girls."

"So you met James Hunt and you went out with him?"

"Yes."

"And hooked up with him?"

"Yes."

"Meaning you had sex with him."

"I did. I thought he was nice at first, but it turned out I was wrong." *So goddamn wrong.* "I broke up with him. And then he came to my house and raped me." Anger blazed inside her and shot out through her fingertips, her eyes.

"I'm sorry this distresses you. I'm required to take a statement as soon after the incident as possible. You went out with Jimmy prior to last night?"

"I just told you. I was with the girls at a honky-tonk the night we met. A couple nights later, I fixed him dinner and he stayed over. The next day, he offered to take me to the shooting range."

"Shooting range? Are you a fan of shooting?"

"Don't know the first thing about it. It just sounded kinda cool, like something to do." She stared at her lap. Her borrowed top was all wrinkled. It was exhausting, the way the detective wanted her to go over and over this. "We never went, though. I had second thoughts. I decided we weren't a match."

"What made you decide that?"

He hadn't bothered to help with the dishes. Left his towels on the bathroom floor. And then . . . "I asked him to use a condom and he didn't."

"You're sure about that."

"Yes. You can ask him. He won't deny it."

The detective gave her a look. It was brief but Margie noticed.

"I told him later that day I didn't want to go to the shooting range after all. I didn't want to see him anymore." She thought about the raging text messages that had blown up her phone after that, before she blocked his number. She rubbed her throat. Her own voice sounded like a stranger's. She ached all over. "Can I go now? I need to feed my cat," she said, rubbing her wrists. "You don't rescue someone and then neglect to feed him."

A pause. "Let's get through this," the detective said. "Now. You got home. And then what?"

It seemed like a hundred years ago that she was making barbecue sauce, the mason jars lined up like soldiers along the kitchen counter, the cutting boards and peeler and knife at the ready. She remembered singing along with the songs on the radio—Brandi Carlile and Dave

Grohl and the Plain White T's. She loved those artists but she knew she would never be able to listen to them again.

There was no strength in her voice as she described seeing headlights outside, thinking it might be the neighbors—

"Are you good friends with the neighbors?"

"Friendly, I guess you'd say. They have teenagers."

The detective asked for their names and wrote them down. "But the headlights—it wasn't the neighbors."

"It wasn't the neighbors. It . . . Jimmy startled me."

"Did he sneak up on you?"

"No, just . . . I wasn't expecting him."

"Did he force his way into your house?"

"No."

"You let him in?"

"No. I guess the door was unlocked. I'd just come home."

"Do you typically fail to lock the door?"

"I lock up at night. I was planning to work for a bit, is all. Making my sauce. But he walked in unannounced, and I was . . . startled."

"Do you recall what was said?"

"No. Small talk. He got a beer from the fridge."

"He was drinking?"

"He was already drunk."

"What made you think that?"

"The eyes. His eyes were bleary. He was slurring his speech."

"What kind of beer was he drinking?"

"Shiner. In the stubby bottle, not a longneck."

"You had beer in your fridge. Where did you get it?"

"From Jimmy. He left a six-pack in my fridge before."

"Before what?"

"Before I broke up with him." She was starting to confuse herself. He'd brought a six-pack the night she'd made him dinner. He'd been nice enough that night, if a bit boastful about himself and his family. *My big brother, Briscoe, is a lawyer. Gonna be state's attorney general one day, just you wait. Maybe even governor. He's that smart. I'll be the family football star.*

"Were all the bottles in the six-pack last night?"

"What?" She felt tired. She yawned, desperate for sleep. Would she ever sleep again? "Five. There were five."

"Who drank the sixth one?"

"I opened it to drink while I was cooking."

"So you were drinking."

"Yes."

"How much did you have to drink?"

"Hell, I don't know. I was in my own house. I was . . . It was after work." Jesus, a guy had raped her and this woman was worried about her being underage and drinking?

"Do you drink a lot?"

Margie frowned. "Hardly at all. Anyway, last night, Jimmy was drunk and looking to get laid. He wasn't very gracious about being dumped, but I didn't expect him to show up and attack me."

"Tell me about that. He showed up and surprised you."

"He'd been drinking." The eyes. The slurred words. "I asked him to leave. I tried to be nice but he was pissed."

"How could you tell?"

"He was rough. Grabbed me and tried to kiss me."

"What were you wearing?"

Margie blinked. "Excuse me?"

"Street clothes? Did you change when you got home from work?"

"Why would it matter what I was wearing? I was making barbecue sauce."

"Every detail is important."

"Boots and a skirt. I had a top on that I didn't want to ruin with the grease, so I took it off and put on an apron. One of those bib aprons from Cubby's." She touched her neck. "He choked me with the apron strap."

"Right away?"

"Not just then. When he wouldn't back off, I grabbed a knife."

"What kind of knife?"

She described the knife, and how he cut himself grabbing for it. "I didn't mean to hurt him. Then he said I was stupid to bring a knife to a gunfight. I thought he was kidding but he showed me his gun."

"What kind of gun?"

"I don't know. A handgun, you know? In a holster strapped to his side. I couldn't tell if it was loaded or if it had a safety or what that even looked like. I was just— I don't know guns." Remembering the incident made her flinch.

"But you were interested in guns. You mentioned going to the range with him."

"I also mentioned that I canceled that plan. Seeing the gun in my kitchen scared me. I asked him to put it away."

"And did he?"

"Uh-huh."

"Back in the side holster?"

"Yes. He still wouldn't go away, though. I realized he wasn't going to leave me alone so I pretended to go along with him." She described the different ploys she'd attempted. Asking to go out with him. Saying she needed the bathroom. Saying she'd sleep with him again.

"You said before you didn't want to."

"I wanted him to leave me alone. I tried to act like I was cooperating. You know, until I could get away."

"Away from your own house?"

"I figured I'd go to the neighbors'."

"So you could have walked away before things escalated."

Margie felt a tic of annoyance. "Believe me, I tried. He kept me cornered, though."

"Can you tell me what you said and did at that point?"

"I offered him another beer and invited him to the bedroom. To buy time. I suggested we could have sex like before."

"You invited him to have sex with you?"

"He was stupid drunk, and I figured it would be a way to distract him until I could get away. I thought . . . I don't know what I thought. That he'd get it over with quick. That he'd fall asleep and I could go for help. I don't know." Spoken aloud, her plan sounded idiotic. Offer a guy sex so he'd leave you alone? Really?

She twisted the drawstring of her pants. "I went to the fridge for the beer. My phone was there on the counter so I dialed 911. He saw me do it. Got really mad again and attacked me."

"Can you be more specific?"

"Yanked the apron strap, pulled my hair. Dragged me to the bedroom." Margie started to hyperventilate. She drank some of the water and almost puked again. She breathed through her teeth and stared at her broken nails. "I scratched him as much as I could." She'd seen enough crime shows to know why that was important.

She described his hands on her, twisting the strap around her neck. Pinning her wrists. Hitting her when she cried out. Ripping the front closure of her bra. Ripping her panties. Holding her down. The feeling that she was dying from lack of air.

Her hand finding something hard against his rib cage. The gun in its holster.

"He had his gun while you were having sex?"

It wasn't sex. It was rape. "I kept trying to push him off me, and I touched it," she said.

"Was it snapped in the holster?"

"I don't know."

"Did you unsnap it?"

"No. Maybe. I don't know."

"Did you take it out of the holster?"

"I don't know." Her hand came up and touched her cheek, tender and swollen with a bruise. She remembered him tightening the strap around her neck. Seeing stars. Feeling her bladder weaken and release. "I felt the trigger. With my middle finger. I felt the trigger."

"Was the safety on?"

"I don't know. I don't know anything about guns."

"You don't know how a safety works?"

"No."

"Do you know how a trigger works?"

"I . . . It's a trigger. You squeeze it. Pull it back. Everybody knows that."

"You say you felt the trigger. Did you pull the trigger?"

She flexed her right hand. Looked down at it. Fingernails broken but clean, thanks to the shower. She opened and closed her fist. The gun was little, like a toy.

"Yes," Margie said. "I reckon I did."

"Did what?"

"I reckon I pulled the trigger."

"And did it discharge?"

Discharge. Angela said she should expect some discharge after the exam and the meds she'd been given.

"Did the weapon discharge?"

Bang.

"Yes."

"Once? Or more than once?"

"The one time is all. I think."

"Are you sure?"

"No."

"What happened then?"

"I . . . don't remember." She rubbed her elbow, tender with bruises. "I couldn't breathe. He was squeezing me, pushing down." All two hundred fifty pounds of him, all that heat and his terrible grunting rutting sounds. Then silence, and his full weight crushing her.

"What happened to your elbow?" the detective asked.

In the ER, they had done an X-ray and found that it was dislocated. She'd howled in pain, and then somebody—a short doctor and an assistant—had given her arm a tug and she'd yelped like a wounded animal and then the elbow joint was back in place and the pain subsided.

"I fell," she said.

"Where did you fall?"

"On the floor. The . . . bedroom floor." It was slippery, like an oil slick.

"Did you get up? Did someone help you up?"

She remembered flickering lights. Bobbing flashlight beams. A knock at the door. The pain so furious that she went light-headed, maybe even passed out. More lights and thudding footsteps, a mask with a peculiar smell, backboard and rolling bumping *on my count* and the crinkly paper and glare of the ER. The brown curtain, scissors, and swabs.

Margie was trembling so hard she had to grip the edge of the table to hold herself steady. "I'm really tired. I need to get home. I got a split shift at the restaurant today." Anything that felt normal. That felt like her real life.

Detective Glover went to the door again and murmured something. A few minutes later, there was a document in a manila folder. "This simply says your statement is true to the best of your knowledge." She laid a business card on the table. "You can call me anytime if you think of anything else or if you want to make any amendments or corrections."

Under her title it said *Criminal Investigations*.

I'm not the criminal here, Margie thought.

"You need to sign and date it at the bottom and I'll get this filed."

This statement, consisting of six pages, is true to the best of my knowledge and belief, and I offer it knowing that, if it was tendered in evidence, I shall be subject to prosecution if I have willfully stated herein anything that I know to be false or do not believe to be true.

Margie had never felt so tired in her life. She wanted to sleep forever. She wrote her name and the date. There was a time stamp on the printout. "The time is wrong," she pointed out, thinking of the clock in the reception area. "It can't be 1:45 P.M. yet."

The detective glanced at it. "Probably a printer glitch. I'll fix that later."

"Can I go home now?" She needed a ride. Maybe the rape crisis woman would give her a ride. Brenda Pike. Wasn't she supposed to be here? And what about that pink tub with the brochures and pills? *Take exactly as directed.*

"Sit tight. I'll be right back."

"I'm done sitting tight." Margie surged to her feet so quickly that the chair fell over behind her. "I need to use the bathroom." She felt like puking again. "Where's the bathroom?"

The detective stood swiftly, watching Margie like a hawk. The door opened and two cops entered—a woman with her hair in a tight bun, and a guy who looked vaguely familiar.

"Marjorie Salinas," he said. "You're under arrest for the murder of James Bryant Hunt. You have the right to remain silent. Anything you say or do can be used against you in a court of law. You have the right to an attorney. If you cannot afford an attorney, one will be appointed to you."

She wasn't sure she was hearing this correctly. Her knees nearly gave out. "What the hell—*no*." Margie cast a wild, confused look at the detective by the door.

With a metallic click, the cold bracelet of the handcuffs circled her wrists.

13

Margie lay on a bunk facing a wall made of cinder block, painted beige pink, the color of Silly Putty. She pressed her hands together between her knees, smearing the fingerprint ink on the oversize gray jumpsuit they made her wear. During the booking, they'd taken everything from her, little as that was—the bin from the hospital, the borrowed scrubs, plastic shoes. There was a mug shot and a backhanded slur from the woman who did the body cavity search. Though she wanted to jump out of her skin, Margie gritted her teeth and submitted to being intimately examined. They strapped her wrist with a bar-coded inmate bracelet and checked her hands for residue.

In a daze, she had stood before a judge on a TV monitor, blinking in confusion as he told her she'd be held in general population until an undetermined court date. *Held*, she came to understand, meant caged. The pods were units full of minuscule cubicles and cracked plastic lawn furniture that looked as if it had been left out in the weather too long.

You have the right to remain silent.

She had told the detective everything that had happened to her. *A witness statement*, they'd said. Detective Glover, with her weary-hippie empathy, had put her at ease, saying she needed to take a statement. She'd been a sympathetic listener, and her questions had prompted Margie to reconstruct the whole horrific evening in detail.

You have the right to an attorney.

She didn't have an attorney. Who had that? Not anyone Margie knew. Rich people hired lawyers to write their wills and settle their frivolous lawsuits and help them with their divorces. Last year, some woman got drunk at Cubby's, broke a barstool, and fell backward, fracturing both wrists, and she had sued him. Even though his liability insurance had covered the settlement, he'd nearly gone bankrupt paying for the things that weren't covered. She'd overheard Queen telling Tillie, the house manager, that they had to take out a second mortgage on their house in order to raise money. Margie barely knew how a mortgage worked but she looked it up and learned it was a huge loan people took out to pay for their house. It took something like thirty years to finish paying back the loan. She couldn't imagine doing anything for thirty years. Sitting in jail, wrongly accused?

She couldn't imagine buying a house, either. Sometimes she wished the tiny furnished cottage by the creek belonged to her so she could fix it up a bit, maybe install a better stove and nicer countertops. She would paint it a cute color and replace the floor of the bedroom that had been ruined by all that blood, rivers of it, so much blood that it had created an oil slick, and she'd slipped and fallen in it—*splat*—dislocating her elbow in her rush to get the hell out of there.

the murder of James Bryant Hunt

He was dead, then. But . . . murder? He had been trying to murder *her*.

There was one other person in the cell across from her, a skinny, agitated woman who couldn't keep still. A tweaker, probably, haunted by cravings. Margie stayed on her side, turned to the wall, curling her body to try to fend off the horror of being in jail.

She slept for five minutes. She slept for a hundred years. She woke up feeling sick and they scanned her bracelet and took her to a communal bathroom where the sink was a trough and the stall doors were missing.

There was no one to talk to. Margie found a pencil but had no paper. She used her inmate handbook to write down her jumbled thoughts. And so many questions. No one was available to answer all the questions exploding from her mind. There were civilian workers, and inmates known as "trustees," and someone called the watch commander, but she didn't know how to find that person.

The jailhouse pamphlet listed endless regulations. Her eyes glazed over as she scanned the rules about roll call, dayroom, television viewing, two paperback books at a time available to be borrowed from a cart in the pod. Permission forms had to be filled out for every possible request—sick bay, commissary purchases, phone calls. She went to a prayer group meeting, not because she was feeling particularly prayerful but because they had scratch paper she could write on.

Meals were brought on a cart and the women went four at a time to get a tray. Her wristband was scanned and she stood there, looking for a place to sit. The food was a mess of carbs and onion and fatty meat. She nibbled at a piece of white bread. No one wanted to talk to her during the meal. She persisted, trying to get someone's attention, asking questions, changing seats until an officer poked her in the back. "Pick a horse and get on it, missy."

"I just got here. I need to call someone." But who? She

didn't know anyone's phone number by heart. Everyone's number was in her phone. They'd taken Brenda's card from her along with everything else, including her dignity, the last of which died during the body cavity search. "I need to know how to get out of here," Margie said.

"You're gonna be held here until your arraignment."

"What's an arraignment?" she asked.

"The charges against you will be read. You enter your plea and then bail will be set."

"When do I do that?"

"When they say. Eat up, girl."

"But—"

The officer moved on.

To keep herself from going insane, Margie borrowed two books at a time from the library cart. She read voraciously, devouring a dog-eared copy of *The Handmaid's Tale* in one sleepless night. She studied a thick volume called *Teach Yourself Spanish*, and she practiced every day, chatting with civilian staffers and inmates. In school, she'd made top marks in Spanish class and wished she'd been able to learn more.

She soon discovered that she was notorious. The murder of Jimmy Hunt was a local cause célèbre, and the news had spread like a virus through the general population of the jail. She didn't make any friends, but a few women were willing to talk to her. One day, she was making a selection from the library cart when an inmate named Sadie came over and eyed her briefly with a flinty, assessing regard. Margie had already figured out that Sadie was a huge busybody, buzzing around the unit like a hummingbird, collecting random bits of gossip. She was also supersmart and had been in college when she was arrested for something she refused to talk about. She knew things and passed around her shiny bits and pieces of data about the inner workings of the jail.

"You the one who shot Jimmy Hunt," she said.

Margie's heart flipped in panic. She looked from side to side. "I . . . No. That's what they say, though."

"Shooting a Hunt in this county is a real bad idea."

"Why do they say I killed him?" Margie asked.

"Well now," the woman said, "let's see. According to the *Hayden County Star*, the man was found dead in your home. Shot one time in the femoral artery. That's the big one in the groin area. It appears he bled to death."

Through the gauze in her brain, Margie glimpsed flashes of memory. A gush of blood like a hose coming loose. Jimmy had howled and called her a goddamn fucking bitch and his entire weight had pinned her and she squirmed and fought and he kept yelling. Somehow she inched her way out from under the great weight of him and staggered to her feet. She slipped and went down, hearing a *pop*—her elbow dislocating—followed by an explosion of pain.

She was screaming without sound coming out and Jimmy roared and came at her. He staggered and fell, dragging himself toward her. She managed to get out of the room, gulping air through her damaged throat until she collapsed.

After a minute or an hour, there were swirling lights, police and EMTs. "I never meant . . . I just wanted him to stop."

"He's dead 'cause you shot him."

"He was raping me. Once that's sorted out, I'm walking out of here."

"Yeah, that's not gonna happen, not in this county," Sadie said.

Margie winced, thinking of the Hunt family's status. "What do I do?"

"You're supposed to be charged within a couple days. They don't always do that here, you'll see. Folks like us tend to get lost. Things tend to move real slow around here."

"So what happens next?"

"There's supposed to be a preliminary hearing. It's like a minitrial with no jury. Only a judge. He can either dismiss the charges or set a trial date."

"How do I get him to dismiss the charges?"

"You don't shoot a guy in your house."

"I had to. He was choking me to death."

"Then your lawyer'll explain that."

"I don't have a lawyer. I couldn't afford one, even if I knew who to call."

"You're entitled to a court-appointed lawyer, but good luck with that," said Sadie. "There's always a backlog and you have to wait your turn. Maybe your looks will help you at the arraignment," Sadie suggested. "Bat those baby-blue eyes. Get yourself cleaned up. There's two minutes of hot water in the shower. Use every second of it."

Sadie culled through the library cart and gave her a worn copy of a book called *You and the Law*. Margie retreated to her bunk and started reading. In Texas, there were no degrees of murder like you heard on TV legal dramas. There was no separate category like voluntary manslaughter. In Texas, murder was murder—"depraved indifference to human life," a serious crime with harsh penalties, including death. Margie felt trapped. She wavered between frustration at the injustice and abject fear. When the worst-case scenario was the death penalty, terror took on a new meaning.

At the arraignment, a sad army of criminals in their plastic shoes shuffled into the courtroom. They were lined up on benches, each waiting for their turn. One by one, the charges were read, the accused had to enter a plea, and that would be that. You could plead guilty, not guilty, or no contest.

"Case number 14749. *The State of Texas versus Marjorie Salinas*."

Margie stepped up to the lectern the way she'd seen the others do. She tossed the hair out of her face and gazed up at the judge. He was a looker, with a fancy haircut and a long, thin face, keen eyes, and a heavy, flashy-looking wedding ring.

"You're unrepresented by counsel?"

"What?"

"You don't have a lawyer?"

If you cannot afford an attorney, one will be assigned to you.

"No, but I want—"

"You are charged with the murder of James Bryant Hunt. How do you plead?"

She froze. *He's dead because you shot him.*

"How do you plead?"

"Not guilty, Your Honor," she said, but her voice cracked from her still-damaged throat. According to the book she'd read, a not guilty plea meant she was refuting the charges against her. The words she spoke were hollow, so she repeated them, rasping louder. "I'm not guilty, but—"

"Bail is set at two hundred fifty thousand dollars cash."

The number was too big to get her head around. Margie knew the term *bail* but had no idea how it actually worked. And even less idea about where to get two hundred fifty thousand dollars. "Is that how much it takes to get me out of jail?" she asked.

"Cash bail can be posted with the court clerk."

"But I don't have—"

The gavel came down. "Next case."

"But—"

"Next."

The first time Margie cried was when Queen came to see her. They were separated by a Plexiglas shield, but Queen's sweet, sad smile floated through the barrier and touched Margie in a tender spot, and something broke loose inside her and she cried.

"Oh, child," Queen said. She held her purse in her lap, her fingers strumming it like a guitar. "Look at you."

Margie stared at her hands in her lap, cuffed at the wrists. "There are no mirrors in this place. Guess that's a blessing, after what happened." There were sheets of stainless steel above the sinks in the bathroom and sometimes she caught a glimpse of her reflection in the wired glass dividers in the hallway, but she never looked close. She didn't want to scare herself any more than she already had.

"What'd he do to you, baby girl?"

"Aw, Queenie. I reckon you can guess."

"I suppose I can, honey. I won't make you talk about anything you don't want to talk about."

"I'm scared. I'm worried about Kevin—my cat. They said I have to stay here until I meet with a court-appointed lawyer. There has to be some kind of hearing and they won't say when that is."

"Just doesn't seem right."

"Can you go by my place? Feed my cat?"

Queen's gaze shifted, and she leaned forward toward the Plexiglas.

"What?" asked Margie.

"Nobody's allowed near your place. On account of the investigation. I'll see what I can do about the cat."

"Thanks," she said to Queen. "Oh, lord, I hate it here so much."

"Did they set bail?"

Margie told her the amount. "In cash," she said. "Nobody has that kind of money. Some woman here named Sadie said it has to be that high because I'd be considered a flight risk on account of I have weak ties to the community, and apparently, I pose a danger to society. Doesn't matter, anyway. I couldn't post bail even if it was an option."

"Now, you know we'd front you the money if—"

"I wouldn't let you." Margie was firm about this. Cubby's was thriving, but she knew the Watsons' margins were tight. She was not about to take their money.

"Just as well you stay out of sight anyway," Queen remarked. "The whole town's gone crazy over that boy's death."

"What do you mean, crazy?"

"I mean like this." Queen opened her purse. A monitor stepped forward, and Queen scowled. "I'm showing her the paper," she said.

The monitor raised his hands, palms out, and stepped back. Nobody dared to mess with Queen when she had that fierce look. She held up an issue of the *Hayden County Star.* There was a big front-page picture of flowers and candles and stuffed toys and football memorabilia piled around the entry to the high school stadium where Jimmy Hunt had been the best player on the squad. The fence and kiosks were decked with hand-lettered poems and Bible verses, and a huge banner that read JUSTICE FOR JIMMY HUNT.

There were smaller photographs of his mother, Octavia Hunt, her face behind a veil, crumpled against her husband in grief. Other pictures showed weeping football players and cheerleaders staring in disbelief. Outpouring of love for a local hero, the caption read.

Margie felt a twist of dread in her stomach. She had pulled the trigger, and he was dead. He was choking her and she was fighting for her life, but no one seemed to know that side of the story. How did you convince a whole town that their homegrown hero was a vicious rapist?

Someone had made a poster with a blown-up picture of her mug shot, her miserable frightened bruised face starkly lit, with the stenciled phrase *Death Penalty.*

"The funeral was something to see," Queen said, shaking her head as she folded the paper away. "The whole Aggie marching band played. You'd think he was a war hero, the way they carried on."

"Folks do like their football," Margie said.

Queen leaned forward. "You look a touch green around the gills."

"I think I'm dying of anxiety." Margie sighed. "I'm hungry all the time, but the food is horrible. And I feel sick all the time, too."

"Can you go to the infirmary?"

"I filled out a form to request it, but they keep saying I have to wait." Everything here was a wait.

"You need to eat. You're too skinny. Make sure you eat something, you hear? I left a little money in your inmate trust account. It's not much, but I wanted you to have something."

"Oh, Queenie." She nearly sobbed the name.

"And get yourself to the infirmary. The way you look—they got to do something. I'm real sorry this is happening. I'll be praying hard for you."

As she whispered goodbye, Margie felt sick in her throat as the tears gathered force again. Since her mom had passed, she hadn't felt this—the caring, fussing love that seemed to emanate from Queen like the warmth from an ember.

The ensuing weeks were filled with unexplained delays and ignored pleas. The court set a mandatory hearing date, but the date kept getting pushed back with no explanation. According to Sadie, the delays were illegal, but there was no one to complain to, and they happened anyway.

Margie kept hoping Queen would come back. Or that someone else she'd known from Cubby's would visit— one of the girls from the front of the house, maybe. Or Nanda, who headed the cleaning crew, or Jock, an older man who was in charge of the wood supply, who always seemed to have a kind word for Margie. But no one came. Maybe they were busy. Maybe the girls at the restaurant weren't really friends after all, just people she worked with.

She just didn't know anymore.

14

Margie's situation was not unique. Like her, most of the women in jail were lost in a bureaucratic limbo as they awaited magistration. Like her, most—more likely *all*—were poor. The cash bail system made it impossible for anyone to afford to post bail. It didn't seem to matter that the law required charges to be brought within a reasonable time frame, and that a public defender would be assigned to her case. There was no one to ask, no one to complain to.

The food was beyond awful. Nothing tasted good to her. She tried to eat, but everything was starchy and gluey and barely edible. One of the women in the cafeteria said she looked like a scarecrow.

Her inability to eat turned out to be a blessing of sorts. After filling out numerous request forms, she was finally allowed to go to the infirmary. The nurse on duty, Mrs. Renfro, checked out her injuries and offered the first kind words she'd heard in this place. "Food, rest, and exercise," she said. "Spend as much time in the yard as you can. Remember to breathe."

There was a kitchen garden in one corner of the yard. Margie welcomed even the smallest distraction and busied herself tending the herbs and greens, peppers, and cherry tomatoes there. When she was late getting back to the pod one day, the cafeteria supervisor said she should be put on kitchen duty. This was supposed to be a punishment, but Margie embraced the assignment.

She was not a trustee but "unclassified," meaning, she supposed, she had not been labeled a troublemaker yet. At least the work gave her a break from the unrelenting tedium and worry. Food preparation consisted of opening pouches and cans and pouring the contents into stainless-steel serving vessels on a warming bar. No actual cooking took place. Clad in a hairnet, apron, and gloves, she opened the food chute to place the trays for lunch, which usually consisted of something like potato salad, chopped beef on a bun, pudding, and juice. Most of the chopped beef came back, the sandwiches only picked at.

Margie's Spanish was fairly basic, but she could express herself to the staff. She could always find a way to talk about food. The kitchen help treated her like a human being, at least. The manager, Ninfa, approached her one day at the condiment bar, where Margie was mixing sugar and salt with mustard and pepper and a splash of vinegar in a small cup. She added some dried onion flakes and pimiento. Then wordlessly, she offered the cup to Ninfa. With a vague shrug of one shoulder, Ninfa tried the concoction.

She gave a nod. "Better. Yeah."

There was nothing to be done about the quality of the food-service ingredients, but there were ways to improve the taste. Margie helped with the breakfast of biscuits and sausage gravy. She sauced the bland chicken with lemon juice from a bottle and thyme from the garden. She added seasoning to the fried catfish.

The horror of her circumstances didn't fade. But two things saved her—the books on the library cart, and the cafeteria work. The kitchen project—fixing food for her fellow inmates—kept her tethered to earth. Without a project, she probably would have faded into despair.

She kept track of the days with pencil marks on the notepaper she cribbed from prayer group. On the forty-fourth day, she was handcuffed and taken to a window-less conference room with a table and two chairs. The officer said this was where she would meet with her court-appointed lawyer.

A lawyer. Finally.

The public defender's name was Landry Yates. He looked like a Boy Scout—clean-cut, apple-cheeked, and maybe even too young to raise a beard. His gaze darted around the small conference room as if he sought an emergency exit. His hands fiddled with his briefcase, and he dropped his pen twice. Beads of sweat shone on his smooth white forehead.

Was he scared of her? Maybe he thought she really was a murderer.

"I've been here forever," Margie said. "What took you so long?"

He set his briefcase on the table and took out a phone and notepad. "I'm real sorry about the . . . situation you've been through," he said. "I can take a statement from you now."

"That woman took a statement from me weeks ago. Can't you get a copy of that?"

He frowned. "What woman?"

"Detective Glover. Right after it happened. Right before they locked me up."

He pressed his lips together. "Shoot. A witness state-ment, then?"

"That's what she said."

"Before you were Mirandized?"

She knew the term from all the books she'd been reading. "Yes."

Landry's face drained to a paler shade of white. He made a note on his yellow pad. "No good can ever come from giving a statement. I guess the reports are here but I haven't had time to read them yet."

"They said I had to. Didn't know I had a choice."

His lips thinned into a line. "Making that statement was voluntary."

"Didn't seem that way at the time. I thought it'd help them nab the guy who raped me. They said I *had* to."

"What'd you tell them?"

"I answered all her questions. I told her what Jimmy Hunt did to me. Please," she said. "I've been here so long. I want to go home."

"I'm going to need you to tell me everything you told the detective, only now, anything you say is privileged. Just between you and me. You don't have to hold anything back. Once I get all the information, I'll see what can be done."

"How long is that going to take?"

"It varies. Depends on what else is going on at court."

"I just want to go home," she repeated.

He dropped his pen again and leaned down to pick it up off the floor. "I'll see about filing a writ of habeas corpus, but it's up to the court scheduler to get it on the calendar, and then it's the judge's call. Right now, I need to hear from you. Everything."

Margie went through the night of horrors again, up until the gun went off. Mr. Yates's phone kept vibrating with calls and text messages. He kept checking it. He didn't seem to listen nearly as well as the detective had.

"I didn't mean to hurt him," she said. "I couldn't

breathe. I had to get him to stop." Her stomach heaved. She had never killed anything other than a mosquito or a cockroach. Yet that night, she'd shot a man with his gun.

His phone vibrated again. "This has already been looked at by the felony review unit. We need to schedule another hearing." He gave her a form to sign.

She glared at the form. "I'm not writing my name on more legal stuff."

"This is to help you. I'm going to try to secure your release until the trial."

"They said I have to post bail. It has to be cash," she pointed out.

"We'll see what we can do about that. There's no case yet. No indictment. So far all they have is a crime, a suspect, and an arrest."

Margie had zero confidence in Landry Yates. He seemed sincere and even sympathetic about her situation. But he was distracted, juggling too many cases, and he admitted that he lacked the staff and budget for extra support services to help him out.

When Landry Yates finally got her a court date, Margie felt sicker than ever. She cleaned herself up as best she could. Ninfa lent her a hair tie and found her a clean jumpsuit. A deputy took her to court from the jail. Given the climate in town, the rage, Landry didn't want her to be stuffed into a police car and marched into the courtroom.

"You're nervous," Margie said to him. They were waiting on a hard bench in the marble hallway outside the courtroom. The air smelled of furniture polish, and the soaring dome over the lobby magnified the *tick tick tick* of the ceiling fans. Landry looked even worse than she felt. "I can tell by the way you keep studying that sign on the wall." It was a glass case with a list designating the presiding judges for the day.

"It's not the judge I was hoping for. This one—Shelby Hale—ran on a platform of being a law-and-order guy. Likes putting people behind bars. Plus he plays golf at the Hayden Country Club."

"Let me guess. The Hunts are members of the country club."

"Octavia Hunt is on the board of directors there."

"Isn't that like a conflict of interest?"

"You'd think."

She wished he had more confidence, but come to find out, he was so busy that he didn't have time to be confident or anything else. With all the folks he had to help, a public defender got no rest. Landry was juggling cases and hearings and pleadings, and he was short-staffed and there was nothing she could do about it.

In the courtroom, the gallery was full, more than usual to hear Landry tell it. They all wanted to see the monster who had gunned down their favorite son. Deputies and bailiffs moved through the room, intent on keeping order. Landry made a breathy noise that sounded like *shitfire*.

"What's the matter?" she whispered.

"I figured they'd send an ADA—an assistant. Looks like we got the DA—Ursula Flores."

"Is that bad?"

He pressed his mouth into a thin line. "She's a good DA."

Margie eyed the woman at the long table in front of the bar railing. She was perfectly groomed, with shiny dark hair and a fitted suit, her movements deliberate and efficient as she organized her materials on the table.

"Don't we want a good one?" Margie asked.

"Not if she's in charge of bringing an indictment against you. A good DA can indict a ham sandwich."

A few minutes later, Ms. Flores was joined by an associate, a tall guy with a military bearing and a politician's falsely earnest expression, which couldn't hide a tinge of hostility. He shot Margie a seething glare, as if trying to roast her alive by will alone. He looked familiar.

He looked like Jimmy Hunt.

My big brother, Briscoe, is a lawyer. Gonna be state's attorney general one day, just you wait. Maybe even governor. He's that smart.

She noticed a couple with their heads together, murmuring. The woman looked familiar. Margie had seen her at Cubby's every Tuesday. "Jimmy's parents?" she asked in a whisper.

Landry gave a brief nod.

She doubted the high-and-mighty Octavia Hunt realized that Margie Salinas had been her waitress numerous times at Cubby's. She shuddered and kept her eyes on the surface of the table in front of her.

When it was time to address the judge, Landry said, "I'm requesting my client be released in order to better prepare for her defense."

"That's completely ludicrous, Your Honor," said Ms. Flores. "We've already provided evidence that she is a flight risk and a danger to the public. She has no ties to the community other than a part-time waitressing job. She fled her parents' home in another town and came to Banner Creek as a vagrant. She's a school dropout. Lied about her age to get a job at some honky-tonk, and when she got found out, she worked as a waitress. She has nothing to keep her here. Nothing at all."

Margie winced. Was that how she was perceived? As a dropout, a liar, a vagrant? On the surface, everything

Ms. Flores said was accurate. But it wasn't who Margie was. So far, all the judge knew about her was what the prosecutor had told him—that she was a drifter with no education, trading on her looks to get by, sleeping around with different boyfriends, drinking and partying after work every night. By her own admission in the witness statement, she had been walking around scantily clad in her kitchen when Jimmy came to call.

"She was Jimmy's girlfriend," the DA continued. "He was completely smitten with her, but she shot him dead. As he lay bleeding to death in a pool of blood, she failed to render aid. She made no attempt to stop the bleeding or to save his life in any way. By the time help arrived, this young man, this shining star of the Texas A&M Aggies, was beyond saving."

"Objection," Landry said. "She's giving testimony, Your Honor. That's not the purpose here—"

"Sustained," the judge said quietly.

"Miss Salinas acted in self-defense," said Landry. His voice sounded tremulous as he consulted some papers on a clipboard. "A total of thirty-three injuries were documented by the sexual assault liaison task nurse. My client was strangled, beaten, raped—"

"Nothing but hearsay," snapped the DA. "She was the victim's girlfriend. They'd had sex before that night, and this particular occasion was no different, right up until she shot him and tried to flee the scene."

"I wasn't fleeing," Margie whispered. "I—"

"Hush, please." Landry made a motion with his hand to quiet her down.

The district attorney described a night that was nothing like the night Margie had experienced. The DA spoke about the lighthearted fun Margie and Jimmy had when they'd first met. There was something called a sworn affidavit from Ginny Coombs, her coworker, describing their budding romance. Text messages retrieved from mobile phone records proved that their dinner date had been eagerly anticipated by both parties, and that he'd spent the night just a short time before she shot him dead. A screen in the courtroom displayed enlarged slides of their flirty exchanges, and then her abrupt rejection, which had broken Jimmy Hunt's tender heart.

Worst of all, there were pictures of the crime scene, including Jimmy's body. Margie couldn't bear to look.

A hundred times, she wanted to surge to her feet and explain what had really happened. Landry had warned her not to say a word. *Exercise your right to remain silent*, he'd admonished her, again and again. Margie had to settle for furiously scribbled notes on his legal pad, which she punctuated with underlines and exclamation points.

The prosecutor laid out the case as Landry had predicted. The judge examined the documents submitted, scowling over the pages and asking the occasional question. *It must be hard to be a judge*, she thought. *Hearing about all the terrible things people did to each other must be depressing.*

There were statements from her coworkers, along with text messages and accounts from casual observers meant to show that she had sought out Jimmy and was his eager partner. The implication was that her injuries were the result of consensual rough sex. She was portrayed as a careless woman who thrived on attention by partying, wearing revealing clothes, and inviting a man into her home. They claimed she was a blatant opportunist, eager to take advantage of Jimmy Hunt's status and his family's wealth.

Landry objected to the characterization, but the judge allowed it.

Margie managed to keep her cool during the expected

questions and prompts from her attorney. Yes, she had met Jimmy Hunt at a honky-tonk. He was good-looking and charming, and yes, she had invited him home, fixed him dinner, and yes, she had slept with him. The questions and her replies were meant to preempt the issues that would be brought up on cross-examination.

"You were scantily clad. You were drinking, even though you were under twenty-one. You'd been promiscuous with Jimmy and with other men as well. These are the facts. So could the alleged rape have been caused by your conduct?"

This was the question that would haunt Margie. She would shy away from it for years, hiding from the deepest doubts inside her—*She had it coming.* She didn't want the memories. She didn't want them to be part of her story. She didn't want to relive how the incident had made her feel. She didn't want it to affect who she was at her core.

". . . and here we are, with no witnesses other than the accused, who is known to be a liar," the DA added. "How convenient that the only other person present at the incident was killed at the scene."

She scribbled *I did not lie* on Landry's pad.

"Your Honor, she was defending herself from a deadly attacker," Landry said. "She had no duty to retreat. Her use of deadly force was justified under Chapter 9 of the Texas penal code."

"A person who uses deadly force after provoking someone cannot be protected. The defendant provoked the victim into attacking her and then she shot him. If she felt threatened, she could have escaped without harming anyone," the DA insisted. "Could've run away. There was no rape. She just got mad and shot him, and now she's lying to keep herself out of trouble."

I need to feed my cat, Margie thought.

"And remember, she shot her lover at close range. Clearly she poses a danger to others."

Margie wasn't allowed to speak so she quit trying. Languishing in jail had taught her to detach and go someplace else in her mind. She thought of her mom singing "You Are My Sunshine" in her smoke-roughened voice. She thought about adding kiwi fruit, a natural tenderizer, to barbecue sauce. She thought about her cat's fur, downy under the palm of her hand.

During a brief recess, she told Landry, "You're letting them make me out to be a murderer in there. Why aren't you explaining what really happened? Who did you line up to vouch for me?"

He was checking his email on a BlackBerry device. "We're going to let the facts speak for themselves."

"So nobody then. Not Cubby or Queen? Not somebody from the church?"

"I did ask. But you need to know it's a big ask. In a situation like this, things can get mighty unpleasant for people of color."

The suggestion chilled her blood. "You mean they'd be intimidated? Harassed?"

"There's a lot at stake for your friends. They've got a lot to lose." He went back to his email.

Maybe Sadie was right, and this was the reason Queen had not returned after the first visit. Could be someone had threatened her for being friendly to the woman who had shot Jimmy Hunt.

"Holy hell, Landry, do you not have a problem with this?" Margie demanded.

"Doesn't matter if I do or not."

"What about finding other girls Jimmy dated?" she persisted. "I'd be willing to bet I'm not the first one he roughed up."

"If there's a trial, we might have the personnel to look into that. I'll have more time for discovery."

"What do you mean, *if* there's a trial?"

He put away his BlackBerry and looked at the clock. "We have to think positively. Time to go back in."

Back in the courtroom, Landry portrayed Margie as a hardworking young woman whose jars of gourmet barbecue sauce had made her popular at the local barbecue place. Yes, she'd been with Jimmy a time or two, but her phone records showed that she had broken up with him in no uncertain terms.

Margie wished she'd been more explicit with Jimmy. Instead of trying to soften the blow—*I'm just not in a good headspace right now*—she should have told him he'd acted like a jerk and had shown utter disrespect and irresponsibility about the condom the night he'd stayed over.

"She also made a 911 call," he pointed out. "She clearly felt unsafe when James Hunt showed up."

Landry spared no sensibilities when he documented the results of Nurse Garza's report and showed the stark images of her injuries on the screen. Margie tried not to feel the pain all over again. *You're okay now*, she kept telling herself. *You're okay now.*

There was one moment, a glimmer, when Ms. Garza seemed to address the judge directly.

"It's my testimony that the rape was caused by only one thing—the rapist."

The DA reared up and objected.

Then Landry concluded that she had been attacked in her own home and feared for her life. While fighting off his deadly attack, there had been a struggle for Jimmy's gun—the gun he'd threatened her with—and she had managed to save her own life by firing a single shot.

The judge announced he would read all the documents and evidence and render his decision regarding probable cause. Then her case would be sent to a grand jury. And since the grand jury wouldn't convene for several more weeks, the wait would continue.

Finally, Judge Hale concluded with the gavel. His ring flashed turquoise, and Margot noticed that the setting was a heavy silver longhorn, the icon of UT. She didn't move from her seat as the courtroom emptied. "I feel as if I've been raped again," she said in a quiet, shaky voice to Landry afterward. "And did I hear that right? They're not reducing the amount of the bail?"

"That's right. It means you'll be fighting your case from a jail cell."

Her heart beat like a caged bird. "No. I can't . . . You have to do something."

"There's nothing more to be done until the grand jury meets, and that's six weeks from now. After that, we'll hear from the prosecution."

"Hear what? She already made me look guilty as hell and convinced the judge to keep me locked up."

"To be honest, staying here might be the only safe place for you."

"What's that supposed to mean? Like the Hunts are out to get me?"

His silence was assent.

"They'd better not hurt my cat."

"The cat is the least of your worries. Look, it's a DA's ploy to avoid a trial. A trial takes a long time and it's messy and expensive for the state. The system is always backed up. So keeping you behind bars is meant to weaken your resolve. It gives the prosecutor a ton of leverage to get you to accept a plea deal."

"So they're keeping me behind bars to wear me down? Weaken my resolve?"

"We don't need to have this discussion unless the grand jury sends an indictment."

"You mean they might not?" He didn't answer, so she knew the possibility was slim. "What kind of deal?" she asked.

"They'll likely make you an offer if you plead guilty to a lesser charge."

"Why would I do that? I'm not guilty of a damn thing."

"To avoid waiting for months on end for a trial date. Years, maybe."

"I don't want a plea deal. I want to be found not guilty. I fought off a guy who was raping me in my own home. My own bed."

"The fact is, you shot a guy."

"Yes, because—"

"—of you. He's dead because of you."

"He's dead because he was raping me and I fought back."

Landry held up a hand to cut her off. "If you don't want to be stuck behind bars, you should keep an open mind about a deal. Based on the fact that you don't have any priors, you could end up with a more moderate sentence."

"I don't deserve any sentence at all," she said.

"It's not up to you. If you get a heavy sentence, it'll be because we didn't plead it out."

"I'm not going to plead guilty on your say-so."

"The prosecution will make the case that you shot a man during a lovers' quarrel. Ultimately, it's going to be for the jury to decide."

The jury. Her heart sank. Any jury in this county was

bound to be made up of folks who thought the Hunts walked on water. "Then what are you doing here?"

He looked weary and distracted. "Here's the deal. You gave a signed statement—"

"As a victim. Shitfire, I told them everything so they would arrest Jimmy for raping me. I didn't even know he was dead. How can they use that to convict me?"

"The statement is admissible. I can argue that it's not, but they'll argue that it's testimony. I did request the video footage from that day, but apparently the equipment was faulty and there's no video, just your statement."

"The detective made a recording of it," Margie pointed out.

"I can request that, but I doubt it'll be admitted. Ultimately, it's up to the judge."

"I thought judges were supposed to uphold justice."

"Look, the Hunts are famous around here. Civic leaders. Movers and shakers. Known all over the state as upstanding citizens."

"Which is exactly how I know you're lying about getting a lighter sentence if I plead guilty. They'll make sure to have me locked away for life. Or sent to the electric chair."

"There's no electric chair in Texas."

"Well, whatever they use, I'm sure that's what the Hunts think I deserve."

Landry's expression was bleak. "I'm not going to pretend this is an easy situation. Jimmy was their golden boy, a hero on the field and off."

"Jimmy was a rapist."

"The prosecution will attest that you were in a relationship with him. They'll find witnesses to say you went out on dates together."

"He forced me. He choked me, bit and hit me."

"That could be characterized as rough sex." He flushed and shifted in his chair. "Some folks . . . well, that stuff happens sometimes between intimate partners, and it's not a crime."

"It was self-defense. I stood my ground."

"Stand your ground is not a thing in Texas. Now, there's a similar concept known as the castle doctrine that serves the same purpose—"

"Fine. Then that's what happened."

"We can ask the judge to rule on that basis, but it's risky. It could be argued that you were not in imminent danger, that you acted aggressively. That you provoked him."

"*I* was aggressive?" Margie pressed the palm of her hand to her neck. "He was trying to kill me. I had a right to defend myself. Mr. Yates, I need you to do better. Please."

Margie was sick to her stomach, and she hadn't been sleeping much. She read more books—*To Kill a Mockingbird*, which Sadie said was outdated but still a classic. Margie liked the books with the Oprah logo on them, which were as dark and serious as she felt. She was also drawn to the romance novels that fed her fantasies about having a different life, a life in which people followed their hearts and solved all their troubles in the final chapter. She studied her Spanish, whispering phrases under her breath. More books on Texas law. One of them had an article about the recent castle doctrine legislation, which stated that an individual had no duty to retreat when faced with a threat in her home.

Jail was a horrible nightmare, but not in the way it was on the TV shows. There were no plots to escape or intrigue among the inmates. No gangs or fighting. Just endless time to be bored and worried and to scrounge for something—anything—to read, or to stare at the mind-numbing game shows on the TV in the dayroom. She helped in the kitchen, finding ways to make sauce on a budget with the extra produce or stone fruit that had been delivered overripe. She learned a few tricks from Ninfa and the staff, who could work wonders with a sack of masa harina and a few cans of adobo sauce. She lived for the morning and afternoon hours when she was allowed to walk around in the yard and tend the garden. Anything to hold on to her humanity, her individuality.

As Landry had predicted, a plea deal was offered. A trial and an uncertain fate could be avoided if she would plead guilty to murder in the heat of passion.

Sadie walked with her in the yard after the meeting. "Bad news?" she asked.

"My lawyer thinks I should take a plea deal. Says it's my best chance."

"Chance at what?"

"Best chance to spend fifteen years in prison." The prospect freaked her out. She wanted to puke. "Maybe more."

"And what do you think?" Sadie prompted.

"I don't care if it's fifteen years or fifteen minutes. I'm not going to say I'm guilty of a crime when all I did was defend myself."

"That's it, then?"

"I reckon. Landry Yates thinks I should do it."

"Can you ask for a different lawyer?"

"They said no, I can't."

Margie felt tired and sad all the time. She was hungry and then she was sick, and for some reason her concentration was shot. Maybe she had a bladder infection because she had to pee a lot. Maybe she had an STD. They'd given her pills at the hospital that morning, but she'd thrown up in the shower that morning so maybe the pills hadn't worked.

Something had been nagging at the back of her mind and she couldn't put her finger on it. During shower time she spotted a tampon wrapper on the floor by the waste can, and that was when the horror struck her like a punch to the stomach.

She was late.

15

I have to get rid of it. Gone, I want it gone," she told the
nurse in the infirmary. "I need it to go away. It's an
emergency."

"I hear you, honey," said Mrs. Renfro. "I get it." She
was the nice nurse. All the girls in the unit liked her.
Judy Renfro was older, and she wore a pink cancer survivor pin on her lab coat. She had a way of looking at
each visitor to the infirmary that seemed to magically
turn them from an inmate into a person.

When Margie had first arrived, Mrs. Renfro had
asked about her injuries and Margie had told her straight
up all the ways Jimmy Hunt had hurt her, and Mrs. Renfro had looked as though she hurt right along with her.

All through the previous night, Margie had lain
awake imagining the minutes ticking by in a relentless
march, the cells dividing in secret, hidden inside her by
a monster. She thought about Jimmy Hunt's hard-boned
face, his insolent grin and cruel voice, his big hands
and feet, his cold eyes. He had implanted his seed like
a parting shot, a final *screw you* to punctuate his hate-
ful act.

First thing this morning, the nurse had hypothesized
that Margie had probably missed her period due to being
so skinny and stressed out. But the test strip had shown
otherwise. The second test only confirmed it.

"The sexual assault nurse said they did a pregnancy test," she said. "It was negative."

"False negatives are rare. My guess is, it was too early in your pregnancy to give an accurate reading."

"I need to get rid of it," she said. "I need an abortion. There's no way I can have a baby by the guy who raped me."

"I'm so, so sorry. I can't imagine what this must be like for you. And I'm real sorry to ask, but I want to make sure. Were there any other partners since your last period?"

"Absolutely not," she said. "I don't sleep around. The night with Jimmy wasn't typical for me. And, holy hell, do I ever regret it now."

Mrs. Renfro frowned. "After the incident, didn't they give you something when they did the rape exam? An injection or pills?"

"Yes. Pills for STIs and an emergency contraceptive pill, but . . ." She shifted her gaze. She had such vague memories of that morning. "I threw up in the shower right after I took the meds."

"Could you tell if the pills came back up?"

Margie shook her head. "I was in the shower. It never occurred to me to check. And I was supposed to have a second dose after twelve hours. She said it was real important to follow directions. But by that time they had taken everything away from me. They put me in a holding cell and I lost track of my stuff."

"After the assault, where were you treated? Remind me."

"St. Michael's."

Mrs. Renfro's lips thinned into a line of disapproval.

"I didn't have a choice where they took me," Margie said. "Should they not have taken me there?"

"Well, it's just . . . in my opinion, it's not the best choice for emergency contraception. Some Catholic hospitals use a pill that prevents fertilization but doesn't act against a conceived zygote. So it wouldn't be effective for an embryo that's already implanted."

Margie recalled the process from her health education classes—ovulation and a slow journey through the fallopian tubes. If a sperm happened to be swimming around, fertilization might occur and the egg would implant in the uterus. "Why would they use a pill that might not work?"

"Because of the tenet that a fertilized egg must be preserved like a live human being whether or not it's viable. If conception can be prevented, they're okay with that. But if there's a fertilized egg, they would be morally obligated to preserve it."

"*It?* You mean preserving a zygote or blastula or whatever? *That's* their moral obligation? Not their obligation to a living, breathing woman who just got raped?" Her heart pounded with panic.

Mrs. Renfro checked her temperature. "Different hospitals operate under different leadership."

"And they didn't think to tell me they were using something that might not work?" Margie felt dizzy with rage. It blew her mind that no one had bothered to explain this to her. It was a violation of a different kind, a complete disregard for her as a person.

"I'm sorry. It's hard when medical science has to compete with religious dogma."

"Hard? Yeah, especially when they don't tell people their treatment might be bullshit. Is it too late to get another pill?"

The nurse nodded. "I'm afraid so."

"Now what do I do?" The thought of having a baby was completely surreal.

"You can request a furlough to go to a clinic where you can terminate your pregnancy."

Relief flooded her, softening her shoulders and neck. "Fine. I'm requesting it. What do I have to do?"

"You fill out a kite. That's a sick call request form. It's similar to the slips you fill out when you need to come here. If it's approved—"

"If? You mean it might not be?" Margie's pulse thundered in protest.

"Well, since it's not a medically necessary procedure—"

"What? I was raped. So yeah, it's necessary. I can't have a baby because I got pregnant from a rape."

"Physically, you can. For that reason, an abortion is considered elective."

"And I *elect* to have an abortion. What do I have to do?"

"There's a process. First, you apply to the jail administrator. After approval from there, you'll need to secure a court order to be transported off-site. You'll have to cover the cost of security and transportation up front, as well as the cost of the abortion itself."

"You're talking about hundreds of dollars."

"Yes." Mrs. Renfro checked Margie's pulse and blood pressure. "You go try to eat something and get some rest. Think about a way to cover these expenses. I'll get a list of the approved clinics."

Margie was reeling. She already knew the charges would be insurmountable. At last tally, she had less than a hundred dollars in the bank. Most of her wages were garnished to pay off her bill from the accident, and the rest went to rent and expenses.

She thought about Cubby, but no. She couldn't ask him for a loan. When would she ever repay it? In desperation, she considered asking Del. Could she? Would he agree to help her? Probably not. After Mama died and the shock had worn off, Del had been pissed because she hadn't left anything behind except unpaid credit card bills. Margie doubted he'd find a lick of compassion for her situation.

She had to do something, though. Having Jimmy Hunt's baby would be an abomination. Avoiding that was more important than anything else.

Gathering courage, she used precious funds from her commissary account to call Del, finding his number through the beer distribution company he used to work for. When Mama was alive, Margie and Del got along okay. She thought he might remember that.

"I heard you were in trouble," Del said. "It's all over the papers and the internet."

"I need your help," she said. "It's urgent. A medical issue. You know I wouldn't ask if I could figure out any other way."

"You sick, girl?" he asked, his lazy drawl bringing back unpleasant memories.

"I . . . Yeah," she said. "I need a doctor and I have to come up with the money."

"I can't help you. Especially after all this time."

"I never asked you for a thing after Mama passed. All I'm asking for now is a loan."

"I said I can't." His voice sounded sharp. "I'm not even supposed to be talking to you."

"Supposed . . ." She felt a chill of apprehension. Oh god. "They got to you, didn't they?" Her voice shook. "The Hunts." Landry had warned her that if they went to trial, the DA would dig up as much dirt as possible about her. He'd said they would track down people from her past. "They want you to testify against me."

"Now, Margie—"

"Yes or no, Del? Did you get a new truck, maybe? A set of fancy golf clubs?"

He said nothing. His silence was all the answer she needed. She hung up the phone and leaned against the wall, shaken. Of course they'd contacted Del. They knew they could use him to make her look bad. He was weak and had a big ego. If they made him think he was helping out the Hunts, he would feel flattered and important. Later, her attorney confirmed her suspicions. Del had given a deposition claiming that even as a young teen, Margie was provocative with him, parading around the house while scantily clad and sneaking out after curfew to meet up with boys. He said she skipped school and dressed slutty, showing no gratitude to him for putting a roof over her head after her mother died.

She hadn't expected much from Del. But she hadn't expected him to be in the enemy camp, either.

There was no response to Margie's initial written request for the procedure. Just no answer. Nothing. And there was no way to compel the jail administrator to respond. After a week, she begged Mrs. Renfro to intervene. The nurse reported that Captain Graham, the administrator, was "looking into it."

A few days later, an officer came back with the original form she'd submitted. "You didn't fill it out properly."

"What the hell is that supposed to mean?"

"This is a medical procedure request. You have to fill out forms requesting an *elective* procedure."

More paperwork. More delays. The restrictions on getting the help she needed popped up like roadblocks every step of the way. The jail was a petty fiefdom under the iron rule of Captain Graham. As it turned out, the administrator was known to be an extreme antichoice activist who insisted that a ball of cells the size of a garbanzo bean should supersede the will of a living, breathing woman. If that woman happened to be an inmate at his jail, then no one could stop him from taking his own sweet time to deal with her.

As she struggled to navigate her way through the labyrinth of obstructions, Margie sensed his game. He was procrastinating, putting her off so the unwanted pregnancy would advance.

She tried talking to Landry about the situation, but he kept saying his job was to defend her against the murder charge, not secure her right to an abortion.

She spent hours and hours poring over books specially borrowed from the central library of the prison. According to her reading, the Supreme Court had ruled in a case to uphold the reproductive rights of an incarcerated woman.

Margie took the book to her next clinic visit. "Right here," she said, pointing to a passage in a journal article. "I have a serious medical need and it's my right."

"The captain might say you're not incarcerated," Mrs. Renfro said. "You're awaiting trial." She wrote down Margie's weight. "You gained a pound. You should be taking these." She handed her a bottle of pills.

"I don't need prenatal vitamins," she said. "I'm not planning on being pregnant."

"Your body needs them. Do yourself a favor. Just take them until you're not pregnant anymore. They're for your health, not just the fetus."

"Mrs. Renfro," Margie said, her voice trembling, "I'm desperate. Someone in the unit said there's a way to force my period to come—"

"Good lord above, don't you dare." The nurse looked

aghast. "Promise you won't harm yourself. I mean it, Margie. Dear god, this is one reason abortion was made safe and legal, so girls won't hurt themselves trying to get rid of a pregnancy."

Margie thought about the whispers she'd heard in the kitchen, folk remedies that probably didn't work but were oh so tempting to try. "Legal for which girls? All of them? Or just the ones who can afford it?"

Mrs. Renfro said, "Listen. I'm supposed to report all talk of self-harm to Captain Graham."

Margie shrank toward the door, where an ever-present officer waited to escort her back to the unit. "Don't. Ma'am, I'm begging you—"

"Promise you won't try any of that nonsense. I need to have your word."

Margie nodded. "Yes, ma'am."

Mrs. Renfro stood with her back to the door and lowered her voice. "I made some inquiries. There's an agency I contacted—the Amiga Foundation. It's an inmate advocacy group centered in San Antonio. Let's see if they can help."

The Amiga Foundation sent an advocate within a few days. Truly Stone was her name, and she wore her hair in pigtails and chewed gum and looked like she was still in high school. She seemed really smart, though, and had a way of listening with her whole body, leaning toward the visitor window, her lightly freckled face a picture of total absorption.

"I totally understand your sense of urgency," she said when Margie explained the situation. "No one can order you to carry a pregnancy you don't want. It's illegal."

"This is jail. We get ordered to do all kinds of things in this place," Margie said. Only this morning, there had been a predawn roll call because the early shift watch officer had misplaced her mobile phone. The women in her unit had been up since four, turning out their bunks until the phone was found in the staff bathroom.

"I get that. However, restricting you from having an abortion and forcing you to give birth to a rapist's baby cannot be part of your punishment. You still have rights."

"I should have *all* my rights and I shouldn't even be in this place. I'm not guilty of anything but fighting for my life."

"The administrator is not required to consider those circumstances. So long as you're a ward of the system, you have to abide by his rules. Bottom line—you do have the right to make this decision. That's the good news."

"Which means there's bad news to balance it out."

Truly pursed her lips, then blew a small bubble with her gum.

Bang. Margie winced.

"The corrections staff here have plenty of leeway to ignore and obstruct your request. Also, there's a dearth of licensed facilities you're entitled to access. For reasons they don't have to explain, only certain clinics are authorized to treat inmates. There could be quite a wait just to get on the schedule. I'm worried that the administration officials might drag their feet and draw out the wait until an early, safe abortion is no longer an option."

"I think that's exactly what they're doing."

"Welcome to the patriarchy. I'll try to help you. It's . . . Sometimes it's hard to work with the system."

"Can you be my lawyer?" Margie thought about how harried and overwhelmed Landry seemed all the time.

"I'm not a lawyer," Truly said. "I'm an intern. I'm working toward my master's in public health. Anyway, this is not a legal issue. Your right to choose to terminate this pregnancy is a procedural matter."

"What do I have to do?"

"I'm going to see about getting funds for your transportation and security. The foundation can take care of things left undone, too—rent and bills, up to a point."

"Can somebody find my cat? Make sure he's fed?" Margie gave her the address.

Truly wrote it down. "Yes, and we'll keep the rent on your place up to date. I'll see what can be done about expediting the administrator's approval for the procedure."

"Soon," said Margie. She twisted her inmate band around and around her wrist. "Please."

"I'll do my best." Truly popped her gum again. "I know I don't look like much, but I'm scrappy. I don't walk away from a fight when I know I'm on the right side."

For the first time in weeks, Margie felt a flicker of hope. Yes, she was still locked up. Yes, she was still pregnant and scared. But finally she sensed that there was a path forward with someone who wasn't beholden to the jail administrator.

"Truly Stone," she said, peering through the Plexiglas shield. "Is that your real name?"

"Since the day I was born." Her cheeks turned pink. "And yes, people are forever calling me Truly Stoned. To be honest, I've never been stoned. You?"

"I got stoned one time," Margie admitted. "I was thirteen, and stupid."

Margie hadn't thought about that day in a long while. She'd gone with her mother to help with a catering gig. To Margie, going along on a job didn't seem like work, but a glimpse into another life. Sometimes the drive would take them through the elegant, winding hill streets of

Austin where the millionaires lived—Westlake, Bee Caves, Driftwood, Rocky Cliffs. It used to be that big oil money was the source of the incredible mansions. Nowadays, the rich folk were tech millionaires and media types whose money flowed through the meticulously landscaped streets.

She had fantasized about life behind the elegant wrought-iron fences and limestone walls. She and Mama had worked at places with infinity pools and pool houses, homes that had an entire room just for a grand piano, and others with a theater, its rows of cushy chairs lined up facing a screen.

One time, Mama got a gig to work a summer party at one of the mansions at Rocky Cliffs. Reverend Beauregard Falcon was a TV evangelist who had, Mama joked, more money than God. Perched high above the Colorado River, it was one of the swankiest areas of the capital. At thirteen, Margie knew how to make herself useful. She dressed like her mother in plain black slacks, a crisp white shirt, and an apron, her long blond hair pulled back and neatly braided. "Look at us." Mama had beamed at her. "We're twinning." Mama always loved it when people said they looked more like sisters than mother and daughter.

It was a croquet party, which apparently was a thing with the superrich. The only requirement seemed to be that the guests all dressed in white from head to toe. It was like stepping into a storybook world where every single person was headed for a happy ending.

On a lawn that looked like a flowing green carpet, they played their old-fashioned game while sipping mint juleps and lavender lemonade. There was a guy performing ragtime music on a painted upright piano, and it all looked so jolly and elegant. A food pavilion had been set up on a flagstone patio adjacent to the kitchen. Margie heard heaps of praise for Mama's sliders and rollups, her piadinas, vegan shawarma wraps, and soft tacos. Everyone was supernice to Margie, complimenting her on how pretty she looked and what a good job she was doing, passing out trays of snacks and picking up after people.

The kitchen was vast and busy, a humming contrast to the tranquil scene out on the patio and lawn and pool deck. She couldn't help noticing that the people keeping the kitchen and house in perfect order were Black. The ones tending the gardens and lawns were Latino. As far as she could tell, every single guest at the party was white.

After bringing in a heavy tray of used glassware and utensils, Margie needed the restroom. Someone told her where to find the powder room, which was a fancy name for a bathroom—down the hall from the kitchen, under a coved doorway. It was like a tiny oasis of elegance with a beaded chandelier that turned on automatically. There was a stack of clean towels you were supposed to use only once and then discard in a little basket. The wallpaper resembled a French painting, and the place smelled so nice you'd never know it was a bathroom. She lingered over washing her hands with the scented soap, rinsing them in the painted porcelain sink with its gleaming fixtures.

When she stepped out into the hallway, there was no one in sight. Looking left and right, she decided the coast was clear for more exploring. Just a little. She followed a hall that led to the grand entryway with marble floors and pillars and a massive, sparkling chandelier high above. The space was surrounded by not one but two curved staircases that seemed to float clear up to heaven.

Margie tiptoed up the stairs. The air was filled with the scent of lemon oil and clean laundry and fresh flowers.

On the upper level, there were long hallways leading to elegant rooms with soaring ceilings and fancy beds and fireplaces. At the end of one hallway was a Romeo and Juliet–type balcony with a view of the croquet party, where the catering staff bustled around with their serving trays. Margie's mom was all smiles, and people—especially men—sought her out to help themselves to a sandwich and exchange a pleasant word. This was Mama in her element, making folks happy with the food that she fixed.

Margie watched with a mixture of pride and yearning. Why did some people get to live a life like this while others made sandwiches and cleaned houses and trimmed hedges to keep the world looking beautiful for them? She knew how Mama would answer that question, because they talked about it sometimes.

"Oh, baby," Mama would say, "everybody has their own happy place, and it's different for each person."

And when Margie would ask, "What's your happy place?" Mama's answer was always the same: "You, baby. You're my happy place." .

I could be happy here, thought Margie. She poked her head inside several more rooms—a library, a dimly lit alcove with a bar and a pool table, a home gym. The next room was an explosion of pink. Not syrupy pink but a tasteful shade, with gold-flecked wallpaper, deep, soft carpet, and a canopy bed with fancy drapes and a collection of stuffed animals. A strange, piney scent filled the air. There was a fireplace and beyond that was an adjacent sunny room, filled with daylight.

Margie knelt down to inspect a magnificent dollhouse

on a display table. She was too old for dolls, but this was fascinating, with tiny details—a grand ballroom, a dining room, even a gourmet kitchen with what looked like a pizza oven. The little chef with his paddle lay on his side. She reached in to set him upright.

"Oh, hey," said a voice.

She shot to her feet and nearly peed her pants. She glanced at the door, wondering if she should make a break for it. But she was too scared to move.

At the far end of the room near an open window, two girls were looking at her. One was Asian and one was a blonde. They were lounging in beanbag chairs and smoking, letting the smoke drift out the window. Margie clapped her hand over her mouth, then edged toward the door. "Ah . . . sorry," she said through her fingers. "I was— I didn't mean . . . Um, I was looking for the restroom."

"Nuh-uh." The blond girl, a teenager, didn't seem mad. She just grinned. "You were snooping."

"I wasn't," Margie blurted out. Then she looked down at her scuffed shoes. "Actually, I was. Sorry."

"It's cool. We don't mind. What's your name?"

"Margie Salinas."

"I'm Autumn, and this is my sister, Tamara."

"You don't look like sisters."

The girl named Tamara laughed. "A brilliant observation. I'm adopted, obvee."

"Oh, okay. Well, I better go."

"No, stay," Autumn insisted. "It's totally cool." She held out the cigarette. "Ever smoke weed?"

"You mean pot? No." The very idea was ridiculous. Where would she ever get pot?

"Want to try?"

She hesitated. "What's it like?"

"Fun," Tamara said. She looked younger than her sister, and just as friendly. "It makes you happy and silly."

Margie edged closer. She was flattered that these wicked cool girls were being so nice to her. "Okay," she said.

Autumn showed her how it was done. "You need to inhale like you're about to jump into the water. Then hold your breath. It's kind of harsh at first but you'll get used to it."

Margie breathed in the pine-scented smoke, and her head nearly exploded. She held her breath, then let go with a fit of coughing. "I can't believe you like this," she confessed.

"You'll get used to it. And then you'll see," said Autumn.

"Cough to get off," Tamara said.

Margie gave it another try. And then another. After a few minutes, a strangely pleasant feeling came over her, and she smiled.

"See?" said Tamara. "It's cool, right?"

"Mmm." Margie's lips felt numb and thick, her mouth filled with invisible cotton. She wasn't sure of the point of feeling this way, but she was fascinated by this family and their storybook castle, their white friends all dressed in white, their nice things and perfectly ordered house.

"Are those tattoos real?" she asked. The sisters had identical tattoos on their wrists—a small line drawing of a bird in flight.

Autumn nodded. "They're falcons. We're the Falcon sisters."

"Our parents went ballistic when we got them," Tamara said. "They threatened to send us to military boarding school." She shuddered, then looked over at the door, and her face changed. "Oh," she said, moving to block the bowl with the joints and lighters. "Hey, Missy."

A housemaid in a dark skirt and white apron bustled toward them. "Don't you oh-hey me," she said. "You kids put that stuff away and get it out of the house."

"We're sorry," said Autumn.

"And you." Missy rounded on Margie, who was now shaking in terror. "Who the devil are you?"

"I'm . . . I'm Margie," she squeaked.

"Well, you don't belong here, brewing up trouble with these delinquents." She studied Margie's face, her hair, and the logo on her apron. "You're that sandwich lady's girl. You ought not to be here."

"I know," Margie admitted. "I'm sorry."

"It's not her fault," Autumn said. "We invited her to hang out with us."

"We practically forced her," Tamara added.

"Girl should have had the sense to say no. Don't be stupid, you hear? Ain't nothing but trouble for you if you do that stuff."

Margie stood there shamefaced, feeling as if she were floating in a cloud.

Missy turned to the Falcon sisters. "Do you know what would happen to you if your folks found out? Do you?"

Autumn and Tamara looked down at the floor. "Military boarding school," Tamara mumbled.

Margie didn't know much about military school, but it sounded unbearable, like prison.

"What's going on here?" Mrs. Falcon strode into the room. She was a tall, fierce-looking woman with beauty-parlor hair and sparkly jewelry that looked real. She sniffed the air like a coonhound on the scent. "I smell marijuana."

Autumn's face drained to pasty white. "Mama—"

"You were smoking marijuana."

Tamara started to cry. "We weren't, Mama. I swear."

Their mother seemed to swell up with anger, like a sorceress conjuring a spell. "Do you have any idea what this will do to your father? To his reputation. To our reputation as a family?"

Both sisters looked so miserable that Margie blurted, "It was me."

Mrs. Falcon swung around, seeming to see her for the first time. Her eyes and nostrils widened almost comically. "And you are . . . ?"

"Margie Salinas. Your daughters didn't have anything to do with this." She spoke on total impulse and felt almost defiant, defending these two strangers from a fate that seemed to terrify them. "It's all my fault, so please don't blame them."

The mother seemed eager to believe her. She probably didn't want to actually go through with sending her girls away. She swiveled to face Missy. "Well then, there's nothing more to be said. Please escort Miss . . . *Salinas* to the exit." She spoke the name with a hiss of anger.

The sisters stared at Margie with wonder-wide eyes. Tamara pressed the palms of her hands together in a silent gesture of gratitude.

"I swear," the maid said to Margie. "You're nothing but trouble. Come on." She motioned her to the door and nudged her toward the grand staircase.

Margie kept reaching for handholds and missing the railing. Missy delivered her to Margie's mom as if taking out the trash. "Keep this one out of trouble," she said to Mama.

Her mother took one look at Margie's eyes. Though

she thanked the maid and apologized, Margie could tell she was furious by the way the veins stood out at her temples. She almost never got mad, but when she did, it was like a blast from a hot oven.

On the way home, Mama lit into her. "Do you know how bad that could have been for me?" she demanded. "What the hell were you thinking?"

While Margie shrank into the bucket seat of the catering van, Mama lit a cigarette with an expert flick of her lighter. She cracked the window and blew out a gray-blue cloud. "And don't start with me about this," she said, preempting Margie's comments. "At least it's legal. What were you thinking?" she asked again.

"I was curious. I was exploring and the girls invited me."

"And you just fell in with them. What a stupid thing to do, so unbelievably stupid."

Margie picked at her fingernails. "I shouldn't have done it. They were really nice, like they wanted to be friends."

"You *don't* know. Those girls are not your friends. They don't know the first thing about you. If they get caught with pot, it's no big deal. Maybe they'd be grounded from horseback riding lessons or going to Europe. But you? If you get caught, you'd be sent up to juvie. You know what that is, right? Reform school, with uniforms and razor wire and lord knows what else. You would end up with a record, and your life would suck forever. Is that what you want?"

"No, ma'am. But they were really, *really* scared on account of their dad's a famous televangelist. If they got caught, they were going to have to go to military school. So I told Mrs. Falcon it was my fault."

"Jesus Christ on a fricking cracker. Why would you do that? They're not your friends," she repeated.

"They were scared. I just kind of blurted it out to protect them."

"Great. My daughter's Joan of fricking Arc. Juvie would probably do you some good."

Margie leaned back and stared out the window. She didn't feel high anymore, just worn-out. Thirsty. Although she knew her mom was right about kids getting different treatment for doing the same thing, she didn't understand why it had to be that way. "One of the daughters is adopted," she said, by way of changing the subject.

"Yeah? Did they tell you that?"

"It was obvee," she said, borrowing Tamara Falcon's word. "She's Asian and the other sister is Caucasian."

"That's probably one lucky kid," said Mama.

"Because a rich family adopted her?"

"Well, sure."

"What if she'd rather stay with her original family instead of being rich?"

"Well, maybe that wasn't an option. Maybe the birth mother didn't have a choice."

Margie was quiet, looking out the window. "When you got pregnant, did you think about giving me up for adoption?"

"Sure. I thought of every possible option, including adoption and abortion. Hell, honey, I was sixteen years old. My folks said I was on my own, and my boyfriend ran for the hills. So yeah, I weighed my options. And I gotta be honest—by the time I actually realized I was knocked up, I was in the second trimester. If I'd figured it out sooner, and if I'd had the scratch, I for sure would have chosen abortion. Most days—maybe not today—I'm glad I didn't."

"I'm sorry about today," Margie said.

"I know, baby. Even when I was a dumb kid like you, I knew the best choice for both of us would be for me to raise you and love you forever."

"Oh. I'm glad you kept me."

"Do you wish I'd given you to some rich people to raise like that Falcon girl?"

Margie thought about the fancy house and swimming pool and gardens and horses. Then she thought about the single-wide at the Arroyo where she and her mom lived, and the kitchen where Mama went to make sandwiches every morning. She thought about giggles and snuggles at bedtime, dancing to "Waltz Across Texas" and jumping into the chilly clear water at Barton Springs on a hot day, and how she loved the sound of her mother's laughter, and she couldn't imagine any other life.

"Nah," she said, thinking of the girls in the mansion. "I reckon those two sisters didn't seem any happier or sadder than any other kid. And their mom was scary."

"You're an old soul, Seesaw Marjorie Daw. I'm glad you're mine."

"Same," said Margie. "And I'm sorry about smoking weed."

"I'm just glad there wasn't any real trouble over it. There better not be a next time."

It was not much longer after that day that Del came into their lives like a guest star on TV, swaggering onto the scene. Margie was used to guys wanting to go out with her mother. She was so, so pretty. She was super-picky, though, and none of them ever lasted.

Del was different, or at least he seemed to be. Treated Mama like a queen. He drove a beer truck delivering kegs to restaurants, but then he hurt his back and went on disability and never returned to work.

They moved to a bigger unit at the Arroyo, a double-wide. It had an extra bathroom, but it was still in the Arroyo. Del said he didn't want to take Margie away from her friends or switch schools in the middle of high school. After she graduated, they'd get a house, he promised. He used to promise a lot of things.

Pulling away from the memories, Margie gazed at Truly Stone through the Plexiglas window. "My mom had me young," she explained after telling her the pot story. "She said it was a total accident and she never even knew she was pregnant until it was too late to do something about it." That was the part that messed with Margie's head. If her mother had realized plenty early, if she'd ended the pregnancy, then none of this would have happened. *Margie* would not have happened. She wouldn't be here, Jimmy Hunt would still be alive, and the world would keep turning.

Truly studied her with quiet interest, almost fascination.

"I swear," Margie said, "that's the only thing I ever did that was against the law. You're looking at me like I'm some kind of criminal."

"No, it's not that. It's . . . Have you thought about being a mother?"

"Have you?"

"Only in the abstract," Truly admitted.

"I always figured I'd have a kid but not like this. Shit-fire." Margie felt torn between curiosity and wonder about having a baby and terror and loathing of giving birth to Jimmy Hunt's child. She sighed. "I miss Mama every day. She was my best friend. I was just getting big enough to share clothes with her. People used to say we looked like sisters. I don't know, though. She was really pretty."

"You do look a lot like her. You're superpretty, like her."

"What? How would you know I look like her?"

"One of the articles in the paper ran side-by-side pictures of you and your mother."

"Articles? What articles?"

"Oh my gosh. I guess you wouldn't have seen, being in here."

"I saw something right after it happened. But . . . articles?"

"The incident made news. It was even mentioned in *Texas Monthly*. And there's a blog I follow—*Lone Star Justice*—"

"That's Buckley DeWitt's blog."

"You know him?"

"He's kind of a friend, I guess." She was surprised to hear that he'd been writing about her. As a friend, she wondered, or did he think she was a murderer?

"The things in the papers and online are not very flattering." Truly popped her gum. "It's to be expected. The family doesn't want to believe their golden boy could be guilty of rape. I imagine they want the DA to build a case by swaying public sentiment."

The idea of articles and pictures circulating made Margie's skin crawl. She couldn't stand the thought of people speculating about that night, jumping to conclusions, assuming the worst about her.

"I'm sorry. I wish I hadn't said anything. I thought you knew. I thought your lawyer was keeping you updated on everything."

"He barely talks to me. He's barely my lawyer. And it sounds as if they're already trying and convicting me in the paper. How can that be right?"

"It's not right. I'll see if I can find someone to help you connect better with your lawyer. And I'm not going to rest until we get your procedure authorized."

"Please," Margie said, trying to keep the glimmer of hope alive.

"I'll see what I can do," Truly said.

Each day of waiting was an eternity, elongated by anxiety and dread. Margie fantasized about getting her period. She tried to will it to happen. She mulled over the remedies and home procedures she heard about in the kitchen and around the pod, like eating papaya or cinnamon or skipping rope until she dropped from exhaustion. Sometimes she thought she was losing her mind, but she wasn't sure what that felt like.

She had gone crazy the day her mama had dropped dead. She'd seen Del's truck parked in the driveway, and he came out on the porch and was completely wrecked. But no, that wasn't crazy. That was grief. She knew what grief felt like. It felt like trying to breathe after her mom had breathed her last.

Now she was starting to think she knew exactly what crazy felt like: Her heart beating out of her chest. Her lungs too full of fear to inhale anymore. Her hands tingling, her legs restless and ready to run wild, though there was nowhere to run in this place. The kitchen work was a godsend because it gave her something to do. Even washing dishes, the lowliest of jobs, created a temporary distraction. But work only lasted a few hours. The rest of the time, she fretted.

Margie hated every minute that passed, because every minute made the pregnancy seem more and more real to her. She threw up all the time, haunted by the twin demons of nausea and panic. She had to pee every five minutes and her boobs felt weird and achy.

She read constantly and studied her Spanish, practicing with women in the pod and kitchen. She wrote down her thoughts on the blank pages she took from prayer group. Then she started writing down her recipes, the ones she'd developed and others that she'd learned from her mother.

After her mother had died, Margie's greatest treasure became that thick, disorganized notebook stuffed with recipes torn from old books and magazines or passed along by friends. She was haunted by her mother's hand-written notes. "Too much heat—overpowering," she'd written next to a recipe clipped from *Southern Living*. "Made for Adam's 12th birthday" was jotted by her honey butter chicken and biscuits. Who was Adam? When had he turned twelve?

A certain recipe was bookmarked with a strip of black-and-white photos from a booth. Each shot featured Margie and her mother making silly faces. They'd taken the pictures on what Margie remembered as the best day of her life, the day Mama had driven her to the beach at Corpus Christi to see the ocean for the first time.

The recipe archive gave Margie tantalizing glimpses of her mother's thoughts, but now she had no chance at all to ask her questions or dig deeper.

Writing down the recipes was something she had always meant to do in a more organized way. Now she had no idea what had become of her personal belongings, the ones left behind in the house that had become a crime scene. She hoped the notebook was still there on a shelf over the kitchen counter.

She tried to reconstruct recipes from memory, and to dream up others on her own. There were different styles of barbecue in different parts of the country. She had never been anywhere, but she used to check books out of the Hayden County Free Library. Even though the sauce started with the basic ingredients—sugar and salt—there were endless varieties. In Kansas City, their barbecue was known for rich, robust sauce with a reduced tomato base. There was an area of the Carolinas known as the Low Country—she didn't know why it was called Low Country—where they favored a light yellow mustard sauce. Here in Texas, folks went for heat—from jalapeños, serranos, or even fiery ghost chilies—the kind of deep, flavorful pepper that sent the waitstaff at Cubby's scurrying for pitchers of beer and sweet tea by the gallon.

In the dayroom, Margie found a travel magazine with an illustrated map of the whole United States, showing all the iconic foods in each city. She wished she could travel to every single place, even the wintry spots like Milwaukee and Ann Arbor, Vermont and Montana. Her most desired destination, though, was San Francisco, California. She'd never seen the place in person, of course. But she knew she'd love the famous city, the cable cars, sourdough bread and painted houses, the hills and bridges and the Pacific Ocean gnawing at the coastline.

A school trip to the capital in Austin was a big deal for Margie when she was growing up. Mama liked to take her wandering through the HOPE Outdoor Gallery, where no one was required to pay money to look at the art. One time, they went to the city to stand on the bat bridge at dusk, watching in horrified wonder as thousands of bats swooped into the orange sky. Her mother used to set aside one entire Sunday every April to take a drive into the countryside to look at the bluebonnets. They both found the glorious fields of deep indigo flowers mesmerizing.

Sometimes they'd talk about the places they'd like to see, just the two of them together—Cancún and Cozumel, where the waves from the Gulf of Mexico rolled up on miles of sandy beaches. The Rocky Mountains, Big Sur, the Oregon coast, the Carolinas, and even New England. Everything sounded so far away, but Margie had never doubted they'd see those places one day.

During the agonizing wait in jail, she began to fear she'd never go anywhere at all.

16

"It's good news," Truly Stone told her on the phone. "The appointment has been scheduled for next Monday."

"Thank heavens." Margie slumped against the wall at the phone bank. She was exhausted by worry and by constantly feeling sick, heaving not only in the morning but after every meal, it seemed. The emotional toll itself was exhausting. Her dreams were haunted by visions of the rape and its aftermath, the violation of everything that made her human. "And the cost . . ."

"It'll be covered by the foundation."

"Wow, that's . . . I'm really grateful." She was, but Margie also felt a struggle in her heart. The cells dividing inside her hadn't harmed a soul, yet they were the result of the biggest harm imaginable. *Lord*, she thought, *the sooner this is done, the better.* "Did you go by my place? Did you see my cat?"

"Yes, and your rent's paid up for another month. And . . . no. I'm sorry. Didn't see a cat. I left several types of food out."

"Thanks for trying." Margie let out a long sigh of relief and resignation. After Monday, it would be over. She would be free of Jimmy Hunt and his brutal attack, and the attack of the county jail system on her rights. She felt more hopeful than she had in weeks, and even offered a smile when Landry Yates came for a meeting later that day.

"I hope you have good news for me. Like the grand jury met early and there's no indictment."

He shifted in his chair. Adjusted his glasses. His phone went off as he set his briefcase on the table and took out some papers. "It's about your furlough on Monday."

Margie felt a curl of apprehension in her stomach. "What about it?"

"It's been postponed. A temporary restraining order has been filed."

"What the hell is that supposed to mean?"

"It's to stop you from terminating your pregnancy."

The gut-level apprehension seemed to harden, like ice. "What? Who—"

"The family. The Hunts," Landry said. "It was filed on their behalf."

"Well, I hope you'll tell them my personal, constitutionally protected decision is none of their damn business."

"It's not that simple. The procedure will be delayed to hold a hearing."

"A hearing? About *my* private health decision about *my* private body? Let me guess. The judge is one of their country club cronies, right?"

Landry's phone vibrated again. "I couldn't say."

"And what on earth is the purpose of this hearing? Do I get to be present? Do I get a say?"

"The purpose is to appoint a guardian for the preborn child."

"The *what*?" She couldn't believe her ears.

"The legal papers claim the preborn child is entitled to a guardian."

Margie's head was spinning. She was unschooled in the law, but she'd been reading voraciously, and even she could tell the situation was patently ridiculous. "How the hell did the Hunts even find out about this?"

"They're the Hunts. They hear things."

"Well, they're not going to restrain me from my right to choose to have an abortion."

"You do have the right to contest the order. However, there are legal guidelines to be followed. Now, you can file an emergency appeal—"

"Fine. Then do it. *Immediately.*"

"You need a lawyer for that."

"What are you, chopped liver?"

"I told you before, I'm the public defender in your criminal case. This is a separate issue. You'll need to hire a private practice lawyer to handle this, because it's not part of my defense for you."

"I can't afford a private lawyer."

"You could try to challenge the order without a lawyer. It would be an uphill battle, though."

"What, like *this* is not an uphill battle? Being locked up? Ignored? Lied about? Worrying about my cat? Pregnant by my rapist? You think filing a damn appeal is more challenging than *this*?"

He had the grace to flush. "I'm real sorry."

"Then help me, Landry. Tell me what to do."

He pulled in a deep breath and gave a slight shake of his head. "I have an ongoing relationship here in the county. My job is to defend you in the criminal case."

"I'm not asking you to do this as a job. I'm asking you to do it because it's *right.* No one, not even the Hunts, can force me to have a baby against my will. That's . . . It's barbaric. It's like . . . *Handmaid* shit." She now felt different from the dazed and traumatized girl who had arrived at the jail. The Hunts were letting their crazy out, but they were also hardening her sense of righteousness and confidence. "So yeah, I get that defending me is your job. But helping me fight this bullshit restraining order is . . . It's your duty as someone who knows how the law works."

He looked away again, and then back at her. "That's not how *I* work."

And in that moment, in his slightly narrowed eyes and thinned lips, she finally understood. She felt the truth like a punch in the gut.

"Oh my god," she whispered. "Oh my sweet lord. You don't believe a woman should be allowed to make private decisions about her own health."

Landry didn't say anything. He didn't have to. She felt a draining sense of defeat.

"I suppose you think I'm a murderer, too. You think I meant to kill Jimmy Hunt."

"It's not up to me to determine that," he said. "I'm here to defend you as is your constitutional right."

"You know what else is my constitutional right? To get an abortion. You don't get to choose what rights belong to me." She hoped her gaze gleamed as cold as steel as she looked him in the eye. "I am pregnant because a monster attacked me. Right now, the procedure is safe and simple, but time is running out. If you let them force me to carry this to the end, how will that work? What'll that look like, Landry? Tell me that. Will I be forced to give birth to a rapist's baby in prison?"

"Of course not. You'd be transported to the hospital."

"Oh, that's right. I get to pay for my own transport and security—which you know I can't afford. Will I be handcuffed to the bed? And then what about the baby? Will it be handcuffed, too? Do I bring it back to jail with me? Raise a rapist's child behind bars?"

"The Hunts are asserting the father's rights." He indicated the file on the table.

"They're *what*? That's absurd. There is no father. Right now, there is no viable baby."

"The Hunts have made a commitment to taking custody of their grandchild—"

"Oh, my god. Do you hear what you're saying? You want me to incubate this thing like a broodmare, and then hand it over to a family so they can raise it to turn out like Jimmy. A drunk, violent rapist—"

"I don't want anything," Landry said. "I'm merely here to inform you of the TRO."

"How long is temporary? How long do I have?"

He drummed his fingers on the file. His phone buzzed yet again. She knew then that she was screwed, not just about the abortion, but about her own defense. Landry had too many cases to deal with and not enough resources. He didn't believe in her. He didn't believe in women's rights, but in controlling women. He wasn't going to fight for her. She was just an obligation to him.

She glared at him and called for the guard.

"I don't know what to say." Truly sounded mystified when Margie called her in a panic. "This is a horrible dilemma for you. I've made like a hundred calls to various sources and I hope this gets resolved in time."

Time was the enemy. The minutes dragged, but the days flew by.

Based on the reading she'd done about rape trauma, Margie knew she wasn't crazy, but suffering from PTSD. She was already racked with terror and worry. And now she had this new disaster unfolding in her life. The delay in the procedure had already inflicted extreme emotional distress, and she would face increased medical risks with each passing day. The expected mental health consequences of forcing a woman to carry her rapist's baby to term, and having to raise it despite an uncertain future, were well documented. Could be, she'd end up crazy after all.

She didn't think she could survive much more waiting.

Truly reached out to advocacy groups and women's health centers and legal aid volunteers. No one disputed that the restraining order was objectively wrong and would be thrown out.

But the process took time, and Margie didn't have time.

Eventually, she was granted a visitation with a legal aid intern named Harry Brooks. He was as young as Truly and just as sincere. There was a glimmer. He gave her encouraging news when he cited case law chapter and verse, justifying the clear legal right of a woman— even a woman in jail—to make her own private health decisions.

She had to file a motion to challenge the order, though. It was all a matter of filling out the correct paperwork and filing it properly and in a timely manner.

They faced roadblocks that seemed engineered by a corrupt system. They would get a hearing on the calendar, and then the schedule would suddenly change. Things got pushed back. They were at the mercy of the court scheduler, whose name was Karen Castro, who happened to be best friends with a sheriff's deputy named Belle Fields. The deputy's maiden name was Hunt. Everything came down to the Hunts.

Harry filed two sets of emergency appeals, one of them directly to the state supreme court. The appeals court declined to take immediate action.

"We have a tentative date with the appellate judge in four weeks," he told her.

She recoiled. "We can't— I can't wait that long. What part of *emergency appeal* do they not understand?"

"That's the soonest they could offer."

"No. That puts me into the second trimester. You get what that means, right?" She felt her face drain of color. Terminating a more advanced pregnancy meant a higher risk of complications. More regulations and limitations. More restrictions. More nightmares about what would actually happen.

More creeping awareness that the fetus was getting closer to being viable. Not a cluster of cells but a separate person.

"I stressed that it's an emergency," he told her before she could ask.

Margie tossed and turned, night after night. She threw up and lost weight. When she lay on the thin mattress and stared at the pockmarked ceiling, she tended to think too much about the informational literature Mrs. Renfro had given her. She thought about cell differentiation and limb buds and the idea that a tiny cluster inside her was completely taking over her body.

Then she would ruminate about the fact that half the DNA came from Jimmy Hunt. College man. Star athlete. Son of the richest man in the county. *Rapist.*

One night, she woke up from a fitful sleep and tried lying flat on her back, doing the breathing exercises Mrs. Renfro had said might help with her anxiety. She lay there breathing in, two, three, four, hold, two, three, four . . . and in that moment, she felt . . . something. A ripple, not from anxiety—lord knew, she was familiar with that sensation. But . . . a ripple of something else, something vital inside her. An otherness.

Although she ran from the feeling and all it implied,

her mind wouldn't quiet. Her mind kept asking her *What if?* If she did nothing, if she simply surrendered and gave up control of her personal rights, she would be signing up for a major life change—giving birth to a rapist's child. Her mind, her body, and her soul would be forever changed by the fact that she would suffer through months of a forced pregnancy, an ordeal she would never endure if given a choice.

If the Hunts got their way, then in just a matter of months, a baby would appear. She would still be in jail awaiting trial. Jimmy's family would lay claim to the child. Unless she did something drastic.

The next day, Margie filled out an urgent request form for the infirmary. Hollow-eyed from lack of sleep, gaunt from anxiety and illness, she was permitted to go right away. So far, no one seemed to notice that the only time she went to the infirmary was when Mrs. Renfro was on duty. She was the one person who truly saw Margie, whose compassion seemed real.

Mrs. Renfro tried appealing to the administration for more medical care, but she got nowhere. "This proves the Hunts don't care about the fetus," Margie said. "If they did, they'd make sure I'm healthy. All they really want is revenge."

Mrs. Renfro gave her shoulder a squeeze. "I'm keeping detailed records, Margie." She leaned forward so the guard wouldn't hear. "What's happening is probably illegal. I'll keep the records safe in case you ever need them."

The idea of seeking justice seemed far-fetched, but the nurse's kindness brought tears to Margie's eyes. "How can this be my life?" She gestured wide with a sweep of her arm. "I feel so damned helpless. So trapped. They're deliberately causing a delay to close the window on me getting an abortion."

"It seems that way, yes."

"Early on, it was a no-brainer. Now . . . it gets more complicated every day." Margie pushed her knuckles into her lower lip. "So last night, as I was lying in bed, I think I felt something."

"Something?"

She lowered her hands to her lap. "A movement. More like a . . . flutter."

"You felt the baby move?"

Margie shrugged. "I think maybe I did."

"It's early yet, so you might be feeling a touch of indigestion. Gas, maybe. It's common enough."

"This seemed different. I was lying flat on my back and I felt it."

"Well, you're real skinny. And there are two potential dates of conception."

She twisted her hands in her lap. "So . . . um . . . when I first realized I was pregnant, I knew exactly what I needed to do. For me. It was plain as day. There was no hesitation. No debate about what I knew was the right decision."

"You were very clear with me. And the law is on your side." Mrs. Renfro checked Margie's blood pressure. "Now what are you thinking?"

"That I so. Don't. Want. To. Be. Pregnant." Margie enunciated each word, yearning to make the wish come true. She dropped her gaze to the floor. "I can't undo it on my own, but now I get why women from the beginning of time have—and always will—seek to end a pregnancy they don't want."

"Oh, Margie. I'm sorry."

"They made me wait so long that all I can think about

is that I can't stop time from passing. At first I was like, 'I have to do this.' Now it's advancing to 'Can I do this?'"

"What are you thinking?"

"About what would happen if they put me off so long that I end up having it."

"Do you *want* to have a baby?"

"God, no, not now. And Jimmy Hunt's baby? *Never.* I realize it's not the baby's fault that the father was a violent monster, but *I* would know. I would carry that knowledge every damn day."

Mrs. Renfro used the ear thermometer to check her temperature. "Mm."

Margie recognized the noncommittal sound. The nurse used it when she wanted to show she was listening, but didn't want to let on what she was thinking.

"I'm so scared," Margie said. "But I'm not stupid. I know that the longer they make me wait, the higher the risk of complications. Still, being forced to have a child is even riskier, right?"

"With proper care, the risk would be minimized in either case."

"Proper care. In this place?" Margie inhaled a breath for courage, then exhaled the question: "What happens when an inmate has a baby? Just . . . hypothetically, I mean."

"The baby stays with its mother for up to eighteen months. Then it's sent to live with relatives or foster parents until the mom is released."

Margie had no relatives. Foster parents, then. Could she pick the foster parents? Queen and Cubby? Maybe someone from their church? "What if getting released takes a long time?"

Mrs. Renfro glanced away, checking things on her cart. "While the mother is incarcerated, there would be visitation like anyone else."

Margie tried to picture the situation playing out. A little kid, dragged into the visitation room, squirming and recoiling from the stranger behind the Plexiglas. That was no life for a kid. "I've seen it with other inmates," she said. "And those are women who *want* their kids. It's a nightmare."

"I'm sorry, Margie. It's far from ideal. Children are resilient."

"They shouldn't have to be. They should be *kids*." Margie watched the blood pressure cuff deflate and the needle count down the dial.

She took a deep, shaky breath and said the quiet part out loud: "What about . . . giving it up for adoption?"

The notion had come to her in the night, swirling into her thoughts like a stealthy intruder. She'd remembered her long-ago encounter with the girl named Tamara Falcon, adopted by a wealthy family, living like a princess in a tower.

"Are you saying adoption is on the table?" Mrs. Renfro asked quietly.

"Everything except what I need is on the table," Margie said, swiping at an errant tear. "I don't know anymore. Giving it up for adoption is one of a very limited collection of options, right?"

"It could be," the nurse agreed. "Just so you know, the current preferred term is 'placing' a child for adoption, not giving it up."

"I don't prefer the term at all. But I'm scared that time will run out and I'll end up having a baby I don't want."

"The Hunts have offered to take the baby," Mrs. Renfro reminded her.

"No. God in heaven, no. I wouldn't give a rabid dog to that family to raise. They already raised a monster. Why would I give them another shot at it? No. *Never*." A horrible thought occurred to her. "Oh, shit, would they try to take the baby from me?"

"In an adoption situation, that'd be illegal even for the Hunts. As the birth mother, you have the absolute right to choose."

"As a human being, I also have the absolute right to defend myself when I'm being raped, and yet here I am," Margie pointed out. "Sorry, but I don't trust anything about this system."

"Let's work through this one piece at a time. I hear you saying you're considering other alternatives to abortion, is that correct?"

"I . . . No. Or yes. Maybe I am. Lord knows, it's not my first choice, but these delays are pushing me there. If I were to do this, if I went through with adoption, I would make sure it never went anywhere near the Hunts. I'd want to find total strangers who would give the kid a great life and not make him live with the fact that his father got shot while raping his mother."

Margie was shaken by her own words. She felt as though she was hearing them for the first time from the mouth of a stranger. She was quiet for a bit, contemplating the scenario playing out in real time—bearing the unwanted pregnancy, giving birth, handing over the baby. What would that feel like for anyone? She shivered and twirled the inmate bracelet around and around her wrist.

"Are you sure you want to explore this option, Margie?" Mrs. Renfro prompted. "Because once the TRO is lifted, you'll still have the right to terminate your pregnancy."

"Hell, no, I'm not sure of anything. If offered the chance to get the abortion right now, I'd jump at it. But I . . . Pretty soon it'll be too late, you know?"

"If you want, I can reach out to social services and get you information on adoption procedures."

"Okay, yes. I'm not saying that's my choice, but I'm not saying it's *not* my choice. The way things are going, I'm losing hope. I need a damn plan B."

17

Getting someone's attention about adoption was way easier than getting justice for a crime she didn't commit. A social worker showed up the very next day to explain how a private adoption would work and offered to connect Margie with adoption services. As it turned out, plenty of families were waiting to adopt a newborn.

She was presented with a bewildering array of agencies. Most were run by lawyers, because apparently the process of giving someone a baby was legally complicated.

Looking over the information, Margie felt a subtle shift in attitude. As a knocked-up, locked-up young woman, she was at the mercy of the system. Yet as a potential birth mother holding the fate of an entire family in her hands, she wielded enormous power. She was not expecting this. Suddenly she was the source of someone's deepest desires.

"All this time I've been begging for a lawyer," she said to the social worker, "and no one would give me the time of day. All it took was the right kind of currency, I guess."

"Well, let's be clear. These are not criminal defense attorneys, and they're not allowed to represent you in anything but this specific matter. They're strictly concerned with organizing a private, legal adoption."

"I hear you," Margie said. "I know I can't trade a damn baby like a commodity for the services of a lawyer."

She was given special permission to hold lengthy phone conferences with prospective adoption specialists. One was a fire-breathing man who warned her that she'd burn in hell if she had an abortion. He was also opposed to allowing non-Christians and same-sex couples to adopt. She couldn't hang up on the guy fast enough. No child should be raised by people chosen by a man like that.

Another lawyer claimed she had a high success rate, yet she didn't offer any testimonials. She seemed distracted, as if she was working at her computer while Margie talked to her. She kept deferring all the questions to her associate, who wasn't able to be on the call. Her favorite phrase seemed to be *I'll have someone check on that for you*. Margie wasn't impressed. She wanted someone who already had the answers. The level of trust she needed was sky-high. She was still teetering about this decision. Terminating the pregnancy was still on the table, assuming the restraining order was lifted in time.

Eventually, she spoke with Maxine Maycomb, Esq. Maxine was both a lawyer and an adoption coordinator. Her record of completed adoptions was one of the highest in the state, and she had certified testimonials to prove it. Throughout the call, she listened and didn't seem to judge, and she gave clear, confident answers. When Margie mentioned that she might still choose abortion, Maxine said she supported a woman's right to make her own health-care decisions and was in fact an active volunteer in Planned Parenthood. Margie didn't feel rushed, or pressured, or obliged to give certain replies.

After all the dragging weeks, it was remarkable how

quickly things moved once Margie settled on an adoption coordinator. Ms. Maycomb came to meet her in person that very evening. With high-teased silver hair and hoop earrings, she looked a bit like Margie's mama's favorite governor—Ann Richards. Mama used to have a signed picture of the governor stuck to the fridge. Ms. Maycomb didn't seem at all put off by Margie's beige prison clothes and handcuffs, or her story of rape and a shooting, or the fact that they met in a bleak, windowless conference room with a guard stationed outside.

"My stars and tiny catfish," said Ms. Maycomb. "You're no bigger'n a minute. How are you feeling, honey?"

"Terrible. Nauseous half the time, and anxious the other half."

"I'm real sorry to hear that. And I am so, so sorry you're going through this. It must be several kinds of awful."

"Sometimes I can't even believe this is my life. I was a waitress. I make barbecue sauce and take care of my cat. And now this. I've tried my best to figure out how to deal with it. I've read everything I can get my hands on. I'm getting help from the Amiga Foundation. But I'm still stuck in jail and I'm running out of options. I feel like I'm in hell."

"You know what Winston Churchill famously said? 'When you're going through hell, keep going.'"

Margie fiddled with the cuffs. "Just so you know, I still haven't made up my mind a hundred percent. I need to learn more about how this would go before I decide what I'm going to do."

"You deserve to give full consideration to all your options. I promise, there's a way through this," said Maxine. "I'm here to help, but ultimately, you'll make the choice that's best for you."

"Can you help get me out of jail?" Margie knew the answer but asked the question anyway.

"I'm not that kind of lawyer. But . . ." Maxine stopped, and her gaze shifted away for a moment.

"But what?"

"My sole focus is helping with a secure, legal adoption, creating the best possible outcome for the mother and child. Right now, let's talk about your questions and concerns."

Margie handed over some dog-eared pages. "They let me have a pencil, but paper costs money at the commissary. So I wrote them on notepaper from prayer meeting."

"I'll make sure your commissary account has enough for paper," Maxine said.

"Uh . . . thanks." Margie was surprised to feel a rush of emotion. Not since Queen's visit had anyone offered to give her anything, even something as humble as paper to write on. Her emotions felt like a ride on a runaway skateboard, swiftly changing and out of control. Mrs. Renfro said it was probably caused by hormonal changes from the pregnancy.

Margie hated that Jimmy Hunt still had a kind of power over her emotions.

"How about I start by showing you how the process would work, should you decide to choose adoption." Maxine took out a lap-size flip chart showing the steps. "The most immediate need is to find the best possible prenatal care for you."

Margie gazed at the picture on the chart, showing a mild-faced young woman with a doctor and nurse in a fancy medical suite. She thought about the low-income clinics she went to, with their glaring lights and plastic furniture and harried workers. "Looks like a five-star hotel."

"The stakes are high for everyone involved, so the care team is going to be selected especially for you."

"They're sending a care team to jail?"

"We'll work out a schedule to take you to regular appointments."

"Did they tell you what it costs to send me with a security detail?"

"This will cost you nothing. It's standard for the adoptive family to cover all your medical costs, before, during, and after the birth. Transportation, safety measures, counseling, and personal care are all part of every arrangement I coordinate. There might be a stipend for other expenses as well, though it's not required."

"Hold on a hot minute. Counseling? Personal care?"

"These are vital needs of all birth mothers. It's an established fact that a well-supported birth mom results in a successful placement."

"And the jail administrator is okay with this."

Maxine gave a curt nod. "Once you choose a family, you'll make a legal contract with the adoptive parents. You have a lot of choices to make. For instance, you can choose what level of involvement you want with the family before the birth and how open you want the adoption to be. After the birth you'll sign a final termination of parental rights—followed by a waiting period and a home visit to the family—and the adoptive parents will take full custody."

"And then what? I walk away as if it never happened? Well, guess what? I can't walk *away*." Margie shuddered. "I walk in circles around the yard out there." It was crazy to think that after incubating a baby and giving it to someone else, she'd still be here, awaiting trial.

"I think you'll find that it doesn't work in quite that way," Maxine said. "Not for any birth mother I've ever met. You don't ever walk away. You don't ever forget. This is one of the biggest things that will ever happen to you. One of the biggest things in your life. It will always be part of you. That's one reason counseling and self-care are part of the process."

Margie stared down at her lap, rubbing her thumb on the edge of the handcuff.

"Now, that doesn't mean it weighs down your whole future," Maxine said. "Quite the opposite. You can move ahead with your life, knowing you did a selfless, loving thing for another human being."

There were no secrets in the unit. Gossip made its way through the invisible network of whispers and signals among the inmates. When word got out in the pod that she was thinking about adoption, Margie's choice became something of a cause célèbre among the inmates and staff. The other girls offered their advice from the sidelines. Whether out of boredom or true compassion, Margie's fellow inmates became deeply invested in the process. Pick this. Pick that. You want a family with big bucks. A family with other children. A couple who wanted an only child. A single mother who knew better than to get involved with a man. Dogs. Horses. A guaranteed college fund. A plan for the kid in case the parents split up or die. Everyone had an opinion.

Margie was distracted by all the chatter, diverting as it was. After lights-out, she lay still and blocked out the noise and truly focused on the choice she was facing. She rolled her limited options around and around in her head. She still wished she could get an abortion and reclaim her body. She pictured being a mom behind bars, and her heart broke not just for herself, but for a child forcibly separated from its mother after eighteen months. She fantasized about winning her freedom and leaving Texas forever. She could go to Vermont and make maple syrup–based sauce. To Seattle or San Francisco or Denver.

But with each passing day, freedom seemed less and less likely.

Yet now suddenly she had more support than ever— her adoption lawyer, her jail caseworker, and a social worker. There would be a designated mediator appointed by the jail administrator. Maxine must have a silver tongue, because she sweet-talked her way into extra visitation time, and she was even allowed to bring a laptop computer. Under strict supervision, Margie was permitted to view profiles and watch videos of prospective families, a bewildering array of people yearning for a child. She listened to their hopes and dreams, their outpouring of love and desperation. She studied their photographs, read their letters, and tried to imagine their everyday lives. Their heartfelt, sometimes heartbreaking stories and videos showed glimpses of these strangers. Margie observed them relaxing in their lovely homes, taking walks together, celebrating holidays with friends and relatives.

It felt surreal, choosing a life for a person who didn't even exist yet. She spent every waking hour imagining the path in life she could give to a child.

City life or country life? A mom who was a doctor. The dad, a DJ for a radio station. A bilingual household. A big house with a garden. A condo in a high-rise. Only child. Siblings. Baptists. Buddhists. Vegans. World travelers. Homebodies.

Each family Margie read about seemed wonderful and touching. There were wrenching stories of people who couldn't conceive because of a health condition.

Women who had lost their pregnancies, time and time again. Gay guys who wanted to be dads. Couples yearning to be parents so bad they promised to love any child at any age with any special needs.

She realized the profiles were meant to make them sound ideal. She wondered what they were like when one of them got mad or sick, or if they went broke or got in a wreck.

Ms. Maycomb encouraged Margie to ask those questions of the people she wanted to learn more about.

Not one prospective family lived in a trailer park. None of them seemed to worry about where the rent money was coming from or if they'd be able to fill the car with gas. Margie wondered what her life might have been like if her mom hadn't had to struggle just to get through the week. Sometimes she had to catch her breath, because seeing all these stories made her think long and hard about the way she'd grown up. They'd had nothing—a rented spot in a trailer park and a car that was older than Mama herself. And yet Margie had never felt deprived. There was a richness to their lives that had nothing to do with the bank account. Their world was built on a foundation of love and trust between the two of them. Where they'd lived didn't matter. What they'd meant to each other—that mattered. The two of them had the one thing these sad, eager, affluent couples yearned for with all their hearts.

Thank you, Mama, she thought. *I hope I appreciated you enough.*

Maxine advised Margie to narrow her choices to a few families that felt like a good fit, and she would set up video interviews. She wanted Margie and the parents to build trust through disclosure, honesty, and mutual respect. A successful adoption would not be easy, but there were things that would make the process meaning-ful and rewarding.

"Most families want to know a health history," Max-ine explained. "The rest is up to you."

"They should also know what I told you—that my mind is not a hundred percent made up."

"That's completely valid," Maxine said. "Adoption is the start of a bittersweet and difficult emotional journey. It's also the most rewarding and selfless thing I've ever done."

"*You've* ever done?" Margie's jaw dropped.

Maxine nodded. "I was even younger than you. This was a long time ago, when there was a lot of secrecy and silence about the process. I didn't have a support system. That's why I became an attorney and why I specialize in adoption placement. It's also the reason I volunteer with Planned Parenthood. To help prevent situations like this."

"Do you know what happened?" Margie asked. "Af-ter the adoption, I mean."

"It was a closed adoption, so no." Maxine shut her laptop and tucked it neatly into her briefcase. "I never got to hold the child in my arms. Nowadays, we've found ways to make things better for the birth mom, to give you as much closure as possible."

Margie studied the lines in Maxine's face, the hand that went to her heart as she spoke. She was lovely, like a picture book grandmother. It was hard to imagine her with a broken heart, a broken life. *We all have our sto-ries*, she thought.

"These six." Margie placed her penciled notes—on thick, smooth stationery from the commissary—on the table in the conference room. "I want these six families to know more about me."

"More," said Maxine. "How much more?"

"Everything," she stated. "I want them to know exactly who I am—a high school dropout who makes the best damn barbecue sauce in the world. I want them to know where I am and why I'm here. I want them to know that this baby was conceived in a violent act and that it has the DNA of a rapist. I want them to know I shot the sperm donor dead while defending myself. And I want them to know I'm in jail."

"Well, that's your choice, of course. I assume you realize some families might find this information difficult."

"Exactly. If they can't handle who I am, if they can't handle what brought on this pregnancy, then they're not the right choice for me."

Maxine studied her. Took a deep breath. "You're an old soul, Margie Salinas."

Margie was startled. "My mama used to say that about me."

"She knew you well."

Margie's insistence on full disclosure culled the field to three families. Apparently the other three had reservations about her background or circumstances. The remaining couples assured Maxine that they had zero qualms about the way the baby was conceived and about the accusations leveled against Margie.

Jason and Avery of Abilene even sent a personal message via Maxine, assuring her that the father's crimes did not taint the new soul developing in Margie's womb.

They were parents to a disabled son and had suffered several miscarriages. Judging by their profile, they were attractive in an easy, approachable way, looking like a happy couple in a real estate ad. They owned a successful sporting goods store and sponsored the local Little League organization and went to church every Sunday without fail.

Brent and Erin met while in the Coast Guard Reserve, and they lived in San Francisco. They loved the outdoors and had a big extended family. Erin was a general surgeon and Brent was in nursing school. The video reel made them seem smart and unpretentious as they hiked with their two rescued dogs along the California coast or in the redwood forests. Erin had to have a hysterectomy at age thirty. She said her gratitude for Brent increased tenfold, because he was so steadfast in his support of her. Margie loved the look of their house—beautiful but not superfancy, nestled amid towering trees on a cul-de-sac. She could imagine a kid running around and exploring there. They seemed like the kind of people who would surround a child with love.

The third couple had been married for fourteen years—Lindsey and Sanjay. Lindsey was the CEO and founder of a tech start-up, and Sanjay was a concert pianist and triathlete. They lived in Austin. They already had a prenuptial agreement in place, which they admitted was unconventional. They had drawn up a parenting plan as well, because even though they never expected it to be needed, they wanted the birth mother to know that if anything happened to their marriage, there was already a plan in place for the child. With a cheeky grin, Lindsey said, "Marriage might be fleeting, but divorce is forever." Sanjay added, "You know what else is forever? Parenthood. Family is forever."

Margie was drawn to their candor. To her, it meant adoption was the clearest, most conscious choice to be made for a couple wanting a child.

Maxine set up the meetings, securing special permission from the jail administrator. There was a computer program called Skype that could connect people live on video, so it would be kind of like a face-to-face conversation. Margie was nervous but hopeful. The girls in the unit had placed bets and lobbied for their favorites. Once again, Margie found herself struggling to tune out the noise and speculation in order to make sure the decision was hers and hers alone.

On the day of the first meeting, she sat in a conference room facing Maxine's laptop. Jason and Avery appeared with a bright country kitchen in the background. They sat shoulder to shoulder in a sunny spot, smiling hard. Behind them was a shelf lined with jars of homemade pickles and preserves, which Margie instantly liked. There were plaques on the wall with affirmations in fancy lettering, and a collage of family pictures. They talked with sincerity about their lives and their community. They briefly introduced their little boy, who was in physical therapy after surgery. They spoke about the importance of good schools and going to church and having youthful, active grandparents on both sides. Their obvious love for each other made Margie's chest ache with yearning.

When the meeting ended, she had no doubt in her mind that this would be a wonderful, loving family for any kid.

Then she turned to Maxine. "They're not the ones."

"What makes you say that?"

"They didn't ask a single question about me."

"They're not adopting you."

"I get that this is not about me, but there wasn't any interest at all. I'm just the incubator."

"You told them every last thing in your disclosure form, so perhaps they didn't have any lingering questions. Could be they didn't want you to feel interrogated." She paused. "It's fine, though. You should trust your gut."

"I hope my gut is right, because they really do seem fantastic and they'll be a great family for some lucky child."

Erin and Brent were great, too, sitting on their back patio overlooking San Francisco Bay. The setting looked magical to Margie, one of those places you saw in travel magazines. They said all the things she hoped to hear and a few things that surprised her. There were tremulous tears along with Erin's smile. Brent held her hand. She kept looking at him with hope swimming in her eyes. They promised a safe and stable home life. They were committed to meeting all the child's needs, and their connection to each other and to their extended families looked genuine and powerful. They invited Margie to tell them anything she cared to share about herself. They wanted to know what kind of future she hoped for, and Erin asked if she was getting help dealing with the rape and its aftermath.

"I appreciate you asking," Margie said, "but the answer is no, I'm not getting any special help and it's pretty certain I have PTSD. Special help doesn't seem like something that's available to me where I am."

"It must be so scary," Erin said, glancing at Brent. "I hope the justice system serves you well and that you get through this. And we would definitely see if there's some way to find some help, not just for your medical care but counseling about the rape as well." She turned to her husband. "Right, honey?"

Brent said, "Sure, babe. I'm sorry to hear about what happened to you, Margie. You don't deserve it. You're such a beautiful young woman."

What if she wasn't beautiful? Margie wondered. Would they still want her baby?

Maybe something showed on her face, because he added, "I mean, I wouldn't have said anything but . . . well, you and Erin could pass for sisters. I couldn't help noticing the resemblance."

Erin had long blond hair and big blue eyes. Like Margie. Like Margie's mother. "Is that important?" Margie asked.

"Absolutely not," Erin said quickly, glancing at her husband. "We want a child, don't we?"

Brent nodded. "I'm adopted myself. Growing up, folks would tell me I looked just like my daddy, and I always thought that was cool, since we weren't related by blood. But it didn't define our relationship. What defined our relationship was that my dad was fantastic. *Is* fantastic. He lives in Sausalito, just across the bay"—he gestured beyond the patio—"and he'll be an amazing granddad."

"Do you know your birth mother?" Margie asked.

Brent stiffened slightly. "We met when I was eighteen. She . . . She's always struggled with mental health issues. I'm grateful to her for placing me with my adoptive family. I know it wasn't easy, but it was the ultimate loving act."

"We hope you'll reach out to us anytime," Erin said. "If you have questions, or just want to talk, or need to know more about us. We're here, Margie. Anytime." She looked at Brent. "Isn't that right?"

"Absolutely, babe." He gave a thumbs-up sign.

After the interview, Maxine turned to her. "Well?"

"Wow. Just . . . wow. They seem terrific, and they asked me about myself." Margie felt herself edging close to tears. "Like I matter for something more than just a baby maker." She wasn't sure if she was being flooded by pregnancy hormones, or if this strange, sad, bittersweet process was getting to her.

"I'm glad you hit it off with them. Remember, though, that there's absolutely no rush. You're just beginning the process. You have lots of time to find the right fit."

The San Francisco couple had set the bar high. Margie felt ambivalent as the third interview started. Nothing about this process was simple. Or certain. She didn't expect it to be, but she'd been hoping for a moment of crystal clarity, when she knew exactly what she was supposed to do. So far, all she felt was a nagging self-doubt interspersed with flares of hope. The girls in her pod would probably go nuts for Brent because he was as gorgeous as a movie superhero. His wife was a doctor and they lived in a city Margie had always dreamed of visiting. Yet she still thought about the other two options— keeping the baby, or ending the pregnancy.

When Maxine logged onto the next meeting, Margie shut her eyes and took a deep breath. Then she waited for the third couple to appear. It was such a strange way to meet people, looking at their nervous smiles on a screen. Could you really get to know someone like this? Maxine had said that if she did find a family, an in-person meeting might be arranged, with permission from the administrator.

Lindsey and Sanjay were seated side by side at a shiny black grand piano. The background was a wall of glass and what looked like a tropical forest.

By now she was prepared for the anxious, earnest, darting glances, the small talk meant to reassure her. "We both come from close families," Sanjay said, referring to a group of framed pictures on the piano. "What about you, Margie? That is, if you don't mind sharing."

"I don't." She folded her arms, as much as she could

with her wrists cuffed. "So I guess you know what brought me here."

"We read every word of your statement, over and over again," said Lindsey. "We're so very sorry. No human being deserves what happened to you. I can't imagine how hard it must be."

"This extraordinary, unselfish thing you're doing is amazing," Sanjay added.

Maybe she was exhausted from the first two meetings. Maybe she was hungry because she'd missed lunch service. Whatever it was, Margie was in no mood now and the words of praise annoyed her. She decided to say whatever the hell was on her mind.

"I'm not extraordinary. I'm not amazing," she told them. "And being an unwed mother is not the worst thing that ever happened to me. I had the shit judgment to hook up with a guy who turned out to be a violent criminal. And when he wouldn't take no for an answer, he raped me and got himself shot. So no, I'm not extraordinary. I'm somebody who had to do something terrible just to survive."

There was a pause. They looked at each other like maybe they were freaking out a little. They might be having second thoughts based on her attitude. Well, if they couldn't handle her anger, then they probably couldn't handle raising a kid.

"To be honest, I tried everything in my power to avoid having this child. I wanted an abortion, and there's a chance that I still might have that choice. But time's running out, so I reckon I'll be stuck. And I'm pissed as hell about that."

They turned to each other briefly, then back to the camera. "This is a terrible burden for you. We won't try to steer you one way or the other," Lindsey said. "If you decide to place your baby with us, we'll do everything in our power to support you."

She studied their faces on the small screen. Good-looking and sincere, like the other couples. "Anyway, I get that the baby didn't have a choice, either. It didn't ask for this mess any more than I did. So all I can do now is make a good decision out of a rotten situation. Maybe you're my good decision, maybe not. You can say I'm unselfish, but I'm not. I'm trying to get through this, is all."

Like the other two couples, they talked with wrenching sincerity about their hopes and dreams for a family. They loved the great outdoors. Hiking and camping. At one point in the interview a little dog scampered into view. They had rescued Wally from a local shelter. They didn't spend much time watching sports, though Sanjay trained hard for his races, and they liked playing tennis and waterskiing. They said they had a yard and a house with plenty of room, good schools nearby.

The two seemed utterly sincere, and they were saying all the right things, from their favorite taco place (Torchy's, of course) to their ongoing dispute over the best kids' movie—*Toy Story* or *The Lion King*.

Beauty and the Beast, Margie thought, the movie she'd watched over and over again with a faulty DVD player and a secondhand TV while her mother worked. She didn't speak up, though. If she handed over this child, she would have no say in that, or any other matter.

And then there was a moment, unplanned, seemingly spontaneous, toward the end of the interview. The little dog jumped into Sanjay's lap, and he leaned toward Lindsey and they shared a gaze that nearly took Margie apart, it was so tender.

"There are so many things I love about this man,"

said Lindsey. "I could keep you all day and put you into a diabetic coma, telling you about them. I'll spare you, though."

"The point is, the child we adopt will live in a world of love and acceptance," Sanjay added. "We won't be perfect parents but we'll do our best each and every day."

I could be saved if I ever found a love like that, thought Margie.

18

Margie was surprised when a guard came to escort her to the visitor center. She wasn't expecting a visit today, but since the pregnancy whirlwind, she drew a lot more attention. She spied Truly waiting in the visitors' lobby, energetically chewing gum and pacing back and forth, pigtails flying out at every turn. When she saw Margie, she scurried right over.

"I have news," she said. "Two things. First off, the order barring you from getting an abortion has been thrown out. The judge who finally reviewed it was appalled, and he lifted it immediately. It was a really stern ruling, too. He said no one has a right to overrule a woman's choice. He also said it's unconscionable that this process took as long as it did, and it's shameful that every court in the system touched this case and still didn't apply the law. Not only that, the judge who originally granted it was censured. Harry delivered the official document to the administration office this morning." She let out a long breath and leaned toward the Plexiglas. "You get what this means, right? The way is clear once again for you to terminate your pregnancy."

Margie sat with this for several long moments. So. The option was back on the table. It would be safe and legal. The whole ordeal would be over in half a day. Her body—her life—would be her own again. The possibility blew her mind.

"Wow," she said quietly. "Wow, that's . . . exactly what I wanted."

"You seem kind of shocked, Margie."

"Well, four weeks ago, I would have welcomed the news. I would have been so relieved."

"You're not relieved now?"

"To be honest, I'm kind of freaked out. I need to think this through. See, it's different now. I've been thinking about other options."

Truly's eyebrows shot up. "Such as?"

"Well, other than abortion, there are only two that I can think of. I could keep the baby. It would stay with me for eighteen months, and then it would go to foster care."

"What?" Truly's face drained of color. "Oh my gosh, Margie—"

"Calm down, I'm not keeping my damn rapist's baby. And I'd never give it to the Hunts, for Chrissake."

Truly slumped back in her seat. "Well, thank god for that."

"So that leaves adoption. A legit, private adoption." She told Truly about choosing an adoption specialist and interviewing prospective parents. "Believe me, this situation was not on my bingo card, but here I am."

"That's amazing," said Truly. "You're amazing."

"I'm not," Margie said. "I completely resent the bullshit system that set me on this path. I've been forced into a horrible position." She stopped and looked down at her lap. Lately, there was a subtle but undeniable thickening around her middle.

It could be gone in a matter of hours. She now had the right to pursue what she'd wanted in the first place—to end an unwanted pregnancy that had resulted from rape.

She didn't know she was crying until she saw her reflection in the Plexiglas when she looked up at Truly. "What I'm about to do is going to be horrible for me, but now it feels like the only choice. I'll have to find a way to make my peace with it."

"Oh," said Truly, "you must be so relieved. Do you want me to help you with a new appointment at the clinic?"

Margie shook her head. "Maybe one good thing can come of the shit show I'm going through. In the midst of all the terrible things happening to me, over which I have zero control, I can make something good happen. There's a family waiting, and they're going to be wonderful."

This was the first time she had stated her intention aloud. She hadn't told anyone else, but somehow, she'd already decided. It didn't even feel like a decision. There was a moment just now when she had felt like she wasn't even in charge. Something else was driving her—a firm, incontrovertible knowing in her heart.

"Holy cow. I . . . Just, wow." Truly paused. "But I have to ask—are you one hundred percent certain? I want to make sure you haven't been pressured or promised something in return. Or . . . threatened."

"I'm totally freaking out," Margie admitted, "and it *is* going to be horrible for me. But it's my decision. Completely, I swear. Nobody pressured me or promised me anything. I haven't even told the adoption lawyer or the parents yet. I'm still getting used to the idea. You're the first person I've told."

"I won't say anything. It's your story, not mine," Truly said. She was crying now, too, dabbing her eyes with her sleeve. "And I know you don't want people to think you're amazing, but you are, so there."

"Whatever."

"There's something else," said Truly. "Whoa, don't look at me like that. This is a good thing. It might be the best thing ever. You're getting a new lawyer."

Margie frowned. "I don't understand."

"Well, it's up to you, of course. You can stick with the public defender, but now there's another option. An anonymous donor has provided funds specifically for your legal defense. You get to hire your own criminal defense lawyer."

"You mean for the murder charge?"

"That's right. A private attorney who works only for you. At no charge. The donor is covering the entire cost through Amiga. You can pick any lawyer you want."

"Somebody came to you out of the blue?" she asked. "Just like that?"

"Just like that."

"And you have no idea who it is."

"I don't. The foundation director does, but it's being kept confidential."

Margie squinted at her. "What's the catch? Why would someone throw down for my lawyer costs?"

"We don't know. Maybe the director does. I swear, there's no catch. No strings attached. Your case has been covered in the press—even *Texas Monthly*. Somebody knows you're getting the shaft and wants to help."

"Somebody with a buttload of money."

"The foundation has donors like that. It's for real, I swear, Margie."

"Seriously, who would do this?"

"Someone who cares about you. Or maybe someone who cares about justice."

Other than Cubby and Queen, no one cared about her. Margie doubted they could afford a lawyer for a murder trial, though—unless they took up a collection at their church, maybe. But the anonymity was a clue. Could be they wanted to help but didn't want any attention from the community.

"Damn." She leaned back in the plastic chair. Her stomach—or maybe the baby—did a little roll and flip. "Suppose I agree to this. How does it work? I don't know any lawyers."

"I brought a recommendation from the foundation's general counsel. He's what they call a superlawyer. Somebody who can give you a real defense." She set a business card on the counter.

Margie looked at it through the Plexiglas. Terence Swift, Attorney-at-Law. An address near the courthouse in Austin.

"You're not obligated to hire him. You can hire anyone you choose, or no one at all. He does come very highly recommended. All you have to do is tell your public defender and then it's handled. If you want, you can meet with this guy before you make up your mind. He's available whenever you say."

Margie thought about Landry Yates and how he seemed to have a million things going on and never had time and was always in a rush. She thought about how he had refused to help her with the restraining order from the Hunt family, and with the abortion.

Then she looked at the new lawyer's card. "I reckon he'll do just fine."

Terence Swift was a good old boy. That was what they would call him at Cubby's or at the icehouse across the road from the barbecue joint. He wore a fine-looking suit, well-buffed cowboy boots, and a conservative tie. He was probably a good tipper. He didn't seem particularly warmhearted or kind.

He offered something Margie needed more than warmth or kindness. He had total focus. And he exuded confidence as he gave her a document to sign, making her his client and stating that the Amiga Foundation would provide a hundred percent of his compensation.

"I've never been anybody's client before."

"Count yourself lucky, then."

"What happens next?"

"I'm going to get the charges against you dismissed," he said.

"Dismissed. Does that mean charges dropped?"

"Yes, ma'am."

"When?"

"Soon. We'll file grounds for dismissal, get an expedited hearing, and you'll be released when the judge rules."

"Wow, I . . . Okay, then. What do I have to do?"

"Sit tight. Stay positive. My office will keep you informed."

As he got up to leave, she asked, "What if you don't get the charges dropped? Do I still have to stay here, waiting for a trial?"

"There won't be a trial."

"You're not going to make me plead guilty," she said. "The other lawyer said that's the only way to avoid a trial."

"It's not *my* way."

"Who sent you to do this? It's just . . . This all seems too easy. The charges are simply dropped? Just like that?"

"It's a process. I've got it handled."

The thought of freedom overwhelmed her with yearning. When she was in the yard later, Sadie approached her. "You met with Terence Swift," she said.

Margie no longer wondered how word spread through

the unit. Its gossip mill was more efficient than high-speed internet. "You know him?"

"I know of him. You don't?"

Margie shrugged. "Not before today. Should I?"

"He's like the Clarence Darrow of Texas. That's the guy who—"

"The Leopold and Loeb guy," Margie said. "I read that book. But he made them plead guilty."

"Damn, girl," said Sadie. "Is there anything you don't know?"

"I've been reading a *lot*."

"Well, okay, so he's no Clarence Darrow, then." She studied Margie's expression. "Maybe Atticus Finch?"

"That's a made-up character." She did love *To Kill a Mockingbird*, though. It was one of those books that, when she finished, she had turned back to the beginning and read it all over again. "But if my guy is anything like that, I guess it's a good thing I got him on my team."

The morning of the hearing, a watch officer showed up with a white blouse and a navy skirt and a pair of slip-on canvas shoes. "Put these on before court," she said.

The clothing was labeled Neiman Marcus. Margie had never owned anything from Neiman Marcus before. The outfit was basic, but the fabric was luxurious and expensive-looking. The skirt had an adjustable waist.

She threw up a little but it was mostly dry heaves.

Her decision about the pregnancy was settling into reality. No, she didn't want it at all, and she resented that the pregnancy had been forced on her. Still, she was prepared to go through with the plan for this child. She was beginning to think of it as a person now. Against her will, she was growing a whole person inside her.

Mr. Swift seemed to be singularly uninterested in

this situation. He was focused like a laser on the murder case—specifically, on the fact that no murder had been committed at all. He and his assistant had spent hours with Margie in the conference room, going over every second of the incident.

Going through it all again was like reopening a wound. Swift was not apologetic, and he didn't back off. Not for a moment. His assistant also took statements from the neighbors, from coworkers. People at church.

"I hope you know," she said, "the Hunts run everything in this county."

Mr. Swift had offered a brief smile without any warmth. "Roy Hunt and I go back a ways," he said.

"Roy Hunt has done nothing but attack me in the papers. Probably online as well," she said. "And he's a retired judge."

"I'm the reason he retired," said Mr. Swift.

The DA made a motion to curtail the proceeding, claiming Margie's new representation didn't entitle her to a new hearing.

"Your Honor, the facts of this case have not changed. They've been established by the defendant herself. On the one hand, we have a woman who murdered her boyfriend in some kind of lovers' quarrel. On the other hand, there's James Bryant Hunt, a lifelong resident of Banner Creek. He was a promising athlete, a member of an upstanding, churchgoing family, coldly murdered by a vengeful woman. There is more than ample evidence for an indictment."

Margie kept her eyes straight ahead. By now she ought to be inured to the impact of the words, but each one felt like a bludgeon blow.

Mr. Swift didn't make a sound. He didn't object to a

single thing the DA was saying. He sat there like a bump on a pickle. She started to fear that she'd made a terrible mistake. This was a plot by the Hunts to get her to plead guilty. Maybe they were the anonymous patrons. She started to panic. She should have asked Swift more questions, demanded to know who he was really serving.

He rose slowly and carefully to deliver his remarks.

"For the moment, we'll set aside all the ways the system has failed my client," he said. "We'll set aside its failures to bring charges within a reasonable time frame. The manipulative tactics employed by investigators. The failure to provide an attorney promptly, as is her right. The failure to provide medical and mental health assistance to her in the wake of a brutal sexual assault. The failure to admit key elements of the rape kit as evidence."

"Objection," the DA said. "This is testimony, Your Honor. It's got no place—"

Swift waved his hand as if swatting at a fly. He introduced information about Jimmy Hunt himself. The DA objected but was overruled because she had already touted the excellence of Jimmy's character, so the door was open to the defense as well. There were complaints filed by women at his college—the ones that had been buried by the athletic department. There were two DWI citations as well.

"Fine, we'll set all this aside as well," Mr. Swift said magnanimously. "The matter at hand can be dispensed with through an examination of the facts in this case. My client was assaulted in her own home. The attack was unprovoked and clearly life-threatening. She fought off her assailant, and as she struggled for her life against a man twice her size, the firearm in his possession—the firearm he used to threaten her life—was discharged. She had no duty to retreat. Under Texas law, specifically the 2007 legislature's revision of that law, she is immune from prosecution."

"That defense clearly does not apply," the DA pointed out. "By her own admission, the accused knew the victim. That's not in dispute. She went on a date with him. She had sex with him. That is also not in dispute. And on the night he came to visit her, innocently assuming they were in a romantic relationship and that she'd welcome his attention, she taunted and provoked him." A selection of text messages went up on the screen.

A close-up of a hand appeared on the display. "As you can see, this wound was inflicted by a kitchen knife belonging to the accused. Ms. Salinas slashed his hand with a knife." The DA also showed pictures of her house in the aftermath. Margie recognized her home and yet she didn't recognize it at all, with upended furniture, numbered markers set in key places, smears of blood, a handprint at the front door. Someone—Jimmy's mother or sister, maybe—sobbed and sniffed softly. Margie's throat was closing, and she struggled to breathe.

Detective Glover testified to the statement she'd taken from Margie. The statement itself appeared on the screen. Margie recognized her own signature at the bottom, attesting to its accuracy. She squinted, just able to make out the file path at the bottom of the printed page.

She grabbed a pencil and scribbled a note to Mr. Swift. He gave it a dismissive glance. Then he addressed the detective. "The arrest report states that Miss Salinas was Mirandized at 12:40. Is that accurate?"

"As far as I know, yes."

"And what time did you say the witness statement was taken?"

"The document is time-stamped—13:45," Ms. Glover said.

"I can see that. The question is, what time did you take it?"

"I . . . Again, the document has a time stamp."

"So it's your testimony that Miss Salinas signed it at that time." He didn't wait for an answer, but referred to his screen. "Here's a video clip of the defendant signing your document—9:58 A.M."

Margie stared in amazement. Landry had told her the video didn't exist. Yet there it was, plain to see.

Terence Swift took a step closer to the witness stand. "Care to revise your statement, Detective?"

The DA requested a conference with the judge. Margie noticed that Swift's demeanor changed ever so slightly—a certain tilt of his chin, perhaps. He wasn't gloating or looking smug. Merely . . . satisfied.

The medical examiner testified to residue on Margie's right hand. And that, she realized, gave Terence Swift another opening. "Did you also examine samples from under the defendant's fingernails?"

A pause. "Yes."

"And the result?"

The witness glanced to the side. "I don't think I have that data."

"Well now, that's interesting, because I do."

There was a vigorous objection from the DA and another conference with the judge.

Mr. Swift stood and walked to the bench. In the flurry of discussion, Margie could tell from the slight upward angle of Swift's chin that he got his way. She had noticed Angela Garza, the rape kit nurse, in the courtroom earlier. When Mr. Swift called her to testify, she walked with confidence and swore to tell the truth in a strong, clear voice.

Her credentials were quickly established. Following the attack, she had documented thirty-three specific injuries. Margie resisted the urge to cover her ears. Hearing the details, so clinically stated, brought back the horror of that night. Predictably, the DA challenged and objected, but the facts were irrefutable. Mr. Swift questioned her several times about her findings, drilling down on the material extracted from under Margie's fingernails. Apparently the medical examiner had failed to note that the skin samples—deep scrapes of skin, not just the surface layer—came from Margie's attacker.

The DA objected to the term *attacker*, but Swift waved his hand and called him *the deceased*. His point had been made. "There is ample evidence to show that Miss Salinas put up a nonlethal defense when he first started the assault. A preponderance of the facts proves she acted in self-defense and had no duty to retreat. Phone records show she dialed 911. When that failed to deter him and he escalated the attack, choking her and pinning her down, she was in fear for her life. In light of the many errors and omissions of the prosecution, this case must be dismissed. My client is entitled to immunity from prosecution."

There was another heated conference at the bench. The judge spoke sternly to both attorneys. Margie made the mistake of glancing over her right shoulder at the gallery. Briscoe Hunt, an older, harder version of his brother, Jimmy, was drilling a hole through her with his stare.

Then Mr. Swift returned to the chair beside Margie. She couldn't tell if his chin was tilted. She didn't understand why his jaw looked so hard.

The judge folded his hands and scanned the courtroom. For the first time, he subjected Margie to a lengthy stare. She resisted the urge to look away.

"Based on the information presented today, it's clear the defendant was in peril of losing her life. Her injuries are consistent with being sexually assaulted. She acted in her own defense and she had no duty to retreat. This case is dismissed." The gavel came down.

Bang.

19

In a daze, Margie left the courthouse with an escort from the sheriff's department. She didn't understand the reason for the escort until Mr. Swift walked with her to the exit.

"It's over?" she asked, incredulous. "For real? For sure?"

"Yes, ma'am."

"I'm . . . I don't even know what to say. Thank you. From the bottom of my heart, thank you."

He put on an expensive-looking ten-gallon and a pair of shades. "All in a day's work."

"And please . . . thank the person who paid your fees. I don't know if I'll ever get to do that, because they're anonymous." There was no word for the intense relief and gratitude she felt. It made her weak in the knees.

"Just because the case is over doesn't mean your ordeal is done," Swift cautioned Margie.

And he was right. Jimmy Hunt—football hero, favorite son—was dead. The family still wanted her punished, as if surviving rape and bearing his unwanted child was not punishment enough. Seeing her walk free would surely enrage the Hunts.

Truly Stone was waiting to see her. For the first time, they greeted each other without the Plexiglas barrier, and they fell together in a lengthy hug. Simple human contact felt strange and wonderful to Margie. She still felt shell-shocked as Truly conferred with Terence Swift.

A cluster of local news organizations bustled toward the courthouse portico. Mr. Swift and his assistant went to address them while Margie followed Truly in the opposite direction.

Margie shuddered as they hurried away from the crowd. "It doesn't matter that my case was dismissed today," she said. "It doesn't matter what he did to me. I'll always be judged by what I did to defend myself."

"I'm sorry about that. You deserve to make a fresh start. My car is on the other side of the building," Truly said. She gave Margie a wide-brimmed sun hat and a pair of sunglasses. "Let your lawyer deal with the rubberneckers."

Margie followed her to a silver Prius and they drove away. *Away.* After all this time, she was simply riding away. "Where are we going?" she asked.

"That's up to you. Where would you like to go?"

"I'm homeless," Margie said. "I mean, it was amazing that the foundation covered my rent, but I can never spend another night in that place. I do need to go back there and see about my cat." There were only a few things she was desperate to save from the wreckage of her former life—her cat, her mother's canning set, and her recipe collection. Finding Kevin would be a long shot after so much time had passed, but there could be a chance that he had stuck around, haunting his usual spots around the porch and down by the creek.

"Tell me how to get there," Truly said. She smiled from ear to ear as they turned onto the farm-to-market road. "I'm really happy for you, Margie. You must be so relieved."

Margie gazed out the window at the sorghum fields

and meandering streams, the pastures and storage lots, pale with Hill Country dust. She couldn't believe how much she'd missed even the most simple scenery while she was locked up—a hillock topped with a live oak, a tin-roofed barn, an old farm with an aeromotor windmill, a yellow school bus lumbering past. The world looked different. In a matter of months, everything had changed. And the biggest change of all was inside her.

"Speaking of phones," Truly said, "I have one for you from the foundation. That's one of the first things a woman needs when she's making a new start. You have to be able to function in the world again. It's in that box by your feet. All activated and ready to go. You just need to create a pin and personalize it."

"Wow, that's— Thank you." Her own phone had been seized when she was arrested. It had been returned to her, but it no longer worked and her data plan had been canceled. She opened the box and saw a flat object with a black glass screen. "What's this? An iPod?"

"Something better," Truly said. "It's an iPhone. A brand-new style that just came out. There's this Austin company called Rockler that provided them to everyone at the foundation. You're going to love it, I swear."

During the drive to Banner Creek, Margie figured out the new phone—a state-of-the-art device with a screen instead of a keypad, and more functions than a computer. She was able to log in to her mail account and find her contacts, but for the moment, there was no one to call.

"So now that you're free, how do you feel about the baby?"

"Pregnant is how I feel." Then she realized what Truly was asking. "You mean, will I change my mind about the adoption? Get an abortion? Too late for that, thanks to the stupid county jail system. Keep it? Absolutely not. No matter where I am or what I'm doing, I can't raise Jimmy Hunt's child. It'd be too painful for me, and that's not fair to the kid."

"I understand." Truly kept her eyes on the road.

Margie sent a text message to Maxine, letting her know the case was over and that she still intended to go through with the adoption.

The WELCOME TO BANNER CREEK sign was still in place at the edge of town, but at its base was a memorial marker to Jimmy Hunt. The high school stadium was staked out with JUSTICE FOR JIMMY signs, tattered and weathered now. Margie was shocked to see that Cubby's barbecue had a sign out—CLOSED FOR RENOVATIONS.

"What the hell?" she asked. "Pull over, will you? My lord, what happened here?"

"There was a vandalism incident. It was in the paper," said Truly, parking across the street from the building. They peered into a new plateglass window with the backing still attached. Inside, workers in white jumpsuits were installing fixtures. There was a new ceiling with a constellation of half-moons, each containing a security camera.

"What happened?" Margie asked.

"Looks like broken windows, mainly. And . . . some, uh, unpleasant substances thrown inside."

"Shitfire, is it because the Watsons were the anonymous donors?"

"I doubt it," Truly said. "I mean, I don't know for sure, but it's not likely."

"It's because that was where I worked," Margie said. She felt ill. Cubby's life's work, his future retirement, had been attacked because of her. Although she was worried about bringing the Watsons further trouble, Margie had to see them. They'd been like parents to her. She noticed parts of the n-word that hadn't quite been scrubbed off the wall. Race made them even more vulnerable.

Truly waited in the car while Margie crossed the street and went in to find Cubby and Queen. She kept the hat and sunglasses on in case someone was watching. They embraced her, but she sensed an element of caution in them. "I know I brought y'all a world of hurt," she said. "I'm real sorry about that. You know I didn't mean to."

"Of course not, baby girl."

"The new place is going to be better than ever," Cubby said. "Don't you worry, we got insurance."

Margie's hand wandered to her midsection, a subtle soft mound. "So I guess maybe you heard . . . there's going to be a baby."

Queen nodded. "I was hoping it was idle gossip."

"No such luck." Margie told them about the wrenching choice she'd faced, and how she'd finally opted for adoption.

"You listened to your heart. You know what I always say. If you listen hard enough, your heart won't steer you wrong."

"I hope you're right. Now I better go." Margie wrote down her new phone number and handed it to Queen. "I'll be moving on," she said. "I can't stay here in this town." She never wanted to see or hear of the Hunts, ever again.

"We understand," Cubby said.

"I learned so much from you," she said. "I plan to keep working in the business. I had a crazy idea that one day I might open a place of my own."

"I bet you'd do just fine at it," he said. "You keep making those sauces. You got a gift, girl."

"I hope you're right."

"Come here, baby." Queen gathered her into a generous hug. "I wish you well. I wish you well."

Margie was overwhelmed by the sensation of warm, human contact. Queen's kindness was imprinted on her soul, and she knew she would never forget it.

She felt raw and vulnerable as she told them goodbye. Everything felt so complicated, and so final.

Margie's stomach clenched as she and Truly drove over the creek ford, where the water spilled across the road after a big rain. She pointed out the gravel driveway just past the ford, and Truly turned in. The small house looked neglected, its two front windows like blank stares, the porch furniture in a heap. Her car was parked where she had left it, under the lean-to next to the house. Sticker bushes had grown up around the tires.

Waves of horror engulfed Margie as she got out of the car. There was the spot where Jimmy Hunt had parked his truck, nearly ramming the porch steps. And there was the door she'd stupidly failed to lock the night of the attack.

Her hand shook as she keyed in the door code and stepped inside. The house was a mess, furniture and boxes. She pictured the vans from the state crime lab rolling up, the investigators declaring the house and yard an active crime scene. As she surveyed the kitchen, she gulped in air, fighting off shudders of nausea. In the bedroom, the mattress had been removed, and the floor was covered with dirty tarps. A brownish handprint marred the doorframe. Her hand, covered in blood.

No sign of her cat anywhere. His bowls and bed had been shoved into a corner of the kitchen.

"You okay?" Truly asked her.

Margie waved her off, walked into the bathroom,

and puked. By now, it was a reflex, like sneezing. She used some paper towels to clean herself up. The cabinet under the sink had been ransacked, her belongings scattered—a spray bottle of cleaner, disposable razors, a half-empty box of tampons. The objects of an ordinary life. A life that no longer belonged to her.

She walked outside and told Truly, "No sign of my cat. I'm going to check with the neighbors."

Raylene Pratt answered the door, and when she saw Margie, she took a step back, her hand on the doorknob.

Margie quickly explained that her case had been dropped.

"I know. It's already out on Facebook."

Great, thought Margie. Truly had advised her to delete her account to avoid seeing all the hate posts and speculation. "I came to look for my cat," she said. "Have you seen him?"

"Not lately," Raylene said hastily. "I reckon he run off when all the emergency and crime folks were here."

That night. The blood. The dizzying strobe of emergency lights. EMTs and police draped in gear. Her cat must have been so scared. *Oh, Kevin.* "You sure, now? You haven't seen him since?"

Raylene shook her head. "I got to go. Sorry." She glanced over her shoulder and shrank back into the doorway.

"Here's my mobile number." Margie wrote it down on a slip of paper. "You'll let me know if—"

The door snapped shut.

Margie sighed and left the note tucked in the doorjamb. It was strange to realize she inspired fear. That people looked at her and saw a monster. A killer. The whole world was turned upside down.

As she walked away, she heard a sound from her new phone. A ringtone.

She fumbled, trying to answer it, until she realized she just needed to tap the screen. "Maxine," she said.

"My stars and tiny catfish, you're a free woman."

Margie felt a rare grin unfurl. "That I am."

"Well, this is simply the best news in the world. You've been my number one priority, and I have the preliminary documents all prepared just like you wanted. First thing is to let the adoptive couple know your decision. Would you like me to tell them? Or you? Or both of us together?"

Margie had agonized over which couple to choose, but ultimately, she went with her gut. The couple she'd chosen were going to be great parents. She wanted to give them the news herself. It was kind of exciting to know that the next time she spoke with them, it would be to tell them they were going to adopt her baby.

"I want to let them know," Margie said. "I'd like them to hear directly from me."

"Of course." Maxine arranged for Margie to come to Austin to sign the papers. She insisted on putting Margie up in a hotel, safe and secure, far from Banner Creek.

She sank down on the porch steps and gave Truly the news. "I guess I won't need to stay at your place after all. Maxine said she'd get me a hotel in the city. I'm about to call the parents."

"How do you feel?"

"Freaked out, right now," she said. "But good. At least one of us has a future." She touched her stomach.

"You both do. I swear, you're going to be all right. I know that sounds like a platitude but I really think the future is going to be wonderful for you. I meet a lot of women through Amiga, and I have a sense about these things."

Margie looked down at her phone. "I barely know how to use this thing."

"Want to call them now?" Truly asked. "Hey, what about a video call on my laptop? I have Skype, and it's on my mobile network."

"Would that work?"

"Sure." Truly brought out the laptop and set it up. "You just put in the number here, and talk directly to the screen. I'll give you some privacy."

"I don't need privacy," said Margie. "I got nothing to hide."

"I know, but . . . it's your moment. I'll wait by the car."

Margie perched the laptop on her knees, leaned back on her elbows, and looked up. It was the same sky she'd seen from the beaten-earth yard at the jail, but from here, it looked completely different. Everything looked different. She used to sit out here for hours, reading a book or tending her plants. On the three steps up to the door were her potted herbs and peppers. She used the fresh herbs and spices in her sauce—cilantro and cumin, laurel and thyme, bird's-eye chilies for a surprise burst of fire. Some of the pots had spilled, probably knocked over by the crime scene people. Most of the plants had gone to seed, desiccated by neglect. She plucked a dried twig of Kevin's favorite catnip and swirled it in the dust by her feet, idly tracing random shapes as she gathered her thoughts.

The call she was about to make was going to change four lives forever.

I found the best family I could for you, she told the stranger inside her. *I think you're going to like the life you get to live with them.*

After a few burbling sounds, the screen flashed *connected* and a face appeared. "Margie! How are you feeling? Is everything all right?"

She wanted to puke. Was he asking because he cared, or because he wanted her to give birth to a healthy baby and hand it over to him?

"I got out of jail," she said. "The case was dismissed."

"Wow, hey, that's wonderful news. I mean, it's beyond wonderful. I'm sorry for everything you had to go through, but it's fantastic that you're a free woman. Where are you calling from?"

"The house where I used to live. I came to look for my cat," she told him. "No sign of him, so I guess he ran off." She sighed, and tears welled up. "I really loved that cat."

"Oh, Margie. I wish I could help you."

"I wanted to talk to you both," she said. "Is this a good time?"

She had truly agonized over the decision. Erin and Brent in their Bay Area home? Or Lindsey and Sanjay, with their piano and garden? Both couples were great. Both seemed smart and kind. Any kid would be lucky to join either family. In the end, though, she had felt nudged in one direction. She hoped with all her heart that she'd picked the right family.

"Sure, hang on . . ." He carried his laptop as he walked through a big space with marble floors and pillars. Maybe he was at the bank or something. No, it must be their house because suddenly they were both sitting in a big outdoor space—a patio at the edge of a bright green lawn.

"Hey, Lindsey," Sanjay called. "Margie wants to talk to us."

She knew Erin and Brent would be disappointed. They

were great, but there was something about them that made her hesitate. Maybe it was the way Erin always seemed to be checking with Brent, looking his way and saying, *Right, honey?* Or maybe it was because Brent had called her *babe*, which reminded Margie of Jimmy Hunt. Brent couldn't have known that. He was probably a great guy. But Margie was drawn to Sanjay and Lindsey, whose partnership felt more equal. Somehow, in ways she didn't yet understand, she had connected on a deeply personal level with this couple.

On the screen, she saw the dog scampering into view with a tennis ball in his mouth. Behind him came Lindsey in athletic shorts and no shirt, his chest gleaming with sweat. He grabbed a gray T-shirt from the back of a chair and pulled it on.

She suspected that a big factor in her choice was the fact that they were both men. They had exactly zero interest in attacking a woman. But it was more than that. It was the love she read on their faces when they looked at each other, their commitment to openly and fiercely love each other even though society might disapprove. Given its conception during a violent rape, this child might also need that strength of commitment and acceptance.

She took a moment to study their faces on the screen. "Hey, guys."

"Hey, yourself."

"I'll get right to it," she said, feeling the weight of the moment as she gazed at the two strangers. "Lindsey Rockler and Sanjay Rai, I'd like to ask you to adopt my baby."

They both gaped at her and then seemed to melt into each other, their emotions mirroring her own. She didn't bother to hide the tears pouring down her face. "Maxine has the papers for us to work through to make it official, but I wanted to tell you right away."

Truly, over by the car, was crying, too.

"I'm speechless. There will never be words enough to thank you," said Lindsey. "Never in a million years. To be entrusted with this sacred gift is completely overwhelming."

Margie nodded, still making random patterns in the dirt with the branch of catnip. "It's all pretty overwhelming, but I've given this so much thought. We'll get through it, right?" *When you're going through hell, keep going.*

"Absolutely. We can't wait to meet you," Sanjay said. "I mean, if you're open to that."

"Totally. Maxine said we could meet at her office in Austin." She still felt disoriented from her abrupt release. What a strange feeling to have nowhere to go.

"We'll do whatever's most convenient for you," Sanjay told her.

"I literally just walked away from the jail. I need to see if my car will start and figure out where to go from here."

"Do you have someplace to stay?"

"A hotel in Austin tonight. After that, I'll figure something out."

"We want you to have everything you need to move ahead with your life," said Sanjay. "We can offer to help at any level you're comfortable with."

"And by help, he means anything and everything— medical care, counseling, housing, school—just say the word, and we'll make it happen," Lindsey added.

She glanced over at Truly. "I'll let you— *Oh my god.*"

Truly rushed forward. "What's the matter?"

Margie set the laptop aside. A ginger-colored paw extended out from under the porch steps and batted at the catnip sprig she was holding.

"Kevin," she said, waggling the catnip. "Hey, boy, you're here. You're here." He delicately slipped onto her lap—thinner, his fur dusty, but he was purring as he relaxed against her.

"Everything all right there?" asked Lindsey.

"Yeah," she said, holding up Kevin to show them. "Everything's okay. I think everything's going to be okay."

Rebooting a life that had been derailed was not a simple process. From the abandoned house, Margie grabbed a change of clothes, her knives, and her canning set. She broke down again when she found her mother's overstuffed binder filled with recipes and notes. Everything else could be replaced, but not that.

The Toyota's engine coughed a few times and then turned over. Margie left it running and got out to tell Truly goodbye.

"You've been a lifesaver," she told the other woman.

"Well, I think you're incredible. I've never known anyone like you, Margie. I'll never forget you."

"Same here. Maybe we'll stay in touch."

"I'd like that. It'd be nice to hang out without a window between us."

"Oh, hell, yes," Margie said and gave Truly a big hug. "I better get going. Maxine got me a room at some hotel in the city." She checked her phone. "The Driskill."

"You're kidding. Have you been there?"

Margie shook her head. "I've never stayed at a hotel in my life."

"Brace yourself, then. The Driskill is quite a step up from county jail."

"Really?"

"Wait until you see." Truly smiled and offered her a stick of gum.

Her next stop was to meet with Maxine at her office in Austin. Margie got lost several times looking for it and then discovered that her new phone had a map feature. The office was in an old-fashioned, unassuming building not far from the courthouse. The outer office had a display wall with pictures of happy families and testimonials about successful adoptions. Maxine greeted her with a hug. Margie couldn't believe how much she missed hugging.

"This is going to go so well," Maxine said. "I have such a good feeling about it." She explained the documents in detail and reassured Margie that nothing would be final until after the birth. "Sanjay and Lindsey want to be close allies," she said. "It's your choice. Entirely up to you."

"I guess I don't mind having allies."

"Now, in addition to covering all your medical expenses, this couple is prepared to offer additional support. You're under no obligation to accept their help, but their offer is exceedingly generous. They would like to provide any housing of your choice, as well as counseling, education, and training in any field you choose."

"That's . . . I don't really know what to say. It seems like too much." Housing of her choice? Education? Seriously? It sounded too good to be true.

"They're fully committed to this process with you. Remember, there's no pressure to accept any of this, and there are no strings attached."

"Unbelievable. I don't know what to say."

"You chose well. I've been doing this for a long time and I believe you've made a wonderful choice for your baby. Even more important, *they* chose well, Margie."

"They said they want to meet with me in person," Margie said.

"That's up to you entirely. I've met with them several times, and they are exactly as nice as you want them to be."

"I do want to meet them." Yes. She wanted to see where the child would live. The rooms where it would play and eat and sleep. What the air felt like in the house where he or she would grow up. The quality of the light. The smell of things.

"Does tomorrow work for you?"

Her future was entirely blank. No job. No home. A hotel room for the night. "Sure," she said.

"All right. You get checked in to your hotel. I bet you'd love a nice hot shower and room service, and a good night's sleep."

"Sounds like heaven."

"If there's anything you need—from a toothbrush to a nightgown to a change of clothes for tomorrow—you can get that at the hotel and put it on the room tab. I mean it, Margie. Don't hesitate."

"Um . . . so do I just walk in the hotel and check in?" It was kind of embarrassing that she had literally never stayed in a hotel or even a motel.

"Exactly." Maxine paused. "Find the registration desk and they'll help you out. Get used to reaching out for help, Margie. You're going through a lot of changes all at once, but this is a good one. I promise."

"I need to bring Kevin," she said. "He'll be in his crate, but he's coming with me."

"I'll call ahead and make sure they can accommodate your cat."

Margie's new phone navigated her to the Driskill Hotel. As she drove up to the hotel entrance, two guys in doorman uniforms instantly opened the car door and greeted her by name. Maxine must have called ahead. There was a valet to park her car—another first. She was embarrassed at how old and dusty it was. They carried the cat crate and her bag—a reusable sack from H-E-B—into a palatial marble and pillar lobby with a stained-glass dome and a sweeping grand staircase, and artwork that looked as if it belonged in a museum. She signed a card and was escorted to a suite with a balcony overlooking a trendy downtown street abuzz with cafés and shops. She was overwhelmed by the pristine furniture and fixtures, the gleaming bathroom, complete with a litter box, the bucket of ice and bowl of fruit and snacks with a card—compliments of the manager. It blew her mind that, only the night before, she'd been in a cinder block hellhole. This didn't even feel like real life.

"Oh, Kevin," Margie said. "We're not in Kansas anymore."

20

The next morning, Maxine arrived in her SUV to take Margie to meet the chosen parents. "How was your evening?" Maxine asked.

"Unbelievable," Margie said. "I took a two-hour bath and read a book called *Eat Pray Love*, and ordered room service, and watched TV, and slept really well for the first time in five months." She was wearing a simple tunic dress and sandals, which she'd found in the hotel gift shop. "I can't thank you enough."

"Don't thank me," Maxine said. "The hotel is courtesy of Lindsey and Sanjay. They want you to have a safe, comfortable place. You can stay as long as you like, so there's no rush to figure out where you want to settle."

"That's . . . Wow." She'd seen a card on the door—three hundred dollars a night. The tab for her room service order had been breathtaking. "It's really expensive."

"Don't worry about the expense. They don't want you to worry about anything."

"And it's okay if I bring Kevin in his crate? I can't leave him alone in the room."

"Of course. He's part of the family."

Margie loaded up the cat and buckled herself in. She flipped down the visor and peered at her reflection in the mirror. The hotel's fancy shampoo was way better than the harsh soaps at the jail, and she'd taken special care with her hair. "Do I look okay?"

"Sure you do. You look beautiful."

She was quiet as the freeways and busy commercial arteries and subdivisions glided past, eventually giving way to an old and beautiful section of town. Stately live oaks shaded the boulevards, and the streets had interesting names like Paloma Avenue and Bull Mountain Cove and Toreador Drive. Most of the homes weren't visible from the street but were protected by ivy-clad walls built of Hill Country stone and wrought iron. Margie caught the occasional glimpse of vast, well-kept gardens.

When they turned into a deeply wooded driveway and passed a gatehouse marked *Rockler & Rai*, she caught her breath. "This is where they live?"

Maxine nodded. "It's lovely, isn't it?"

"Shitfire," said Margie. "You didn't tell me they're rich."

"They are a wonderful couple and they've been very successful." Maxine drove forward slowly.

Margie gazed at the sweeping gardens and focused on what looked like a château in the distance. "Are they too good to be true?"

"Not this pair," said Maxine. "They're the real thing. I've been working with them for several years. They have shown superhuman patience and understanding every step of the way, and they've endured a lot of challenges."

"You mean the two other adoptions that didn't work out."

"They told you about that?"

"When I called them yesterday. There was a surrogate who had two miscarriages, and a birth mother who decided to stay with the baby's daddy. I guess that must've been tough."

"This entire process is filled with risk. The rewards are amazing, but sometimes it can be a hard and heart-breaking journey."

"I'll try not to break their hearts."

Pulling up to an iron gate, Maxine touched a keypad, and the gate rolled open with a mechanical whir. The driveway took them past manicured lawns and a tennis court. Beyond that was an infinity pool overlooking the west Austin hills. They parked on the circular drive in front of the elegant stone house. Twin curved staircases led to the grand entryway.

"Okay, we're *really* not in Kansas anymore," Margie whispered to Kevin in his crate. "Shitfire," she said again. "Excuse my language, but shitfire. Why didn't you tell me?"

Maxine glanced over at her. "I think you know the answer to that."

Margie nodded. "You're right. I'm glad I didn't know." A nervous hum started up in her gut. The Hunts were rich, too. Rich people knew how to work the system and how to take advantage of people like Margie. *These guys had better be different*, she thought.

As soon as they got out of the car, Lindsey and Sanjay came rushing out of the house and down the stairs. They stood with arms open in welcome and tears in their eyes.

"I'm Lindsey," said Lindsey.

"I'm Sanjay," said Sanjay.

"I know," said Margie. "It's real nice to meet y'all."

There was paperwork and chitchat and a delicious meal. Margie had missed good food more than she could have imagined. "We didn't know what you liked so we asked Rosalia to make a bit of everything," Sanjay said.

Compared to jail food, this was a five-star feast. There

was tender chicken in an intriguing adobo sauce, served with tortillas fresh off the griddle, a cheeseburger with all the fixings, shrimp and grits, a salad with a cheese she'd never had before—burrata, it was called—and three kinds of cookies with ice cream for dessert.

In a matter of hours, Margie's life changed from a morass of uncertainty and despair to an unexpected situation that offered something that felt like security and hope. Maybe. She still felt vaguely cynical and suspicious. They were rich guys—like the Hunts. She was a girl with nothing but the scars from being assaulted by Jimmy Hunt and abused by the system. And these guys had just swept in with the ultimate ask: they wanted her baby.

Yet so far, Lindsey and Sanjay were respectful of her every wish. They claimed they didn't want her to feel that this was a transaction, that she was trading a child for the advantages they could give her.

They offered to provide a home during her pregnancy—anything she chose. A cottage near the UT campus. A condo close to the hospital. A guesthouse on their property with its own private garden, and daily maid service.

She chose the guesthouse. It reminded her of the perfect miniature dollhouse she had seen that long-ago day when she'd met the Falcon sisters, Autumn and Tamara. Now that she was going to place her own baby for adoption, she often thought about that day. A life could be determined in the blink of an eye. The tap of a finger on a mouse pad. An entire life. Would the child love it here, surrounded by luxury, with every need fulfilled by eager, indulgent fathers? Or would he or she turn into a cynical teenager like those girls?

Margie would never know. But for the next few

months, she was happy enough to bring Kevin into the perfectly ordered little guesthouse with its shelves full of books and crisp linens and tiny efficiency kitchen.

"You set the boundaries and we will respect them," Sanjay said to her after she was settled in. "Our goal is for you to feel supported, whatever that looks like to you. Come and go as you please. We'll just be your mostly quiet neighbors."

With regular medical care for the first time in her life, Margie was learning all kinds of things. She had no cavities and 20/20 vision. Her blood type was A-positive. Basically, she was healthy—if somewhat underweight—and despite the weeks of sickness, the baby was healthy, too. The baby. The *baby*. Margie was still trying to get used to the idea. She'd always assumed that one day, she would be a mom, but it had been a vague, distant notion. And this wasn't like that. This was like . . . renting out temporary space in her body.

The issue of greatest concern was anxiety, which might be the reason she puked so much. The doctor recommended counseling with a sexual assault trauma specialist. Seeing a therapist was such a foreign notion to Margie that she didn't know what to expect. The therapist's name was Elke Taylor and she mostly listened and validated. She said it was important for Margie to find her own way so that she felt empowered to make decisions and move forward with her life. There was no magic formula to make the nightmare of the past go away.

Elke recommended a course in self-defense tailored to survivors of assault. At first, Margie was intimidated by the drills, which were conducted by masked and padded assailants; then her confidence grew as she learned that when confronted with a threat and de-escalation wasn't possible, there were ways to kick an assailant's ass, no matter how large and powerful he might be.

Even though they wouldn't let Margie practice any risky moves because of the pregnancy, the class and the therapy sessions helped. She learned to detach from the relentless flashbacks to the night Jimmy Hunt had raped her. Her memories of the attack were gradually becoming new memories of mastery and control over the situation.

Every once in a while she felt something like a warm light inside, and she realized that this was what hope felt like.

Sometimes in the evening, Lindsey and Sanjay would invite her over. They were tentative at first, not wanting to intrude, but she liked their company and their amazing house. Her favorite room was their library. Every single wall from floor to ceiling was lined with books, and she went crazy reading. Lindsey seemed to have read every book in the room, and he loved discussing them with her. She was glad for the company, and she especially loved listening to Sanjay play the piano. One night, he set up a karaoke screen for a sing-along. Her voice wasn't much to boast about, but she could carry a tune. She performed a passable rendition of what she now considered her anthem—"Irreplaceable" by Beyoncé.

One night after dinner, she drummed up the courage to speak up about the food. It was healthy and mostly well-prepared, but Margie missed cooking. Elke encouraged her to find meaning in self-expression of all kinds. For Margie, that meant drawing and sketching her fantasy restaurant, the one she and her mother used to dream about, pretending it would actually happen one day. She missed being in the kitchen, so she took a chance and said, "Listen, I know you guys have a really good chef and all, but I wish you'd let me cook for you sometime."

"We thought you'd never ask," said Lindsey. "Make a list of everything you need."

It was the kind of feast she loved to fix. She made her falling-apart-tender ribs, smoked on the way-too-fancy patio barbecue and finished in a slow oven. She prepared three kinds of sauce and her very best sides—homemade cornbread with pepper jelly, plates of slow-simmered greens in pot liquor, and a salad of heirloom tomatoes and grilled peaches and herbs from the local farmers' market, topped with a scoop of burrata cheese. Hummingbird cake for dessert, because who didn't like a hummingbird cake?

As they sat down to the meal, Margie vacillated between shrinking apprehension and grand self-confidence. When the guys tasted her food, their faces told her she had nailed it.

"This is so damn good I might break down and cry," Sanjay said.

"It's utterly delicious," Lindsey agreed. "You, young lady, have an amazing talent."

"Thanks. I really love what I do." She told them about her small-batch sauce production, and they seemed intrigued.

After that, they invited her to showcase her skills anytime she felt like it. She made them honey butter fried chicken and buttermilk biscuits the way her mother had taught her, with White Lily flour and the butter shredded on a box grater. She served charred eggplant with cilantro pesto, polenta pasticciata, grilled corn, and fried dill pickles. Eventually Margie got out her mother's pressure canner and took up her sauce-making operation again.

They went bonkers over her cooking. One night, Sanjay asked, "What do you want your life to look like after the baby is born?"

"I guess I'll get work someplace. Restaurant work. I'm good at it and it's what I like to do. The manager of the breakfast place at the country club down the hill already said they'd hire me." Sanjay and Lindsey were members of the club, and she was authorized to dine there on their membership anytime she wished. She never did, though. The dining room was so fussy and ostentatious. She felt more at home with the tattooed cooks and waitstaff who lounged in the alley behind the kitchen.

"You want to work there?" asked Sanjay.

"I've always worked. Longest time I ever took off was when I was in jail."

"Suppose you could do anything you wanted. Anything at all. What would *that* look like?"

She thought about that for a while. Her mother used to praise her for being so smart in school, for always getting high marks. "Whatever you do," Mama used to tell her, "follow your star."

"What's my star, Mama?" Margie loved asking the question because she loved her mother's answer.

"Well, that would be whatever keeps drawing you to do what you most want."

Now she looked at Sanjay and Lindsey. "Well, I reckon whoever made me figured out that I should fix food for people."

"Makes perfect sense," said Lindsey. "The happiest people I know are people doing what they love to do."

She showed them the overstuffed book filled with her recipes. She had also added pages with her drawings and sketches for the restaurant she'd always fantasized about. At night when she couldn't sleep and was haunted by anxiety, she worked on the project. The drawings became more intricate, her vision sharper.

She laid the pages on the kitchen bar and took them on a tour through her dream. "I've always wanted a restaurant. A barbecue restaurant," she said. Working at Cubby's place, she knew how challenging it would be. But she also knew the deep satisfaction of creating a good kitchen and a fine dining room. It was hard to describe the feeling she got from serving delighted patrons, or the creative rush that came with making her sauces. To Margie, it felt like a life that made sense and kept her heart connected to her mother—fixing tasty food and making people happy.

She told them about her mother's sandwiches and about how much she'd learned from Cubby Watson. Then she said, "San Francisco." She blurted it out, flashing on an article she'd saved from a tattered old magazine. "That's a place I'd like to go. That's where I'd open a restaurant."

"I like the way you think," said Sanjay. "I hope it happens for you one day."

"What's your plan?" asked Lindsey.

She gathered up her notes and tucked them away. "I don't have a plan. Just a ton of ideas."

"If your dream is to have your own restaurant, then that's what you should do."

"It'd sure be nice," she said.

"You don't think it's possible?" asked Lindsey.

She shrugged. "I mean, come on. We're talking about something that would be years in the making. It'd take more money and know-how than I have. It's too big to get my head around."

Sanjay leaned back in his chair and eyed his husband. "Uh-oh. He's all fired up now."

"I can't help myself," Lindsey said. "I was about your age when I had the idea for GreenTech, my first start-up. I had run out of money for tuition, so I had to leave school to save up for more. And I did it by following my dream."

Lindsey Rockler's success was a big story, big enough that several books had been written about it. And a documentary was produced for TV. It had even been on *60 Minutes*. His company now developed apps—applications—that worked on the iPhone everybody was so crazy about.

Whoever this baby turns out to be, Margie thought, *is going to be one lucky kid.*

"I won't tell you it was easy," Lindsey said, "because it wasn't. It's all a matter of wanting something bad enough that you're willing to make a plan and work your ass off to get it."

"I know how to work hard," she assured them. "I'm not so sure about business and finance, though."

"That can be learned," Lindsey said.

In her therapy sessions, Margie came to realize that the most important component of her recovery was taking responsibility for her own life. Loss of control was at the root of her deepest issue. Reclaiming that control was key to conquering the demons that sneaked into the darkest corners of the night. Elke also reminded her that knowing how and when to reach out for help was empowering, too.

"I know what I know," she told them. "But maybe more importantly, I know what I don't know. I could use your help figuring that out."

They exchanged a glance and said it again: "We thought you'd never ask."

Margie listed everything she would need to learn—not just how to make the best barbecue in the world but how to run the whole house, front to back. She knew it would be a steep climb, taking years, probably, but if it was worth having, it was worth working for.

Lindsey and Sanjay were all in with her plan. This was a revelation to Margie. She'd never had someone to help her connect the dots from where she was to where she wanted to go. Her mother had lived simply from day to day, like a butterfly in summertime, gathering nectar. Mama never worried about the future. With Lindsey as her mentor, Margie realized that making a plan gave her the sense of security she'd never had before.

Mapping out her future wasn't easy. It wasn't perfect. It didn't fill the deep void of loneliness that haunted her in the middle of the night. But it was a start.

When she enrolled in her first community college classes, Lindsey and Sanjay uncorked a bottle of champagne and a bottle of Topo Chico for Margie. "To new beginnings," Sanjay said.

"New beginnings," Margie echoed, regarding them with a sudden wave of emotion. For these few short months, they were more than mentors. They felt like family. She'd always known leaving her baby would be hard. Now she realized it would be hard to leave Sanjay and Lindsey, too. She tapped her glass against theirs. "How's the champagne?"

Lindsey put a cork in it. "You're too young and too pregnant to drink."

Margie's doctor recommended a daily walk, and Elke encouraged her to explore the practice of yoga. She joined a studio that offered a class for pregnant women, and it was a half mile down the road from the house.

"Mind if Wally and I join you on your walk today?" Sanjay asked as she came out of the cottage.

"Sure," she said, shouldering a bag with her mat and water bottle. She put on shades and a floppy-brimmed sun hat. "I'd love the company."

"You don't socialize much." He clipped a leash on the dog. "By choice? Or because you haven't met anybody?"

"I'm social," she said. "With people from work at the country club. And I made a couple of friends at school. But . . . now that I'm showing, I get all the questions, you know?"

Wally scampered along the row of bursting pink crape myrtles that lined the driveway. They went out to a hiking trail that wound down to the main road.

"I don't know, but I can guess. Like when are you due, and do you know if it's a boy or girl? Have you picked out names yet? Are you planning to be a stay-at-home mom . . . ? That sort of thing?"

"Exactly that sort of thing. I mean, I have no trouble explaining that I'm a birth mom and the baby will be placed for adoption. That either creates an awkward pause, or a slew of other questions. People don't mean to be rude, but sometimes I feel like they're judging me. Like, you look perfectly healthy and comfortable. Why would you give your baby away? Of course, I could also explain what happened to me, but how far down the rabbit hole do I want to take people with me?"

"I'm sorry. That must suck sometimes."

She gave him a sideways glance. Sanjay was remarkable-looking. He said he was forty but looked much younger, with an elite athlete's build and wavy golden hair. "You're probably going to get your share of awkward moments when you and Lindsey start going around with a little kid."

He grinned. "I can handle it. I'm looking forward to having to handle it."

He and Lindsey had not yet gone wide with their news. They probably didn't want to jinx their chances to adopt the baby. The adoption would not be complete until the moment Margie signed over her parental rights.

There was virtually no part of her that wanted to keep the baby for herself.

Still, she was learning that the whole world could change in an instant, whether you wanted it to or not. There was the tiniest sliver of her soul that was reserved for the possibility that the baby she was incubating inside her might be the most powerful force in the universe, so powerful she wouldn't be able to walk away.

Then she would remember Jimmy Hunt and think, *Yeah, right.*

The hike down through the ravine took them to a busy road lined with upscale salons, dim sum places, taquerias, boutiques and home goods shops, and fitness centers.

It was a gorgeous fall morning. They passed nannies pushing prams, joggers, and yard guys getting to work on the edging and pruning. It was a far cry from mornings at the Arroyo, where people went around cleaning up broken bottles and fast-food wrappers and drug paraphernalia. This was the world her baby would be born into.

Margie wondered how her life might have unfolded if she'd grown up in a neighborhood like this.

Across the tree-shaded boulevard, a woman got out of a late-model car and crossed the road, heading purposefully in their direction. She carried a manila envelope with a clipboard, like maybe she was collecting signatures on a petition. Wally stood stiff-legged, and a defensive ridge rose along his back as he emitted a soft, cautious growl.

Sanjay gave the leash a tug. "Hey, boy," he murmured.

"Margie Salinas?" the woman asked with a falsely bright smile.

Margie stepped back. How did this stranger know her? "Who are you?"

The woman passed her the envelope, pressing it into her hands. "You've been served."

Then she pivoted on her heel and headed back to her car.

"Hey," Margie called. "What's this about?"

The woman didn't turn, but waved a noncommittal arm, then got in her car and drove away.

Margie looked up at Sanjay. "What the hell was that?"

"She acted like a process server."

Margie knew what a process server was. She'd read about it in jail. It was someone who made sure a legal summons was placed directly into the recipient's hands.

"Let's see what she handed you," said Sanjay.

They sat on a nearby bus stop bench. With shaking hands, she opened the envelope. A legal summons sounded scary. Together, she and Sanjay scanned the papers.

The Hunts again. They had registered with the putative father registry on behalf of their deceased son.

She knew her face was dead white when she faced Sanjay. "What the hell is that?"

"It's a way to document paternity," Sanjay said.

There was a statement from Jimmy's parents, declaring their intent to assume the father figure role, providing support and custody, to retain parental rights.

"Wait, so the Hunts are still saying they have the right to this baby?" she demanded. Her stomach felt as if it had flipped over. Then she realized it was the baby moving.

"Let's go back to the house and sort this out." The normally affable, cool, and chill Sanjay had turned as white as chalk. He sent a text message to Lindsey, and his strides were long and agitated as they headed back home. Margie half ran to keep up.

Lindsey met them at the door. He grabbed the multi-page document and scanned it to send off to one of the many lawyers who worked for them.

"They're claiming parental rights," Sanjay said, and then dug deeper into the document. "They claim we're not qualified because we don't embrace Christian values."

"What?" Margie gave a bark of joyless laughter. "Sorry, I know this is not funny. But *what the hell*?"

Apparently the Hunts had somehow unearthed details of her adoption. "Christian values," she spat. "I know what real Christians are like. I worshipped with them in Cubby and Queen's church, and none of them went around raping women and putting the victims in jail. I can't believe they're saying these things about me, and especially about y'all."

"Trust me, we've heard it all," said Lindsey. "Sometimes from people who actually matter to us."

"I'm sorry. That sucks. For the record, I think you're fantastic."

She had been judged and criticized plenty for being poor, and a dropout, and a white girl attending a Black church, but she'd never been put down for who she loved. Not that she had ever loved anybody the way Sanjay and Lindsey loved each other, but if she were ever to find a love like that, she wouldn't be condemned for it.

"That's nice of you to say," Lindsey told her. He was usually so upbeat, but now his voice was weary.

"I'm being honest. I read like a hundred profiles before I found you guys, and almost all the couples were awesome. But you led the pack." Now that she knew them better, she admired them even more for putting up an honest profile that showed who they were without flaunting their wealth.

"We're going to get this dismissed so fast their stupid heads will spin," Lindsey declared.

And sure enough, within minutes, his phone came to silent life on the table. He touched the screen to dismiss the call, but not before Margie noticed the caller's name. A knot hardened in her stomach.

"That call came from Terence Swift."

He nodded. "That's right."

"The lawyer who got the charges against me dropped."

"Yes."

"He's your lawyer?"

"We do business with his firm."

She mentally connected the dots. "You paid him to get me out of jail."

"He was paid via a private grant."

"And let me guess. You made the private grant." She looked from one to the other. "Were you planning on telling me? Ever?"

"We didn't mean to deceive you," Lindsey said. "Our only goal was to get you the best representation available. It's a sad fact that sometimes money can buy a better defense."

"I hadn't even decided on you guys yet."

"Doesn't matter. If you hadn't chosen us, we still would have funded your defense."

"It's too much," she protested. "Why would you do that?"

"Because it's the right thing to do," Lindsey said. "We've worked hard all our lives. We've been lucky enough to have the means to furnish the best possible help for you, and that's what we did. It's not a handout, Margie. You're entitled to justice. This is not a transaction. It's an act of love."

"Is it?" she asked. "I don't even know anymore. It feels like an act of survival." She pressed her hands to her stomach. "Don't get me wrong—I'm grateful for everything you've done for me. All this"—she gestured around the room—"seems too good to be true sometimes. I've never had a reason to trust in my own luck."

An associate from Mr. Swift's firm showed up right away. He was in the civil division, and he explained the action in more detail. "They're trying to check all the boxes," he said. "They've set aside an escrow account to prove they're serious about providing support. They're furnishing statements from character witnesses, like their pastor and community leaders."

Margie cringed. "All I know is that the boy they raised turned out to be a bully and a rapist. And now they want to raise another kid? Because they did such a good job on Jimmy?" She felt angry and ill. *Please don't be like the man who fathered you*, she silently told the child, over and over again. "What am I going to do? Can I just throw this in the trash?"

"Once you get served, it's a bad idea to ignore the summons."

She shuddered. "Do I have to go back to the courthouse? Will I have to see those people?"

"Absolutely not."

In fairly short order, Mr. Swift's associate found that the Hunts had accessed confidential information to find out Margie's plan and track her down. Even more appalling, they had used material from her rape kit to verify paternity. It probably hadn't been hard, given their connections in the county. But no judge, not even the Hunts' good buddies, could allow the suit to go forward. To her relief, the action was quickly dismissed. She wasn't sure how, and she didn't much care.

After the summons scare, Margie's life settled into a routine that was happily uneventful. Mornings were a pleasant, almost surreal surprise as she awoke in a beautiful cottage surrounded by a garden with her cat slumbering nearby. She felt like Snow White, hidden away from the world by men whose only aim was to protect her. But unlike the fairy-tale princess, Margie didn't dream of Prince Charming.

Instead, she designed the future she wanted for herself. She worked the lunch service at the country club and attended school, following a restaurant management track. She took her vitamins and went to the doctor, to her yoga practice, and to her self-defense class. She studied gardening and sourcing, bookkeeping and hospitality management. It was as if she was exploding with newness, her mind expanding along with the new life inside her. Sometimes her dreams felt so big they nearly crushed her with their weight. Other times, she nearly floated away on a cloud of grandeur.

Most nights, Margie's anxieties still closed around her throat like Jimmy Hunt's big hands, choking off her airway, starving her brain of oxygen. She took deep yoga breaths. Inhale, two, three, four. Hold, two, three, four. Exhale, two, three, four . . . There were a few blissful nights of sleep, and she savored these.

The baby grew willfully. Uncomfortably. A force beyond her control. When she looked down at her body, it didn't even seem like hers. It was strange and misshapen.

Her OB's office signed her up for childbirth preparation classes. Though apprehensive, she showed up for the first session at the hospital. There were five couples and Margie, and almost immediately, she could see the speculation in their glances. The instructor, a labor and delivery nurse who looked like a storybook grandma, invited each couple to introduce themselves and say a bit about their anticipated birth. There were Sonny and Zoe, who cuddled and giggled. Chad and Sally, bashful and blushing even as they burst with pride. Cindy and Peter—newlywed triathletes. Margie missed the names of the others due to the panic that crescendoed in her ears.

The introductions turned into touching tales of falling in love and conceiving a child, picking out names and dreaming of the family they were creating. By the time Margie's turn came up, she was on the verge of a full-blown anxiety attack. After all the heartwarming stories, she couldn't quite bring herself to tell the group *A guy raped me and I shot him dead, missed my chance to have an abortion, and now I'm giving the baby to a gay couple.*

Instead, she mumbled something about not feeling well, stepped out of the room, and ran all the way to the parking lot. In her car with the doors locked, she broke down, deep sobs roaring through her and engulfing the hard orb of her baby bump. There was no end to what Jimmy Hunt had taken from her. She would never find a love like the couples in the class. She would never have a sweet origin story to tell about her baby. This child had been conceived in violence and pain and injustice, and its story was a dark tale that could never be rewritten.

Once she managed to calm down, she left a message with the doctor that she wouldn't be attending further classes. She knew the importance of being prepared, but she was learning to listen to herself. If something didn't feel right to her, then it wasn't right. She simply could not sit with a group of happy couples so eagerly awaiting their babies with joyful anticipation.

When she got home, she invited Sanjay and Lindsey to tour the hospital birthing center with her and to attend a private meeting with her birth coach.

At her next checkup, the doctor asked if she wanted to learn the baby's sex. The fetus looked like the inner curve of a baseball mitt, but she couldn't work out its sex.

No, thank you, she said. She was trying not to imagine the child in her life. It seemed easier that way.

21

The baby came in the middle of a storm, an epic Texas blue norther that walloped the city with lashes of wind-driven rain and sleet barreling in from the west.

Margie went to grab a bagel—her second of the day—when she peed herself. Realizing what was happening, she froze for about three seconds.

Then she whispered "shitfire" under her breath and went to find the dads.

The ride to the hospital passed in a blur, and within minutes, Margie was in a private birthing suite. Labor was hard and swift, the contractions gathering force and rolling over her in great crashing waves. The pain was so intense that it didn't even feel like pain, more like a force of nature that felt powerful enough to lift her off the bed. The birth coach brought her through the contractions like a lifeguard throwing out a line, waiting for her to grasp on, and reeling her back in.

In the lull between contractions, she felt strangely detached from the situation. Despite the busy personnel around her, she was alone here. She had no supportive partner or best friend or mom by her side. Oh, how she missed her mama in those moments. For the first time, she wondered who had been there for Mama when Margie was born. Margie regretted that she had never asked her. Mama had been all alone, too. Probably not in a fancy

suite like this, though. Probably not with a hired coach
and doula and private nurse to ease her through the ordeal.

The plan was to have an epidural to block the pain
from her waist down. When they had first explained the
process to Margie, it had sounded risky and painful, but
now she couldn't wait for something—anything—that
would take away the explosions that racked her body.

But just like everything else, when it came to birthing a baby, timing was everything. When you were making pecan-smoked honey brisket at Cubby's, you had to
cook the meats slowly and then, at just the right moment,
finish them in the radiant salamander broiler to achieve
that delicate caramelized crust. In the birthing center,
when you needed to inject something into the spine of
a woman in labor, it had to happen at the optimal time.

"Your labor went faster than average, and you're already at eight or nine centimeters," said Dr. Wolf, holding up her gloved hand in what looked like a Vulcan
salute. "And the anesthesiologist is delayed with another
patient."

Margie's teeth chattered. "How long . . . ?"

"I can't say. You have to be able to sit up and hold still
for a three-inch needle stick, and then it takes about ten
minutes to set in. The birth is imminent, so we might
have missed the window . . ."

The rest of the explanation disappeared into the fog
of the next contraction. Margie understood only that the
thing that was supposed to take the pain away was no
longer an option. She opened her mouth, and what came
out was some kind of howl that echoed like a sound ef-
fect in a horror movie.

"There is a silver lining," said the birth coach. "Now
that you're fully dilated, you can push."

They had told her that with first babies, the pushing

sometimes lasted for hours and hours. The prospect of straining all day in the grip of this agony was unacceptable to Margie. The moment they gave her the green light, she bore down with everything she had.

There was a commotion at the end of the bed. People in scrubs and masks moved quickly into position. The labor nurse, a technician, and the nursery nurse gathered around. The pediatrician arrived, her shoes making purposeful squishy sounds on the linoleum. Another nurse stood by at the computer stand by the door.

As Margie wound up for another push, another woman arrived, introducing herself as Dr. Wolf's OB tech. She pushed a wheeled tray covered with instruments in sealed parcels. In her long coat and mask and face shield, Dr. Wolf positioned herself between Margie's legs like a baseball coach at home plate.

"Nice work," she said. "We're nearly there. How you doing?"

"Can I be done?" Margie gasped.

"You're in charge. Here we go," said the doctor. "You're doing great. Total rock star."

They coached her through the final breathing and pushing. There was a rush of movement and another flurry of activity, and the baby was suddenly there, out in the world, dark red and slick with pasty vernix. The room was curiously silent except for Margie's own gasps for breath. A thundering pain rolled over her one more time, this one muted and quickly gone—the placenta, part of the baby's temporary home, evicted for good.

The pain ended instantly, as if it had never happened, and a floating sense of wonder took its place. People in the room were murmuring to one another, their gazes connecting over the pleated masks, eyes crinkling behind the shields.

Then there was another sound—the staccato bleating of a lamb.

"Ready to hold your little one?" asked the coach.

Margie was weirdly numb, but also loose and relaxed, her body unburdened at last. "Yes," she said. "Yes. All right."

She had been advised to hold and bond with the child she was going to give away forever. It was the start of the ritual of letting go. Grief would be inevitable, and hiding the newborn from its mother would not make it less so.

The lights had been dimmed for the sake of the baby. Margie could see its smear of dark hair and slightly pushed-in face, colorless unfocused eyes that were somehow trained on her face. Her arms came up and around, and a tiny foot escaped the turquoise draping and was, for a moment, silhouetted against the ceiling, looking impossibly vulnerable and powerful at the same time.

A feeling rolled over her, something so powerful that she couldn't even think of a word to name it, as if a new emotion had been invented just for this moment.

She took it all in, the sweet weight resting on her chest, the oddly familiar stretching movements of the baby now emerged from its dark cocoon, the quiet snuffling sounds, the surprised starfish shape of a tiny hand.

After a long time, the birth coach moved in close. "How you doing, sweet mama?"

"Good," Margie said, her voice cracking over the word. She cleared her throat, tried again. "I'm good."

"You did it. You were amazing. Absolutely amazing. It was a dream birth—fast and focused."

Margie couldn't stop staring at the bundle in her arms, warm and vibrant and flushed with the color of life. There was no force in the universe powerful enough to take it from her.

"Boy or girl?" she whispered, shocked to realize she didn't know yet.

"A boy," said the coach. "A perfect little boy."

The unnameable emotion shuddered through her again, trailing over every cell in her body like the tail of a comet. The feeling settled into her bones, and she knew it would dwell there forever, a connection with this baby despite the circumstances of his conception. *Look what I did*, she thought. *Look what I did*.

There was a powerful urge to curl herself around the child and let the world fade away. Adrift in a dreamlike state made of exhaustion, relief, and elation, she yearned for hours and days and weeks and decades to be able to process what had just happened, to discover each and every detail of him.

But there was something she had to do. Her arms didn't want her to do it. Her heart and soul didn't want her to do it.

Margie looked at the beautiful face, the nose, the rosy little mouth, the delicate neck and clavicles of her little boy, this stranger who had grown under her heart and was now a fully formed, separate human being. She leaned down and put her lips to his perfect seashell ear. The scent of him was like nothing else in the world, and she knew she would remember it until her dying day. "You're here. I can't believe you're here," she whispered, her breath making no sound. "I wish someday you could know that you saved my life. Really, you did. When I didn't want you, when I wanted to get rid of you, when all I wanted was for you to be gone, you gave me a purpose. You made my life matter. Carrying you was the only thing that kept me alive."

The gratitude she felt was powerful enough to move mountains, yet at the same time, she was filled with the deepest grief she'd ever felt, deeper even than her grief for her mother.

Yes, there was something she had to do.

This is the end of our story together, she said to him, her heart speaking to his as she pressed her lips to that tiny ear again, and then to his forehead.

The sweat and tears were drowning her, but Margie pulled the words from a reserve of strength she didn't know she had.

"He needs to meet his dads," she said.

Lindsey and Sanjay must have been only a few steps away, because they were there in a flash, draped in gowns and masks. Sanjay seemed to stumble against Lindsey, who propped him up.

"Margie, honey," Sanjay whispered.

She knew her smile was tinged by the wrenching emotions pressing at her chest, almost too big to contain. "Would you like to hold your son?"

The nurse brought them chairs, which was probably a good idea because the guys both seemed unsteady, weak in the knees.

Margie's arms did not want to surrender the baby, but somehow she allowed the nurse to scoop him away. Within moments, the child was encircled in a pod between the two men. She took off her mother's hospital bracelet and put it on Lindsey's wrist.

The new parents held each other and the baby, their hands and arms strong but trembling. Tears dampened their masks as they stared at the little stranger with the same intensity she had felt. Like her, they couldn't look away. Like her, they couldn't bear to let go.

Part Four

To tell the truth is a beautiful act
even if the truth itself is ugly.

—Glen Duncan, British author

22

Margot looked out at the view of the bay, with the orange web of the Golden Gate Bridge scoring the horizon. In the distance, a schooner sailed past under a sunset sky of deep gold and purple. The cypress-scented breeze had turned chilly as evening fell, and she tucked her arms around her drawn-up knees. The air smelled of the ocean and the scent from the wind-harried evergreen trees. She couldn't read Jerome's expression. Shock? Sadness? Pity?

She felt drained and raw, as if she'd run too far in the hot sun. "Now you know," she said. "I wish it wasn't my story, but I'm stuck with what happened. I spent a long time trying to run from it, but the past is always with me. A part of me. I wanted to tell you now because . . . well, we're getting close, and you have kids, and you deserve to know."

"Ah, Margot. I hate what happened to you, but I don't hate your story, because it's yours. This is . . . I'm sorry as hell to hear what you went through." He stood and helped her to her feet, then caught her against him in a hug that was so tenderly fierce and so encompassing that she ached to melt into him. She laid her cheek against his chest. Pulling back the shroud from her past was exhausting.

"I'm glad you're here now," he said, his words muffled against her hair. "I'm glad you got through that."

"I didn't, not really," she admitted. "What happened . . . it's never really over. It stays with me, no matter where I go or who I'm with."

He took both her hands in his and held on tight. "Damn, girl. Just, damn. I hate the thought of you being hurt like that."

Margot touched her neck, then noticed what she was doing and placed her hand back in Jerome's. She looked down at their joined hands. Her finger had pulled the trigger that had ended a man's life. Would Jerome think about that, now that he knew? "You probably have questions."

"About everything," he agreed. "But the main question is, are you all right?"

She shrugged, looked out over the crumbling cliff. "Sometimes I think I'll never be okay," she said. "Sometimes I think I'm already okay. Most of the time, I'm a mess. I'll always be haunted by the fact that I took a person's life."

"You didn't have a choice."

She touched her neck again, rubbing the lump in her throat. "And all it took to prove it was a lawyer I couldn't afford. When I was in jail, there were delays I thought would never end. I guess I always took equal justice for granted. It was kind of a shock to realize how much depends on access to money and power."

She caught his look. Of course he knew that. As a Black man, he'd seen and experienced inequities. She tried to imagine the outcome of that night if she'd been a woman of color. She probably would have been shot dead the moment the police arrived.

"I'm so damn glad you got through that," said Jerome.

"I . . . Yes. But I traded a baby for my freedom. I have to live with that."

"Come on, now. That's not how it happened."

"Okay, not quite. I did try to get an abortion early on," she reminded him. He had to understand this, because if he had a problem with it, then there was nothing further to discuss. "The idea of being forced to have a baby, giving birth in jail, having the child of my rapist . . . it was horrifying. With every cell in my body, I didn't want to give birth to his child. All I could think about was terminating the pregnancy. I don't know how you feel about that, but I won't apologize for wanting it."

"Not my call to make," he said quickly. "I'd never judge you for ending a pregnancy you don't want. And the fact that you chose adoption—that's amazing."

"No," she said bluntly, "that was an act of desperation. The decision was taken away from me. It did cause something unexpected to happen—it gave me some control over my situation. Turns out a woman choosing adoption, even a woman behind bars, gets a lot more support than a woman who needs an abortion or who plans on keeping her baby."

"What you felt, what you did . . . it's okay, Margot. It's okay."

She shivered, and he put his arm around her and they started walking to the car. "Now it seems . . . appropriate. A life for a life."

"Are you . . . You don't have to answer if it's too confidential. Are you in touch with the child?" His question awakened memories that were as vivid as yesterday, even after so much time had passed. She recalled sitting in a hospital rocking chair and holding the infant against her full, aching breasts as she prepared to let him go. That last goodbye, whispered to the swaddled bundle in her arms, had torn her to shreds.

Her hand had shaken as she signed the relinquishment papers. Although she understood that there was no path back from that point, she couldn't help thinking about the life she might have had with the child, what it would have looked like. Maybe it might have resembled her own childhood with her mother, scratching out a living but finding happiness with each other. Or maybe she would look at the child and see the brutal rapist who had impregnated her. The choice she'd made had taken both options from her.

Even so, her fate was entwined with the little human being she had created. She would never forget the sweet weight of him in her arms. She would never fail to wonder about missing the milestones—birthdays and holidays, his first steps and first words, starting school and learning to ride a two-wheeler, watching all the events of his life unfold. Wherever he went, a part of her went with him.

Sometimes Margot yearned to breach the boundary she had created between herself and the child. His dads would not have objected if she'd wanted to stay nearby, or to keep in touch so she could watch the child living his life with them. But always, she pulled herself away from those impulses and reminded herself to let him live the life she'd chosen for him.

Most of the time, she was at peace with the choice she made for her baby. Still, it was a pain that would never go away, but she managed it.

She tried to explain it to Jerome. "I'm not in touch," she said. "But something happens when you create another being. You have kids so you know this, right? Your fates are entwined. But with adoption, your most sacred creation disappears without you. You can't hold him in your arms, you can't claw at the boundary between you.

It's . . . a hollowness. Like I'm missing a piece of myself."

"Ah, sweet Margot." He tucked her closer to him as they walked.

"At Christmas, I get an annual letter from his dads. They named him Miles. A few years ago, a sister came along. She's a little girl named Jaya, adopted from India. Sanjay—one of the dads—he's from India, too." She brushed at her cheeks.

"That's . . . I wish I knew what to say to fix this for you."

And there it was. She needed fixing. She didn't want to be the girlfriend who needed fixing. "I'm taking care of myself as well as I can. Therapy. Self-defense class. Working my ass off."

"Yeah, but how are you *doing*?"

It was amazing, even a bit disconcerting, to finally talk with someone who wasn't paid to listen to her troubles. "I am clear-eyed about what happened and what I did about it and how it turned out. But to be honest, I can never say I have no regrets. I think about what it would be like to have that child in my life. When I was with your boys today, it really hit me. Not in a bad way," she quickly added, noticing his expression. "It was a reminder. There's a part of me that doesn't ever want to get over missing my child—a little boy I held in my arms only a few times. He's too important to simply forget. I think about him and imagine how it would be if he were here, going for a picnic or learning martial arts moves or being silly like your boys. I picture what his room would look like, and little things like taking him for a haircut, teaching him to swim or ride a bike, all the things you do with a kid. It's a kind of longing, this feeling that washes through me. By now I know better than to fight the feeling. Sometimes I close my eyes and hold still and send out love and kindness from the deepest part of me, and I hope it makes its way to him."

Jerome stopped walking. He swallowed hard, and she saw the gleam of tears in his eyes. "Damn," he said in a broken voice. "I don't know what to say. I wish I'd known you then. I wish I could have protected you."

She wished that, too. Yet if it hadn't happened, she never would have met him.

"I'm glad you're here with me now," he said. "I love the way you put your new life together. I love *you*."

Margot pulled back and looked up at him, her gaze riveted to his. No one, other than her mother, had ever uttered those words to her. He would never know how much it took for Margot to learn not to recoil from getting involved with him. He was worth the effort. He was. If she tried to say something, her voice would break, so she stayed quiet, blinking back tears.

He cupped her cheek in the palm of his hand. "I mean it. This feeling has been building for a while and I've been thinking about it a lot, and wondering if I should tell you or not. You don't have to say anything or do anything, but I wanted to say those words to you and now—"

"Stop," she whispered, placing two fingers against his lips. "Just stop." She put her mouth there and kissed him, and they kissed each other, and the world stopped spinning. After a few minutes, she pulled away and leaned her cheek against his chest. She could feel his warmth and hear the steady rhythm of his heart. "That might be the best kiss ever," she said.

"Plenty more where that came from."

"I have trust issues," she said.

"Understandable. I'll earn your trust."

"It's not you. What I distrust the most is myself—my judgment. I wasn't some random rape victim," she said. "I *chose* him. I went out with him. Invited him into my home, fixed him dinner. What does that say about me?"

"That you were young. That you didn't recognize the red flags. You had no reason to think some guy would hurt you." He tipped her face up to his. "I won't ever hurt you. I swear."

"I want to say the same to you. But I've never been in love before. No one's ever been in love with me before. I'm not sure how it's done."

His soft chuckle warmed her. "You know what I think? I think you've had a hard time in your life. Harder than most. But this isn't the hard part. It's the easy part."

Margot thought about Jerome constantly—his eyes, his hands, his lips. She wasn't falling for him, because falling implied something sudden—an accident, a mistake. No, she was leaning into her feelings for him, and it was exhilarating and scary and it preoccupied her even when she was supposed to be focused on work.

Finally, she screwed up her courage and crossed the kitchen to the Sugar side and found him hard at work at his computer. The air always smelled so sweet in the bakery. "Am I interrupting?"

"Yes." He swiveled around in his chair. "And it's fine. I was just wrapping up for the day."

"Can you come over for dinner on Monday? Also, I'd like you to spend the night." She could feel the licks of color flaming high in her cheeks. Maybe she should have invited him via text message instead of cornering him like this and forcing him to make a snap decision.

A smile spread slowly across his face. "What can I bring?"

"Just your good self."

"That'll be just fine," he said. "See you then."

Margot served Jerome shrimp and grits with a full-bodied Sonoma chardonnay, and lemon chess pie for dessert.

"Oh, honey," he said, helping her clear the table, "that was so good, I feel like you've made love to me already."

"Oh, honey," she said, "I'm just getting started." She took his hand and led him to the bedroom. The cat regarded them quizzically, then slipped off the bed and minced away. Margot was smiling, but her heart was pounding. She had gone on dates, but they had fizzled when she balked at intimacy. She'd tried before and failed, and she didn't want to fail Jerome, because he meant too much to her. He was the first person to make her crave more than intimacy and release. He filled her heart. She gasped softly, and it sounded like a sob.

"You okay?" he asked, holding her against him.

"Yes, I'm . . . Yes. But this is a lot. You're a lot." She took a breath. "You have a lot of love in your life, Jerome. You know what that feels like. But me. I'm just finding out."

"For what it's worth," he said, "I've never felt this way for anyone. Until you."

He went slowly. He made her feel safe as they found their way to each other. She was entirely caught up in the moment with him, her heart and her mind filled with nothing but him. They were new together and there was bumbling and awkwardness, but also humor and affection and, ultimately, joy.

It was a long night, and they scarcely slept at all. Margot felt intoxicated, light as air, and she laughed when she saw the dawn shining through the window. Jerome stretched and nuzzled her. "I'm taking the day off work today," he said.

"Let's spend it together." She gave a happy sigh.

"What do you want to do?"

At the moment, everything seemed possible. "You know something I've always wanted to do? Get a tattoo."

"Whoa. What?"

"You know, a tattoo. I've never had one before."

"Guess I wasn't expecting that. I like the way your mind works."

She chuckled softly while her fingers lightly played over his bare chest. "My mind is not working. My mind is playing."

He shivered. "Uh . . . where were we?"

"Tattoos."

"What kind of tattoo?"

"I . . . Don't laugh. I'm thinking about a shaker of salt." She grabbed a pad of paper from her nightstand and sketched it out for him. "What do you think?"

"Geek tattoo," he said. "It's cool. Where? Please don't say your neck or your lower back."

"No way. What's the point of a tattoo if you can't see it? I'm thinking calf, right above my boot line."

"You should do it, then." He rubbed his morning-shadow cheek against hers.

"Will you come with me?"

"Are you scared?"

She shrugged. "You might have to hold me down."

They went to Red Dog Tattoo on the corner of Perdita and Encontra Streets. The tattoo artist, Nickel, recognized Jerome. "The kolache man," she said. "You satisfied my every craving when I was pregnant. How can I help you?"

"I'm just here to have my woman's back," he said.

"Oh, I'm your woman now?" Margot couldn't stop smiling. Nickel made a template and got to work. The noise and pain and blood wiped the smile off Margot's face, but she held fast to Jerome's hand and powered through. It was like nothing she'd ever felt before, both searing and cold, leaving her feeling oddly vulnerable when it was done.

"How about you, big guy?" Nickel asked Jerome.

"I'll have what she's having," he said, baring his ankle.

"Really?" asked Margot. "That's so cool."

"I need a different symbol." He showed her on his phone.

"What's that?" asked Nickel.

Margot felt a rush of delight. "It's a sugar bowl."

By the time their tattoos healed, they were a couple. It was completely different from the few other guys Margot had dated. She could already feel it. This was something special. She chafed with impatience through every minute she couldn't be with Jerome, and when she was with him, time flew by. They both had busy careers, and sometimes they had to content themselves with passing each other in the kitchen and exchanging a secret look.

She'd always assumed she didn't understand how love worked. Lately she'd been thinking of her mother a lot, missing her, wishing she could tell her about Jerome. She vividly remembered the soft tone of Mama's voice when she would say *You're my happy place.* And then Margot realized that she did know how love worked after all. She understood how it was supposed to feel. Thanks to her mother, she'd always known, but the chaos of the past had made her forget.

"If this doesn't work out," she whispered to Jerome

one day when she encountered him in the restaurant kitchen and he started nuzzling her neck, "we're going to be so screwed, having to share this space."

"Oh, it'll work out, don't you worry."

"You sound very sure of yourself."

"I'm older and wiser. You'll have to trust me," he said.

Another day, Margot was engaged in her least favorite chore, paperwork, currently a stack of forms for a community college in Oakland. "Tuition assistance for employees," she told Jerome.

"It's really cool that you started that," he said. "Everything about you is cool."

"Stop it."

"Seriously. You made this kitchen a place to work. A safe place. Since you told me what happened in Texas, I get it."

She felt a surge of pride. "Thanks for saying that." She had also dedicated a percentage of her profits to Planned Parenthood and to the Amiga Foundation. Each year at Christmas and Easter, the Banner Creek Church of Hope received a large contribution from an anonymous donor.

"Question," Jerome said. "How do you feel about weddings?"

That caught her off guard. What was he asking? "Weddings. I've catered a bunch of them."

"Want to go to one with me? Not as a caterer. As a guest."

She gasped. "Ida and Frank?"

"Yep."

"Wow, really? Yes, a thousand times yes. I'd be honored to go to their wedding with you." She was thrilled for them. Since their reunion Frank and Ida had been inseparable. Jerome was getting used to the idea of Frank.

He'd found freakish similarities between them, not just the asthma, but the fact that they were both left-handed. Their favorite ice cream was maple walnut, and they both disliked the taste of cilantro. They both played the ukulele, and in school, their favorite subject had been chemistry.

From the very start, Ida and Frank had refused to keep secrets. They put their children and grandchildren together and hoped for the best. Margot and Jerome met Frank's kids and grandkids. They were all new to one another and cautious, but like Jerome, after the initial surprise, Grady and Jenna were happy for their father and Ida. That was how it looked to Margot, anyway. When it came to understanding the inner workings of a family, her knowledge was limited. Being with Jerome gave her tantalizing glimpses of what it might be like to have a family in all its messy, heady glory.

Margot was at her desk one day, agonizing over what to wear to the wedding, when an unfamiliar number appeared on her phone screen. A Texas area code. She instantly recoiled and was about to dismiss the call. Then, almost defiantly, she answered.

"It's Buckley DeWitt," said a voice with a subtle drawl. "Remember me?"

She broke into a smile. "Are you kidding? Of course I remember you, Buckley. You wrote the first review of my sauce, a hundred years ago. I'd never forget that. How did you find my number?"

"I'm an investigative reporter these days," he said. "I've come up in the world since I was the barbecue editor's assistant with a legal blog on the side."

"Is that right? Good for you."

"I'm a senior writer now for *Texas Monthly*. I saw that

piece on your place in *Travel Far* and recognized your picture. Congratulations, Margie. Seems like you're doing great."

"I go by Margot now," she said.

"I noticed. Margot Salton, owner of the outstanding new restaurant called Salt. Care to say why you changed your name?"

She wasn't sure how much of her story he knew. From the moment of her release from county jail, Lindsey and Sanjay had been vigilant about protecting her privacy. "I imagine you know, Buckley."

"The Jimmy Hunt incident."

Her year in hell was an "incident." Her pulse sped up and her hand went to her throat. "What are you after, Buckley?"

"I want to do a piece for *Texas Monthly* about the night Jimmy Hunt died."

"Absolutely not. Shitfire, Buckley. Why would I want to dredge that up?"

"Because a lot of folks still don't know the real story."

"And it's not my job to enlighten them. Sorry, Buckley."

"Margie—Margot. I could get a lot of the story through the Freedom of Information Act, but I want to be collaborative and respectful. I'd rather have input from you. I know what I'm asking—"

"You don't know the half of it," she said, her voice shaking.

"Then tell me. Tell the world. Your lived experience is important. I want you to tell your story instead of me writing what I can glean from documents."

Margot did not want her story to be the thing that defined her. She'd never wanted that. But wasn't that what she was doing, what she had done since 2007? Wasn't that the reason she'd never let herself fall in love, the reason she was being so cautious with Jerome? Still, she balked. "What happened is old news, Buckley. The world doesn't need to hear from me now."

"The Hunt family just submitted plans for a new football stadium," he said quickly, before she could hang up. "They've been fundraising for years and recently got final approval."

She rolled her eyes. "Football's like a religion in Texas. Let them build the damn thing. I don't care."

"They're going to name the stadium after Jimmy Hunt, and the plans include a twelve-foot-high statue of Jimmy in front of the place. I'll send you a link to the illustrations they submitted to the county planning commission."

The old burn of outrage flickered to life. "That's disgusting," she said, cringing at the image of a twelve-foot rapist.

"You can do something about it. Or let the Hunts control the narrative. The reason I decided to cover the story is that they had some PR firm contact the magazine about it, wanting some kind of self-congratulatory puff piece. Briscoe Hunt's getting into politics, so he's trying to polish up his reputation. They're painting Jimmy as some kind of tragic hero."

That gave Margot pause. She thought about the message it would send to girls, to the world, to memorialize a man who had died while committing a brutal rape. Her silence enabled this situation. Maybe Buckley was right. She needed to have the courage to say aloud what she'd held in for so long. She needed, once and for all, to speak her truth. Still, the idea of revisiting the incident repulsed her. "I don't know, Buckley . . ."

"Oh, and did I mention Briscoe's on the zoning commission? He's asserting eminent domain over Cubby

Watson's restaurant to make way for the stadium parking lot."

"Shitfire, Buckley," she said, feeling a surge of rage at the thought of a monument to the man who had put her through hell. "Buy your ticket and get up here now before I change my damn mind."

23

Margot's in-box was filled with search engine alerts about the article, which had recently been published. Buckley had shown her the piece in advance and she'd read it swiftly, with a strange detachment. Seeing her words in print created an odd sort of distance between her and what had happened. The old feelings of violation began to harden into vindication.

The interview had taken place over three days, not only because of her work schedule but because revisiting the incident had been a rough ride. Finding the fire to speak up for herself was incredibly liberating. It was different from telling Jerome what had happened. That had been a private conversation. With Buckley, she focused on the facts, and the facts alone had brought back fresh waves of pain and trauma. Buckley had quietly gained her trust, creating a safe space for her to speak and feel heard. Revisiting the facts of the case had felt profound, compelling her to dig deep, to peel down to a place that was still raw and unhealed, even after years of struggle to regain her balance in the world. She'd bolstered her courage by reminding herself that somewhere out there, the piece would be read by women who might someday be in a similar situation. She wanted people everywhere to know they had a right to tell their stories, and to keep telling them until someone finally listened.

To give her a modicum of privacy—and to keep the trolls from targeting her restaurant—Buckley had concluded the piece with "Margie Salinas is a restaurateur in California."

Margot knew there would be fallout once the story broke, and she was prepared for that. At least, she thought she was. The groundswell of reaction started in Texas as the papers and news media picked up the story, and it quickly reached California. It had the expected polarizing impact. There were those who were genuinely moved and outraged on her behalf, and others who claimed she was just another woman scorned who had gotten away with murder. When she learned that the plans for the stadium and statue were under review, she opened a bottle of imported Lambic beer and drank the whole thing while staring up at the night sky.

The next day, Anya interrupted Margot's media scrolling with a tentative knock on the office door. "I have news," she said.

Margot's stomach clenched. She'd taken a risk, exposing her story to the world. "Is it bad?"

"Not unless you think being the recipient of this year's Divina Award is bad."

"What?" Margot shot to her feet. "Me? *No.*"

The Divina was more than a chef's award. It was meant to honor not just culinary skills, but it acknowledged a person's character and humanity, the fundamental character of a chef—her values and business practices, her management style, the kitchen environment, and the way her colleagues and employees perceived her. The days of chefs who threw tantrums, who bullied and underpaid their workers, were numbered. Those nominated for the award had been vetted not only for their skills, but for the work environment they created for employees and their contributions to their communities.

In that moment, she wished she hadn't finished that Lambic beer the night before, a rare import from Belgium.

"I need a beer," she said in an awed whisper.

"It's ten o'clock in the morning," said Anya.

"I just need something to cry into," Margot told her.

Jerome and his boys had all shined their shoes for Margot's award ceremony. As he told Asher and Ernest, it wasn't every day you got to see someone win the coveted Divina Award for Best New Chef. The kids weren't overly impressed by the ceremony, but the promise of a gourmet reception afterward had them salivating.

He was proud of how handsome the boys looked in their suits and shiny shoes. Most of the other attendees were culinary royalty—food writers with international reputations, restaurant magnates, bloggers and influencers with massive followings, and representatives from the nonprofit groups that supported restaurant workers. The Culinary Channel was covering the event to air live. The magazine writer from Texas, Buckley DeWitt, was present as well. His story had made huge waves in Texas that had rippled outward, all the way to California. Reading the piece had reminded Jerome of how hard it must have been for Margot to put herself back together after what she'd endured. It made him want to fold her into his heart forever.

This, honey, he thought, looking around at the chattering crowd. *Let this be the thing that puts the past to rest—achieving a dream, being surrounded by friends.*

This was Margot's moment right now. She had worked so damned hard. He might never fully know the depth of her struggles, but it was clear she had pulled herself up by her fingernails, enduring challenges and sacrifices that would destroy most people. This was such a fine validation for her.

Jerome noticed a message from Florence on his phone, but he decided to deal with it later. This was Margot's time to shine. The cameras were rolling as they gave her a medal on a rainbow-colored ribbon, and the head of the society made a speech extolling her accomplishments. The praise made her cheeks turn as pink as his mother's favorite rose.

An event photographer captured the moment, and people held up their phones to take pictures of their own. At the reception afterward, coworkers, investors, people from the media, and friends thronged around her. Some were fans, wanting her to sign their commemorative menu.

Jerome's heart seemed to expand in his chest. It felt good to get to this place where he had complete clarity. He loved her in a way that felt like forever, and there was no mistaking the feeling for anything else. It was a welcome contrast from the wary and bitter disappointment that had haunted him after his divorce.

He leaned over to Ida B and Frank, who had shown up for the event. "Look at my girl. She's all lit up."

"Yes, she is," Ida said. "You picked a good one."

"I did indeed," Jerome said.

"Who's that woman?" Ida asked. "The one waving her Sharpie marker and menu."

Jerome shrugged. "Don't recognize her. Another fan, maybe?" He got up and wove his way toward Margot. He had big plans for her tonight. Ida and Frank were going to take the boys back to the city. Jerome was going to whisk Margot away to the Grande Patron Suite at

Hacienda Bella Vista for a private celebration. He had the ring in his pocket.

He approached her just as the strange woman walked up to her from the opposite side.

"Margie Salinas?" She intoned it as a question.

Jerome saw Margot sway a little. She frowned, tilted her head to one side. "Sorry, what?"

"Margie Salinas aka Margot Salton," the woman said.

Margot froze. The color visibly dropped from her face. Her eyes darted around, but she didn't seem to see anything. She looked like a trapped animal.

Then she glared straight at the woman. "Who the hell are you?" she asked.

The woman passed her the manila envelope, pressing it firmly into her hand. "You've been served."

"Defamation of character?" Margot stared at the printed document and tried not to hyperventilate. Inhale two three four exhale two three four.

She had taken refuge in the luxurious suite at Hacienda Bella Vista. Jerome had booked it for a romantic evening, but romance was the furthest thing from her mind.

Roy and Octavia Hunt, Plaintiffs, v. Margie Salinas AKA Margot Salton. They had come at her with a lawsuit spurred by the magazine article. They wanted financial restitution from her for telling the truth about their dead rapist son.

If Jerome hadn't slipped his arm around her and propped her up, she probably would have crumpled to the ground. "Let's not panic now," he said. When he caught her look, he quickly added, "Sorry. Never the best thing to say to someone on the verge of panic. We can deal with this together."

"I'm going to throw up."

"Deep breath, honey. I got you."

No, he didn't, but she appreciated the sentiment. "This family, though. They're a nightmare."

She took off the medal and set it aside. Jerome placed the folded envelope on a side table by the door and loosened his tie. She took hold of his hands and looked up at him, feeling every beat of her heart. She'd been cautious, settling into the idea of loving him. But she knew what she was feeling, and until the envelope had arrived, she had begun to believe that a future with him was possible.

Now the Hunts' action made Margot question her right to live the new life she'd built after the rape, after jail, after placing Miles with his parents and moving on. Jerome probably didn't understand the storm she'd stirred up back in Hayden County, Texas.

He struck a match to the fire that had been laid in the hearth, and the beautiful, antique-furnished room glowed with life. Then he drew her over to the sofa facing the fireplace and pulled her down next to him. He slipped her shoes off one by one and gently massaged her feet. "What's on your mind?" he asked. "I hope it's the award, but I have a feeling it's not."

"I'm so proud of that award," she said. "And the thing I'm most proud of is that you and Ida and the boys were there. It felt . . . It felt like having a family, and I don't even have words to explain what that means to me."

He set her foot aside and slid his arm around her. "It means you don't have to do this alone," he told her. "I'm here for you. I'm here for the hard things, and for the easy things, and everything in between."

"I don't deserve you," she whispered.

"I'll tell you what you don't deserve, and it's that bullshit summons."

"Bullshit or not, I have to deal with it. Legal matters, no matter how vengeful or frivolous, don't resolve themselves."

"I'll come with you."

Margot shook her head. "The Hunts are my problem, not yours. It's about them, trying to ruin me. I won't let you be part of this. I won't let you expose yourself and your assets to a possible judgment against me."

"That's not going to happen."

"In Hayden County, Texas, anything can happen because the Hunts are in charge. I almost got sent up for life because I shot a guy who was raping me. I was forced to have a baby because they wouldn't let me end the pregnancy in time. The Hunts are looking for a way to take everything from me—and from you and your boys, if they find out how much you mean to me."

"That's not how it works. They can't touch me, and I won't let them touch you."

Margot slept in Jerome's arms that night, but it was a fitful sleep. She realized with a sinking heart that she would never outrun what had happened. All she could do was try to keep it as far from the present as possible.

Jerome had said *I won't let them touch you.*

She turned the phrase over and over in her mind. She could do no less than that for him.

"Jerome."

Standing in the front room of his house, he turned at the sound of his ex-wife's voice. He'd been expecting Margot, not Florence. Margot was leaving for Texas without him, insisting that this problem was hers to deal with on her own. His every instinct urged him to go with her, but he resisted. Given what she'd been through, Jerome did not want to insert himself into the situation or take away her independence. He had to trust that she'd manage without him. She'd promised to stop and tell him goodbye on her way to the airport.

"Florence." He held open the screen door and motioned her inside. She looked around the home they used to share, her face unreadable. It was a hot day, and he had all the windows open, trying to catch a breeze.

They rarely saw each other and almost never spoke. After working out their divorce and parenting plan, they kept their distance. The boys shuttled between them like commuters on the BART, with the sliding door closing behind one parent and opening to the other. It was routine now. Communication was managed through text messages. So when his ex-wife asked him to meet with her in person, he suspected there was something on her mind.

This house used to be their place. Ten years of memories were bound up here, shared routines and celebrations, parenting pleasures, frustrations, and fights. Now Florence was a stranger, like someone he might occasionally see at the gym or at church. And she was pregnant. Seeing her, all rounded and pretty as a ripe pear, reminded him of those times back in the day when everything had seemed possible. When *they* had seemed possible.

"What's on your mind?" he asked. He hoped it wasn't something about Ernest again.

"The boys tell me you're in love. You're probably going to marry her."

If she'll have me, he thought.

"They get along great so far," he said. "They didn't tell you otherwise, did they?"

She scowled at him. "According to them, she's some kind of action figure Barbie doll."

"She's cool," he said. *Don't oversell her*, he thought.

When Florence had first moved in with Lobo, Jerome had taken it like a punch to the gut. It meant the permanent closure of a door that might have been open a tiny crack. Any thought of the family he used to have was forever changed. Now it was his turn to move on, and Florence's turn to make her peace with it.

"I'm concerned, Jerome," she said. "When I googled her—"

"You googled her. That's great, Flo."

"Tell me you didn't google Lobo when we started going out," she challenged him.

He didn't say anything. Of course he'd checked the guy out.

"Anyway, I am concerned," she said. "Not for you—that's none of my business—but for the boys."

"Because she's white?"

"That doesn't help, but no, that's not the problem."

"Because she's young?"

"Please. No. It's this. This is the problem." Florence slapped a copy of a magazine on the table between them.

He'd been so proud of Margot when it was published. The cover featured a hand-tooled cowboy boot with a stylized blond woman on it, and the shoutline "Don't Mess with Texas Women." It was ironic since the Hunts were doing just that.

In the surprised silence, Jerome heard a car door slam. "She has a past," he said to Florence. "So do we. Everybody has a past."

"Jerome, will you listen to yourself? She shot a man, for god's sake."

"She defended herself from a rapist."

"What happened to her is horrible, I'd never deny it. Still, these are my children I'm talking about. I'm not comfortable with the boys being around her."

"I never liked Lobo, but I trust your judgment. You need to trust mine."

"Lobo didn't kill anybody . . . I'm sorry, Jerome, but I just can't. If you choose her, I'm going to want to renegotiate custody of the boys."

"You wouldn't."

"These are my kids. I'm not playing games, Jerome. You're a fine, fine man. And a good father. You deserve a new love. But this . . . I can't have her around my boys."

"You don't get to make that call," Jerome said.

"Maybe she does." Margot stepped inside the front door. Her face was hard and ghost white. It was clear she'd overheard. "I'm Margot," she said to Florence. "I don't mean to interrupt. I stopped to say goodbye on my way to the airport."

Florence touched her belly in that unconscious gesture all pregnant women seemed to make. "Listen, it's nothing against you. I trust Jerome's judgment, and I want to be okay with whoever he's with. But this . . . the situation in Texas. It must have been awful, but . . . it was a shooting. That scares the hell out of me. I'm thinking about my boys, is all."

"Because you're a good mom," Margot said. "I imagine you'd do anything to protect your kids, and I respect that."

"Your point is taken," Jerome said, pointedly holding the door for Florence. As she left, she shot him a look he remembered, a look that said she wasn't finished.

"I need to go, too," said Margot. "My Lyft driver is waiting outside. And, Jerome, I'm not going to argue with your ex. She's not wrong. Her feelings are her feelings. I don't want to be the reason you get less time with your boys."

"That's not gonna happen," he said, frustrated with Florence, hurting for Margot. "I swear—"

"It's not just that," she said. "It's me. I'm . . . I don't think I can do this, Jerome."

"This."

"Us."

"Come on now," he said. "You don't mean that, baby."

"I need to go to Texas and get through this, and frankly, I have qualms about whether I'm ready to be with someone. I can't ask you to wait for me."

"You didn't ask."

The Lyft's car horn sounded. "I'm sorry. I have to go," she said.

24

The Hayden County courthouse was haunted by nightmares. Margot instantly recognized the smell of wood polish and floor cleaner, the steady *tick* of the ceiling fan overhead, and the whispery echo of voices under the marble dome. It didn't matter how much time had passed. It didn't matter that she was no longer a frightened girl in plastic shoes and a jailhouse jumpsuit. This place was all too familiar, and it brought up memories of terror and pain.

How ironic that she had circled back to this place. She had gone from a life in which she had to fight off a rapist, to prison, where she'd fought to get a grip on a defense when the forces against her were so huge. She'd felt so powerless, having to depend on others to help at every turn—advocates, nurses, officers, judges, attorneys, the baby, the prospective parents. She had been buffeted along like a leaf in a storm, trying to grab her power where she could. And just when her life finally felt like her own, the Hunts had come at her once again.

Margot missed Jerome. Thanks to him, she had discovered all kinds of things about love, including something new—the pain of leaving. She had closed that door before it had fully opened. The ache of missing him was enormous, but she knew she would survive it. After saying goodbye to Miles, she realized there was no goodbye she couldn't handle.

Still, she hated how she had left things with him. She hoped one day he would understand why her confidence in their relationship was faltering. There was no disputing the boys' mother's doubts about her. She was not about to let her boys anywhere near a woman who had killed a man. Margot couldn't help feeling intimidated by Jerome's ex. This was a woman who had been married to him for ten years, who knew him in ways Margot never would. The mother of his children. Margot did not want to force him to choose between her and his kids.

And if this trial went badly, it would underscore her fear that she would never truly be free of what had happened.

He would have come with her if she'd asked him to, but continuing her relationship with him would put him at risk, and she refused to let him be part of this. One of the demands of the lawsuit was a claim on her future income and assets. She would not drag him into her darkness.

She tried not to feel defeated before the proceeding got underway.

"Margot." Buckley DeWitt strode across the rotunda. "You didn't get my text?"

"Oh, I . . ." She patted her handbag. "Sorry. As you can imagine, I've been distracted."

He nudged her over toward a waiting area with some benches. "I'm sorry as hell you're going through this."

"Someone once told me, when you're going through hell, keep going. Listen, I knew the risk when I decided to speak out. I had to, though, Buckley. You did the right thing, giving me a way to tell my story. I couldn't let them erect a damn stadium and a statue to Jimmy Hunt."

She folded her arms and shivered from a blast of air-conditioning. "I am not looking forward to this settlement conference, though."

"Better than going to trial, though," he said. "The judge will hear both sides and give you a sense of how he'd rule if it ever did go to trial. The Hunts won't get anywhere with their bullshit annoyance suit. The magazine's legal counsel agrees. I'm just sorry you have to deal with it."

"Does the magazine's counsel know the Hunts? My attorney says it's all up to the judge we get at the settlement conference. And since all the judges in the district are cozy with the Hunts, I'm going to have a fight on my hands."

Terence Swift, the lawyer who had dealt with the murder charge, did not handle civil cases. He'd referred her to Blair Auerbach, who seemed very smart and well-prepared, although she didn't exude Mr. Swift's brash confidence.

"Best-case scenario, the whole thing will get thrown out," Buckley said.

Margot glowered at him. "Worst-case scenario, it goes to a jury trial and the jury's packed with Jimmy Hunt fans." This was what she feared. The Hunts had bullied their way through life in Hayden County, and she doubted that would ever change. Jimmy's brother, Briscoe, was a lawyer and the head of the county planning commission. The lawyers and judges of the county were cronies, going to the country club for golf, making their deals.

Her lawyer arrived, expensive shoes tapping on the marble floor. "Don't forget to turn your phone off," she said. "Judges don't like it when phones go off."

"Got it," Margot said.

Blair checked a glass-front letter board listing the room numbers and judges for the day. "Maybe we'll get lucky and he won't be one of their cronies. A different judge could be a game changer."

"You're going to be all right, Margot," Buckley assured her. "Don't forget to breathe. I'll see you on the other side."

"There's time to stop in the bathroom if you want," Blair suggested.

"Good idea." Margot went down a hallway and ducked into the ladies' room. Bracing her hands on the edge of the sink, she checked herself in the mirror. This morning, she had put on makeup with plenty of concealer under her eyes, and she'd used drops to get rid of the redness. Skinny black slacks and a white silk blouse, the kind that came with concealed armpit pads, because she fully expected to sweat. Flat-ironed hair and low-heeled shoes. Nothing to draw attention to herself. She didn't want to make today's settlement conference about the clothes.

The toilet flushed and a woman in jeans and a T-shirt came out and stood at the sink washing her hands. Their gazes met in the mirror and skated away. Then the woman—young, Asian, attractive—turned to her. "Sorry, I don't mean to stare. Have we met?"

Margot tucked away her makeup bag. "Not likely." Then she felt a stab of familiarity when she saw a small bird tattoo on the woman's wrist. An old memory flashed to life. "Tamara Falcon," she said.

"Hey, that's me." She finished drying her hands. "Remind me where we met."

"I doubt you'd remember. It was years ago, when we were kids. My mom was catering a party at your parents' house."

"Wow, oh my gosh, I totally remember you. Wow," she said again. "It was . . . a memorable day."

Margot felt her cheeks flush as she recalled the pot smoking incident. "It's been a while," she said.

"Well, you look fantastic." Tamara glanced at her watch, then gathered up a thick stack of documents. "So are you a lawyer? You look like a lawyer."

"No. I, uh, I'm here on a legal matter." She forced a smile. "You?"

"I work here. Had to come in unexpectedly on my day off to fill in for someone." Tamara moved toward the door. "On that note . . . I'd better go. Nice seeing you."

Margot rejoined her lawyer, and they went down a long hallway and into a conference room. The Hunts were already there, shooting the breeze with their lawyer.

Octavia Hunt watched with laser beams of hatred as Margot set down her handbag and struggled to project a calm, confident demeanor. She could feel the rage rolling off the woman like waves of heat off the highway on a hot day. Mrs. Hunt was middle-aged and attractive, perfectly dressed and groomed, with a swirl of auburn hair and shell-pink stiletto nails. Margot noticed a tell—three of her fingernails had been chewed to the quick. Mrs. Hunt appeared to notice Margot's regard, and she tucked her fingers into a fist.

Her husband, Roy, wore a suit with a string tie that curved out over his prominent belly. Their son, Briscoe Hunt, looked eerily like Jimmy, so much so that Margot felt a jolt of terror in her gut.

He leaned back in his chair, subjecting her to a lingering, up-and-down inspection. His expression was laconic as he said, "Well, well, well. If it idint the famous Margot Salton." He exaggerated his drawl as he studied her from head to toe.

She said nothing. There was nothing to say to the family of the man she'd shot. They would never, ever accept what had actually happened that night. They had lost a loved one, someone they remembered as a little kid growing up. They had known a different Jimmy than the one who attacked her that night. Margot felt a tiny glimmer of sympathy, but it quickly dimmed. This family had tried to keep her in prison, to steal the baby they'd forced her to have, and now they were suing her. It would take too much from Margot to forgive that.

She took a seat next to her lawyer at the long conference table and waited for the judge to enter. There was a blank pad of paper and some bottles of water in the center.

"You've had a chance to look over our settlement offer?" asked the Hunts' lawyer.

Blair regarded him with a blank expression. "And you have my answer. We're requesting that you withdraw the suit."

"I won't have it," snapped Octavia.

The lawyer leaned over and murmured something to her.

"You have no idea," Octavia said. "We'll see what Judge Hale makes of this situation."

Margot wanted to throw up. Judge Shelby Hale had been the judge who wouldn't release her before trial when she was first arrested; she knew he was a fixture in the county, and undoubtedly a longtime friend of the Hunts.

The door opened, and a clerk entered. "I apologize for the delay. Judge Hale has a family emergency. A different judge will hear your case. She'll be with you shortly."

"She?" Roy turned to his lawyer. "You mean that new one?"

"Youngest judge in Hayden County," Briscoe said with a nasty curl of his lip. "Squeaked into office last year with fifty-one percent of the vote."

"In that case," said the Hunts' lawyer, "we're going to reschedule this proceeding."

"I'm afraid that won't be possible." The new judge entered in her robes. Unsmiling, she surveyed the room and pressed her hands on the surface of the table. Under the hem of her sleeve, a small tattoo of a bird in flight was visible.

The clerk produced several file folders. "The Honorable Tamara Falcon presiding," she said.

25

Margot couldn't wait to get out of Texas, but there was something she wanted to do first. She drove her rental car to Cubby's and found him busy at the pit. He looked as magnificent as she remembered, a god surrounded by a cloud of blue-gray smoke, wielding his tongs like a symphony conductor. When he saw her, he did a double take, then nudged his assistant and hurried over to her.

"Well now, look at you, Miss Margie. Just look at you. And me all sweat and smoke."

She hugged him, anyway, remembering with aching gratitude that there had been a time when he and Queen were her only family. "You look so good," she said. "And here I am, in and out of trouble again."

"It's been in the papers." He wiped his hands on a towel and they went to his office, which had been renovated along with the rest of the place. Judging by the state-of-the-art equipment, business had been good.

Queen was there, working at a computer. There was a high-speed menu printer, an electronic inventory screen, and a display of images from all the security cameras.

Queen crowed with delight when she saw Margot. "My, my. Don't you look wonderful." They drew together in an embrace; then Queen gestured at a chair. "Sit a spell."

"The case got thrown out," Margot said. "No hearings, no trial, just dismissed."

"Of course it was," Queen said. "The truth is your defense, and you finally got to tell the truth."

Margot was still stunned by the outcome. She told them about the last-minute change of judges. "That's exactly what Judge Falcon said—when it comes to defamation, slander, or libel, the truth is an absolute defense to the allegation. Since what I said is true, then there is no case."

"Well, then. I'm glad I voted for her in the last election," Queen said.

Margot shuddered. "The Hunts are already threatening to appeal. They think they can get it before a different judge—their friend, Shelby Hale."

Cubby shook his head. "Wouldn't be allowed. He's been carrying on with Mrs. Hunt for years. Everybody knows it. They come in every Tuesday, because that's Roy's regular league day at the golf course." He gestured at the display from the security cameras. "Eventually, the truth catches up with folks. Maybe even the Hunts."

Margot paused. Maybe that was why the judge suddenly had a family emergency.

"There's more news, too. I got word just as I was leaving the courthouse. Buckley DeWitt said it's official—the stadium project's been scuttled. There's not going to be a memorial to Jimmy Hunt. No damn statue. And they're not turning your place into a parking lot."

"Really?" Queen and Cubby exchanged a glance. "Are you sure?"

"Buckley said it'll be in tomorrow's paper."

Queen's hand fluttered to her brow, and Cubby gave her shoulder a squeeze. "Thank the lord."

"And thank our girl Margie," Cubby said, beaming at her. "If you hadn't come out with your story, our place would be paved over."

"Well, I don't know about that," Margot said.

"I do," Cubby said.

"We both do," Queen said. "You're a treasure is what you are." Margot felt a welling of affection for them. They'd opened their home to her, shown her a path in life, brought her into their faith community. "Y'all are more than I ever deserved," she said. "I can't thank you enough for being there for me when no one else was."

"Oh, baby girl." Queen favored her with the sweetest of smiles. "It's good to see you again."

"I'm sorry I was away for so long. I didn't think you needed the kind of attention I'd bring. You've always been in my thoughts, though, and that's a fact."

"You come see us anytime, you hear?" Cubby said.

"I might just do that. And I'd be honored if you could pay me a visit someday."

"We'll keep that in mind," said Cubby.

Queen walked her to the door. "Are you happy, baby girl? I know you're doing good, but are you happy?"

Margot knew better than to give her a flip answer. Queen could always read her. "I'm getting there," she said, her voice rough with emotion. "I've been working harder than I ever thought possible. I opened a good restaurant and made a few good friends. I even fell in love with a good man."

"Well, isn't that nice?"

"It . . . was. Maybe one day it could be. He's got kids, and I got a past, and . . . it's complicated." She mustered up a smile for them. "I guess I'm about as happy as I deserve to be."

Margot spent her final night in Austin at the Driskill. The opulent hotel had once been a safe haven for her and Kevin, and although it seemed a grand indulgence, she decided to treat herself. She felt dog tired, as if she'd run a marathon or worked a twelve-hour shift. The day had left her mentally and emotionally exhausted, and all she wanted was a drink and maybe a bite to eat in the dark, cavey hotel bar.

She headed up the wide staircase to the bar. It had a hammered copper ceiling and a longhorn mounted over the fireplace. A few couples and clusters of men were gathered around the bar. Margot took a seat in a secluded booth and ordered a Wild West, which contained four shots of alcohol. The fiery flavors soothed her and she sat listening to music from the speakers and the occasional burst of male laughter. A text message came in from Lindsey Rockler. *We would like to see you if you have time.*

She hesitated, trying to picture what it would be like to see the boy she had placed in his fathers' arms at birth. He'd be half grown by now. She took a sip of her drink, then replied, *Okay.*

There was a bit of back-and-forth. They invited her to their home, but she demurred. There were unforgettable moments in that place, memories of the light-filled garden cottage and vast kitchen, evenings spent with people who saw the best in her. But the memories needed to stay there.

Besides, she didn't trust the Hunts. For all she knew, they were stalking her in secret. She didn't want to lead them to Miles's house. She arranged to meet them in the morning at Zilker Park near the botanical gardens. It felt strange, being back in Texas after such a long time, seeing the landmarks she used to visit with her mother. There was no sense of nostalgia tied to this place, but she felt the old ache of missing Mama.

Margot had only ever seen Miles in pictures. His

parents had told him about adoption from day one, and as he got older, they answered his questions honestly. They told him he could ask them anything. Eventually, he would learn everything he wanted to know about his birth, and Margot supported this. He deserved to know his personal history, even the difficult parts. Even the story of how he had been made. Right now, they assured her, he was simply a happy kid, a big brother, the pride and joy of his dads.

Someone slid into the booth across from her and set down a highball glass, half full of amber liquid. "Thought I'd stop by," said Briscoe Hunt. "See if there's anything else you're planning to ruin for my family."

Margot felt a chill like an icicle to her gut. He looked more like Jimmy than ever, his eyes glassy from drinking and his mouth slick. "You followed me here."

"It's a free country."

"Go away," she said.

"I don't think so, baby doll. You found my favorite watering hole."

The expression on his face—both laconic and hostile—triggered a response in her. Without even thinking, she felt her body assessing the situation and weighing her options. Her pulse sped up and her skin flushed. "Are you really looking for more trouble?"

"That what you think I'm doing? Lookin' for trouble?"

Margot knew there was no getting rid of him and she was in no mood. She left her drink on the table and walked out of the bar. Best not to lead him to her room. Seeing a sign to the ladies' lounge down a marble-floored hallway, she ducked in there. It was mercifully empty, and she leaned against the counter in front of the mirror and shut her eyes. Her heart was beating a hundred miles an hour.

Calm down, she told herself. *Calm down*. He was a drunk bully like his brother had been. But she wasn't a victim anymore.

She opened her eyes and looked in the mirror. Blue eyes, like her mama. Would Miles have blue eyes?

As she was thinking about seeing him in person for the first time, the door opened and there was Briscoe Hunt. She spun around, shock giving way to anger. "Seriously?" she asked loudly.

"Haven't you figured it out yet?" he asked. "I don't take no for an answer." Then he lunged for her.

Oh, hell no.

All the years of training and practice kicked in as she executed a four-direction throw. She used his own momentum to slam him to the marble floor, hearing the air rush from his lungs on impact. His eyes widened as he tried to draw breath. She stepped around him and said, "You sit tight now. I'm calling security."

The next morning, Lindsey and Sanjay arrived at Zilker Park on their bikes. They looked virtually the same, all smiles and couture cyclewear as they locked their bikes and hurried over to her.

They each gave her a hug. "Thanks for meeting us," said Sanjay. He gestured at the shady path. "Miles is over there, helping his sister. She just got her training wheels off."

Margot's heart sped up. She watched a golden-haired, willowy boy trotting alongside a dark-haired girl who wobbled along on a little pink two-wheeler. *Hi, Miles.*

A bittersweet ache rose in her chest. "Your kids look wonderful."

"The center of the universe," Lindsey said.

The sunlight glinted over them, and Margot shaded

her eyes. "My mama used to bring me here. On market days, the food truck would be over there by Barton Creek."

"She would have been proud of you. You've done so well," said Sanjay. "And it sounds like you sent the Hunts home with their tails between their legs."

Margot shuddered, thinking about the previous night. She had informed hotel security that there was a drunk guy on the floor of the mezzanine ladies' lounge, and then she'd gone to her room. It had taken three shots from the minibar to calm her nerves, but after that, she'd fallen dead asleep.

"I'm not cut out for drama," she told the guys. "Just glad it's over. I hope it stays over."

"So do we," Sanjay said. "You look incredible. I feel as if a theme song should start playing every time you appear."

"Stop it." She glanced over at the bike path.

"Ready to go say hi?"

She nodded. Took a breath. "I'd love to," she said. She felt strong enough now, stronger than the grief that had consumed her when she'd given the baby to his parents. She could do this.

"Miles and Jaya, this is Miss Margot," Sanjay called. "She wanted to say hi to you."

The boy slowed down and brought the bike to a stop. Then, seeming to forget his sister, he turned to Margot. "Hi," he said.

"It's nice to meet you," she said.

Miles regarded Margot with big blue eyes. They were the same shade as her mama's eyes. And maybe it was force of will, but she did not see a single trace of Hunt in him. She never wanted him to feel shame or guilt. A kid deserved to take pride and joy in his identity. That was all she wanted for him. Everything else would blossom forth out of that.

"You're my birth mother," he said.

"I am."

He took a step back. His cheeks colored up and he dropped his chin in a bashful way. "Oh. Um, okay."

"I wanted to see how you're doing," she said. "I told your parents that you should feel free to ask me anything, anytime. So . . . is there anything you want to ask me?"

He shrugged. "Don't think so."

"You probably know this, but I wanted to tell you myself. I've done a lot of things in my life so far, and I suppose I'll do a lot more. But you're the most important. Being your birth mother is the very best thing I ever did. Placing you with your dads is the second best."

"Okay," he said again, still blushing. "Uh . . . thank you?"

His uncertainty touched her heart. "I don't need thanks." She handed him a photo strip in a cellophane envelope. "This is a copy of my favorite picture of my mother and me, from back when I was about your age. You're welcome to keep it if you want." It was the picture she and her mother had made in a booth in Corpus Christi. She'd written a message on the back. Maybe he'd see it. Maybe he wouldn't.

Miles studied their faces for several long moments. Margot wondered what he saw, what he was thinking. She knew she couldn't be part of it, yet at the same time, she would always be a part of it.

"Thank you," he said again, and this time it wasn't a question. "Dad," he said, "can you keep this for me?"

"And, Daddy, can we get some ice cream?" the little girl asked. She wore her shiny hair in lopsided ponytails, and she was ridiculously cute.

"In a minute," Lindsey said, carefully sliding the photograph into his backpack. "Want to join us, Margot?"

Yes. With all my heart, yes. She shook her head. "I need to get going to the airport. I'm glad I got to meet you, Miles and Jaya."

"Yep, me too," he said, and his sister latched onto his hand.

Margot turned to cross the street to the parking area, feeling such a mixture of intense emotions that she couldn't sort them out. Bittersweet pride. Yearning and relief. Miles was a wonderful, beautiful boy. He seemed as sunny and guileless as a flower in springtime. *Try to stay that way*, she thought and sent out a silent farewell. *I wish you everything good.*

At the other side of the street, she turned to watch them go, the four of them holding hands in a chain, flickering in and out of the sunlight through the trees.

26

The world looked different to Margot when she returned to the Bay Area. She felt as though she'd been away for a hundred years and aged a decade. It was Sunday morning when her flight touched down, and at home, she scooped Kevin into her arms and cuddled him close. A neighbor had been feeding him, but he was as starved for affection as Margot was. Despite the hour, she curled up in bed and slept until dark.

She woke up slightly disoriented. It was after ten at night, but now she felt too wired to sleep. Work, then.

She showered and changed and drove to Salt. The place was deserted, so she decided to use the time to tackle the myriad chores she'd ignored while she was away. Emails, paperwork, and general catching up. Staff had come and gone in her absence. The menu had changed here and there.

A tap at the door startled her. Ida and Frank were outside, waving at her to let them in. "We saw the light on," Ida said. "Welcome home."

Margot admired their eveningwear, a tea-length dress for Ida and a formal suit for Frank. "Have you been out on the town?"

"We have," said Frank. "There was a revival of an old play called *Bus Stop*. We went to opening night. Coffee? I make a mean decaf cappuccino."

"That sounds good," Margot said.

"Put mine in a to-go cup," Ida said. "I'll be looking for bed soon."

"Yes, ma'am." He went over to the bakery to use the big gleaming espresso machine.

"Now then," Ida said to her in a brisk, no-nonsense tone, "about you and Jerome."

"You read the story?"

"I did."

"Then you know why I had to leave." Margot felt the raw burn of tears. "Even though I left Texas, what happened there will never leave me. Jerome made me forget that. I got caught up in him, in this family, in the life I dreamed about with him, and I lost myself in that dream. I'm sorry. I wanted so much for this to work, but it's just too complicated."

"You're talking about Florence, then." Ida pressed her lips together. "She was my daughter-in-law for ten years, and I know her. She needs to get used to the idea of you. What you did to save your own life—that was you being fierce and protective, the way she is with her boys. She'll settle down and realize that. Just takes time."

"I don't know, Ida."

"Well, *I* do. Now, listen, if you leave, it'll break his heart and yours, too. But if you stay, you might just end up with something that took me fifty years to find."

Frank brought the coffee, and they chatted about other things—the play, the weather, their grandchildren. Margot liked seeing how happy they were together, how much they adored each other. That kind of happiness could change the world, she thought.

After they left, she surveyed the cramped work area she'd carved out for herself. The corkboard over the desk had the picture of her and Mama, a few of Kevin, and a new one—a shot of her with Jerome and his boys on Angel Island. They didn't look like her family, but her heart had fooled her into thinking it was possible.

The desk was stacked with unopened mail, boxes, and parcels that had been delivered. She grabbed a box cutter and went to work methodically, opening and dealing with each piece. It was not her favorite part of the business, but it was unavoidable. When the large blue bin was filled with discarded paper and cardboard, she got up to stretch her legs and take the recycling out back.

By now, dawn was touching the sky, and she could hear the sounds of the city rumbling to life. She'd lost track of the time. She unlocked the big metal container and emptied her bin. When she turned to go back inside, she was startled to see a looming male figure.

She put up her hands in defense, then she recognized him. "Jerome."

"So here we are again," he said. "You can put your guard down, Margot. You've been here all night, haven't you?"

"Couldn't sleep, so I came in to start catching up on work."

"How about catching up with me."

He looked so good to her, so handsome that her heart skipped a beat. He was wearing especially nice clothes today, creased slacks and a pressed white shirt. Maybe he had something going on. "Your mother told you to find me here."

"Let's go inside."

Margot thought about the first time she'd met Jerome and fought him off in a panic. She thought about something he'd said the first time he took her sailing—*You have to trust that I'll always come back for you.* He turned out to be the last person who would harm her. He turned out to be the one person who saw who she was and didn't look away.

They sat across from each other at one of the café tables. The early morning quiet of the empty bakery surrounded them. The air was filled with the gentle, homey scent of coffee and baked goods. "Talk," said Jerome. "Or do we not do that anymore?"

She winced at the hurt she heard in his voice. "I was scared to bring you into my life, so I ran. I'm sorry. I didn't know what else to do."

"How about trusting me?"

"I do. I always have. But the Hunts—they're vicious. And vindictive." She shuddered, recalling the look on Briscoe's face when he'd lunged for her. "You've got kids. A house, a business. People who depend on you. And the boys' mom—admit it, if you didn't know me, would you want a person like me in your children's lives?"

"I do know you," he countered. "And I do want you in my children's lives. Which brings me to my next point. There's something else we should talk about."

"What's that?"

"A wedding."

She gasped. "Jerome—"

"Calm down," he said. "I'm talking about Ida's wedding. You said you'd come. Did you change your mind?"

She loved him so much that it hurt. Maybe that was how love worked. If you could handle the pain, you'd find the sweetness. "I haven't changed my mind."

Jerome walked Ida down the aisle. It was unconventional, but everything about his mother's love story was unconventional. Margot had never experienced a sense of family like this, two disparate tribes, now united. To her, it seemed like something out of a fairy tale.

Ida wore a beautiful ivory dress, and Frank was tall and stately in his tux. The venue was incredible—Hacienda Bella Vista, surrounded by the orchards and vineyards of Sonoma. The best men were the bride's grandsons, and the officiant was Frank's son, Grady.

"The moment I met you," Ida said, looking up at Frank, "you took up residence in my heart. I've been blessed with a rich and beautiful life, and you've made it even richer." She paused, and her gaze flickered ever so briefly to Jerome. "In some way, you were always with me, even when I didn't know where you were. Now we're together, with our families' support, and every dream I've ever had is finally coming true."

Frank cleared his throat a couple of times, then took out a handkerchief to dab at his forehead and then his eyes. Margot's throat felt thick as she watched him. She didn't know the man well, but she recognized the emotions written on his face. "Our love feels as strong today as it did long ago," he said. "I still know you, Ida. But I know there's so much more to learn. I intend to spend the rest of my life discovering you all over again."

Watching Ida and Frank and their surrounding families, Margot marveled at all the ways the joy of true love could change a life—not just one, but many, radiating outward in widening rings.

She glanced at Jerome, tall and straight beside her. Finally, she could see what might be possible if she let herself follow her feelings for him. It had been a long journey to get herself to this point. She'd lost her bearings, blown off course by a horrible event, and it had taken her years to adjust her sails and steer her way back. Maybe it was the beauty of the ceremony, replete with the music and the bright humanity all around, but maybe, Margot thought, she was so moved because she could finally imagine that kind of love happening in her own life.

"Why so many tears?" Jerome whispered, handing her a packet of tissues from his pocket.

"I don't want fifty years to go by and then realize you're my person."

He cupped his hand over hers. Though he stared straight ahead, though he said nothing, she felt a wave of warmth emanating from him. And a sense of possibility that suddenly felt very real.

The reception took place under twinkling lights in the Bella Vista apple orchard. The menu was prepared by Bella Vista's legendary kitchen, and wine came from the neighboring Rossi Vineyards. The lavish banquet featured a locally sourced menu and a magnificent cake made with organic lemons and buttercream icing. A golden glow from the setting sun bathed the atmosphere in gold, and the toasts ranged from silly to awkward to heartfelt. There was live music, including covers of songs from the San Francisco sound of the early seventies. Jerome and Margot tried some of the moves they had learned in their ballroom classes, but she left the dance floor in a haze of self-consciousness.

"You look like you could use a drink," said Ida, handing her a champagne flute.

Margot gave her a grateful smile. "Thanks."

Ida drew her over to a table. "Have a seat. Tell me what's on your mind."

The wall went up. A reflex. Margot simply wasn't used to getting close to people. Especially people who mattered greatly—like Jerome's mother. "It's a wonderful wedding," she said. "It's definitely too wonderful to be subjected to my dancing."

"You're fine," Ida said. "The only way to be bad at dancing is to have a bad time doing it."

"I'm going to keep that in mind. Jerome's really good."

"Could be the connection to his partner." Ida smiled at Margot's stunned expression. "I've never seen him like this. He's bursting with happiness. It's real nice."

"It means a lot to hear that. Ida, this is what I always picture when I think of family." She gestured to encompass the sunlit orchard, crowded with happy guests.

"We're all on our best behavior," Ida said. She focused on Asher, currently filling his pockets with Jordan almonds from the dessert table. "Most of us, anyway. But thank you for saying so. My concept of family has certainly evolved now that all this is happening."

"What are you two beauties gossiping about?" Jerome strode over to them.

"You," said his mother. "Now I need to go rope my new man into dancing with me again."

Jerome watched her go on a flutter of ivory and lace. "About me, eh?" he said.

"You're what we have in common, your mom and me. She's really cool, Jerome."

"So are you." He drew her in close and pressed his lips to her temple. "Let's go to another wedding together," he said. "I like going to weddings with you."

"You do? Well, I like it, too." She searched the crowd for Frank's daughter, Jenna, who had caught the bride's bouquet. She was newly single after a rough breakup, but Margot knew what yearning looked like in a woman. "Jenna? Is it too soon for her? I mean, she's been divorced less than a year. Maybe, though . . ."

"Margot. Mark my words—one of these days, I'm going to marry you."

"Knock it off. You are not." Her pulse started to race, and in spite of everything, she felt a rush of joy and hope.

"You think I can't handle you?"

"I figure you can handle just about anything, Jerome. You're not the problem. I am."

"How about you let me be the judge of that?" He took her hand and led her to a corner table away from the crowd.

She stared down at her lap. "I've never been in love before. I might be a bad risk."

"And yet you opened a barbecue restaurant in the most expensive city in America. You don't shy from risky things," he said.

"In work, no. With you . . ." She looked across the table at him. Dear lord, that face. "Sometimes . . . most of the time, I feel completely overwhelmed by my feelings for you," she said.

"And that's a bad thing?"

"I was afraid if you got to know me, really know me, you wouldn't want to be with me. Not just because of the lawsuit, and not even because of your ex. But because . . . I'm that person. I'm that person who took a man's life."

"No. That's not who you are. That's what you did because you didn't have a choice. And I'm so damn grateful you survived and that you're here with me. *Now* what are you afraid of?"

She realized then that there were worse things than her ordeal in Texas. "Losing you. When I was away, I missed you so much I wanted to die."

"Did you, now?" He took a small, rounded box from his pocket.

She gasped, unable to speak. She forgot how to breathe. Her heart seemed to stop, though she knew that wasn't possible.

"Don't panic, now," said Jerome. "I thought this might be a step in the right direction." He flipped open the top of the box. Inside was a pendant set with a diamond so bright it looked like a piece of the night sky. "This is not the way I thought this would go, but I don't want to wait another minute. This is my promise to you. A promise. I'm not asking for anything right this minute. You don't have to do anything more than just be yourself."

He didn't seem to know what to make of her stunned silence. "It's a Kalahari diamond," he said. "I picked a square cut because it looks like a crystal of salt."

Margot reached across the table and touched two fingers to his lips. "It's the prettiest thing I ever saw." She faltered, feeling an ache in her chest. She felt too raw and fragile to bear the weight of a love that felt so huge. The Hunts made her question her right to a love like that. To a life like this. This was her first experience falling in love and she didn't know if she could do it. The trauma was scarred indelibly upon her heart. There was an age gap between her and Jerome. A race gap. He had kids. She'd be a stepmom. If she had a child with him, she would face the delicate challenge of raising a biracial child. All her misgivings blew up inside her.

"I'm a mess, Jerome. And I don't want to mess this up."

"Something bad happened to you," he said. "We can make something good come out of it. I can handle a mess. I know how to be careful. And patient. Listen, you're not a criminal. Or a victim. You're a survivor. Love yourself, honey. Love that girl who lost her mama too young and picked the wrong guy and had to fight for herself. Love that girl—because I do."

Margot pressed the palms of her hands on the table and felt her heart beating like a bird in a cage. Then she closed her eyes because she couldn't bear to look at him.

"Jerome, if I . . . if we do this, it isn't going to be an easy ride," she whispered.

"Hush now. I love you," he said. "I love the broken parts and the parts that are perfect and everything in between. I won't ever abandon you. I won't let you lose yourself in me." He stood and drew her up and into his arms.

She laid her ear against his chest and listened to his beating heart. And in those few moments, Margot felt something shift. Yes, she was a mess, but she wasn't fragile. She would not be broken.

So many times in her life, she'd felt powerless, but once she grabbed hold of her power, she realized it had been there all along, waiting for her to find it. And Jerome seemed to know that. He was her safe harbor. He defined, at long last, who she belonged to, who was there for her, who saw her and cherished her. "You feel like a dream to me," she whispered.

"Then you keep on dreaming, honey. Keep on dreaming."

AUTHOR'S NOTE

Although Margie/Margot's situation seems unlikely, it was informed by real events. The case of Brittany Smith, who in 2018 shot and killed her rapist and was subsequently indicted for murder, was covered in the national press. The only way for her to gain her freedom was to plead guilty, thus branding herself a felon. Cyntoia Brown was sentenced to life in prison at age sixteen for the murder of the man who subjected her to abuse and sex trafficking; she was later granted clemency by Governor Bill Haslam. Chrystul Kizer, at seventeen a survivor of sex trafficking and abuse, was charged with first-degree intentional homicide. LadyKathryn Williams-Julien of New York State killed her husband during an act of domestic violence and was charged with his murder. At thirty-six, she had no prior criminal record, only a history of abuse from her father and then her husband. She lobbied the state legislature to pass the Domestic Violence Survivors Justice Act, which gives judges discretion to consider the role of abuse in situations of sexual violence. There is troubling evidence that dismissal on the grounds of self-defense is far more common for men than women.

It's also true that certain medical organizations treat rape survivors with a drug that prevents fertilization but fails to act against a conceived zygote, thus opening the possibility that a pregnancy could occur as the result of the rape.

Due to the system of mandatory cash bail, people in jails across the US have not yet been convicted of a crime, according to the Prison Policy Initiative. Even the innocent might remain in jail for days, weeks, or even years simply because they cannot afford their bail.

If You Need Help

RAINN (Rape, Abuse & Incest National Network) is a confidential, free, supportive resource for those dealing with sexual violence. If you or someone you know has been sexually assaulted, help is available 24/7. Visit online at rainn.org or call 800-656-HOPE (4673).

Sugar and Salt Recipes

collected by Susan Wiggs, inspired by the novel

Cocktails

Welcome to Salt

1 part lime juice
smoked sea salt
1 part smoky mescal
1 part Cointreau or Grand Marnier
1 jalapeño slice

Dampen the rim of a glass with the lime juice and dip it in smoked sea salt. Put the glass in the freezer to frost it. Combine the ingredients in a shaker with ice and shake well. Strain into prepared glass, garnish with the jalapeño slice, and serve.

Baja Oklahoma

¼ to ½ ounce freshly squeezed lime juice
coarse salt
2 ounces blanco or reposado tequila
4 ounces Jarritos Toronja, Squirt, or Fresca
grapefruit twist

Dampen the rim of a tall glass with the lime juice and dip it in coarse salt. Fill the glass with ice cubes, add the ingredients, stir, and garnish with a grapefruit twist.

First Friday

> 8 cucumber slices
> 8 mint leaves
> 6 ounces tonic water

Muddle the cucumber and mint together in a shaker, then fill with ice, stir in the tonic, and strain into a tall glass filled with ice.

Mains, Sauces, and Sides

Red Hot Raging BBQ Sauce

Since you're already angry, this will set your hair on fire.

> 4 cups packed brown sugar
> ½ cup molasses
> 1 cup maple syrup
> ½ cup honey
> ½ cup orange juice
> 2 pounds fresh apricots, halved and pitted (or use canned)
> 3 tablespoons salt
> 2 tablespoons Worcestershire sauce
> 2 tablespoons soy sauce
> 4 cups cider vinegar
> 1 can (29 ounces) tomato sauce

2 cups ketchup
1 cup prepared mustard
3 tablespoons chicken bouillon granules
4 tablespoons crushed red pepper flakes
2 tablespoons garlic powder
2 tablespoons onion powder
1 tablespoon ground black pepper
2 tablespoons liquid smoke

Combine everything except the liquid smoke in a large Dutch oven; bring to a boil, stirring so it doesn't burn the bottom. Reduce heat and simmer, uncovered for one to two hours, stirring occasionally. Puree with an immersion blender. Stir in liquid smoke. Ladle into jars and store in the refrigerator or preserve using traditional canning methods.

Adapted from *Cowboy Cookbook* by Bruce Fischer

Your Mama's Moist Cornbread

Life is too short to eat dry, crumbly cornbread. This is the one you've been looking for. You don't even need a mixer for this. The leftovers can be split crosswise, toasted, and served with pepper jelly or tomato jam.

Preheat the oven to 350°F. Butter an 8 × 8 pan, or use a seasoned cast-iron skillet.

Combine the wet ingredients in a small pitcher and let the cornmeal soak to soften it:

4 tablespoons melted butter
1/3 cup oil
1½ cups buttermilk or plain yogurt thinned with milk

2 eggs
½ cup cornmeal

Let that sit while you combine the dry ingredients in a bowl:

1½ cups flour
½ cup sugar
1 tablespoon baking powder
1 teaspoon salt
¼ teaspoon cayenne pepper

Combine everything to moisten, but don't beat or overmix.

Then fold in:

1 small can diced green chiles
1 cup shredded cheddar cheese
1 cup fresh, frozen, or canned and drained corn
*   kernels*

Gently fold in but don't overmix the optional ingredients—any combination:

sliced green onion
sliced jalapeño peppers
sauteed red, orange, and green sweet peppers
dried sweetened cranberries
Texas pecans
snipped fresh herbs, such as rosemary, sage, or
*   thyme*

Pour batter into the pan and bake for about 30 minutes. If it's still damp in the middle, bake for another 5–10 minutes. Serve warm with butter and tomato jam or pepper jelly.

Honey Butter Fried Chicken

It's worth the trouble.

2 pounds chicken pieces (or have the butcher cut up a
   whole chicken)
1 pint buttermilk
½ teaspoon kosher salt
¼ teaspoon ground black pepper
¼ cup potato starch
¼ cup all-purpose flour
½ teaspoon baking powder
peanut oil for frying

Brine the chicken for 8–12 hours in a bath of water with
a cup each of sugar and salt. Add other flavorings if you
like—lemon, peppercorns, herbs. Remove from brine,
pat dry, then place the chicken pieces in a bowl with
the buttermilk. Combine the dry ingredients in a wide,
shallow bowl. Dredge the pieces in the seasoned flour.
Heat the oil in a deep skillet or fryer to 350°F. Use
tongs to place the chicken pieces in the oil, starting
with the dark meat. Fry for about 5 minutes per side,
turning with tongs. Chicken is done when the internal
temperature is 165°F. Drain on a rack over a sheet pan.

For the honey butter sauce:

4 tablespoons butter
3 garlic cloves, minced
¼ cup brown sugar
2 teaspoons soy sauce
2 teaspoons honey

Melt the butter in a skillet, add the garlic, and sauté for about a minute. Whisk in the other ingredients and simmer until it bubbles vigorously. Drizzle over the chicken pieces and serve.

Lazy Biscuits

No need to get out the cookie cutter. These aren't as pretty but they taste better.

2 cups White Lily flour (this is made from winter
    wheat and yields the fluffiest biscuits)
2 teaspoons baking powder
½ teaspoon baking soda
1 teaspoon sugar
¾ teaspoon table salt
1 cup cold buttermilk
8 tablespoons unsalted butter, melted, plus
    2 tablespoons melted butter for brushing
    biscuits
Maldon (or other flaky) salt

Heat oven to 475°F. Whisk dry ingredients in large bowl. Combine buttermilk and 8 tablespoons melted butter in pitcher, stirring until butter forms small beads throughout. Add buttermilk mixture to dry ingredients and stir until just until batter pulls away from sides of bowl. Using a greased ¼-cup dry measure, scoop level amount of batter onto parchment-lined baking sheet. This should yield about 12 biscuits. Bake until tops are golden brown and crisp, 12–14 minutes. Brush biscuits with more melted butter and top with a pinch of salt flakes.

Brisket Kaisers

Do not skimp on the not-so-secret ingredient
of crushed barbecue potato chips.

4 kaiser rolls, buttered and grilled
1 cup barbecue sauce
1 pound brisket or grilled portobello mushrooms
1 large onion, caramelized with butter and salt in a
*   heavy skillet*
½ cup remoulade
4 pepperoncini peppers, sliced thin
crushed barbecue potato chips

Brush the rolls on the top and bottom with barbecue
sauce. Then layer the meat or mushrooms, caramelized onion, remoulade, and peppers on the bottom of
the bun. Add a layer of crushed potato chips and top
with the rest of the seedy bun.

Happy Endings

Texas Sheet Cake

2 cups all-purpose flour
2 cups sugar
¼ teaspoon salt
½ cup buttermilk
1 teaspoon baking soda
1 teaspoon vanilla extract
2 eggs
2 sticks butter
4 heaping tablespoons cocoa powder

For the icing:

> 1¾ sticks butter
> 4 heaping tablespoons cocoa powder
> 6 tablespoons milk
> 1 teaspoon vanilla extract
> 1 pound powdered sugar

Preheat the oven to 350°F. Combine the flour, sugar, and salt. In a separate bowl, mix the buttermilk, baking soda, vanilla, and eggs.

In a medium saucepan, melt the butter and whisk in the cocoa. Bring 1 cup water to a boil and pour it into the pan, allowing it to bubble; then remove from heat. Pour this mixture into the dry ingredients and stir. Add the egg mixture and stir. Pour into a rimmed 10 × 13 cookie sheet and bake for 20 minutes.

Meanwhile, make the icing. Melt the butter and add the cocoa powder, then the milk, vanilla, and powdered sugar. When you remove the cake from the oven, pour on the warm icing while the cake is still hot. Cool before serving.

Handwritten by my friend Janece

ACKNOWLEDGMENTS

Due to the pandemic, the lonely process of writing a book became that much lonelier. For me, the void was filled by my fellow writers, who are always there for me, even if it has to be on a small, glowing screen. Thank you to Anjali Banerjee, Lois Dyer, and Sheila Roberts. A special shout-out to K.B. for the lively discussions sparked by the issues in this novel.

The real Candelario Elizondo, a talented lawyer, answered key legal questions for me. Poet and writer Faylita Hicks's observations about being an indigent arrestee were eye-opening and elegantly expressed in the *Texas Observer*. An extra-special thank-you to Kashinda Carter for her wise and insightful sensitivity read on an early draft.

Thanks to Laurie McGee for smart and perceptive copyediting, and to Marilyn Rowe and Kirsten Weisbeck for proofreading help.

I'm grateful to Cindy Peters and Ashley Hayes for keeping everything fresh online.

Every book I write is enriched and informed by my literary agent, Meg Ruley, and her associate, Annelise Robey, and brought to life by the amazing publishing team at HarperCollins/William Morrow—Rachel Kahan, Jennifer Hart, Liate Stehlik, Tavia Kowalchuk, Bianca Flores, and their many creative associates who make publishing such a grand adventure.